ALLY OR ENEMY

When a series of thumps below announce[...] ontact's entry into the airlock, Galvanix swung his [...] und and stood uneasily. Proximity to violence made [...] eply uneasy, and the contact almost certainly had [...] past.

The airlock hatch puffed open. A heavily suited figure, wearing armor scalloped like a carapace, stepped through and stood regarding them. As it raised arms to remove the helmet, Galvanix and Danziger saw with shock that the figure appeared female.

A face black as oil appeared beneath the helmet, earplug wires trailing through cropped woolly hair. The woman looked back at them in impassive appraisal.

Danziger spoke first. "*You're* 'City Boy'?" he asked incredulously.

The woman produced a metal disk and slapped it against the bulkhead, where it stuck. "This is armed, and will detonate if I don't send it frequent signals. I am here to complete a mission, and shall not be stopped by anything as small as a person. Turn and face your consoles, *now*."

THE
OXYGEN BARONS

GREGORY FEELEY

ACE BOOKS, NEW YORK

This book is an Ace original edition,
and has never been previously published.

THE OXYGEN BARONS

An Ace Book / published by arrangement with
the author

PRINTING HISTORY
Ace edition / July 1990

All rights reserved.
Copyright © 1990 by Gregory Feeley.
Cover art by Dave Archer.
This book may not be reproduced in whole or in part,
by mimeograph or any other means, without permission.
For information address: The Berkley Publishing Group,
200 Madison Avenue, New York, NY 10016.

ISBN: 0-441-64571-2

Ace Books are published by The Berkley Publishing Group,
200 Madison Avenue, New York, New York 10016.
The name "ACE" and the "A" logo
are trademarks belonging to Charter Communications, Inc.

PRINTED IN THE UNITED STATES OF AMERICA

10   9   8   7   6   5   4   3   2   1

Gardens on the Moon

ONE

Galvanix came awake when the water clock, punctual as only an engine driven by celestial mechanics can be, released a clear stream of night-cold water over his head. He jackknifed forward in a reflexive spasm which he immediately suppressed lest his quickened musculature, overdeveloped after a regimen under Earth-level weights, fling him against the far wall and break his neck. Galvanix groped overhead and yanked the pullcord, stifling the trickle. The joke was to have been on Rona, toward whose side of the bed Galvanix had somehow gravitated during the night in—he now noticed—her absence.

Shaking his head vigorously, Galvanix climbed from the bed and quickly pulled on clothing. He paused while stepping into sandals to consider the fruits of another pet device, a shaft in the ceiling leading to the greenhouse dome, into which he had fitted a prism. The disposition of spectra on the tiled floor could presumably tell him the position of the sun and the phase of the Earth, but he suspected that the temperature changes overhead were warping the glass.

The water clock, simple in principle, comprised two buried tanks on opposite sides of the house connected by a slender pipe. The water tended toward the tank closer to the Near Pole, but Galvanix corrected for that by adjusting their relative depths, so that the water level would register the solar tides. These tides were weak—a fifth the force the Moon exerted on Earth—but they did vary, unlike the enormous tidal bulges at the Poles, passing from high to low in a week and running water back and forth through his pipe with astronomical regularity. Stopcocks gauged to give beneath a certain pressure would open with clockwork predictability, initiating loud gurglings or the dousing Galvanix had arranged. Most impressively, as he had told Danziger, it required no energy at all, and the larger models Galvanix hoped to build upon the surface like the mythical Martian *canali* could actually generate power.

There was no time for such fancies now. Galvanix wondered who would call up the plans for his various projects when they probated his will, and whether any of them would be built.

The 'phone chimed as he was finishing breakfast, and Galvanix caught himself glancing at the comm screen (dead, of course, like most of the house's energy-drinking extravagances) before he remembered. Rigging the ferrophone with the same chime the comm system had used had been another display of Galvanian wit that Rona had not appreciated, and Galvanix reflected with a moment's bitterness that the next citizen to occupy his house would doubtless disconnect it. He listened for a second tone, which would indicate an emergency warranting use of the comm line, but heard none. Galvanix rose with a glimmer of anticipation and set about kindling the steam telephone.

As he worked Galvanix wondered whom the call was from. The ferrophone summons could only have originated at Constitution House, where the slender steel rod encased in its oil-filled sheath found its terminus. But Burunde had a lovely set of semaphore flags set atop a fifty-meter tower, which was additionally fitted with a periscope that could spy the semaphores of every other house on the South Shore. Burunde could easily be alerting Galvanix that somebody else wanted a word.

Galvanix troweled the coals that had heated his coffee into the steam phone's brazier, and craned his neck to read the tiny pressure gauge. The steam phone system was larger than any of Galvanix's other projects, and he took perverse glee in the thought that it was mostly empty. It was a particular point of pride that the Moon's low density, which had created the long crisis that would probably kill him before week's end, had allowed him to drill lines connecting all the houses on the South Shore. He had even sunk one through the lunar crust that tapped enough heat to maintain a steady steam pressure. The citizens of the Lunar Republic might see their hard-won world taken away, but Galvanix would wrestle surprising concessions from even the circumstances that doomed them.

Galvanix lifted a metal panel under the brazier, revealing a dozen thin pipes running beneath the floor. He touched them lightly in turn, finding the fourth one warmest. Burunde after all.

Replacing the panel, Galvanix shook the pan of the brazier and then worked vigorously at what resembled a bicycle pump.

Pressure had to be high enough to force all air from the sleeve containing the resonating rod, and a steady heat source maintained to offset predictable dissipation. Galvanix expertly adjusted various valves with an eye on his gauges, working quickly and with deep satisfaction.

When his apparatus was hot enough, Galvanix opened it to the trunk line leading to Constitution House, which the caller had already heated. Cracking the valves always caused some slight drop in pressure, and Galvanix pumped it back up before trying to establish a link. He wondered who had sent the chime over the ferrophone, smiling as he imagined Burunde swinging the mallet that would send a shock wave across twenty kilometers of rigid rod.

Galvanix leaned toward the speaker, an orchid-like device he had fashioned to resemble an antique ear trumpet. "*Moshi moshi,*" he said clearly.

"*Moshi moshi,*" replied a voice after several seconds.

"*Ogenki desu-ka, Burunde-sama?*" Galvanix teased. As a member of the non-Japanese minority, Burunde had to bear up under her colleague's ironical greetings.

"I am well, Galvanix-san," said Burunde, recognizable more by character than by voice, which was coming through in the strained pitch of too much steam. "I wish you well in your journey, and also call to inform you of an advance in your departure time, which should be no later than 13:41."

"Where did you hear this?" Galvanix demanded.

"On the telephone, of course. Do you wish to confirm details yourself?" Burunde had a low opinion of conducting crucial business on low-tech apparatus.

"Just speak clearly, my friend. Why are they moving my time up?"

"It is owing to an earlier than anticipated injection of your mission contact into circumlunar orbit. Danziger is launching within the hour, and shall rendezvous at 13:41." Burunde was spelling everything out, intent that nothing be lost to weak communications. "I can imagine that a mission so clandestine as this must be unusually subject to vicissitudes."

"*Ho.* Fortunately I have left plenty of time."

As he spoke, Galvanix lifted his gaze to a painting on the far wall. Painted when he was thirteen with pigments ground by hand from lunar minerals, it portrayed a dark crescent moon rising behind a featureless blue-green world. The moon was Triton, where the crazies lived, a satellite scarcely larger than Luna yet possessing an atmosphere a third that of Earth's. Galvanix kept it to remind him what the Moon would be like if the Consortium did not stifle its development.

"Have you anything further to tell me, Burunde?"

"One thing, Galvanix." The faint pause could have been simply Burunde's enunciation, but Galvanix was sure he detected hesitation. "I got a message from Rona an hour ago, which I am asked to relay to you should you wish it."

An involuntary smile pulled slowly at Galvanix's cheeks. "Did she use the steam phone?"

"She did, yes. I am not sure of her motivation, but doubtless she knew that it would please you."

"You are conciliatory to the end, Burunde. I am sorry that war leaves so few opportunities for diplomats. You would otherwise be thriving now. No, I shall not hear her message. If I am not back later to play it at leisure, it is best left undelivered."

"Your sister Hiroko . . ."

"My sister Hiroko is dead, damn you." Interruptions were futile when sound took four seconds to carry, except to preclude hearing further. Galvanix paused for his outburst to clear, then spoke in a more measured tone. "Do you have advice for me to carry?"

"Simply the observation that you shall have more time now to complete your mission before your orbit carries you to Farside." The deteriorating vacuum was slowing the rod's vibrations, making Burunde's voice sound like a man's. "Perhaps you will be less tempted to regard it as a suicide mission."

"That is a thought, my friend. Let us then look confidently toward seeing each other next week," said Galvanix, steering the conversation to a conclusion. He was disappointed with Burunde's advice, the implications of which he had seen immediately.

"Do not be brash, Galvanix. Should you fail, we shall have to resort to the most extreme measures, and I at least would have to live with their consequences."

"I do not plan to fail, Burunde-san. Go to your telescope and watch: Danziger and I shall keep the ice off your head."

It was not perhaps the most gracious way to end the conversation, but Galvanix found himself disconcerted saying good-bye to a friend who clearly expected never to see him again. Galvanix shut down the phone, imagining next week's eulogies and wondering why one could not cash in early on some of the benefits of hero-worship.

He took leave of the house quickly, glancing once more about his workroom before ascending the corkscrew staircase to the greenhouse. It was a good house, and Galvanix held a .18 equity in it, granted in recognition of his contributions to the Tycho Basin projects. Nobody, he believed, owned a larger share in a residence, and the 3 percent royalties he had won for his last four patents were probably also a record, although the confidentiality programs in the Grand Files prevented him from confirming this.

The weather outside was mild, something rarely seen since the Farsiders had shot the Dragon Kite Mirrors to tatters. Such calm would be remarkable even during midday, when the storms that accompanied daybreak and twilight were safely at the far ends of the world. The tessellated panes overhead shone a deep limpid blue and the usual drumming of rain could not be heard. Galvanix stepped off the stone pathway to sink his feet into the spongy soil, and inhaled the fragrance of vegetable decay.

A bee hovered close to his ear, one from the tiny hive Hayakawa had shipped him, and Galvanix stepped away from the magnolia he had brushed. It occurred to him that the flora might suffer during Rona's absence, but no, she would of course return within the day. Galvanix impulsively took something from his pocket, a set of small screwdrivers that folded to the size of a thumbnail, and dropped it in the damp soil. Rona would find it when working the earth and make of it what she might.

Airlocks had not been needed on the surface of the Moon since Galvanix's childhood, though the dome exit was a revolving door with pliant edges to minimize loss of humidity. His ears popped as he stepped outside, and the soil underfoot crunched dryly. A breeze from the shore blew briefly past, smelling of water but carrying almost none, and Galvanix turned to face the shore. Tycho, the raised rim of the drowned crater running across the landscape like a levee, breathed a low cloud into the thin air above its surface, which the sun in turn dissipated and fed to the storms.

Pausing a moment to acclimate himself to outside pressure, Galvanix raised his eyes to the stars. Both Earth and the sun were well above the horizon, and as always Galvanix was struck by how apposite and balanced the lunar sky was, the Earth never moving but waxing and waning through the month-long day, the sun unchanging but always moving. Galvanix often imagined how monotonous the Earth sky must be, and nursed the secret conviction that Earth's children must be duller than the Moon's.

Galvanix raised his hand to block the sun, looking just past its limb for a glimpse of one of the suncatchers rising or falling on the solar winds. At their farthest reach, the umbrella-shaped engines could sometimes be seen glowing as they fell toward the sun like enormous parachutes before slowing and then sailing back outward, their vanes filled with hydrogen ions needed to create water for the Inflooding. When the collecting tanks were full, the hydrogen was spewed toward lunar orbit in a soliton stream that sent the suncatcher jetting back toward the sun, where the cycle resumed.

No reddish lights shone through the outer reaches of the corona, itself blurred by disturbances in the upper air. Galvanix thought bitterly that the suncatchers' harvest was now being sent elsewhere, probably into High Venus Orbit, where the Consortium was caching its resources while its members fought over his world.

One of the bicycles was missing from its stand, and as Galvanix approached he saw that Rona had left him the power model. He was not sure how he felt about that, but conceded as he wheeled the bike out that it was better he not tire himself pedaling to Tycho Tower. The gears on the power model were small and inefficient, Galvanix recalled as he pushed unsteadily off, but need only take him to cruising speed. He cycled down the walkway, picking up speed, then turned onto the road and headed east.

Irrigated rows of multicolored scrub flashed past him as he accelerated down the straightaway, varieties of the inedible groundcover the Earthies called green cheese. Tailored years ago by the botanical project Rona now worked for, the plant's virtue was that it produced a lot of oxygen.

Galvanix's cycling cap had a visor wide enough to protect his face, but as the curve of Tycho's shore brought the sun round he was compelled to pull the goggles down. The harshness of the midday sun was a galling reminder that Luna still lacked much of an atmosphere, and as Galvanix increased speed his lungs began to work like bellows. Even on what was quaintly called "sea level" good cycling was impossible without training.

Galvanix knew when the bike's engine was likely to cut in, and as he approached fifty kilometers per hour he listened for the sound of the starter. With a soft burr the single-geared engine engaged, and Galvanix lifted his feet from the pedals. The electric battery would get him to the Tower, where a solar recharger with fresh units waited.

Of course, Galvanix wasn't counting on a return trip.

Tycho Tower, as enormous and slender as a reed might appear to a water bug, began to rise over the Moon's constricted horizon. Even Galvanix, accustomed as he was to low-gravity architecture, was invariably impressed to see the tower rise slowly over him. When the air has all arrived, he had boasted as a child, I'm going to live in a house like that! Perhaps someday such a house would be named after him.

To his left, the lights of an industrial complex glowed on the water, one of the off-shore rigs seining the lake for deuterium. Heavier impurities had long since settled on the crater floor, where scuttler robots gradually collected them, though Callisto's mantle, where most of the early water to irrigate the Moon had come from, contained few soluble elements. Galvanix wondered whether the surface of a deep-crater sea would be safer than land should his mission fail and the ice fall.

The Tower was manned at all times, although with the Embargo the stream of arrivals and departures had been choked to nearly nothing, and most of the personnel dispersed. It was not until Galvanix was within a few hundred meters of the structure and coasting without power that he was able to see Mondavi waiting on the driveway.

"You made good time," were the dispatcher's first words as Galvanix braked to a stop and swung off his bike. Galvanix wondered if the man had worried that the low-tech system might not relay word of the schedule change (which he had of course heard via tightbeam of the Tower antenna), but said nothing. Doffing his cap and tossing it over one handlebar, Galvanix strode rapidly toward the Tower, Mondavi following.

"Is Danziger aloft?" he asked over his shoulder.

"By now, yes." Mondavi was puffing to keep up. A non-native like many transport personnel, he was evidently unused to exerting himself outdoors. "You'll get another confirmation before launch."

"Up we go, then." Ascent facilities for a single passenger were modest, and attractively low-energy: a seat on the shoreward side of the Tower, attached to one of the running cables. Galvanix was strapping himself in when Mondavi caught up.

"Is your suit secure? Here, let me check." Galvanix suffered Mondavi to fit a pressure helmet over his head, seal the collar, and then plug a dangling oxygen tube into a shoulder valve and activate pressure. The suit stiffened, and Mondavi waited several seconds, prodding here and there with a finger, before being satisfied with system integrity. Galvanix removed the helmet and took the tube from his shoulder. Mondavi was attaching the helmet to Galvanix's belt with a length of thin cord. "I know you're not going to put on the helmet until the last minute, so humor me. Can't have you dropping it and dying up there."

"Ready when you are," Galvanix said. Mondavi stepped back, looking uncertain how to take this coolness, then seemed to accept it as stoicism. Galvanix extended his hand, and Mondavi shook it with evident feeling. He stepped out of Galvanix's range of vision, and a second later Galvanix felt a vibration at his back. The seat nudged hard against him, and with exhilarating swiftness the landscape began to fall away.

By the time Galvanix had risen half a kilometer the horizon was curving visibly. The air was not perceptibly thinner; unlike larger worlds, the Moon did not hug its atmosphere to its breast but let it drift loosely, a gauzy envelope. In the first years of the Inflooding, when the sparse winds could scarcely raise dust, Galvanix would stand with his family and look into the night sky. Sometimes the Soliton Tunnel, carrying billions of tonnes of gases like a snake writhing through the heavens, could be seen with the naked eye, a smudge against stars like a nebula.

Below him colored squares and ribbons of road spread out like a quilt, gardens of horticulture and atmogenesis. Most of the shoreline was devoted to the latter, for the rising vapor kept the air-producing scrub from scorching during the long hot days, and every standing pond or runneling stream contained algae. The solar tides sufficed to keep the water circulating, and the CO_2 that had been skimmed from the cloudtops of Venus became carbon for the plants, oxygen for the sky.

Galvanix wondered whether the mites were still working the soil. The microscopic machines were to have continued functioning nearly forever, but the loss of the Mirrors had disrupted the ecosphere, creating sharp temperature differentials that fueled endless storms. But now the mites could be blown permanently aloft, buried in sediment, or washed away to the Near Sea.

Tycho Lake was growing more fully visible as he rose. The Earth was reflected in its center, distorted by the water's tidal pull. Drawn Earthward by tides thirty-two times greater than those the Moon exerted in turn, the lake crept halfway up the north shore's inner slope like a plant yearning toward light.

Galvanix felt the lift continue to accelerate, and after a moment began to feel giddy. He clamped on the helmet and attached the air to feed to its base. The soft hissing it made was the first sound he had heard in over a minute.

Tycho Tower rose a hundred and fifty kilometers above the lunar surface, nearly halfway out of the atmosphere. Before the Embargo it served as the pickup point for the lunar Flywheel, a spinning tether two thousand kilometers long which whipped down every hour to sweep cargo pods into space. When the Orbital Consortium declared Embargo, the Flywheel had retracted and spun away. Now suborbital flight was possible only through spacecraft, and the Republic's few ships rested in their silos, conserving their now-irreplaceable fuel.

Danziger would be coming from the southeast, and Galvanix watched that quadrant for a glimpse of his ship. They would have to change course drastically after pick-up, a waste of fuel that Galvanix felt in his bones. A more efficient trajectory could have been achieved if Danziger were able to complete even one orbit first, but he could not risk venturing round the Farside and exposing himself to Yasuhiro's firepower.

A star was moving in the southern sky, near the threshold of Galvanix's vision. He cocked his head to reduce faceplate refraction.

The mission vessel, a small shuttle with its passenger space converted to accommodate a Snatch, would be coming in eight kilometers above the Tower. Galvanix would launch up on a jet-pack, no extravagance from that altitude. He trusted Danziger's piloting, but was happy to know that the calculus of the actual Snatch would be handled by the ship. Galvanix remembered what the Europeans who developed the maneuver in the last century called it: *the clay pigeon.*

The vibrations at his back ceased, and Galvanix coasted with diminishing speed up the last hundred meters. With a sigh the lift entered an enclosing cage and came to rest. Galvanix watched until the cage light shone green, then unstrapped and stepped out.

The roof of the Tower was a square no larger than his greenhouse, silent on the outskirts of space. Although atmospheric pressure was still nearly half of surface level, gravity was a fraction of normal. Galvanix clutched the railing as a gust blew hard, alone atop one of the tallest, slenderest structures in the solar system.

Galvanix acted quickly. He was a half hour ahead of schedule, but knew that Danziger would make up the time. He strapped a jet-pack onto his back, then checked its pressure and couplings carefully. Turning to look again at the moving star, Galvanix saw it was blinking rapidly, telling him to launch any time.

Galvanix flexed his knees and depressed a switch on his chest. With a roar that vibrated through his suit, he lifted cleanly off the deck of the Tower.

The gentle acceleration of the jet-pack returned him to normal gravity, then increased it slightly as the slow depletion of fuel allowed it to rise faster. Galvanix knew that he need only be clear of the Tower for Danziger to operate the Snatch, but would try to get as high as possible. He also aimed into the same direction as the ship, to minimize his own bruises when the Snatch hit him.

Tycho Lake drifted below him, reflecting stars and shining with its own submarine lights. Galvanix watched his bearings on his wrist compass. Suddenly he was engulfed in blinding light, like a moondog caught in a beacon. Galvanix killed the jets and curled himself into a ball, counting *three, two . . .*

The net of the Snatch hit him like an enormous pillow moving fast as a monorail. Breath exploded out of him, and Galvanix felt a long, hard pressure against one side, as though a giant were grinding him beneath its heel. Because of the elasticity of the Snatch's netting, Galvanix was now trailing behind the ship by a kilometer or more, instead of being smashed when it hit him.

The drag against his body slowly subsided, then after a second began again, although more gently. Danziger was reeling him in.

Ten minutes later Galvanix was disentangling himself from the Snatch's taffylike netting as he lay within the vessel's hold. He groped his way toward the hatch, and was at length admitted through the airlock and into the shuttle's cabin.

Danziger swiveled in the captain's chair to face him. "Welcome to the last flight of the *Corsair*," he said, smiling. "Open your faceplate but keep your helmet on; we've junked most of the safety features to save mass."

"What's a corsair?" asked Galvanix, stepping forward to clasp Danziger's spacesuited shoulders.

"A swift pirate ship, operating with official sanction." Danziger, a small man in his forties with the tanned face of a pilot, grinned briefly. "Did you leave your jet-pack in the hold? Good, we've got to dump it."

"Is that necessary?" Galvanix was shocked at the waste.

"Definitely. In fact—" Danziger touched a series of buttons, prompting a heavy lurch below—"I've jettisoned the Snatch as well. We're traveling light."

Galvanix sat thoughtfully in the co-pilot's seat and studied the displays. It took less than a minute to confirm that course projections called for heavy fuel expenditures. There also did not seem to be much for a return trip.

"When do we head for pickup?" he asked, leaning over to read dials in front of Danziger.

"In thirty-nine seconds. You'll be able to count your bruises during this thrust."

Galvanix sighed and began strapping himself down. The acceleration, when it came, threw him into his seat with greater force than he had ever felt in a shuttle, which he belatedly credited to the ship's lighter mass. At various points during the long seconds of thrust the directional rockets would kick in for quick bursts, prompting brief tugs from unexpected directions. Galvanix was beginning to imagine he felt contused skin separating when the thrusters choked off, freeing him into sudden weightlessness and a dance of motes before his eyes.

"There," Danziger said with satisfaction, pushing back his seat. "That's it for eighty-three minutes."

Galvanix was tapping the display keyboard, summoning a hologram of their target. A translucent green shard appeared in the air before him, its surface ringed with contour lines like grained wood. Galvanix set the image rotating slowly and studied it with interest.

"Looks wicked, doesn't it?"

"Not like the good Callisto ice we know and love." The object was an actual comet, captured millions of years ago by Jupiter's immense gravitational field. During the years before the Inflooding, when ice was mined on Callisto and flung toward the Moon, expeditions were occasionally mounted whenever one of Jupiter's several hundred captured comets reached a point of its orbit that allowed for easy diversion. Cometary densities and tensile properties could never be measured exactly, and the irregular bodies were propelled with simple strap-on boosters, far less accurate than the mass driver that spat the Callistan ice cakes into precise lunar orbits. This one—indifferently named Fenrir by a program working its way through Icelandic mythology—had been sent coasting toward the sun eleven years ago, a few years after Soliton Tunneling made it possible to funnel hot gases across space and inaugurated the Inflooding. The comet had traveled slowly and cheaply in service of a project that would take generations; and now, years after the mining had been halted and the last shipments arrived, was blundering in like a lost parcel, huge, irresistible, and lethal.

Galvanix scanned the trajectory reports, which the ship was revising constantly as the comet approached. Present estimates called for it to fissure deeply as it swung round its first orbit, and then spiral rapidly inward until it broke into halves on the eighth pass, each of which would crash into the Mare Imbrium an hour later. Whether the Farsiders would fire on it could not be guessed, but Danziger had no intention of following the comet that far.

Galvanix replayed the mission scenario in light of latest data. The ship still gave the same moment as optimal for triggering the fusion device, showed the cometary remains hurtling toward the Moon as a cone of superheated gas, raining harmlessly over its surface. He wondered how Rona would greet this bounty, manna from the hellfires of fusion.

"I've picked up 'City Boy,'" Danziger said beside him.

"Ho, let's have a look." The screen before Galvanix came alive with the image of an indistinct shape tumbling against a background of stars. Galvanix leaned forward, trying to make out detail. The form, which the scale indicated must be very small, appeared to resemble a five-pointed star swathed in protective covering.

"That's not a spacecraft at all, it's somebody wrapped in plastic!"

"Looks that way, doesn't it?" Danziger agreed. "The material must absorb radar beams."

Galvanix watched the tumbling form. At intervals he thought he saw a tiny flash, like a penlight peeping through the covering. He said. "The guy's got a beam of his own."

"Well, he has to know that we're out here."

Minutes later Galvanix saw the form stir, then begin to cut its way through the membrane. A silvery figure emerged from the shrouding, which it kicked easily away. Their contact, evidently from one of the big industrial worlds in High Earth Orbit—Danziger and Galvanix had not been told which, and suspected their briefing officer did not know—turned slowly to face the *Corsair*. A hand-held device flashed in rapid uneven succession.

Danziger touched a button and an adjoining panel shone green. "That's the right code. Let's get this guy in here."

Galvanix in fact stayed clear while Danziger maneuvered the shuttle toward the growing figure in the screen. He wondered what kind of person would ride from HEO to the Moon in nothing but a shroud to block radiation.

When a series of thumps below announced the contact's entry into the airlock, Galvanix swung his seat round and stood uneasily. Proximity to violence made him deeply uneasy, and the contact almost certainly had a violent past.

The airlock hatch puffed open. A heavily suited figure, wearing armor scalloped like a carapace, stepped through and stood regarding them. As it raised arms to remove the helmet, Galvanix and Danziger saw with shock that the figure appeared female.

A face black as oil appeared beneath the helmet, earplug wires trailing through cropped woolly hair. The woman looked back at them in impassive appraisal.

Danziger spoke first. "*You're* 'City Boy'?" he asked incredulously. He glanced at Galvanix, his hand still poised over the console.

The woman produced a metal disk and slapped it against the bulkhead, where it stuck. "This is armed, and will detonate if I don't send it frequent signals. I am here to complete a mission, and shall not be stopped by anything as small as a person. Turn and face your consoles, *now*."

The comet was a half-lit chunk of soiled ice, shorn of its corona and tail during its million-year captivity in Jupiter's gravity well. Five kilometers long, it was smaller than most asteroids and less dense, but held the luster of nearly pure ice, flensed and squeezed of gaseous deposits. Galvanix once more pushed the button that bounced a diagnostic off its surface, confirming that no new data prescribed any change in mission plans.

"Stop doing that," the woman said behind him. "Your nervous habits irritate me."

Galvanix considered pointing out that their nervousness was her doing, but noticed her impassive face peering over his shoulder in the reflection of his screen, and decided to keep his ears open and let her do the talking.

"My co-pilot knows his job," Danziger snapped, evidently trying to distract her. The woman took no notice of the remark, and when Galvanix glanced from the displays back to his screen, their gazes met.

"You are Galvanix," she said, clearly at the prompting of a memochip. "What kind of name is that?"

Galvanix swung around slowly in his seat, facing her boldly. "It is my own name," he said, "peculiarly so. My parents chose my genes so that I would not be bound to their forebears, and I chose my name so as not to be bound to my parents."

"And you are designer of the steam telephone, where the caller strikes a rod that will ring a bell in the next county?"

Galvanix looked at her expressionlessly. "You are confusing two different devices."

"Oh?" The woman paused a second. "So it seems. You are very clever with engines, Galvanix. Clever enough to build a bomb?"

"I learned it from a book, City Boy."

The woman smiled mechanically. "You may call me Taggart. Well then, get out your work." She stepped back slightly, as if to show she would not shoot him if he stood.

Galvanix rose slowly, wondering as he studied her whether she was armed. It seemed likely. Glancing at Danziger, who was gazing fixedly at his screen, Galvanix went to the footlocker and brought out a small trunk, which opened at his touch like a mollusk. Inside, resting among an array of tiny tools, was a cylinder the size of his thigh.

Galvanix snapped loose its clasps, allowing it to pop free and float toward the ceiling before he reached up to grab it. He looked at Taggart, who watched without reaction. Standing, Galvanix examined the cylinder, which was open at one end, and held it out for her to see.

Taggart reached behind her back with one hand and drew out a bundled object. Galvanix took it from her, noting its heavy mass, and began to tear away its padding. Inside was a thick metal rod, ribbed with microcircuitry.

"The flame in the furnace," he said. Galvanix felt a childish surge of power, and thought of brandishing it like a talisman.

Galvanix took the device, core, and tools over to a prepared workspace, where he spent the next hour carefully sliding the core into its niche, pausing every few centimeters to run calibrations and systems checks. At one point Danziger announced a course correction, and Galvanix secured the device before returning to his seat, where Taggart insisted on watching them both.

When he finished, Galvanix raised his head in triumph, expecting at last to see the woman leveling a weapon at him. She was merely watching him carefully.

"I've got it, Danny," he said. And then to Taggart: "We have to arm it from the console."

"Tell me what you're going to do," she said as he towed the bomb, like a small but unwieldy zeppelin, toward the controls.

Galvanix cradled the bomb in his seat and then began to explain patiently. "The device will be triggered at the instant selected for maximum effectiveness with minimal fallout. Our diagnostics may change that optimal moment should they discover new data about the comet as we approach. Consequently we will not run the arming program until the last possible minute."

"Do it now," she said. "You are not to run the diagnostics again."

"Ho, and why not? The odds of a late discovery are very small, but why do you object?"

"Never mind." Galvanix began to protest, and she said sharply, "There will be no unexpected data. That is known."

Danziger and Galvanix exchanged glances. "Then I will arm

the device," Galvanix said formally. Taggart watched him carefully as he pulled a cable from his console and plugged it into the device. The arming program was simple, but he displayed it first at Taggart's insistence before she let him run it.

"Ho," Galvanix said as he depressed ENTER. He unplugged the cable and let it slide back into its base. "The fusion device is now armed, and will detonate at—" he checked the readout on his console—"19:55."

Danziger looked sidelong at the fusion bomb, a nervous glint in his eye. Galvanix grinned, slightly giddy at his accomplishment. "Think of it as a surgical device," he said easily. "Like a laser evaporating a brain tumor."

"Get it out of your chair," Taggart said.

Galvanix smiled to her. "Certainly, *Taggart*." The word, he remembered from his study of demolitions, referred to manufacturers's tags packed into explosives that would survive their detonation.

They secured the device in a harness near the airlock, and Galvanix sank back into his chair with a long sigh. Taggart resumed her station behind the control seats. Galvanix, surprised at how easily concentration could strain muscles even in zero gravity, craned his neck to look up at her.

"Is your share of artificial parts so high that you can plant yourself somewhere like a machine?" he inquired genially.

She looked at him without expression. "High enough that I don't lose my temper and injure you," she said.

"Ho, I'm sure that was wit and not just machine language," Galvanix told Danziger. "Is this emulation of an automaton what they mean by military discipline?"

He looked sidelong at Taggart, hoping to find her provoked, but the woman was regarding him with speculative interest.

"Machine language," she said. "I've got it. You're a pre-millennialist, late Western. And that's where Galvanix comes from. There's no *x* sound in Japanese, no traceable etymology for the word. You chose Galvanix because that culture would have thought it 'futuristic.'"

Galvanix stared at her. "That is ingenious," he said after a second. "Your processor must have scanned a lot of data to make that inference."

"Machines don't infer." She still held no expression, but her eyes rested on him, searching his features for reaction. "And I wouldn't need one to tell me about the kid who wrote his way faster than light."

Galvanix knew he did not keep the startled expression from his face, which in any event he could feel reddening. He had been five when, rebelling at the proscriptions of his first astronomy tutor regarding the speed of light, Galvanix had composed a romance, *F'Light*, which made him something of a brief darling among his precocity-loving culture. He had surreptitiously revised it several times every year until he was eleven when, in an access of embarrassment over its persistent faithfulness to his younger self, he purged it from the Grand Files. It was a few years before Galvanix understood the Files well enough to realize that none of the versions had been lost, and he still cringed when remembering how many of the adults he had impressed during his post-adolescent surge through the ranks of the scientific community had indulgently read and remembered the puerile thing.

Beside him Danziger smiled faintly. Galvanix looked back to Taggart, putting full intensity into the gaze. "So we all know me pretty well," he said. "And what of you? You bring our bomb, yet plant another on us. Are you sabotaging this mission, or merely fulfilling your part abusively?"

"You won't goad me into giving data," she replied, though again without malice. "You know nothing of the war that you cannot learn with a telescope. You don't know what is happening on your own Farside. Even your government's allies keep you ignorant of strategic matters, for you cannot communicate between cities without letting anyone in space listen in, and may fall to your Farside enemies before the year is out."

Galvanix started to speak, but Danziger burst out, "It isn't strategic matters we want, we're simply asking whose war this is! We've heard nothing for four years!"

Taggart turned her head to face him, again showing her faint smile. "The last transmission to reach the Moon was actually nineteen months ago, but your Republic did not receive it. Not all your officials know as little as you, but they cannot be entrusted with what they cannot secure."

Galvanix spoke up. "We have secure methods of communication."

Taggart cocked her head at him, as though suggesting sardonicism. "You mean your diaphragms and steam pipes? I can tell you what you ought to have guessed: every major power in Earthspace dropped a monitor on the end of a pointed shaft into the land around Tycho when you set up that system. The monitors buried themselves on impact and listen to vibrations. Your allies would sooner trust you if you used carrier pigeons."

Galvanix thrust out his chin, pugnacious. "How intelligible is a signal that's passed through decameters of loose rock?"

Taggart paused a second, as though considering whether to answer. "Enough for me to know that four hours ago Rona Tsujimaro traveled by monorail to Korovsky, where she took up residence in the agronomists' cooperative. Word has spread among your neighbors by the steam phone."

Galvanix gaped. In the silence, which stretched painfully and caused Danziger to look up from his board, Taggart added, "I gather that Tsujimaro belongs to one of your neo-Buddhist sects that oppose the introduction of nuclear explosives to the Moon."

"It's closer to Shinto," Galvanix whispered. An unsuspected weak point had been lanced.

"If you let those people get the upper hand, you'll never get your canals built," Taggart said offhandedly.

"Enough," said Danziger. "We have arrived."

Matching orbits entailed several minutes of swerving deceleration, which Taggart rode out standing, one hand on the back of each chair. When Danziger declared maneuvers complete, the forward screen showed a wall of rumpled ice, too close to reveal curvature.

"Stay here until I return," Taggart announced, picking up her helmet.

Both men looked at her in surprise. "Where are you going?" Galvanix demanded.

"I have something to do first." She lowered the helmet over her head, forestalling protest. Galvanix and Danziger looked at each other. Danziger touched a button and said, "The mission profile contains nothing on private activities."

The spacesuited figure half turned. "I will tell you when to bring out the device," Taggart said, her voice emerging tinnily through the radio speaker. "Do not attempt to move the craft or call anybody."

She entered the airlock and shut it. Danziger looked again at Galvanix, then turned off the radio. "What is she doing?" he asked.

Galvanix shrugged. He was looking at the disk on the wall, then turned to the screen. A shadow wavered indistinctly across the ice for a second, but Taggart did not come into view.

"Sending a message herself, perhaps."

"She hasn't learned anything from us to tell," Danziger said. "She's *doing* something out there."

"If she planned to sabotage the mission, or if she didn't trust us, she would have killed us," Galvanix noted. "Jettison our bodies, save air and mass."

"As it is, we might end up surviving this mission."

Galvanix looked at his friend in surprise, but saw the point. They had privately agreed to remain with the comet until almost the last minute, retaining their chance to alter the bomb's countdown in the event of late perturbations arising from miscalculation, solar flares, or Farsider interference. Such precaution became pointless once Taggart had vetoed any schedule change.

Danziger unsnapped his harness abruptly and stood. "I think I had better take a look," he said.

"Don't you dare," said Galvanix, startled. "She's murderous."

"Worried about my safety?" Danziger asked, smiling slightly as his hands ran automatically over his suit. The point was irrefutable; they had already counted themselves lost.

Danziger completed his integrity check and reached for his helmet. "If she's doing anything suspect, I'll interfere. Keep your radio open."

"Did she sound like a Namerican to you?" Galvanix asked, nervous.

Danziger shrugged. "There are lots of black-skinned people in space. Besides, we might even be allied with Namerica." He stepped into the airlock, then turned. "If you come under attack—" He gestured toward the device, then slid down his faceplate and shut the door.

Alone, Galvanix sat still for several seconds, then shifted to Danziger's seat and reviewed his displays. Most of the ship's accessories had been stripped, but the bay contained one argus, a tiny self-directed camera unit used for monitoring extravehicular activity. Galvanix depressed a key, and the unit drifted free of the ship on a small puff of air. The screen flickered with static and then resolved into a murky icescape. The camera would fix upon nearby motion, but Galvanix could discern no details.

Keeping one eye on the screen, Galvanix studied the board. The *Corsair* hung nine meters from the comet, anchored by two cables attached to pitons fired into the ice. That "height" gave a good vantage over the ice fields, but Galvanix could see little, and did not dare activate the searchlights or put out a radar pulse. An infrared scope would have picked out the spacesuited figures, but the lightweight ship carried none.

Galvanix watched the screen more carefully, and thought he saw Danziger moving slowly across the uneven landscape. Danziger kept his body parallel to the cometary surface and pulled himself along like a swimmer, turning his head slowly.

A faint movement at the edge of the screen caught Galvanix's attention, and suddenly a line of blue light flashed once across the ice. The cabin alarm shrieked, its pitch announcing a breach in suit integrity. Danziger vanished from the screen, appearing a second later as the camera, veering wildly to follow the alarm signal, fixed upon him flying through space, propelled by a jet of gas and body fluid spraying from his ruptured suit.

Galvanix hit the radio button. "You murdering sow!" he screamed.

The argus, its high beams activated by the emergency signal, pitilessly illuminated Danziger's dwindling figure. Galvanix struck the cancel bar, and the camera angle swung back to its previous orientation, revealing Taggart standing unconcealed upon the ice. Looking up, she raised her hands toward the camera, and the screen went blank.

Galvanix flinched as though struck. She would come after him now. He kicked himself from his seat, grabbing his helmet as he sailed across the cabin. He pulled the fusion device from its harness and strapped it under one arm, then backed into the airlock and pulled it shut.

Inside the coffin-sized chamber Galvanix studied the controls and thought fast. Taggart would be closing in, ready to fire upon the first thing to come through the airlock. Thumbing the override, Galvanix depressed two buttons at once to open both airlock doors.

The pressure blew him out the hatch like a wave, and Galvanix twisted, catlike, to face a mountain of ice coming at him. He struck with knees bent, absorbing enough force to keep from bouncing back into space. A rain of debris pelted him, and a cloud of dispersing air, glistening as its moisture content froze, billowed against the ice.

Galvanix grasped a spur to keep from drifting away, and sought to orient himself in the haze. The sun was blocked by the comet's mass, and green moonlight slanted across the ice at a low angle, creating long shadows and knife-edged contrasts that confounded his attempts to determine distance. Scraps of cabin panel and chair stuffing, torn free by explosive decompression, eddied in the vanishing air.

He knew Taggart would come over the horizon with her gun drawn, and hoped that the cooling gas and debris would muddy his infrared image long enough for him to see her. Galvanix could not flee until he placed his pursuer.

He spun himself with a push of his hand, scanning the horizon. The ice spur beside him burst into chips, and Galvanix pushed himself away as blue afterimages pulsed before his eyes. He activated his radio, shouting, "I have the device!"

Pulling himself by hand-holds, Galvanix moved across the ice fields with the hopeless slowness of nightmare. No blast followed. He thanked God that his superiors had prevailed in insisting that the device not be subject to remote control. Taggart now realized that killing him the way she had killed Danziger would propel the bomb into space, if not damage it outright. Unfortunately she doubtless also knew how to kill him without rupturing his spacesuit.

Turning, Galvanix saw her moving purposefully after him, pulling herself across the ice field with steady arm strokes. At a distance of several hundred meters Galvanix could not see whether she was using her jet-pack as well, but it didn't matter. Her practiced speed would allow her to overtake him within minutes.

Galvanix frantically sought to recall what sort of world this was. No true world at all, to a proud Republican: Galvanix felt as though he were dangling from a cliff face. He raised his head, seeking to orient the ice downward, and the irregular horizon became the rounded edges of a plateau. He reached out, clawed at the ice for a hold, pulled himself sailing forward, reached again. His momentum carried him slowly away from the worldlet's tight curvature, compelling him to break pace every several strokes and haul himself closer in.

Sweat bunched the inner folds of his suit, and Galvanix slapped the heater to its lowest setting. He thought of activating the emergency jets in his soles for a last burst of speed, and suddenly had his idea, as though his subconscious had been waiting, like a skilled assistant, to place it in his hand.

The tiny jets were standard equipment in a spacesuit, simple propellants that would burn out in seconds but might free a worker from entangling wreckage. Galvanix reached back and detached the finger-sized fuel tank from its slot above his right heel. Its contents lacked the thrust of his jettisoned jet-pack, but were still under considerable pressure. Like a grenadier stuffing his musket, Galvanix pushed it into the flaring exhaust nozzle of his other boot.

Taggart was within twenty meters of him. Bringing his foot up, Galvanix straightened his knee and sighted along his leg. He aimed low, straight at her chest.

The explosion slammed his heel upward and for an instant Galvanix thought he had blown his foot off. Beyond the plume blossoming from his boot, however, Galvanix could see the ejected tank shoot across the ice like a Chinese rocket. It vanished in a brilliant flash.

Galvanix turned to face forward, pointing his toes to keep from rocketing tangentially into space. *Got her!* a part of him cheered, while another counseled caution. He had overcorrected for surface curvature, and the missile had struck the ground in front of her. Still the fuel had ignited on impact, blowing out a cone of steam and ice that must have come at her like buckshot. The concussion might have damaged her suit, blown her backward into space, or sprayed her with instantly refrozen ice. With luck she was tumbling blind, and might not recover for over a minute. Galvanix sped.

Within seconds the jet in his left boot began to fizzle, and Galvanix pointed his toes in order to angle himself closer to the surface. He was coasting now, and had judged the degree nicely: the icescape slipping past drew slowly closer, then after several seconds began to recede. Galvanix reached out to snag a spur, although the effort jerked painfully on his arm and snuffed most of his speed. Galvanix skidded against the ice, recovered and began scrabbling across its surface.

His destination was easy to steer for: the fusion device was to be exploded on the site where the Moon stood at the zenith.

Fortunately this was not on the comet's sunlit side; moonlight was dimmer, and would beat less heat on his suit to reflect into Taggart's infrascope. The suit had cooled considerably—Galvanix was feeling the chill despite his exertion—and would present a steadily fainter image to infrared.

Before him, the Moon had almost cleared the oblong horizon, its upper limb climbing halfway up the sky. Only a small world would disclose enough sky for such a sight. Galvanix glanced at it for only a second, but could see that the weather patterns differed sharply from any he had seen.

An irregularity appeared on the horizon and Galvanix looked up to see a churned field of upthrust ice, like the rubble of a crystal palace. He realized at once what it must be: the site where boosters had kicked the comet out of Jupiter's orbit, then blown themselves free for later recovery. Galvanix turned and saw Taggart on the opposite horizon, standing upright for a second while she searched for him. The rubble, he realized, hid his low profile from her view. Eventually, though, her augmented eyesight would pick him out, even if he held still.

Galvanix decided fast. Though the broken field did not lie in the direction of the detonation site, he made for it.

The closest formation was a tilted wedge thrust up between two radial faults, and Galvanix dodged behind it, certain that he had been seen. He peered over the top and saw Taggart coming across the ice. Galvanix pushed himself across to the next, boulder-sized chunk of ice, trying to keep out of Taggart's line of sight. Beyond this the fissured ground widened into a crevice, a meter across and narrowing into darkness below. Galvanix eased himself into it, edging along its length and wondering if it led all the way to the booster site. Panic rose almost immediately—he could not move quickly or see his pursuer's approach—and Galvanix vaulted out, finding himself in a rock garden of rounded forms, ice cakes that had partially melted after rocket fire.

A flash caught the corner of his eye, and the outcropping he had first reached burst into flying shards. A second later another boulder was split by a blue bolt. He pushed away from the nearest projection in a panic. Taggart would know she had little chance of hitting him, so was blasting away his cover hoping to terrify and flush him. Galvanix fought terror, moving through the littered field recklessly, striking his shoulder hard against rocklike ice. He narrowed everything to a single goal: Stay alive until the final countdown, then sprint for the detonation site.

Pebbled ice pelted his suit, close this time. Galvanix told himself that twinkling ice chips in the air would mask his own movement, and a fine cloud of water vapor would confound Taggart's infrascope.

The ground beneath his boots jerked slightly, as though kicked. Galvanix took it for another close hit, but realized a second later that previous strikes had not done that. He was moving through the air before the thought registered, but saw the lips of a crevice stir, and as his gloves touched ground Galvanix felt—*heard*—the groaning reverberations of cracked and brittle ice. Around him everything swayed slightly.

Galvanix raised his head and then heard it: an unbroken wash of static. He had forgotten that his helmet had tuned automatically to the ship's wavelength, and had been dutifully transmitting silence. It took a second to understand: the ship had been destroyed.

Something broke into the wavelength with a snap. "You—!" Galvanix didn't catch the rest, but the tone was unmistakable, out of control. He tilted his head to angle his antenna. Words bobbed in the static. ". . . me the device . . . truce . . ."

Galvanix held still, knowing himself invisible. "Talk to me," he said.

"Your ship has exploded," Taggart said in his ear, her voice strained. "The concussion has altered the comet's course, ruining projections. Bring out the device; it must be set off at once."

"I thought you were trying to kill me," Galvanix said, temporizing to cover surprise.

"I can no longer afford that precaution," she snapped. "I am estimating present deflection. Can you see me?" Galvanix could; she was facing away from him, looking up at the stars as some processor in her suit or skull ran an astrogation check. Standing still, he began to shiver. Taggart looked down. "The explosion has perturbed our approach, which will degrade by zero hour to a position less propitious than the present one. Zero hour must be radically advanced. Do you understand me?"

She was right, Galvanix thought; the *Corsair* had been on the side of the comet opposite the Moon. "Stay where you are," he called hoarsely. "I am heading for the detonation site. No—you precede me. Slowly, in plain sight."

Taggart said nothing, but a second later she lifted off from the surface, blue points glowing on her jet-pack as she veered across the ice toward the rising Moon. Galvanix began to follow, finding after a second that he could move more quickly when not in headlong flight. His muscles were stiffening with cold, and he turned up his heater, knowing he need not worry about later.

He strode easily, each footprint sinking slightly into ice that immediately refroze, holding his boot in place long enough for him to complete the next step. The radio silence did not bother him, for his entire being was occupied, bending his life to this moment. His death was all around him, something he had feared himself ill-prepared for, but now saw bathed in the radiance of his mission. The canister under his arm, an abomination to Rona as it would have been to Hiroko, would save them all.

Taggart was standing on the littered ice, looking up. Galvanix slowed and approached cautiously, one hand resting on the timer's controls. Best detonate now, he thought, before she tries something.

"Set it to three minutes," she said without moving. Galvanix stared, his fingers working at the device. She turned and looked at him. "The difference it will make is nonsignificant, and greater weight must be given to the chance to save our lives."

Galvanix held the device up. "Do you see what I have done?"

"I could defeat your dead-man's switch if I had to," she said. "Before you could think to act. Set it to three and we'll run."

Shifting his gaze from her reluctantly, Galvanix squatted and put the device down before him. He set the timer to three minutes with one hand, and immediately snapped off part of it with the other, preventing reset. One hundred seventy-nine seconds.

Galvanix straightened and looked at her. "We have three minutes," he said. "I think you could answer a few questions now."

Taggart leaped across the ice and seized his arms. "Hold the straps above my ribs," she said. Galvanix—who had raised his hands against the leap, expecting death—complied in surprise. "Hold on," she said, and a cloud of stream erupted about them.

Galvanix's arms were pulled almost out of their sockets as Taggart shot skyward. His helmet was pushed against Taggart's armored chest, and a roar filled his ears, that of rocketry more powerful than a spaceworker's jet-pack. Galvanix looked down, fearing to see his legs dangling near tongues of flame, but Taggart suddenly veered and he was thrown back against her chest. Of course, he thought, she won't lift straight up, but will swing around the comet, seeking protection from the blast. Galvanix sought feebly to protest; he did not want to be robbed of his stand, to die in incontinent flight.

"Cut me free," he called over his radio. "My mass is slowing you; save yourself."

"Shut up," she said. "Your usefulness to this mission is not over."

Galvanix subsided. Part of his mind was counting down the seconds, *143*. Another was kindling, despite his wishes, a nascent hope. He thought with wonder at the hindbrain's intractable grip upon self-preservation. So you will die, he told himself, with your mind still unruly, divided.

A thought struck him. "Taggart," he called over the radio, pulling his helmet clear to dull the roar ringing through his suit. "You must correct course to aim straight away from the comet at detonation. The jets might manage to vaporize most—"

"Quiet," she said. Galvanix immediately wondered what she was concentrating upon. She could not be running an astrogation check; the blast, should they survive it, would blow them imponderably awry. Perhaps she wished to spend her last moments in peace. *Twenty-three*. She could be transmitting on another channel; where? Galvanix wondered if she was expending all her fuel to buy distance from the blast and a hot jet. They might survive detonation but have no room for later maneuvering. . . .

The radio was a sudden roar of static, and the underside of Taggart's suit lit up like a beacon. Galvanix squinted, seeing the light flashing across her armored ridges flicker in intensity and shade. Of course, he thought raptly, it was refracting through an expanding ball of steam and gases.

The concussion struck then, as though they had been falling unknowingly and slammed into the ground. Lights flashed before his eyes—suit alarms? was he dying?—and Galvanix found himself unable to draw breath. He thought with wild protest that shock waves don't travel in vacuum. They were being buffeted, irregular blows from all sides that startled him into flinching, allowing his flattened lungs to inflate.

"You still there?" Galvanix didn't recognize the source of

sound, then foggily realized that Taggart was touching her helmet against his. He tried to speak, but heard an overriding droning from within his suit, which he realized with shock was his voice. "Good," she said. Taggart pulled her head back, then leaned forward again. "By the way, we're getting quite a dose."

Galvanix still felt vertigo. He attempted to focus his eyes, but saw only shifting lights he suspected were afterimages, which resolved at last into darkness. His faceplate had gone opaque, meaning it had been exposed to the brightness of the fireball. Thinking tortuously, Galvanix concluded that they must be spinning, hence the omnidirectional assaults and disorientation.

"Taggart, can you read me?" he called. "My faceplate has fogged, what's going on?"

"We're in a cloud of steam," she replied. Galvanix felt tiny jolts from various sides, and realized that Taggart was stopping their spin. The pull on his arms resumed as she fired her rockets. "Debris is diffusing fast as we move farther out. That first jolt wasn't steam, of course, but a shock wave within the gas envelope. The jets did protect us."

Galvanix, cataloguing his injuries as he waited for his faceplate to clear, reflected that the subliming gas envelope of a dead comet must be highly rarefied at this distance, though the shock wave nearly broke bones. What must the blast have done to the comet itself?

"Is there any large cometary debris remaining?" he asked.

In response Galvanix felt the drag on his arms cease, then a slight pull to one side as Taggart fired a yaw jet, turning them. "See for yourself," she said.

The center of Galvanix's faceplate remained a clouded cataract, but he sensed that Taggart's ignorance of his suit's shortcomings should be maintained. Galvanix strained to see, but could discern no more detail than the curve of the Moon. "That looks good," he said carefully, "but do you know there were no fragments blown beyond visual range?"

"There were, and large enough to reach the surface. The operation was not carried out under good conditions."

Galvanix felt a stab of dismay. "How long will they take to fall?"

"Nothing takes long to fall from this height. We shall impact in about eighty minutes."

"We're falling, too?" Galvanix shouted. "I thought you were angling for a higher orbit. Have you requested pick-up?"

"If you could see through your faceplate, you would know that we are falling toward Farside, and are below the horizon of your Republic's surveillance centers. I doubt your superiors know we are still alive."

Galvanix was silent. Death receded and swayed forward again, and Galvanix could not protest that the long fall frightened him more than being vaporized. He wondered if their suits would be consumed upon reentry, shooting stars across the night sky of Farside. Probably not, he thought with some pride; even his Republican-made suit would survive. He wondered what Yasuhiro's soldiery would make of the remains.

"You are nervous at the prospect of falling," Taggart observed unexpectedly.

"My spirit is at peace," Galvanix told her, hearing Rona in the half-true statement. "I have done what I came to do."

"You are consuming oxygen too rapidly. I have introduced a sedative into your system."

"You *what*?" Galvanix was so startled he attempted to draw back, but Taggart held him like a machine. "How could you violate my integ . . ." Galvanix stumbled over the syllables, feeling his body slip away, relaxing into quiescence even as his mind shouted alarm . . .

There was a high keening, which Galvanix realized he had been hearing for some time before registering it. He was warm, uncomfortably so, but did not feel inclined to waken further until he felt his mouth parched. Turning his head querulously, Galvanix drank from his helmet tube, and was surprised to find the water hot.

". . . awake?" someone said. "Turn your cooler up, and keep still."

The keening wavered slightly as something buffeted them. Galvanix noticed a steady pressure on one side of his body, the warmer side. He came alert then, holding carefully still as he put things together. After a moment he chinned his suit controls to maximum cool, and asked, "How far up are we?"

"Seventeen kilometers." Taggart fired her rockets, jolting him again. The keening decreased in tone but did not cease. Galvanix mused, still sedated. He knew that Taggart's jet-pack could not hold fuel enough to land them safely, despite its great efficiency in the weak lunar gravity. It was a fine ending for a story: making it back *on foot*, falling short by a few last klicks.

The rockets faded and died. Galvanix closed his eyes. "Deploying drogue chute," Taggart said. "Hold on."

Taggart lurched hard against him. Galvanix gasped but thought fast enough to brace himself. The snap that followed a second later nearly dislocated his arms, and Galvanix cried out at what he knew were broken ribs. He was thrown violently against Taggart several times, wondering if the chute was tearing. Long after the jolts subsided Galvanix still felt ringing disorientation.

"I'm giving you an anesthetic," Taggart told him. "It's the last you'll see for a long time."

Galvanix began to protest, but felt his pain suddenly fade. They were swaying softly, descending at a rate Galvanix could not gauge but guessed might allow them to live. He felt dizzily proud that his lunar atmosphere could support a parachute.

"You may as well crack your faceplate so you can see something," Taggart told him. "You're also nearly out of air."

TWO

They descended into a storm, dropping through a canopy of clouds that swallowed the stars and lashed rain at them with increasing force as the air thickened. Taggart, who had her radar to penetrate the murk below, periodically advised Galvanix of their rapidly dwindling altitude, which promised an impressive smash. In the final meters, with the wind dense enough to batter at them, she deftly caught a gust beneath her chute, blunting their fall until they actually glided a distance. She angled downward, announcing: "Ten meters, eight . . ." and Galvanix, raising his legs against a looming ground he still could not see, crashed against the surface of the Moon.

He felt himself dragged, and was released with a snap. The parachute, flapping like a kite, disappeared in the darkness. Galvanix rolled on a spongy surface, which a second earlier had felt hard enough to hurt him. Winds howled about them, although he could not feel the cold or wet until he tilted his helmet up and was stung with spray.

"Are you okay?" Taggart said in his ear. "Report."

"I'm . . . all right," Galvanix replied, giving thought now to some serious pains. "Cracked ribs, but nothing worse. Unless your narcotic is misleading me, and how would I know that?"

"Never mind. We will have to move immediately, before others arrive." Galvanix could hear her only through the radio, and turned awkwardly until he spotted her a few meters away, kicking at the soft vegetation underfoot.

"You shouldn't have jettisoned the parachute," he told her. "Yasuhiro's people will find it."

"It has dissolved by now. However, I had to open it higher up than was prudent, and must assume we were observed." She set off, uncertainly at first in the low gravity, in what seemed to Galvanix an arbitrary direction.

"Where are we?" he asked, starting painfully after her.

"Twenty-eight degrees south, one thirty-one west," she replied.

This meant nothing to Galvanix, who irritably sought to place it against his mental map of Farside. He decided it put them somewhere between Apollo and Mare Orientale. It could have been a good deal worse, but was bad enough.

"And turn off your radio," she added. A click followed the order, then static. Galvanix opened his faceplate wider, loath to surrender its protection from the elements.

"You seem to have a plan, Taggart," he called after her.

"Don't call me that," she said, her voice carrying easily through the rain. "That operation is ended, the names dropped. You can call me Beryl."

Galvanix was amused. "Is that what you're called on ground missions?"

"It's my name. And would mean nothing to anyone who forced it out of you."

Galvanix had no response to that. He stepped through soggy masses of decaying foliage, peering in vain for details of the surrounding landscape. The storm was more violent than any Galvanix had known, even in the twilight zone.

Taggart had stopped and was looking down. "Why is there so much dead vegetation?" she asked.

Galvanix squatted and poked through the wet compost. "Lunar flora tends to lose leaves throughout the night, especially Farside varieties. Some species have month-long life cycles. This, however—" and he held up a plate-sized leaf, now falling apart—"is evergreen. It has spread across Farside as the environment moderates."

"So the destruction of the Mirrors is killing Farside vegetation," Taggart said.

Galvanix stood. "At least those varieties accustomed to Earthlight or Mirrors to get through the night. The hardy pre-Mirror strains will survive, but they are fairly primitive, and were being crowded out by the evergreens." He felt a pang at the carnage around him, a waste of all the efforts of Rona and her colleagues. "If it were not raining so hard, this field would stink," he observed.

"And the weather?" Taggart asked.

"Harsher than normal," Galvanix admitted. "The Mirrors never matched the warming effect of a full Earth, but they brought the

Farside night temperature into better balance, so that the twilight zone wasn't a ring of permanent gale. Now we've lost all that."

Taggart nodded once. "You will lose a lot more," she said, and resumed her march.

Galvanix followed, angry. "Will you explain that? I don't think you can consider me a security risk at this point."

"You are the worst kind of security risk. The enemy would twist you open like a spigot."

Taggart's gait was surprisingly good, but Galvanix guessed it had been acquired in a centrifuge, for she did not lope as high as he, as though still allowing for complications of centrifugal force. Galvanix caught up with her after several strides.

"You killed my friend," he said.

Taggart did not alter her pace. "He didn't plan to survive the mission. Neither did you. You threatened me as soon as I boarded ship, then followed me after I warned you away. Had you both stayed in the ship, we would all three be landing on Nearside now."

"We were not sent as your subordinates," Galvanix said angrily.

"No? I suppose this was a joint mission between peers? Sponsored by cooperating governments?"

Galvanix, though knowing what was coming, snapped, "Yes."

Taggart did not respond for a moment, and Galvanix wondered what her expression was. "You are like children," she said unexpectedly, as though musing. "Insisting on your Republic that nobody recognizes. You cannot claim sovereignty over your orbital space; you do not even own the air and water you breathe."

Galvanix had had the answer to that one since grade school. "None of the governments of Earth ever held title to a share of the atmosphere."

"They never had to. But the Orbital Consortium *owns* your air; they make you formally affirm as much."

"And they also formally deal with us, whether acknowledging the Republic or not."

"That's nothing but a service contract. They could send their own people to maintain the biosphere if it were not more economical to work through squatters."

Galvanix, who had heard his countrymen called worse, did not bridle. "Every nation is derided at birth," he said. "The prospect of its existence is an affront until it becomes an inevitability. We only hoped that this time it would not take a war."

The last remark was meant to elicit some response about the war, but Galvanix was disappointed. Taggart said simply, "This is nothing to me. I have my mission."

"And what is that?" he demanded. "You pursued your own agenda, excluding us. Deferring urgent business while you went after something you would not divulge."

"Nor shall I now," she replied.

Galvanix gave up. The ground beneath them was slanting slightly, and a few bushes, largely denuded, swayed over them in the wind. Galvanix watched as a bough rasped across the side of his suit, shedding leaves with disconcerting ease. He hoped the storm had contributed to their loosening.

Taggart stopped abruptly, and stood a second with one hand raised as though to forestall speech. "Get down," she said. "Cover yourself with mulch."

Galvanix dropped and began burrowing into the soft compost. The ground beneath was friable, and Galvanix had soon opened a trench deep enough to lie in. He sat, shoveled earth and leaves over his outstretched legs, then began with more difficulty to cover his chest and one arm. A few feet away, Taggart was amassing a great mound of leaves. She turned and saw Galvanix watching her.

"Here," she said, and tossed something. Galvanix heard a snap against his helmet and flinched. He guessed then what it was, and resumed settling into the leaves. He had gathered a pillow-like pile near his head, and lay back, wriggling most of his helmet under it.

Lying still, Galvanix listened for the sound of footsteps or aircraft, but could hear only rain drumming against the leaves around him. He felt Taggart pull taut the wire stuck to his helmet, and waited for her to speak. No words came, and Galvanix realized after a moment that she was not going to enlighten him. He settled within his suit lining to accommodate his injured ribs, and realized with surprise that if they lay still for very long he would fall asleep.

It was difficult to remain alert as fatigue flooded him. He felt blessed with life, serene beyond disturbance at this gift of every new moment, but reflected that this condition would not last. Enemies would injure him, so he must flee; but if cornered would he fight? Galvanix sought to order his thoughts, but the first step back to gain perspective swallowed him.

"Wake up," a voice repeated in his ear. Galvanix opened his eyes without moving, his body remembering not to stir carelessly when awakening in a spacesuit. He moved his limbs cautiously, and pain flared everywhere. "Keep still," Taggart added unnecessarily. Galvanix waited, able to hear only that it was no longer raining.

"Okay, let's go." The wire dropped off, and Galvanix, pushing aside loam and sitting up, was able to groan within the privacy of his helmet. He brushed wet leaves from his visor and raised it. Overhead stars gleamed through patches of open sky.

"The storm ended a minute ago," Taggart told him, already standing and briskly attending to suit functions. Galvanix clambered to his feet and did likewise. "You slept over an hour. We have to move before a ground search can begin."

"Why did we take cover?" Galvanix asked.

"A flyer passed over, peering into the storm. I did not want to risk a break in the clouds disclosing us."

Galvanix looked up uneasily. "So they know we're here."

"They suspect a landing, but the storm smeared the possible sites over a wide area. The region they must now search expands every hour; within two days it will be unmanageable."

She kicked loose a clinging patch of loam. "We must move quickly, yet not permit even a brief sighting to narrow their search pattern. We will rest only when taking cover."

Taggart kicked at the mounds of compost, obscuring signs of digging. Galvanix attempted to stretch his stiffening muscles and was speared with pain. His outraged ribs tore at his side like teeth, prompting a surge of nausea. Galvanix fell to his knees, fumbling at the catch for his helmet, and retched.

Taggart stood watching. "If you have internal injuries I cannot help you," she said.

"I heard broken ribs click," Galvanix said after a moment, breathing in sips.

"Strip off your suit and I'll tape them," she said. Galvanix, swaying on his knees as the upper half of his suit dangled like snakeskin, submitted to a binding whose strands numbed the flesh they touched, a mercy of Orbital technology. He hoped the anesthetic was broad in its effects, and, thoughtfully tasting vomit, framed the question so to make its relevance plain.

"Will the radiation debilitate us soon?" he asked.

"Not me," Taggart said, retracting tape back into some recess of her armor. "Your suit is doubtless flimsier. We may both remain functional long enough to get away."

Get away where? he wondered, but did not say, content with relief of pain.

"You will *have* to keep up," she added.

"Where are we going, then?" he asked, rising carefully. He had assumed they were heading straight for the twilight zone, then realized that it would be heavily patrolled.

"Farward," Taggart answered, setting off in easy strides.

The countryside was fitfully visible as the roiling cloud cover opened swaths of starlight, revealing a gently rolling land shaded by bushes and trees. If the meters-high foliage had been more thickly leaved, the shade would be as deep as in a terrestrial climax forest. Instead, drifts of fallen leaves rotted among the smaller shrubs, many themselves dying, around their feet.

Galvanix was able to match Taggart's pace without great difficulty. His broken ribs were immobilized; his pain and his nausea were annulled. He even ate a tiny amount of food from his helmet tubes. These provisions did not contain nearly enough calories for a long trek, but Galvanix knew what flora was edible, though he might soon be too sick to ingest it.

The lunar atmosphere was deep but not dense, and what stars could be seen gleamed like eyes. The colors of vegetation were muted to the palest pastels, but Galvanix recognized varieties he had seen in Rona's and others' greenhouses: Mandragora, green cheese, bastard toadflax, kudzu.

Taggart was bounding ahead of him, settling now into that optimal lunar stride that gained the most ground per step without requiring one to sail through slow arcs. Galvanix knew that this pace, efficiently executed, would be faster and less taxing than a march in Earth-level gravity. Could they cover hundreds of kilometers this way? He regretted not having tried; the first decade of the Lunar Republic had never allowed him the leisure to seek his narrow road to the deep north.

Prompted by this, Galvanix checked his helmet display and saw that an empty memory cube resided in the recorder. Galvanix had no camera, and in any case scorned the thought of shooting a visual record, testament by travelogue. He confirmed that his radio was off, closed his visor and set his microphone to Record. For the next hour he recounted—for whom? posterity? the scavenger who would strip his suit?—details of the mission thus far. He then added:

I am at peace, though in flight. My friends think me dead, and would only be pained to learn my end was more protracted. I am, in fact, a ghost.

Why am I following this ruthless soldier? She cannot lead me home, so I may as easily die alone or under what hospitality the locals afford. He considered his question carefully. *I wish to learn more from her.* It remained a good reason.

Several hours later Taggart called a brief halt. Galvanix meanly suspected she could not empty her bladder without breaking stride. He pushed back his visor. "Where are we going?" he asked. Taggart paused, and he added, "Don't tell me we're running *from* not *to*; I can take a bearing from starlight. We've gone in a straight line for nearly fifty klicks."

"You ask me to tell you something you could divulge under duress. It may not be wise even to ponder your inferences."

"If that's true, I would be foolish to have nothing to placate my interrogators. You must speak if you wish me to continue with you."

This was dangerous ground; Taggart might kill him rather than let him depart. Instead, she asked, "Have you objections to a long journey?"

"Probably not. I never had a chance to take my Grand Tour. How far do you think us capable of hiking?"

"Perhaps only to a means of transportation. I could defeat the security systems of most lunar vehicles."

"And we would race off to where?"

Taggart was silent.

"I have other questions. Why did our ship explode?"

Taggart, examining the seals on her knee joints, did not answer.

"Another secret? The controls hadn't been tampered with, except for my overriding the airlock. And I don't see how cabin decompression would make the ship blow. . . ." Galvanix had it then. "It was *your* bomb that blew!" he said accusingly.

Taggart shrugged. "The disk was anti-personnel, so was designed to operate inside a life-support system. Prolonged vacuum triggered a subroutine for scuttling wrecks."

Galvanix stared at her. "And you didn't know?"

"I have since deduced it. Evidently that knowledge is not provided to all agents, perhaps lest it affect their judgment."

Galvanix, though furious, had to smile. "So although ferociously armed, you are not wholly trusted by your superiors?"

"Complex relationships always admit of ambivalences, something you seem unable to appreciate. An agent must act without the instant's hesitation such considerations impose, for not everyone finds death in action convenient."

"What do you mean?"

"Never mind. Let me ask you again: Are you prepared to make a possibly long journey?"

"With no further specifics? All right, yes. I wish to survey what the Farsiders' vandalism has wrought on our beautiful work."

Taggart stood. "Your flippancy ill becomes you. The Moon may be a toy, but the world isn't."

Galvanix did not feel he need take this from a hired murderer. "My motives are known," he said. "You have still not demonstrated you aren't working against us. *What were you doing?*" The answer came to Galvanix then. "You were looking for something on the comet. Not a message—you could have received one before we picked you up. A physical object on the comet, something you didn't want us to know about."

Taggart was unperturbed. "You and Danziger should have guessed that together," she said. She set off then, at a pace that Galvanix could only match with effort.

Galvanix strode quickly, thinking. A specimen, he thought. It must be. Something found during the Jovian expeditions, and left or placed on the comet rather than reported. Curiosity leaped in him like liquid sloshing.

Winds scattered the thunderheads lining the eastern horizon, revealing a starry expanse undimmed by the coming dawn. Galvanix recalled that the sun had been just past the zenith at Tycho, meaning that sunrise here could not be more than forty hours away. Was that good or bad? Taggart seemed to be bearing due Farward, more northerly than westerly from here, so the dawn would overtake them without difficulty. Galvanix confided these thoughts to his recorder in panting snatches.

He wondered what onset of symptoms Taggart's drugs were masking. This would be a poor time to sicken and die.

They stopped several hours later, where a stream they had been following broadened into a pond. Its surface was overhung by an enormous willow, freed of the Earth-level gravity that once limited its species' growth. Insects hovered low over the drifting water, creating a food niche for the trout Galvanix had hoped to stock his world with.

After questioning Galvanix about the possibility of animals coming to drink, Taggart began to strip off her suit. Galvanix studied her body through her silver undergarment, which she unzipped to the navel before wading in and sluicing water through it. Her impressive musculature did not tell him whether she was from Earth—the Orbitals all maintained Earth-level gravity; that was what ruined the Moon as a permanent settlement save for exiles—but Galvanix hoped for some clue (sun-bleached hair? insect bites?) that would betray a natural environment. Taggart, water streaming comically out the openings between her legs, pushed her garment down to her waist, revealing—as he should have expected—a holster under one arm. Galvanix, fearing that water would dissolve the medication in his rib tapes, reluctantly stayed on the shore.

"The water is cooler than when we first reached it," Taggart remarked, letting it run through her fingers. Galvanix wondered if he was being tested.

"It fell from clouds blown by winds warmed in the twilight storms," he said. "And has traveled over ground that has been cooling all night."

"And where is it running?" she asked, looking at him.

"Downhill, or with the tides," Galvanix said impatiently. "Still bodies will incline toward and away from the sun." He sensed something wrong about this.

"This is running Farward," Taggart said. "That would be uphill, of course, and the solar bulge is elsewhere at present." She let Galvanix ponder this a moment. "I am standing on roots," she announced suddenly. "It feels like a drowned bush." Taggart reached down and drew up a dripping length of briar. She held it out for Galvanix's study.

"That is not an aquatic plant," he said. Taggart nodded slightly. "All right. The water level has risen recently. And is running in unusual patterns."

"Tell me about the Far Pole," said Taggart, wading back to shore.

"I have never seen it," Galvanix replied. "But it is nearly identical to the Near Pole." He felt a chill. "The Moon does not of course rotate about their axis, at least not literally. The Near Pole is slightly warmer, from the Earthlight."

"Indeed."

Galvanix thought. "The destruction of the Mirrors has produced deeper night-time chills than the Farside has seen in decades. The atmosphere cannot hold as much water, and it is contracting besides. Is that right? Cooler air condensing to form a shallower atmosphere?"

"Correct." Taggart looked up as though to point out stars, but the overarching willow covered them like a dome. "The tidal bulge of the Far Pole can now be assumed to protrude through the lower levels of the atmosphere."

"Both poles always have," Galvanix objected.

"Not by much, and not like this. Think about it: Increased precipitation puts more water onto the surface, some of which ends up adding to the bulge's height. The atmosphere flattens, the top of the bulge freezes, then sublimes in the low pressure. The vapor molecules are too heavy and moving too slowly to escape the Moon's orbit; they drift and fall back, further feeding the Farside storms. More water is drawn toward the bulge as its top disappears, creating Farward currents throughout the hemisphere."

"My God," Galvanix whispered. "A storm machine."

"A big one. It is going to make our work very difficult."

Taggart stood on the shore, touching snaps at the feet of her undergarment to allow water to empty through the toes. Then she stripped it off and wrung it like a rag. Galvanix was too dumbfounded to study her further.

"But wait," he said. "There is still a solar bulge, and it continues to move. Doesn't that mitigate the effect?"

"Why should it? That's just a complication, making it harder to calculate tide tables." Taggart quickly climbed into her undergarment and suit. A faint whir started up as her blowers came on.

"Actually," she said, "the friction of all this water being drawn across the surface will warm the crust slightly, weakening the cycle. It's a very real factor on Earth, although the effects only show up over long periods."

"This won't last that long," Galvanix said coldly. "We'll be constructing new mirrors."

Taggart, her face recessed within the frame of her visor, made no reply, and Galvanix could not see her expression. He saw something flicker behind her, and realized that a slender antenna was rising out of her back, ascending like a plumbline until it disappeared among the branches overhead. Taggart held still for a moment, then said, "All clear." The antenna descended rapidly and disappeared with a soft click.

"We have been hiking eleven hours; I propose we sleep for three. This tree provides better cover than most sites." Taggart began walking carefully around the pond, looking into the brush as though checking for enemies.

Galvanix realized he could go to sleep quite easily. He stretched out on the sloping bank, head higher than his feet, and inflated his helmet lining for a pillow. As he settled back, an image of the Far Pole came to him like a preview of a dream: a mountain of water rising above all clouds, its snowcap smoking like dry ice beneath the untwinkling stars of space. Galvanix regarded the apparition with half-conscious bemusement, wondering, *Am I going to see this . . . ?*

And woke up with a hand clapped over his mouth, shaking him. "Get into the water. Quietly." The hand withdrew from his helmet. Galvanix blinked, working out the implications. He stood, wincing, and looked to the pond, so dark now that he could scarcely see it.

Taggart punched him hard on the shoulder. Galvanix waded in as quietly as he could, then realized that the wind was thrashing the willow loudly enough to mask any sound. He slipped in up to his neck, pulling down his faceplate and activating the air system. Taggart, her crouched silhouette almost invisible against the shore, slid beneath the surface with a tiny splash.

Galvanix crouched until the water rose to eye level, then slowly scanned the circumference of shore. Another squall had blown up, blotting the earlier starlight and blowing wet gusts that rippled the water. Light glinted beyond chest-high fronds, swaying in the recognizable manner of hand-held torches. Indistinct figures appeared through the scrim of fronds and mist.

A hand grasped his upper arm, pulling him swiftly underwater. Galvanix drifted away from Taggart, adjusting his buoyancy to keep him beneath the surface. He could see her dimly in the clear water, crouched with the top of her helmet breaking the surface. Since he could not look through the water at an oblique angle to see the shore, Galvanix rested lightly on his back, watching Taggart's tensed body hold still as a sunken statue, serried ripples on the surface breaking against the isle of her helmet.

Are they looking for us? he wondered silently. He felt like a mudpuppy in the pondbottom ooze, able to hide for days while search parties swept past. How long would his air last? he wondered. If necessary, he could push an air-tube to the surface. . . .

There was movement, and Galvanix saw Taggart bring her arms up quickly. Light flashed between her hands, a bolt that lit up the water between them like tinted glass, and then another. Galvanix brought up his knees and kicked against the bottom, breaking the surface in a plume of spray. On the shore's edge a man twisted and fell, the front of his shirt burning.

"My God!" cried Galvanix, pushing up his faceplate. Taggart, weapon in hand, did not turn. "What ha—"

A wall of spray struck him, and Galvanix was thrown off his feet. He swallowed hot water, clawed at clouds of bubbles as his orientation spun dizzily, then broke the surface thrashing. Taggart was firing her weapon against the opposite shore, waving a line of violet light across it like a beacon. Someone screamed, and she swung back again. The scream ceased.

"*What have you done?*" Galvanix stared at her, eyes bulging in hysteria. Taggart, low in the water, turned slowly in a full circle, then stood up and looked at Galvanix.

"Fighting," she said.

Galvanix slogged to the shore, high steps splashing clumsily. Two men lay still on the bank. The nearer one, facedown in the wet soil, smoked faintly.

Galvanix turned him over. He was a young man, Japanese features similar to Galvanix's beneath a severe haircut; he had been shot through the chest with a laser bolt. The cauterized wound bled only slightly.

The other man was older, and had the same cropped hair. He had been shot through the side, as though his arm had been raised.

Taggart came up beside them. "They're soldiers," she said.

"Not anymore," said Galvanix. His voice broke on the last word, and he began to cry.

"They found our tracks. Look." Taggart scuffed at the wet sand with her foot. Galvanix didn't look. Taggart seized the young man's wrist, turned it upward. A display band showed, twelve studs ranged beneath a tiny screen. "He would have given the alarm in another second." A light beside the screen pulsed an uneasy yellow. Taggart studied the display for a second, then pushed a stud. The light became a steady green.

"They were unarmed," Galvanix said.

"You wouldn't recognize a weapon if it was fired at you, which one was." Taggart walked around the older man, picked up something nearby. "That was good tactics, sending their third man around the pond. If you hadn't been underwater and in a pressure suit that blast would have killed you.

"It certainly settles any question of their expecting belligerents," she added, turning the body over and searching its pockets.

"Leave him alone, you carrion bird!" Galvanix cried. Her desecration stung him to fury.

"Shut up and keep out of my way. These are our enemies, remember that." The statement seemed ludicrous in the face of Galvanix's strong resemblance to the dead men, beside whom the black-skinned warrior seemed an alien.

Taggart found foodstuffs in a shoulder pack, examined and set aside a compass, small knife, and a hand torch. "You take these," she said. "I have my own." She fingered the younger man's shirt. "These should fit you." And to Galvanix's horror she began to pull it of.

He turned, sickened, and took several steps along the shore. A wisp of steam curled above the roiled surface of the pond, and Galvanix realized dimly that something had been fired at them. War and butchery were loosed on the Moon. Galvanix found his legs were shaking uncontrollably, and he sat down hard on the packed soil.

He heard a low splashing, and turned his head to see Taggart stepping backward into the water. Galvanix squinted, unable for a moment to recognize what was happening. Taggart was pulling one of the bodies toward the center of the pond, where she released it. Bubbles streaming from its billowed garments, the body disappeared.

Galvanix rose shakily and walked toward Taggart, who was striding back to shore. Glancing at him, she bent over the remaining figure, which was stripped like an animal carcass. "Get me some stones," she said.

"What are you doing?"

"Weighting the bodies. Don't look like that; do you think we have time to bury them?" Taggart stood up. "Here." She tossed bunched clothing at Galvanix, which struck his chest and fell to the ground.

Galvanix turned away, wandering down the shore. Behind him he heard the click of stones knocking together. Making an effort, he bent and picked up several rough stones, never smoothed by river currents.

When he walked up to Taggart, she was bending over the dead man's head. She seemed to be feeling the inside of his mouth, as though he were having trouble breathing. "What," Galvanix began, unable to articulate.

"I am putting them down his throat. He has no pockets."

Galvanix closed his eyes.

Willow boughs sighed overhead, releasing a spray of raindrops. Galvanix's handful of stones dropped to the ground, where Taggart reached to pick them up. After a moment he heard her dragging the dead soldier into the water. Galvanix opened his eyes and saw the bundled clothes near his feet. He picked them up, sorting through them absently in search of a name tag. They were standard issue garments, anonymous and unadorned.

Taggart came up behind him, dripping. "The third one will be messy. You had better stay here." Galvanix did not reply, and Taggart moved away, pausing after a few steps to add, "They were more like me than like you. Take a look at that knife, if you don't believe me."

For several minutes Galvanix stood with the clothes in his hands, then looked at the pile of looted tools. The knife handle was larger than most, and Galvanix picked it up, fitting his fingers around the grooves before touching the release. The blade that sprang forth was wider than Galvanix expected, and when he studied it he realized that it was not flat, but deepened to an elongated diamond at the base. The design seemed odd even for cutting meat, and Galvanix realized with a start that it was intended to punch a wound that would not close. He immediately retracted the blade, unwilling to look on its design.

Thinking confusedly that one must bear witness to atrocity, Galvanix activated his recorder, but found he could say nothing. Words had no force against death. Finally he gave a terse statement that three men had been killed and their bodies sunk in the pond. The tape might be played and the dead recovered by their families.

Taggart tapped his shoulder. "We have to go," she said. "The alarm will be given when the patrol fails to check in, and I cannot find the OK code in the wrist monitor's register. They might even be able to trace the device, so we will have to get away from it as fast as possible. I would float it down the current except that we will be moving downstream too."

Galvanix turned to face her, but only because her suit was making a strange sound. Water was spewing out a vent in her side, evidently under the action of a suit pump that drove it in rhythmic spurts.

"I have to sit down," he said, but lost consciousness before lunar gravity gathered him in.

He woke with a feeling that the world was spinning about him, and realized with a shock that Taggart was whirling him around by his ankles. *She has never been on the Moon before*, Galvanix thought as blood rushed into his head. *She's showing off to herself*.

"Wake up fast, for I will not leave you behind," she was saying. "The bottom of the pond is cold. I've just been there."

Galvanix fluttered his hands, was set down and shoved. He began marching, past the mouth of the pond where it fed into a silted marsh. When they were clear of the willow, Taggart stopped and produced a length of tube with a small loop at one end. She fitted the wrist monitor into the loop, then stretched the tube between her arms, pulling it several times its length.

The slingshot, its payload drawn back behind her ear, was aimed along a course perpendicular to their route and released with a thrum. The monitor shot across the night sky, vanishing from sight before it began its descent toward the horizon.

• • •

The marsh was too wet to bound through, and the drier ground of its border left footprints. They circled the low ground, finding on its far side another stream fed by draining rivulets. Taggart probed the dark water with a rigid wire she had extruded from somewhere, and tapped something hard. She pushed, and a wash surged briefly, as though a dugong rolled over beneath the surface. "Good," she pronounced, stepping into the stream to reach underwater.

Galvanix did not react when Taggart pulled a dark prow up to the bank, though its economy of design might have pleased him. The kayak floated just beneath the surface when flooded, held fast by a tiny barbed anchor. Taggart tipped the vessel and water poured from two openings, carrying with it a flapping shape that splashed around the shallows before slipping away. Galvanix blinked.

"I doubt there's a homing device in this thing, as your Farside counterparts seem to share your predilection for pre-technology," Taggart remarked. "However, if there is—" She laid a hand on either side of the ship, whose dripping surface began to crackle, droplets dancing like cooking grease—"it is now inoperative."

Taggart lifted the kayak easily, hefting it on one palm for balance. "They came upstream as far as they could," she said. "That's good news. It means the edge of their search area is here or behind us."

"They went against the current," Galvanix said.

"And we will have it with us." Taggart flipped the craft around, displaying a screw propeller breaking through the stern below the waterline. "Driven by pedals, quieter than oars. A fair design, for a touring boat."

Taggart set the boat in the water. "Get in back," she said. "We have to send this toy as far from here as possible, so we may as well ride it. At first sight of the enemy I shall sink it, so fill your air tanks. We may have to hike underwater."

Galvanix settled into the waist-sized opening, fitting his feet around the bicycle pedals below. Taggart pushed off with her straight wire, which then disappeared into her wrist. "You want to pedal for a few hours? The gear system allows both sets to work simultaneously, and we could use the speed. You could also use the routine; let you think . . ."

Galvanix tentatively began to pedal, feeling the light plastic components move easily. The gear was too low for moving downstream, but he reached down and found the mechanism for shifting up. The boat began to slip forward, steered toward the center of the stream by whatever controls Taggart found in the forward seat. Galvanix merely cycled, seeking a rhythm that would lull his distress.

Within minutes they were moving swiftly downstream, passing groves of willow and bamboo that lined the shores. Many stood within the shallows, and after watching them drift past Galvanix realized dully that the banks had overflowed. He wondered if this would cause the current to move faster than otherwise, but could not focus his mind upon the problem.

In his fatigue Galvanix thought the craft moving faster than it was, and leaned forward to touch his helmet against the back of Taggart's. "Are you in control?" he asked.

"I am always in control."

Galvanix felt his real question unanswered. "How far are we following this stream?"

"All the way."

Galvanix sat back, disconcerted. He settled into the position most comfortable for sustained cycling, and the relief it afforded his spine dropped him immediately into a doze, from which he awoke bemusedly, uncertain how much time had passed.

They were moving through an eroded countryside, gullies carved by twenty years of weather and steep banks on either shore. Rainwater sluiced through newly etched tributaries and into the swelling stream. Alders stood in small groves, sheltering smaller shrubs. The nitrogen-fixing bacteria symbiotic with alders allowed them to survive in this poor soil which, enriched by their leaf litter, supported an entourage of smaller growths. The slowly widening circles would in time touch edges, if the runneled land did not slice them into islets.

"Taggart," Galvanix said.

"I was beginning to wonder whether you thought I thought you were asleep," Taggart said.

Galvanix ignored that. "Just before I went to sleep you said that we were following the stream 'all the way.' " The sudden memory of a dream brushed against him, very close yet transparent. Galvanix batted it away, distracted. "What does that mean?"

"It means what I said, as always. We are following the current as far as it goes."

"To the Far Sea?"

"Farther."

Galvanix blinked at this, then an image came abruptly into focus. He had been standing near the Tycho shore, looking into a morning sky. The Earth was full, and Galvanix—apparently a child—was watching it with expectation. Without knowing why, Galvanix understood that in the dream the Earth had been rising, though the brief moment had not allowed discernible motion. The moment held, pregnant, all of the dream that he could recover.

"Farther," Galvanix said carefully, "means to the Pole."

"Yes."

"I am trying to think of why you would want to go to the Far Pole."

"What I want is there."

"What is there is an ice cap that pokes through the atmosphere. Water goes there but nothing else does. *What you want is borne on currents*," Galvanix said in sudden realization. "Something floating."

"That is correct."

"So you have moved now to a new target, something on the Moon. Further orders, a message in a bottle?" Galvanix raised Occam's razor, and the answer opened before him. "No, it's *the same one*, isn't it? What you wanted on the comet, you think it's on the Moon now? It survived the explosion?"

"There is nowhere else for it to be."

Galvanix thought aloud, lest his thoughts dart away like minnows, too fast to call back. "An object that would survive the heat and shock of re-entry as well as the blast. An object that floats. Something small, that would be washed into a stream. How did this get on the comet?" No answer. "Something placed there, a message not entrusted to radio? A sample from the Jovian expedition, sent eleven years ago."

Taggart said, "You seem to have recovered your reason after the shock of last evening."

And for Galvanix everything collapsed. Remembrance settled like a fine soot, gradually obscuring the world around him. In the silence that followed, Galvanix disappeared within his misery, a stone in a well.

"Perhaps I spoke too soon," Taggart said. "Listen to me. What happened last night was an early skirmish in what will be a very complex and unpredictable war. There is no point in imagining that you were in some way responsible for it. Had you died upon landing I would have followed the same course and encountered that patrol the same way." Galvanix said nothing, and she added sharply, "You are irradiated, in enemy territory, and loyal to a cause you will undoubtedly contrive to get killed for should you live long enough. There is no point in hobbling yourself with guilt over my actions."

"I am grieving, not guilt-stricken," Galvanix said shakily.

"You know nothing of your emotions or motivation. I am concerned that your depression may incapacitate you, endangering my mission."

"I am no burden to your dubious mission," Galvanix retorted, stung. "You do not know the Moon, and cannot conceal my value to you. We will recover your Jovian sample."

"It is information we are after, not a sample. There were no discoveries of military value smuggled off that expedition, just a database that remains uniquely unrifled because it has spent the last decade beyond human reach. Do not tell yourself you are acting for science."

And Taggart fell silent, as though daring Galvanix to throw himself into new depths. Galvanix feared that himself, but instead thought about the database Taggart had mentioned. Data security was a proprietary concern, the obsession of those who saw knowledge as commodity, or had something to hide.

Galvanix wondered about the last secure database in the solar system and what it might contain. It allowed him to think without pain, and he bent his back to pedaling, the whisk of the gears assuming the rhythm of a mantra.

Galvanix was cycling steadily when water gushed suddenly over his feet, causing him to think wildly that the boat was disintegrating. "What—" he began, but Taggart overrode him, turning her head to call, "Quiet. Look up."

Galvanix looked up. A broken beam of light fell through the sky before them, wavering in an unsteady vertical through the tatters of cloud. Atop it Galvanix saw an airship, approaching slowly as it plied its searchlight. The boat was sinking, though Taggart pedaled unperturbed. The craft and passengers slowly descended, like a submarine slipping under. Galvanix realized that the airship was following the river, fixing its beam on the water and correcting course as winds buffeted the gasbag. That meant it lacked computers, he thought as the churning water rose around his chest. So primitive a craft might also lack scopes to see through water . . . Galvanix remembered to close his faceplate just as the river rose over him.

Underwater was a featureless darkness, with a ceiling of dim grey that receded and vanished. Galvanix had not expected starlight to penetrate the river, but felt alarm at the thought of drifting blind beneath their hunters. Since the ship did not nudge the bottom he knew that they had attained neutral buoyancy, and were continuing to drift downriver. Did Taggart have sonar to steer by? Galvanix tensed for the grinding contact with the shallows.

The water about him was suddenly suffused with ruby light, and the outline of Taggart and the kayak sprang into view. Galvanix looked up to see a brilliant orange glare, then sudden darkness once more. He blinked, feeling rather than seeing dark spots bloom before his eyes.

Something touched his chest, and Galvanix jumped. "Keep pedaling," Taggart said, her voice sounding remote through the conducting metal. "They may double back when they reach the marsh."

"Do you think they are looking for us?" Galvanix asked.

"Probably. That patrol missed their check-in, and somebody will have added that to the other data and inferred our existence."

"Then we are lucky that was only an adapted cargo ship, although—" Galvanix began, then realized that Taggart had withdrawn her hand. He contented himself with listening to the full score of riversounds, which resounded within his helmet as though amplified. After a moment he activated his voice recorder. "*Farsider Walkabout*," he said. "By Galvanix. One. The night-side chill, colder and darker with the loss of the Mirrors, remembers the vacuum taken from this world. When the Farside is nightside, as now, the darkness is complete, and the barren landscape resembles some Earthly wilderness, beyond the limits of edible plant and animal life. Too wordy. Cold streams run swiftly uphill, drawn by the tides that draw all water to the very back of the world, where floes and an eventual icecap await. Without—"

The detonation blew away Galvanix's experience of it, deleting even the preceding seconds as if by backwash. Galvanix remembered water striking his face, the spaceman's thrill of alarm at suit breach. Pain entered somewhere, and vertigo that he felt in his body rather than his stunned middle ears. An insistent noise, penetrating even deafness (it was meant to operate in vacuum), buzzed a bone behind his ear and provoked finally an automatic response. Tumbling backward in a flurry of bubbles, Galvanix pulled a thin tube from his belt and stuck it in his mouth. Air rushed in, strong enough to fill his lungs even if vacuum tore it out his nose and ears. Galvanix started wildly. He was underwater, his collar seal choking the flow of water into his suit, keeping him buoyant as he slowly spun.

The lunar spacesuit, primitive as it was, had provisions for operation in open water which Taggart's might have lacked. Underwater pressure coupled with the breach triggered a subroutine, and the suit filled with rerouted air. Galvanix, his limbs immobilized by ballooning joints, broke the surface, bobbed, and twirled slowly downstream like a reed, sucking obliviously on his hose. Cold rain ran down his scalded face. Galvanix grimaced but kept his eyes closed until his suit bumped twice against the shallow streambed, and the current finally pushed him against its slope and left him wedged.

Returning pain prompted him finally to stir, and when the subroutine shut off, a constellation of pinpricks slowly bled the air from his suit. Galvanix felt himself sag, and his head dipped below the water. The hose slipped from his mouth, thrashing like a snake. Chilled and disoriented, he crawled onto shore, collapsing like a castaway on the streaming earth.

When he woke hours later, the rain had subsided and the quality of light was different. Water had entered the leaking suit, and Galvanix was deeply cold. He fumbled with numbed fingers to run a systems check, confirmed that the heater would not electrocute him, and turned it on. Sitting up with difficulty, he opened the stopcocks at his ankles to let the water run out, unmindful of any echo in the act.

The stream from one boot ran a garish pink, but Galvanix told himself that any serious injury would have left him in shock.

Dulled by pain, Galvanix focused upon himself, and only when he noticed a faint shadow move beneath his arm did he look up to see diffuse light seeping through the shrouded horizon.

Although the rain was resuming, it was dawn.

After examining the inside of his helmet to confirm that his food tubes had been washed empty, Galvanix pried out the voice recorder and threw the rest into the stream. He stepped into the throw to ensure that it carried to midstream; he did not want the helmet washing up like other bits of debris he found along the shore. Most appeared to be fragments of the boat, but one scrap, armored on one side and cushioned on the other, had come from Taggart's suit.

Galvanix retreated to higher ground, then began to strip off his suit. The necessity was bitter, but he knew what would happen if he were found in it. When he pulled it off, he noticed the bundled clothing Taggart had placed in his outerpouch. His undergarment was thin and wet, and Galvanix shook out the dead man's clothes, hardly pausing to examine his torn skin before pulling them on. Rations tumbled out with the knife and compass, and Galvanix sat down and opened one. He ate slowly, feeling unwell as the food touched his stomach. The knife he left on the ground, loath to acknowledge that he would pick it up when he rose.

Galvanix wondered if Taggart would have listened had he pressed his small suspicion. The airship must have been dropping tiny depth charges every few hundred meters, floaters with microprocessors that would detonate at the approach of an object in the right mass range. Seeding the river like that might seem a prohibitive extravagance for a militia relying upon transport balloons, but Taggart had failed to think like a Moonie. The unexploded charges, Galvanix knew, would have been collected at the mouth of the river, to be carefully checked and re-used.

Hefting his suit, Galvanix saw he could not entrust it to the river bottom: the current would drag its limbs like sails. He considered filling it with rocks, and was abruptly sick at the notion. Swaying, he sank to his knees, and after a moment began digging at the earth with the toe of one boot. When the hole was large enough he pushed the suit in, then filled it and dragged rocks over the top. He made the pile as large as he dared, hoping it would quiet the suit's radioactivity.

Returning to the river, Galvanix sought his reflection in the running water. He made out the face of a savage, black-eyed, unshaven. He ran a hand through his hair, and felt strands come away in his fingers. "You only half-escaped death," he told the apparition.

Galvanix stood, turning slowly to scan the horizon until he faced the murky sunrise. It was perhaps a thousand kilometers to Republican territory; he couldn't be sure how far the river had carried him. No point in exaggerating his chances of making it back, he told himself. These last days, as Rona would chide him, were a gift. Maybe he would learn something with them.

As he set out, he realized that only he knew the location of Taggart's precious database. Her superiors might guess at the possibility, but could not be sure it had not been destroyed with the comet, or that Taggart did not still have it and was lying low.

Galvanix wondered whether to bring the dirty secret to his own people or let it die with him. He might not, of course, get the choice.

Walking unsteadily toward the light, he wrapped the dissected voice recorder around his neck. "Early dawn," he told the microphone. "Direction, upstream. Dearest Rona, I do not think you shall hear this, but will speak for my own ease of spirit . . ."

The rain gusted warm and cold.

THREE

Three thousand paces into his journey Galvanix saw a dark line dividing the land before him, which widened as he approached into a featureless road. Alert to the likelihood of some barrier within the libration zone, Galvanix studied it warily, but the meters-wide ribbon seemed wholly inert: a flattened strip packed and baked from the surrounding loose regolith by a mobile roadmaking machine. Galvanix hopped onto the smooth surface, glad for its level firmness.

The road ran straight in either direction, bearing neither toward Nearside nor parallel with it. Reluctant to abandon any path, Galvanix decided to follow it in the direction that obliquely approached home.

The paved surface made moonwalking easier, and Galvanix, who'd had to concentrate on keeping his balance crossing the muddy ground, relaxed slightly. Soon he was bounding automatically, lulled into reverie by the steady numeration of his steps. He had reached the forty-six hundreds when the thrill of vibration beneath his feet roused him. Galvanix kicked to a halt and turned. Behind him a large truck was rapidly approaching.

Galvanix froze a second, then stepped off the road and waved. The driver had certainly seen him, and could doubtless overtake him even across the fields. Galvanix felt his pockets and decided he carried nothing incriminating. As the truck rolled slowly past him to come to rest twenty meters ahead, Galvanix began jogging after it, smiling with good fortune.

The truck was a four-wheeled hauler, tiny cab pulling an open container. It settled with a hiss and blurted a noxious cloud through its tailpipe. Galvanix was startled to see heads pop up over the container's lip. Imperturbable, he trotted up to the driver's window, and was not greatly surprised to find it occupied.

A hard-faced woman leaned out to stare down at him. "What happened to you, citizen?" she asked, giving sardonic emphasis to the last word.

Like the faces in back, she appeared to be ethnic Japanese. Galvanix, who knew his features looked mongrelized to those who cared about such things, smiled stupidly. "Field crew left without me," he said, trying for a Korean accent.

The driver looked disgusted. "What field crew?"

"Cleaning nightsoil pumps." Maintenance of the sewage recycling systems where they fed into the fields was an onerous job, often given to mental defectives.

The driver gestured behind her with a thumb. "In back, fool. You're lucky a patrol didn't shoot you."

Bobbing his head in thanks, Galvanix rounded the back of the container, which swung open. Seven men scowled as Galvanix climbed in, and two pointedly moved over to give him wide berth. Nodding deferentially, Galvanix settled with his back against the container wall, which was faintly slick and smelled of vegetable matter.

The truck shuddered and lurched forward. Galvanix could not see the back of the cab, but guessed it lacked an autopilot, since he could imagine no other reason to use a human driver for so simple a haul. He was less shocked that they were using a container to transport personnel than that they had adapted the truck to burn alcohol. He could only surmise that the Farsiders had run out of superconductor, and could not keep outposts supplied with electrical power throughout the lunar night. Small wonder the driver had refused to brake for him.

The truck slowly accelerated to cruising speed, and the men around him resumed their conversation, ignoring Galvanix. He was grateful for that; their accents all held the tang peculiar to Farsiders, and Galvanix feared that his faked Korean would betray reciprocal Nearside cadences. Rising casually to his feet, Galvanix looked out upon the landscape rushing past. The low sun was about to disappear behind a swell of angry clouds, and the muddy flatlands, uncultivated save for the primitive fronds that could fix their own nitrogen, rippled with winds that boded a storm.

Galvanix looked down upon the road, seeing faint wavy lines whip past the truck—tracks, he suddenly realized, of large vehicles running along the verge. Had he noticed them earlier he could have guessed the road was traveled by trucks. Exasperated, he looked about for other signs he might have missed, then saw the eye of one of the passengers on him. He smiled vacantly and looked away, his gaze resolutely incurious.

Galvanix had not appreciated how his exertion had kept him warm, and within minutes he was shivering. He huddled against the warm container bottom, wondering if the others, one or two of whom were glancing at him idly, would recognize a spacesuit undergarment peeping through the torn clothing. Warmth crept slowly up the container's ceramic sides, and when Galvanix's trembling subsided, consciousness fell from him like a stone.

He half-woke to a gust of rain sleeting over him, and screwed up his face querulously, burying it in his sleeve. Something rustled overhead, and the rain ceased. Later he heard the murmur of conversation, nearly audible now that they were sheltered from the wind. Galvanix kept his head down, eyes on a triangle of azure light framed by his drawn-up legs.

". . . where they want to grow rice. Some peasant will blow his feet off."

"We'll have Nearsiders work those fields." Scattered laughter greeted this.

A third voice spoke, too low to be heard. "Or washed downstream," another said.

Someone made the plosive sound of a bomb-burst, and more laughter followed.

"But if they have fission weapons—"

Galvanix felt his weight shift, and the truck geared up as it began climbing, drowning out further talk. He waited for a return to quieter driving, but the truck seemed to be traversing a series of low hills, and without a focus for his attention Galvanix drifted unwillingly back into sleep.

He woke when the truck jerked to a halt and rocked slightly. Opening his eyes, Galvanix saw the men scrambling to their feet, cyanotic beneath the translucent blue tarpaulin that arched over their heads. The cover began to curl back, and a wet wind blew across the container. Galvanix stood stiffly, and at once felt dizzy and nauseated.

Someone struck his shoulder. "Out!"

Galvanix hopped down from the back, staggering as he came gently down. The truck stood at an almost empty crossroads, a lone building filling one crook of its X. The two straight highways neatly sectioned a landscape of low fields, one running into the foothills the truck had just crossed. Galvanix walked unsteadily around the cab and found his fellow travelers confronting what appeared to be soldiers.

A half-dozen men, wearing odd and identically cut clothes, stared hard at the arrivals. One said something to the driver, who drew papers from her pocket. A short discussion followed, while the others studied the newcomers suspiciously.

Galvanix edged into the crowd, hoping to be inconspicuous. He had not seen actual soldiers since childhood, when diplomatic attachés sometimes came to Tycho. These were not foreigners, however, but slender-limbed sansei, holding themselves with the ease of those born to lunar gravity. Galvanix felt a chill in his stomach contract to a point. He kept his head down.

After a minute they were herded indoors, where warm air beyond the antechamber carried the smell of food. Galvanix's companions loudly approved this, though Galvanix felt sick. They tramped down a hallway, crowding too much for Galvanix to see anything, and were ushered into a small common room. The soldiers took their seats at one long table where food was set and resumed eating. The work crew sat at the other, looking to the hatch at the far end of the room through which meals could be passed.

Galvanix sat warily among them, noticing that the driver had evidently left. He felt uneasy at being in a room containing only men, which seemed to hold a promise of violence.

One of the soldiers was studying him unpleasantly, and Galvanix wondered whether the man had been told he was a sewage worker. Mentally deficient adults were more common on the Moon than elsewhere; pregnancies spent in lunar gravity predisposed slightly to birth defects. Expectant mothers were now housed in full-gee orbital dorms, but the Republic had refused to subject the first-born casualties to the reprogramming methods used on Earth to overcome retardation in infants, calling it a violation of the soul. Galvanix remembered suddenly that Farside reactionaries had once called for euthanasia, and wondered in disoriented alarm if the soldier was considering carrying one out right now.

Somebody shoved him, and Galvanix's attention was directed to the hatch, through which a man was waving. Galvanix got up and unsteadily made his way across, where plates of food were slid toward him. He quickly served the others, hoping not to attract attention. Dinner was steamed rice with bits of vegetable. Galvanix sat down with the last plate. It was not bad for farm hostel fare at the end of a lunar night, but he could eat almost nothing.

He got up twice more, to clear plates and then serve tea to both tables. In the bustle he managed to drink two cups, driven by his burning throat and intermittent chills. He was desperate to sit down before some curious soldier sensed he wasn't part of the work crew. As he cleared their cups, his legs began to tremble.

A gang of women trooped in, wet and smelling of turned soil. The soldiers shouted welcome, but were quieted by a gesture from their officer. At once they rose to surrender their table, and Galvanix was pressed against the wall, nearly sagging in relief. The work crew, heartened by the soldiers' departure, called greetings to the women, who shouted for food. Galvanix, head low, headed back to the hatch.

Over the next hour Galvanix served the women and a further group of workers, who had to jostle for seats when Galvanix's crew declined to surrender theirs. The cook, loading a last plate for himself, waved Galvanix into the kitchen and left. Galvanix edged away from the hatch and slumped unobserved against a wall.

As the clamor outside reached a festive pitch, Galvanix stirred himself and considered his surroundings. The kitchen was dispiritingly bleak; beside the stove gaped an empty space where the sterilizer had been removed. Galvanix set the tea kettle to boil, then immersed the plates and chopsticks in warm water and began clumsily to wash them. Alert for more soldiers, he watched his dinner companions make their way out of the commons, some escorting women.

A gauge was set on the wall, which Galvanix recognized after a minute as a power crimp. The dial stood alarmingly close to the red: the cook had not taken care to conserve in preparing dinner, and wished upon Galvanix the chore of cleaning up with the ration left.

In a dull terror of provoking official attention, Galvanix turned off the heaters, scrubbed harder in the tepid water, then heated the rinse in the kettle, which he saw would hold heat longer. By the time he finished the common room was nearly empty, and

Galvanix crept out to retrieve the last plates, unmindful of his staggering gait.

Music seeped through the thin walls, and the floor panels trembled with the beat of dancing. Galvanix shut down the kitchen and wandered into the corridor, opening successive doors onto tiered bunks before finding a lavatory. He stumbled into a stall and shat messily, a thin gruel brightened with blood. Resting his head in his hands, Galvanix felt the nearness of death, his strength sliding from his body in a collapse of entrails.

At the sink he saw himself in the mirror, and realized with a mortal pang that he would never slip unnoticed into the radio room, or even persist in escaping attention. Hopelessly he combed his fingers through his hair and rubbed depilatory from a dispenser over his face. Rinsing in the cold water shocked him awake; he remembered to wipe the fallen hair from the sink.

The service entrance led him outside, where storm clouds made a dusk of lunar morning. He could still hear workers playing and stamping their feet. Behind a shed Galvanix heard low voices and a woman's sudden giggle. He moved away unsteadily, finding a fuel tank to lean against. In a second he slid to the ground, drawing up his feet.

Sleep's fool, Galvanix thought as wakefulness ebbed from him. If he died here they would bury him incuriously, perhaps thinking to report a feeb worker dying without identification. Rona's children might till the soil his body fed . . .

Galvanix was cuffed awake as a voice over him intoned, "Up, louse." A second blow toppled him onto his side, from which vantage he focused at last on the laced boots of authority. "No bed assignment? You look available to me."

Galvanix rose on hands and knees, vision and stomach turning. He was prodded with something hard. "Fled the city? Do that once the war starts and they'll shoot you. Up now, fast."

Lunar gravity allowed him to rise, though shakily. A middle-aged man regarded him distastefully, baton in hand. "Our heroes blow up the comet, and the bedlice celebrate."

"Sick," Galvanix muttered, mouth foul.

"Not for long. We've got work for parasites like you." The work boss prodded him again, and Galvanix stumbled forward.

"Ever worked hard? Things are going to be different now for your sort. *Into the truck.*"

Galvanix shuffled across the compound fast enough to avoid another poke, and climbed haltingly into the back of a sleek personnel carrier. He curled up on his side as he watched the boss's retreating back. Voices reached him faintly from the commons window, but Galvanix felt no hunger.

Something wrong nagged at him through his torpor, and Galvanix twisted his neck to read the time display on one wall of the carrier. Less than five hours had passed since supper. He concluded with difficulty that the workers would be expected to complete their night's sleep on the carrier, so as not to expend part of the working day in transit. Pondering this Galvanix dozed, and woke to find workmen climbing over him. Later he woke again to humming and the faint sway of motion.

Drymouthed, he crawled over the thicket of legs to the water tap at the front of the carrier, apologizing weakly as the occasional worker woke to kick at him. Still faces lined either side, nodding faintly in the dim light as the vehicle trembled.

Galvanix drank a trickle of warm water, curled up among the legs and was roused as the carrier turned sharply, throwing him against two men. He scrambled aside with an apology, bracing his back against the wall with the others.

The carrier seemed to be climbing a winding road, and the workers began to stir. "Where are we going?" Galvanix asked the man next to him, who disdained to answer. Galvanix looked around, meeting the eye of the man opposite, one of the few not wearing the work blues of a trained cadre. "Will you tell me?" Galvanix asked.

The man hesitated, and Galvanix realized he had created a face trap: the worker could not spurn him before the others, thus presuming to share cadre status. "Vanework," the man said, shamed. Galvanix started, but remembered to thank him respectfully.

The carrier rattled over rough soil and pulled suddenly to a halt, and the workers stood swiftly. Galvanix was the last man out, raising his head as he pushed through the curtain to look across the blotched sky. The clouds had taken on color and depth with the rising sun, but the patches of sky still showed faint stars, as they would until midday. The carrier rested on uneven ground overlooking a broad valley, but Galvanix was looking up the hillside, where the Vanes stood silhouetted like swinging partitions of an enormous wall.

The panels seemed too frail even for lunar gravity, and shivered in the slightest winds, whose strength they could never resist. One Vane was still swinging slowly as a puff caught it, aligning itself with the breeze like a compass needle.

The cadre workers were bounding toward them, while the others began to pull equipment from beneath the carrier. The man whose face he had saved nudged Galvanix. "Stay busy," he warned.

Moving carefully, Galvanix helped unload coils of rope and sealed crates. His head ached when he bent forward, and pains ran up his body like current. He could see men climbing the runged edges of the nearest Vane, moving along the top of its rippling green face. Despite his interest Galvanix turned away, letting fatigue help feign indifference.

Atop the Vane, workers were carefully loosening the vines that crept to its upper reaches. Galvanix, staggering as he tried to pick up a box, was sent to unpack crates set down at the foot of another Vane. He pinched the seam of one crate, which fell open to disclose seedlings packed in loose soil. The smell of earth rose like an exhalation, and Galvanix leaned forward, bringing a handful to his face as though he had discovered a square of his garden.

As he laid out the seedlings before him, Galvánix heard the wire mesh of the Vane thrum as though struck. Looking up, he saw the vaneworkers slipping down its face on anchored lines while working the tendrils free. Lengths of vine dangled, drooping to touch the ground as their workers reached the halfway point. The first vaneworker fully to detach his shoot dropped lightly, gave Galvanix a dismissive glance and bounded to the ladder for a second ascent.

Galvanix helped others bear the tendril some distance away. The vine was a species that grew best when its tropism toward climbing was gratified, and could reach forty meters in lunar gravity. When it reached full growth it was robust enough to thrive as groundcover, and was transplanted nearby. Like many vines, it would then sprout a nexus of roots every meter or so, taking to the soil as though changing species. Eventually the area surrounding the Vanes would be thick with undergrowth, and the Vanes would themselves be moved elsewhere.

They worked in this manner for hours. Once a wind blew up and the Vanes all swung like ponderous floodgates, the vaneworkers clutching their lines. No vaneworker ever severed a tendril; the workers surrounding Galvanix took enormous care not to. Galvanix was allowed to place the roots tenderly into the soil, while others arranged its long limb as gravely as imperial gardeners of another age.

Galvanix knew that a break would be called when a fellow drudge, even frailer-looking than he though doubtless stronger, was dispatched to prepare tea. When the gong sounded, vaneworkers came rappeling down like spiders. The laborers around him dropped in their tracks, uncaring that the respite was not meant for them.

Galvanix rose carefully as the vaneworkers strode forward to receive the first servings of tea and dried cakes. He could hardly stand, but was not too tired to climb a ladder on the Moon. No one remarked as he approached the nearest Vane, clipped on a safety line and slowly began to ascend.

From ten meters up, the valley floor opened before him like a banquet. The rain had flooded the plain, and was slowly draining into an irregular lake that inclined slightly toward the Far Pole. On higher ground the petals of a windmill spun steadily, turning a screw that churned and aerated the crusty soil. A dirigible drifted down the valley's length, pulling at the line that tethered it to its railroad car as a crosswind struck it. The largest feature was a ziggurat of concentric tiers, so luxuriant with foliage that its edges had softened with green.

Moving steadily, Galvanix reached the ladder's top and crawled onto the catwalk. Exhaustion hit him and he sprawled, the toe of one boot extending over the edge. The Vane vibrated slightly as wind ran across its surface, producing a deep keening filled with smaller overtones Galvanix hadn't noticed on the ground. The motion sent a thrill through him, for the height was sufficient to kill even on the Moon, and the catwalk had no handrail. Slowly Galvanix rose to a crouch, calves trembling in anticipation of further tremors underfoot.

From his vantage Galvanix could see beyond the hills framing the opposite side of the valley to farther ranges. Detail was lost in the shadows of clouds. He pivoted carefully and discovered he could see over the crest of the hill they perched upon. Diffuse light seemed to glow through the low clouds beyond, as from a hidden city.

A shout caused him to look down, where a work boss was waving angrily. Galvanix gestured and began slowly to back toward the ladder, but a vaneworker was already sprinting toward the ladder on the Vane's other side. Galvanix descended slowly, taking care to detach and reclip the two safety lines in turn lest weakness overcome him. He had not descended far before the vaneworker appeared above him, his glaring face contorted like a demon's.

As Galvanix touched the ground several men seized him. The work boss stepped forward and struck him hard in the face. "What were you doing up there?" he demanded. "Suspects we shoot!"

Galvanix rocked at the blow, sagging in his captors' grip. "We were given a work break," he protested weakly, voice indignant at injustice. "I went up to look at the view."

The men released him, and he fell in a heap. He was hoisted back to his feet at a gesture from the work boss, who raised Galvanix's head by a handful of hair and pulled back an eyelid. "Another deader," he remarked. "Put him in the van."

Galvanix was carried to the personnel carrier and laid on the floor. His nosebleed had smeared across his face, and the man wiping the tea cups stared wide as Galvanix was deposited beside him like an accident victim. The climb, or the punch, had broken some elastic barrier, and Galvanix as he lay there sensed dimly that rest would not return his strength. A tray of half-empty cups was set down beside his head, and when the steam touched his nostrils Galvanix gestured feebly, and was at length given his midday tea.

Later the carrier was moving, and later still it was at rest, with wind from the drawn curtain stirring Galvanix's hair. He heard workers calling *Ho!* and replies that seemed to come from the air. Galvanix craned his neck, looking up through the curtain at what appeared to be a plane of tilled ground slanting into the sky.

"We're at the pyramid," a voice said, and the frail man's face loomed over him. "They stopped for the crop pick." Galvanix could now see the workers spread through the terraced levels, tossing small objects in long arcs through the air. Sailing too slowly to bruise, the vegetables fell into outstretched sheets held by circles of men on the ground.

Galvanix must have grimaced, for the man was moved to explain: "The pyramid increases arable ground area, and the slopes prevent plants from getting too much sun." Galvanix knew this; it was his weakness that left him prey to incomprehension. His fellow wretch studied him with alarm, perhaps seeing his own end foreshadowed here.

Galvanix ebbed into semiconsciousness. Dregs of cool tea were raised to his lips, and he was helped to the carrier's latrine. Once he stirred when the carrier bumped hard, and felt rows of boot tips jab his side in unison. He woke briefly when a wet wind blew over him, harsh with the tang of volatiles, and saw that the carrier's top had been retracted. Galvanix gestured weakly, and was pulled by anonymous hands to a sitting position.

They were approaching an industrial complex, structures outlined with running lights smoldering behind clouds of steam. Galvanix stared as they stopped by an entrance gate, where hard-faced men brandishing hand tools demanded identification of the autopilot and then swept a search beam across the passengers' faces. The guards waved them ahead, and the carrier rolled into a noisy, sooty plaza, intermittently dark as smokestack emissions drifted overhead.

The carrier drove past hangars, scattered mounds of tailings, and long avenues of tarpaulined material. Workers stepped aside as they passed, and the occasional light vehicles gave way. At one point a shadow swept over them, and Galvanix looked up to see the outline of an enormous dirigible low in the sky, stirring restively against its mooring lines.

The carrier made a long series of stops, dropping off first the elite corps, then pulling up at one site where the remaining workers unloaded the crops, and another where they laboriously took off the equipment. Finally Galvanix was left alone on the floor of the carrier, wondering whether the vehicle was going to go into a garage and shut off.

Instead it stopped outside a small building, and a woman garbed in white emerged to confer with the autopilot. A stretcher rolled into the carrier, and Galvanix felt himself lifted onto it. Vertigo washed him, and when Galvanix saw an elderly face leaning over his, he had to strain to hear what was said.

". . . your extremities?" The doctor appeared to be feeling Galvanix's legs. "Ah, your eyes are focusing. Can you understand me?"

Galvanix moved his lips.

The doctor pulled something away from Galvanix's arm, producing a small sting. He held up an instrument surmounting a red vial and studied its displays. "You have not suffered major vascular or neurological injury, so should be able to answer me. What does beset you, of course, I can see without need of diagnostics."

"It is radiation sickness, Sensei," Galvanix whispered.

The doctor was unsurprised. "Indeed. And do you know how you received such an exposure?"

Galvanix was unused to deception even with his wits about him. He said, "I was close to the explosion that destroyed the comet."

The doctor smiled. "Saw it, eh? You would have to have been in orbit to have been affected by it. I'm afraid your problems are more chronic," he said, turning away. Galvanix tried to raise his hand, but could only move it from side to side. He was in a cot in a small infirmary, four beds and a wall of diagnostic machines. The cots on either side were occupied by unconscious men.

The doctor returned with an injector. "I can treat you for ulceration and loss of blood salts, but hematopoietic failure will have to be taken up elsewhere. I have no medical records for you here; where can they be found?"

"Tycho, Sensei."

The doctor's eyes widened. He looked at Galvanix for several seconds, and seemed about to speak when a door opened. The doctor looked up and stiffened. A scowling man dressed like the work boss entered the room.

"You registered an admission. Has there been an accident?"

The doctor gestured at Galvanix. "A worker from the press gang. Chronic radiation sickness."

The supervisor glanced at Galvanix. "I don't want your last bed filled by a transient. Treat him and set him out."

The doctor bowed slightly. "The most cursory protocol would include an overnight—"

"Don't keep him here, Doctor," the boss interrupted, using a discourteous form. "These facilities are for true workers. If there's another accident, I want this bed open."

The doctor nodded, though the boss was already striding off. He stood stiffly until the door closed, then lifted the injector and turned back to Galvanix.

"Have you been exposed to fissionables for long?" he asked as he directed the dose into Galvanix's forearm.

Galvanix trusted physicians. "Sensei, I have suffered an acute overdose from a fusion explosion. Ionizing and neutron both."

The doctor studied Galvanix's expression, then unclipped the vial from the bloodreader and walked across the room. Galvanix watched him feed the sample into another machine and study the screen. After a moment he returned, his face grave.

"Gastrointestinal failure should not manifest for several days; I can treat for some of the gross effects. Your blood does not show the release of enzymes bespeaking cerebrovascular damage, which would kill you within hours. Your initial symptoms should fade by morning, but will return as the cells of your intestinal lining continue to die without being replaced.

"If you can return to Nearside," the physician said without sign of irony, "I advise you to take a fast ship to an Earthorbital medical facility. If not, you may wish to leave this site, go settle your affairs or make peace with yourself. Drifters get used up, here."

Galvanix nodded, closing his eyes. Confirmation did not deepen his composure, though empirical validation was always welcome. He felt the injector enter his arm once more, and listened to the doctor explain that he was receiving leukocyte supplements and polypeptides suitable for tissue repair. Galvanix was allowed to rest, then helped into a chair.

Beside him a set of clean work greys had been laid out, and when Galvanix lifted them he found his spacesuit undergarment folded beneath. He stared at the incriminating thing, then realized he was being trusted to take it away with him. Atop it lay his recorder, which Galvanix had forgotten. He pushed the undergarment into the greys and pulled them both on at once, glancing nervously at the sleeping forms around him. The recorder he impulsively swallowed.

Watching the doctor remake the cot, Galvanix realized he could not ask him to take a message. He looked longingly at the console keyboard, but knew he did not dare record one either. Dismissing finally all hope, Galvanix sat back and folded his hands over his belly, imagining bemusedly the ruin within.

When the doctor returned, Galvanix stood carefully, surprised he could manage without difficulty. "Thank you, Sensei," he said, wishing to spare the physician the shame of having to put him out. "I feel much better now."

The doctor met Galvanix's eyes. "Don't eat solids," he said. "If you stay, come back when you begin feeling weak." He turned quickly and touched his control panel. "I need a name under which to file your record."

"Taggart Pohl," Galvanix said. None of the other patients seemed conscious. The one nearest Galvanix was missing the outline of one leg beneath his bedsheet, and a small metal disk rested on his throat. "Thank you for healing me."

Galvanix leaped lightly to the door, which opened as the doctor touched the release. A small puff of air billowed with him out of the pressurized ward, and Galvanix stepped into the street.

A warm mist blew across his face, tasting faintly of oil. Galvanix stood in a small courtyard, bordered by the infirmary and what looked like barracks. He hurried off the ramp before anyone could notice him, stepping into a street at the court's end. In a moment he had turned a corner and slipped into a stream of workers emerging through a gate.

Dust caked the workers' clothes, a crumbling powder the color the lunar surface had shown before its earliest atmosphere. Galvanix understood then: they were drilling a thermal tap, exhuming mounds of regolith which others sifted for minerals. Selenothermal energy was attractive—simple and self-sufficient, and the Moon's diffuse mass could be drilled without destructive exertions—but seemed an unlikely option for the shogunate, which favored fission technologies.

A change of wind brought the sound of overhead creaking, and Galvanix looked up to see the tethered dirigible bobbing over its airfield ahead. He looked away quickly. The crowd was thinning as workers turned into side streets, but Galvanix allowed himself to slow only slightly, and merely glanced at the field as he bounded past. What he saw nearly made him start, but his stride carried him through the air for the second it took to recover himself.

Stenciled danger signs covered every upright surface on the field, not security threats but the orange symbol signifying inflammables. A gas tank bore an enormous one above smaller lettering, which Galvanix knew must read *Hydrogen*.

Galvanix continued, eyes straight ahead, past the airfield and into a side street that ran like a valley between hillocks of soil. His composure was jarred, and Galvanix didn't dare show his face. The recklessness of using hydrogen, however cheap it was to produce and however costly helium, affronted him like a violation of physical law. Doubtless the dirigible's lift bag was protected by an envelope of inert gas, but Galvanix was still appalled.

He slowed to a stop and stood a moment in the street, running one foot abstractedly along the rail line set into its surface. Other details emerged to trouble him. Galvanix looked at the earthworks about him. There is too much soil, he thought, almost aloud.

He hesitated, then decided reluctantly that his responsibility was to get out of the camp, rather than risk all in exploring further. Certainly he could not walk through the gate without challenge, but might join a departing work crew, or hide in a rail car. Feeling suddenly conspicuous, he resumed walking.

The rail lines disappeared among the buildings ahead. Beyond the camp they could go anywhere, but Galvanix could leap off if the train headed deeper into Farside. He thought his chances of reaching Nearside pretty bleak, but saw no other way to convey word without risk of interception. "Taggart Pohl" might be picked up by a Nearsider scan running regularly through Farside data entries, but it was possible that Nearside did not know Taggart's name.

Galvanix turned a corner and saw a crowd gathering some distance ahead, calling and clustering round something like spectators at a fight. Since others were hastening toward it, Galvanix did too.

Security guards stood about with their hand weapons at the ready, scowling at the arriving onlookers but making no attempt to drive them away. Galvanix attempted to push into the crowd but was shoved back. He circled the shouting mob, then dropped to his knees and saw through the forest of legs that they stood surrounding an open pit. Carefully Galvanix crawled between the workers' legs, ignoring kicks. Within seconds he reached the edge, stretched flat on his stomach, and peered in.

At the bottom of the pit lay Taggart. The woman was sprawled on her back, undergarment ragged and wet with blood. The black skin of her face shone with perspiration, and her eye whites gleamed. The pit dropped into shadow, and the onlookers played pocket lamps over her body like wavering searchlights. Calls of amazement, mingled with jeers, rained upon her.

Galvanix stared. Taggart seemed semiconscious, and her head lolled drunkenly. At one point she drew up a knee, and exclamations increased. Her eyes stared upward but did not seem to recognize Galvanix. He imagined how he must appear to her, foremost in a ring of contorted faces, and resisted the impulse to wave.

Slowly Galvanix backed out, then stood looking fearfully around him. A flatbed truck idled nearby, squandering its fuel unheeded. Its driver—Taggart's deliverer, he suddenly realized— stood bewildered at the door of his cab, forsaken by procedure. Galvanix understood then that Taggart had been dropped into the pit like a beast for baiting. The guards were right to fear her; were she not so gravely injured she could probably jump even that distance.

Galvanix walked slowly away from the crowd, averting his face from the men who continued running up. Now, he knew, was the moment to pass unnoticed through the gates. A bicycle lay on its side where a worker had dropped it to join the crowd. Galvanix righted it and hopped on without a sidelong glance.

A roar went up behind him, and Galvanix turned his head as he began to swing the bicycle in a wide arc. There seemed to be a commotion at the center of the crowd, a churning of just-visible heads as packed bodies bumped in the low gravity. Galvanix guessed that a surge had pushed someone into the pit. Concerned, he looked on a second longer, and then several things happened very quickly.

A figure bobbed up from the center of the crowd, head and body visible for a second, then came down within the first circles of spectators. Galvanix registered an instant's shocked recognition, and then Taggart burst above the level of the crowd and bounded like a cat across packed shoulders and heads, to land crouched among startled newcomers. Taggart sent the two nearest flying with a sweep of her arm, then bolted.

Galvanix braked, mouth open, and men were suddenly running

between them, crashing clumsily against each other in a gravity ill-suited for panic. Taggart sprinted in low, fast bounds between startled workers who reached after her too late. A security officer raised his handgun, and Taggart was upon him. In a second the weapon was in her hand, and Taggart swung round and fired. A spray of fine particles erupted like steam, and more men screamed.

Galvanix steered toward her, weaving to dodge running men. "Taggart!" he cried. "City Boy!" Taggart looked up, eyes wild. She saw Galvanix and brought up her gun. Galvanix leaped from the bicycle, which was knocked sideways by a volley of shot.

A siren went off behind them, and for a second everyone looked up save for Taggart, who raced across the plaza. Workers shouted and started after her. Taggart took a long leap, turning in mid-air, and fired behind her. Her pursuers threw up their arms, and Taggart vanished round a corner.

Galvanix pushed his way past shouting men and snatched up the fallen bicycle. Around him workers rose slowly, writhed or lay upon the ground. Galvanix mounted the bicycle and pushed off before someone could think to challenge him. He swung away from the gate, pedaling hard as he accelerated back up the street.

He sped past the corner Taggart had turned, glancing up to confirm that the dirigible hovered low to his left. Lights were coming on throughout the complex. Galvanix skidded and hopped off the bike. He was not surprised to see a security guard step forth with a hand raised.

"Has the tank feed been blown off?" Galvanix demanded.

The guard's startled gaze flicked from Galvanix's face to the cut of his work greys. "I don't know, Specialist."

"Can you leave your post?" Galvanix asked crisply, pulling the bicycle's tool kit loose from behind the seat.

"No, sir, not during an alert."

Galvanix made a frustrated gesture and ran on. He expected a challenge or a shot in the back, but none came. In an instant he had ducked behind a shed and was moving on hands and knees. He had to hurry, before a real Specialist thought to arrive.

The Farsiders' hydrogen depot was unsafe, but only one who knew its flaws could easily sabotage it. Galvanix, who had once designed such an irresponsible system and heartlessly defended its economies to his teachers, knew exactly where to go. Thus, he thought, I murder my boyhood sins.

The fueling system was pressure-driven, releasing hydrogen to flow from compressed tanks below. Small motors would assist if diffusion and buoyancy did not suffice to fill an airship, but Galvanix didn't worry about them. A row of nozzles rose from the ground like saplings, and Galvanix ran to crouch beside them.

As he expected, the valves could be opened only when the collar from a feed line was secured to the nozzle. Galvanix knew that the pipes themselves would not be kept pressurized, and any residual hydrogen in them was ripe with air that inevitably seeped in. The flammable mixture would be blown off before pure hydrogen could flow into the dirigible, and Galvanix quickly found the bleed valve. He pried open its lips with a blade from the tool kit and, averting his head, struck hard at the serrated blade with a file. A tongue of yellow flame popped out, vanishing as Galvanix jerked his hand back.

Galvanix stood, his legs shaking. Running his hands around the nozzle, he located the catches that a feed line would depress when snapped into place. Galvanix pressed them with spread fingertips and the valve fell open, a faint breath touching his face. He pulled a cube of patch putty from the tool kit and shoved bits under each one. Then he picked up the blade and file, stepped back, and struck a spark over the pipe.

Light exploded over the nozzle. Galvanix stumbled backward, one hand clutching the other. A meter-high flame danced before him like a gas jet, exposing every object on the field. Galvanix turned and bounded away. He was in middair when the landscape flashed white, etching his shadow below him an instant before the shock wave struck.

Galvanix tumbled, limbs flailing. Behind him a pillar of yellow-white flame climbed roiling into the air. The image spun away, and a second later swept past sideways, now flecked with black. Galvanix tumbled again, and something seared his shoulder and leg. A second later he struck ground, rolling wildly.

Coming to rest facedown, Galvanix felt massive dizziness, planets revolving through his spine's axis. Twin points burned deeply, and he flipped writhing on the wet ground. A white roar swallowed all sound, but Galvanix's rolling eyes picked out the column of light. Smoke billowed from it like a new-born cloud.

Running steps splashed past him, hands hauled him to his feet. "Go to the street's edge and lie down," said someone, releasing him. Galvanix staggered, looking for a way out. The hydrogen pyre spilled quickly into the rarefied air, casting dancing shadows that baffled perspective.

Shots were fired in the next street, just audible through the roar. Men were running in that direction, some turning to stare awed at the conflagration. A ground vehicle abruptly turned a corner, uniformed men hanging from its side. Galvanix started painfully after them.

Miners pushed through the gate entrance to a depot, clamoring like a mob. More shots were fired, and men ducked or dove clumsily for the ground. Galvanix bounded through in the confusion, pushing through an avenue between rows of stacked crates.

Shots came again, this time from a different direction. All the men near Galvanix but one ducked.

"How many are there?" a miner asked.

"He's trying to get away," another said. A crate had fallen and burst, and men bent to pick up metal rods that rolled about their feet. About half the stacks stood less than eye height, and the miners ran crouching among them, stopping to peer around corners. Across the depot Galvanix could see dark shapes moving uncertainly. Another shot was fired, and the shapes scattered. "I saw a gunflash!" someone shouted.

Galvanix was watching the man who had not flinched. The man's clothing was ungrimed and nearly black, and he rested with his back against a crate, apparently listening. After a second he straightened and drew something from his belt. Galvanix recognized it as a high-energy weapon, capable of punching through a crate. Without taking his gaze from the man, Galvanix bent and grasped a metal rod underfoot. The man slipped forward quietly, round a corner and out of sight.

Galvanix started after him, suddenly panicky of losing the man in the confusion. The man was moving purposefully down a side corridor, holding his weapon ready. Without thinking Galvanix leaped, sailing in a silent arc that ended at the man's back. He crashed hard and swung at the head, feeling a thrill of impact sting his hand. The man slumped at once, dropping the gun.

Galvanix fell and recovered, scrambling for the weapon. Something told him not to look at the man. The gun was dull metal, surprisingly heavy. He turned the rings ribbing its barrel, squinting to read the settings.

"Hey!" someone cried. Galvanix looked up to see a dirt-smeared miner standing at the crate-bounded intersection, peering into the dim light. Galvanix looked quickly over his shoulder, where the corridor twisted past lengths of stacked pipe. The miner was calling out, others starting toward them.

Galvanix fumbled frantically with the weapon settings, twisting the aperture gauge all the way. He looked up to see two miners springing at him. Galvanix brought up the gun and discharged it, a brilliant flash that bounced purple splotches off his field of vision. Men screamed and struck the sides of crates.

Galvanix fled, caroming off stacks as he kicked wildly. Alarmed shouts called across walls of crates. He hopped over a low stack, grabbing a corner to pull himself quickly down. Fighting to slow the heaving of his chest, he looked at the gun in his hand, fought an impulse to throw it away, and stuffed it into his waistband.

Shouts and screams behind him were compounding the confusion, and Galvanix moved quickly, looking for the depot perimeter. Abruptly the gloom began to dissipate, and he looked up to see a bank of lights surmounting a slender pylon begin to glow brighter. The light tree, looking too frail even for lunar gravity, was being powered up to its nighttime load. A searchlight at one end began to swivel toward the depot like an eye.

Galvanix took out the weapon, twisted its gauge back, and fired carefully at the lights. The pencil-thin beam missed the pylon, but Galvanix kept his finger depressed and waved it over into range. The lights winked out in a short burst of sparks. A deeper darkness fell over the grounds.

Hand torches came on after several seconds, faint beams sweeping about the stacks and piles, but Galvanix was safely anonymous among cursing miners. Crawling on his belly and navigating by the fitfully glimpsed light of the pyre, Galvanix reached the depot's meshed fence. He slashed an opening, shielding the glow with one hand, then pushed himself through. The metal edges burned as he elbowed them apart.

Workers ran about confusedly. The pyre was burning lower,

and Galvanix could see massed shadows approach cautiously, a long robot arm extending toward it. Across the field the dirigible bucked in the storm of air, tearing at its lines like a horse in a blaze.

A fresh wind had blown the mist away, and the clearer light fell in sharp planes, casting everything not sunlit into deep shadow. Galvanix kept to the shaded sides of buildings, trying to look like a pursuer but also keeping his bloodsoaked back to the walls. He was edging along a sandbagged earthwork when a black arm closed round his throat and pulled him backward.

"Keep your mouth shut," said Taggart in his ear. She released him.

Galvanix turned and stared. Taggart had shed her clothing, and was almost invisible in shadow. "Head for the dirigible," she said. "Keep down." Taggart reached for Galvanix's waistband and pulled out the gun, glancing at its setting.

"What—"

Taggart pushed him away with her free hand and vanished behind a dumpster. Galvanix followed and found her gone.

Men shouted in the street, and Galvanix crouched quickly, keeping his head down. Judging from the voices, his hunters were beginning to travel in pairs. Two stopped and questioned a lone miner before allowing him to pass.

Galvanix felt a cold knot tighten behind his breastbone. He pulled his shoulders in as though willing himself smaller, feeling the narrowing confines of his life closing to a point. The task of reaching the dirigible, his remaining commission, began to fade.

The ground started beneath him, trembling in aftershock before lurching twice more. Galvanix's soles knew the thrill before his mind did—the slow topple of a massive object, a building.

Galvanix leaped upward, sailing past tiers of bulwark like a rising bubble. As he passed the parapet the sound broke over him, a volley of shock waves. Galvanix twisted to glimpse a cloud of debris expand billowing across a row of barracks several streets away. Then he was slowly falling back, a languid target for a second, then past the rampart and dropping into shadow. He landed sprawling on the shuddering ground, shivering for a second as though in sympathy with all tormented matter. And suddenly he saw his chance.

Galvanix bunched and sprang once more, leaping across the street in a blatant arc. Two miners stood a few meters away, gaping at the devastation. Neither noticed him. Galvanix raised his face, likewise aghast, and stumbled a few steps before turning to run for the field.

The dirigible seemed to quiver against the overcast sky, and Galvanix saw with a start that its underbelly was reflecting the flicker of flames. He turned puzzled in a full circle before realizing that the fire was blocked from his sight by low buildings. Oily smoke gathered over the field, spreading slowly toward the balloon like a stain.

Figures bounded between the outbuildings, indistinct among the scythelike sweep of their shadows. The pyre vanished as the long-armed robot lurched forward, wisps of flame curling like fronds round the cap dropped over it. A figure in fire-fighter's garb was crossing the field, unnoticed among the scrambling workers.

Galvanix made for the mooring deck, thinking he could duck behind its barrows of stacked crates. Leaping like those around him, he glanced quickly about at the crest of his sailing arc. The fire-fighter, helmeted gaze unreadable, was looking straight at him. The pistol dangled from one glove, looking again like a hand tool.

Galvanix felt his mind blink, like a flickering screen, as the fire-fighter strode toward him. It's too soon, he thought. Taggart was blocks away, having just finished burning through the framework of a warehouse. And Galvanix, striking ground and bounding again, began to realize there was something wrong with his sense of time.

Overhead, the airship creaked against its lines like the calls of passing birds. Its shadow was invisible in the dim light, but Galvanix felt its mass, which pulled rather than pressed upon him. The helmeted figure gestured once, and Galvanix looked up, saw a line trailing from the cab, and leaped.

Despite his weakness the trajectory was good, and at its crest Galvanix reached and snatched the line. Legs swinging, he climbed hand over hand toward the immensity looming above him like an inverted sky. A shout called across the field, and Galvanix swarmed faster.

Without warning the dirigible tilted sharply, sending a shock racing down the line that shook him like a doll. He glanced down to see Taggart slice through the mooring lines with a slow sweep of the pistol. Galvanix's muscles tightened automatically an instant before the line jolted his arms almost from their sockets as the freed airship tore itself aloft.

FOUR

The wind immediately died, though one part of Galvanix's mind urgently whispered that they had not come to rest, but matched its speed. Cries, growing in number as they faded, rose from below. Galvanix looked down. The field was dropping away, a receding tabletop dotted with upturned faces.

A lifetime's experience in judging heights by lunar standards evaporated, and Galvanix saw with his midbrain a plummet from the highest treetops. His hands locked round the line in a deathgrip. Mist abruptly enveloped them, and within seconds the ground below was blurred, cut only by the brief flashing of a beacon or searchlight.

Galvanix heard a sound behind him. Twisting his neck, he saw the fire-fighter steadily climbing a second line. The figure grimly put one hand above the other without a sidelong glance, vanishing at last into reaches beyond Galvanix's angle of vision. Galvanix heard a series of thumps above, then silence. Obdurately he held on, knowing his hands would not unlock to climb.

His lifeline suddenly thrilled, and Galvanix felt himself pulled upward. He spun slowly, observing a full compass of wet drifting cloud, as a faint electric whine drew him up under the belly of the ship. Hands clasped his wrists, and he was hauled bumping into the cabin.

"Freeze up in heights?" Taggart's voice asked as Galvanix fell to the floor in darkness. His toes boomed hollowly upon the deck, and Galvanix, chest heaving as he lay with one cheek against the cold surface, felt the enormity of space beyond it.

"Nice work with the gun, however. Up," and Galvanix felt himself hauled to his knees.

Blinking in the near darkness, Galvanix wondered why he could not remain on the deck. His heart was pounding, but he felt for the moment no pain. "Why don't you turn on the cabin light?" he thought to ask.

"That would activate the running lights, and we don't want to be seen. We won't be here long anyway." Taggart was rummaging noisily through a compartment below the control panel. The clatter ceased, and the yellow eye of a hand torch blinked on.

Galvanix felt alarm. "Why not?"

"Someone shot at us. Didn't you see it? If the cloud hadn't intervened it might have punched through the envelope, but I think it set the netting smoldering. If it reaches the fabric, this ship will erupt. You hadn't noticed this lady's carrying hydrogen?"

Galvanix climbed quickly to his feet. Taggart had pulled back the visor of her helmet, and was flashing her beam round the extent of the cabin, which was less than two meters wide and crowded with metal canisters. The portholes and open hatch showed an unbroken expanse of grey.

Gripping each side, Galvanix leaned cautiously out the hatch. Streamers of low cloud ran past, occasionally broken by patches of featureless dark surface. "I think we're over water," he said.

"Correct. We're running Farward before a sun-warmed air front." Taggart pulled him in and leaned out backward, hanging by one arm as she swept the beam of the torch slowly round the air about her. After a minute she hauled herself in, brushing past Galvanix without a word.

"We're making good speed, since the hold is empty," she said, resuming her search through the compartment. "But some dangling lines are definitely burning. The polymer only combusts at high temperatures, but the laser sufficed. They're burning up toward the gasbag like slow fuses."

A chill blossomed in Galvanix's chest. "What about when *you* cut through them?" he asked.

"I snapped the embrittled ends off by hand. Can't do that now."

Galvanix looked out a porthole. In the overcast, he thought he could see a line trailing from the airship's bow. "Why can't you slice through the burning end with—" he began, then stopped, feeling foolish.

Taggart didn't reply. She pulled out a soft mass and thrust it at Galvanix. "Put this on."

Galvanix shook open a tangle of ribbon, which resolved into a chest harness. Taggart handed him several fist-sized cylinders, which he slid into loops in the harness. "Not much here," she remarked, stepping back from the compartment and shining the torch into the upper corners of the cabin. "Fortunately, the cabin is not welded to the hold or superstructure."

Galvanix was resting lightly on the balls of his feet, his nerves trying to shrink from both the immensity of air below and the hydrogen above. "How fast are we moving?"

"Can't tell," Taggart replied, leaning out the hatch and sweeping the torch beam once more through the clouds. "The controls are automatic only, except the gas dump." She looked at him briefly. "Any broken bones?"

"No," said Galvanix, suspicion rising.

"Good. Time's up," and Taggart pulled herself back in, stooping to pick up a length of line. She secured one end to a stanchion and tossed the other to Galvanix. "Look up, not down, so you'll know when to let go. Don't let the cabin fall on you."

Galvanix stared as Taggart returned to the control panel and pulled hard on an overhead cord. A faint jolt ran through the cabin. "*Move*," she said.

Galvanix hoisted one of the slim canisters, finding it about his own weight. Grasping it awkwardly between his knees, Galvanix looped the line under one thigh and across the opposite shoulder. The ship was already descending: tendrils of cloud rose gently as they drifted past. Leaning cautiously out the hatch, Galvanix began to descend the dangling line, which dropped almost straight into the packed cotton of surrounding cloud. Below his feet a dark expanse, its distance indeterminable, showed fitfully through the grey.

A series of thumps overhead caused Galvanix to look up. Directly above, Taggart had climbed the outside of the cabin and now straddled a strut, leaning toward the narrow space between cabin and balloon. Galvanix saw a flicker of light, and recognized the violet of the laser's low setting.

He almost let go then. Mastering his impulses with effort, Galvanix rappeled slowly to the end of the line, a dozen meters below the balloon. A sudden jolt made him look upward; a corner of the cabin had come free and hung now like a broken fixture. As Galvanix watched, Taggart fired her beam into the adjoining corner, which slowly separated from the balloon.

A sudden light washed over Galvanix, and as he shut his eyes a hot shell of air struck his face. He squinted to see the airship's aft consumed by flame. A shock wave rolled swiftly down the line, and as it struck Galvanix let go. Looking up in the first slow second of fall, Galvanix saw Taggart, hanging from the cabin's edge as on a listing raft, firing steadily into a remaining corner.

In a second, cloud consumed him. Galvanix felt himself accelerating, and as the roar above faded into the rushing of wind he maneuvered the canister into his arms, where he cradled it while looking anxiously down.

Abruptly he broke through the cloud cover, and was falling over an overcast sea. Galvanix saw the flakes of separate waves, and acted quickly. Raising the canister above his head, he flung it downward with his full strength. The cylinder sped away like a missile, and Galvanix felt the rush of his fall diminish.

Galvanix kicked, angling his body parallel with the sea, and stared for seconds at the uprushing ocean. When he saw the splash of the canister, he drew his body into a ball and closed his eyes.

Concussion smacked him, but Galvanix kept hold of a thought—*Alive!*—as he tore downward in a fusillade of bubbles. His arms and legs were being forced apart, and Galvanix felt panic before realizing that the flotation harness was expanding. The rushing water was still, then abruptly cold. Turning slowly, Galvanix watched its color grow lighter and suddenly broke surface, righted by the shape of the harness.

Diffuse sunlight shone above the veiled horizon, but a second source of illumination was brightening overhead. Within seconds the airship dropped flaming through the clouds, writhing like a self-immolating dragon. The wind of its burning carried it several hundred meters Farward until it touched down in an eruption of steam. The collapsing framework sank instantly, but the boiling surface coughed gouts of flame for seconds until the site disappeared behind an expanding cloud of vapor.

Galvanix had not seen the dangling cabin during the pyre's brief transit, but stared long at the dissipating steam before thinking to turn and scan the waters around him. Fifty yards away, near the edge of the close horizon, Galvanix saw something bobbing above the surface. Kicking clumsily as the harness strove to force him upright, he swam toward it.

He had not covered half the distance when a swell from the splashdown lifted him suddenly. Within seconds the water was hot, and he cried out. The sensation immediately vanished, and a second swell carried him meters high, where he glimpsed the cabin, nearly submerged, glint dully in the mild light. A moist exhalation, sharp with the stench of burnt chemicals, puffed in his ear and was gone.

Bobbing on diminishing crests and troughs, Galvanix struggled to the cabin. Taggart was lying across its highest point, unmoving. The thin material of the fire-fighter's suit clung to her skin, its pockets bulging with salvaged tools. Galvanix pulled himself onto the tilted plane of the roof and crawled toward the half that was not awash. The cabin shifted slightly beneath him, and he felt several deep thumps.

Taggart turned her head toward him. "Have you broken any bones?" she asked.

"No," Galvanix panted, sprawling beside her. The harness prevented him from lying flat, and the motion of waves nudged him down its incline. Galvanix saw that Taggart had wedged a foot against a mounting rail, and did likewise. "Have you?" he asked after a moment.

Taggart muttered something Galvanix could not hear, *rib* or *wrist*. "Lost the pistol," she said, more clearly. Galvanix looked at her, seeing only closed eyes within the helmet. "Taggart," he said.

"Beryl," she corrected. Her eyes opened briefly. "You rest too. We will have to push off soon."

Galvanix was alarmed. "If I went inside and pushed some canisters through the hatch, it would ride higher," he said.

"The raft is visible from the air. Now quiet."

The water's swell stirred aches in Galvanix's body, but he relaxed his limbs as though dropping a load, and lay without start or twitch. Overhead the wind briefly pushed the clouds from half the sky, revealing a deep cerulean with no Earth visible, expected but still unsettling. He let his head loll but kept eyes open, and was startled when Taggart spoke his name, calling him from some dreamless state he had strayed into unawares.

"We must go now," she said, sitting up slowly. She had pulled her visor down once more, and Galvanix could see nothing of her save that her suit seemed free of bloodstains. Favoring one arm, Taggart stood and regarded Galvanix while he rose.

"What about your wrist?" he asked her.

"The suit has immobilized it. The nearest shore is there—"

pointing with her good hand, though Galvanix could see nothing but unbroken water. "Are you ready to swim?"

"If you are."

Immediately Taggart leaped, sailing in a low trajectory over the water with her good arm extended before her like a pointer. Startled, Galvanix dove after her. For seconds they arced through the air like a pair of missiles, then Taggart knifed cleanly into the water. A second later Galvanix struck the surface, and felt the immediate drag of his harness. A deep chill entered him from all sides, and his head was thrust above water. Sputtering as a wave struck his face, Galvanix began to kick clumsily after her.

Face down, her upper body unmoving, Taggart kicked with such regularity that Galvanix wondered if she had mechanical assistance. She also disdained raising her head, breathing evidently through the air valve in the back of her helmet.

Thrashing and winded, Galvanix gave up trying to fight the harness's contours and began to pull it off. Bunching it in his arms, Galvanix rested his head against one of the containers and began to kick like Taggart, who was receding before him. Looking up every minute to orient himself, he swam steadily after Taggart's wake.

A hiss filled the air, and Galvanix looked up, seeing the spatter of raindrops race across the water toward him. Wind buffeted him as the shower hit, and the waves, driven by weather not tides, rose suddenly like hackles. Startled, Galvanix dug his fingers into the harness, feeling his legs pulled off course. Looping the harness around his wrist calmed him—one could not, he reasoned, drown unless pulled under—and Galvanix cast about for Taggart, only intermittently visible between swells.

Quickly he realized that the wind was blowing him parallel to shore harder than he could compensate. A wave rose under him and he slid backward, passive as a film on the water's surface. Panicky, he began flailing, then caught a glimpse of Taggart swimming toward him.

Angling with the current to intersect his course, she reached him only after they had both been carried some distance, throwing out her good arm to hook a strand of the harness. The two bobbed a moment together, bumping as Taggart threw back her helmet and blew water like a dolphin. Pulling his head toward her, she shouted, "I'm dropping anchor."

Galvanix stared at her. "The water's only meters deep," she called. She brought from within her suit a metal object like a stringed charm, which she unfolded into curved tines thinner than birds' bones. Flexed, the thing spanned a half meter like a hooked talon. Taggart held it at arm's length and let go, its threadlike line running swiftly through her fingers as the anchor disappeared.

After a few seconds she pulled back on the line and secured it somewhere about her. "Just hold on," she said. Galvanix watched her lower her visor into the water and appear to go limp.

Pulling his arms back through the harness, Galvanix righted himself and turned his face from the spray. His feet were cold, and he kicked steadily. He closed his eyes and his mind filled with falling flames, shouts, the feel of a weapon. Bouncing lightly against the line like a spaceman, Galvanix swayed and thought, the chill in his legs keeping the images crisp.

Some hours later the wind died, and the whitecaps subsided to swells in the vertical drizzle. Galvanix felt Taggart slosh beside him and opened his eyes. Ocher light seeped through heavy clouds, a varnished seascape—the thought struck him with acute irrelevancy—with buoyant castaways.

Taggart was manipulating some object just under water. Galvanix felt a tiny release, and knew they were drifting free. "Still that way," Taggart said, pointing behind them.

Galvanix kicked, and his legs at once shouted with pain. Weakness coursed through him like a backsplash. Determinedly he began a gentle sidestroke, which he maintained steadily for several minutes. Taggart, he noticed, was swimming no faster than he.

A dozen meters away Galvanix saw a spur of rock protruding just above water level, happily green with algae. Within minutes they passed a lily pad, and Galvanix paused to probe the water beneath with a toe, without touching bottom. Pads were soon drifting past regularly, and after half an hour Galvanix and Taggart were pushing through a false shore of almost-touching circles of green which extended without variation to the horizon. Galvanix was occasionally able to graze the bottom, which seemed to be rising very gradually.

Neither spoke for over an hour. The sun had risen to Day Two, perhaps thirty-six hours since dawn here, Galvanix estimated. He wasn't sure how long since he had seen dawn, or how far from there he had traveled. Galvanix resolved to get their location from Taggart when they reached land.

The bottom rose to allow them to wade waist-deep, but no shore was visible, and it was easier to continue swimming. Taggart scanned the entire horizon, and glanced up frequently. Tiny insects buzzed among the pads, but Taggart pulled at his arm when Galvanix paused to look.

Eventually they had to slog, lily pads brushing their knees as their boots sank ankle-deep into the fine lunar silt. When the sun peered between clouds Taggart turned to glare at their wake, a straight line of disturbed pads that the wind effaced only after a hundred meters. Galvanix doubted it would be readily visible from the air, but agreed to walk in single file.

Once a distant whine reached them from somewhere above the clouds, and Galvanix dropped to the water even as Taggart lunged toward him, both wriggling frantically beneath the pads like frogs fleeing a stork. Galvanix pulled off the harness and thrust it away, digging his fingers into the fine network of muddy roots, trying to pull himself under. Taggart was floating on her back, visor flush with the surface. They held still for long seconds as the whine faded behind the wind, and Taggart insisted they remain motionless a minute longer before they resumed sloshing.

Galvanix never knew when the hectares of lily-choked shallows gave way at last to land, which emerged by centimeters from beneath a film of green broth. It was another hour before the mud was solid enough to retain footprints, which Taggart stared at disgustedly.

"They'll melt in the rain," said Galvanix, gesturing at the resuming drizzle.

Taggart lifted a foot, and the sound of the mud sucking at it made Galvanix's legs ripple with pain. She swayed slightly, and set the foot down. Galvanix, fighting a wave of weariness, turned to peer forward into the rain. "I think I see a hillock," he said.

When they reached the slope, Taggart walked its length before settling to the ground. Galvanix had resisted the impulse to throw himself down at once, and watched Taggart for a second before resting his hands on his knees.

"Don't lie down. We'll be getting up to gather mulch in a minute."

Galvanix was seeking a glimpse into the foreshortened recess of Taggart's helmet. "And what about you?"

"I can get up when I must."

"You seem worse off than you should be," Galvanix observed.

"And you, better." Taggart lifted her head to look at him and slowly, but without faltering, rose to her feet. So she too can hold herself up rather than cede face in a confrontation, Galvanix thought. "Did you manage to get medical treatment?"

"Oh, yes," said Galvanix, surprised to realize the gulf this set between them. "I was briefly treated in the camp clinic before—" Before they destroyed half the camp and fled, leaving dead behind.

"You may live to endure longer. I will hear of this when we wake." And Taggart turned to gather armfuls of rotting ground-cover, which she piled, scrupulously, at the top of the slope.

The wind blew steadily from Nearside, a sun-warmed front that pushed the rain in the direction of their trek, like a faint parody of a current. Galvanix wanted to face Taggart and demand answers, but she had insisted they set out directly after scattering their heaped shelters. Before turning her back and bounding off, she had confirmed only that they had slept over twelve hours.

Galvanix watched her closely as they fell into the overland lunar stride, which did not encourage conversation between hikers. When she paused after an hour to study a threatened break in the clouds, Galvanix said, "You seem better than last night."

"I dosed myself from the suit's pharmacopoeia," Taggart replied. "Tell me how you got treatment."

Galvanix gave his story briefly. Taggart nodded. She turned and seemed ready to spring when Galvanix said, "Taggart!"

"*Beryl*." But she turned to face him.

"I want to know how badly you were hurt."

She inclined her head, then nodded. "I have fractured a bone in my right carpus, but can manipulate thumb and one finger. Multiple contusions, difficult to gauge on dark skin in bad light. I poured nearly a liter of blood from my suit. Radiation injury somewhat less grave than yours, though untreated. I—" She paused as if about to go on, then turned away, hitching at her suit.

Galvanix spoke evenly, leaning the weight of authority into his words. "Beryl, I want you to tell me what else is wrong with you.

If you are overcome by it or otherwise injured, I will have to know." He glared at her in the ensuing silence.

Beryl said, "I think I have become fey." And leaped into the rain in a long arc, making him scramble to follow.

Two hours later they halted by a pile of rubble softened and tinted by a luxuriant coating of moss. Against the surrounding carpet of dying vegetation, its vivid green stood out like fresh paint. "Is any of this edible?" Beryl asked, stepping round the outcropping and out of sight.

Galvanix poked at the moss, expanses of which bore tiny florets. "I don't know," he called. "Can you digest cellulose?" A closer look revealed that much of the rock was in fact lichen, which interpenetrated the similar-colored moss in swirling bands as though competing for space. Galvanix guessed that with the destruction of the Mirrors the advantage had shifted, though in whose favor he did not know.

"Correction, there is lichen." The lunar varieties were all edible, though varyingly nutritious. Galvanix delighted in the plant's symbiosis of fungus and algae, resonant as the opportunism of two breeds scrambling for domination of a rock was merely ugly. None of the twelve thousand varieties brought to the Moon had been altered genetically; those that could thrive in the alternations of temperature and sunlight now covered the lowlands, and failed varieties were reintroduced as the ecosphere grew slowly more clement.

Galvanix peeled away a sodden patch, shivering slightly as he pulled apart the strands of fungal matrix into which billions of algae cells were woven. He brushed the torn edge against his lips; the rain beading its surface was as free of flavor as the droplets on rinsed lettuce.

Reluctant to start eating first, Galvanix circled the mass looking for Beryl, whom he discovered defecating messily some meters away. Galvanix was alarmed; like him, she had performed a similar operation upon rising, only hours ago. Beryl shouted him off angrily, but a shift of the wind threw a chemical stench in Galvanix's face, and he stepped back, then forward.

"Are you unwell?" he called as Beryl, suit still unsealed, stalked silently away. Despite himself he stepped forward to examine the mess, a profound discourtesy. Galvanix, who had turned a lot of soil in his youth, saw immediately that something was amiss here. Geminate lumps trailing dark threads gleamed slickly like tiny sweetmeats in the mucid pool, and Galvanix caught a whiff of something not human as he bent close. He drew back quickly, then kicked foliage over it and returned to the rubble, where Beryl was cleaning herself with wet moss.

"Have you been swallowing incriminating material, or is that indigestible offal something soldiers eat?"

Beryl shivered and flung a wad of moss away from her. "It would have degraded into unrecognizability within minutes, though you did well to cover it."

"It's unrecognizable now. Do you think the bacteria and saprobes in the mulch will eat anything? You've had stuff in your gut that doesn't even smell organic."

"I don't . . ." Beryl made a fretful gesture, a slip in control that Galvanix found frightening.

"Let's eat," he said. "We'll have to stuff ourselves to get any real calories. Maybe the bulk will help you," he added.

They stood peeling strips of lichen like sloths, chewing determinedly while wet strands hung from their chins. Galvanix squeezed water from a wad and popped it in his mouth, searching for a trace of flavor in the cresslike mash.

Beryl, visible from the corner of his eye, was leaning as though nonchalantly against the rock. Galvanix wondered if she was seeking to disguise exhaustion or merely carrying a lot of mass in her suit. Still chewing, he began pressing lichen into damp balls and pocketing them. Beside him, Beryl had begun pulling strips off the rock's underside, which required her to sink to one knee.

"Two minutes," said Beryl after they had worked nearly round the rubble. She had been moving slowly but steadily. Bouncing lightly on his toes, Galvanix hefted and then redistributed some of the lichen in his bulging pockets. He continued watching Beryl, learning only that she did not look up to notice.

"Let's move," she said, and sprang lightly into the air. Galvanix watched her sail through her arc, bringing her legs up slightly to reduce drag and extending them before her for touchdown. He followed close behind, watching her frequently. In three hours of cross-country she did not falter, although Galvanix thought he heard her talking to herself.

The landscape they traversed was typical southwest Farside, if alarmingly sodden: rolling highlands carpeted with a dense groundcover compounded of numerous species, some tailored, many sown to fend as they might. The vegetation smothered the outlines of smaller craters, but strewn rubble and discernible rings broke through the tangle more frequently as they moved over higher ground. Sometimes they would hop or climb over a crater wall running across the land like the crumbling stone fence of some vanished farm. If the wall was part of an intact ring they might cross its mate kilometers farther, returning to higher ground.

Galvanix tried to ascertain where they were, but his recollections of Farside geography—the cratered lakes of its uplands, smaller and more discrete than Nearside's drowned mares— jostled each other without binding. His mind swayed with fatigue and the slow poisons produced by unending fear.

When they halted hours later, Galvanix was too tired to think of questioning Beryl. They had paused throughout their false afternoon only to allow Beryl to drink from clear streams, but Galvanix saw her pace steadily slacken. Clambering over the meters-high scarp of a vanished crater, Beryl found a slight overhang of tilted basalt affording some shelter from the rain. None of the ground was dry, but Galvanix needed only to keep his head above stream level. Beryl was already lying on her side, evidently asleep. Galvanix arranged his limbs, exhaustion muffling their ache, and reflected confusedly that Earthpeople, pressed into the dirt with six times the pleasant lunar force, probably found it difficult to sleep on the ground.

He woke as something crashed against him, driving the breath from his chest. Hands ran over his face in the dark, forcing it down into the mud as Beryl hissed in his ear, "Don't even exhale."

A faint whine droned lazily through the clouds, cutting through the patter of rain. Beryl covered him, her body pressing against his with more than its natural weight, as though she were pulling herself against the ground in order to crush him. The drone grew louder, and Galvanix held still, the traces of some extinguished dream fading in the clamor of alarm. The taste of mud in his nose brought a sudden image of Rona, and as Beryl pressed against his pounding chest Galvanix sensed with horror that he was becoming aroused.

The sound of the aircraft swelled, and Galvanix thought for a second that it would pass directly overhead. For long seconds it held at a steady register, then slowly subsided, while Beryl shifted to touch a finger against Galvanix's lips. Galvanix nodded fractionally, disoriented with excitement and fear.

After a minute Beryl lifted her head. "It may return," she whispered. And as an afterthought: "Stay under me; my suit shields body heat." Galvanix nodded again, his erection straining unconcealably against Beryl's hip. The wraith of his dream had passed, but his body, uncontrollable as a decapitated snake, continued to tremble.

Beryl rose slowly. "Your physiologic response is unusual, though not unprecedented."

Galvanix was flushed, another unseemly rerouting of blood. "My wife and I sometimes made love in our garden."

"Perhaps you should wear a locket of mud," Beryl observed absently. Galvanix looked and saw her shivering. "If we had been caught in the open it would have had us," she said.

"The aircraft? It may not have been seeking us at all."

Beryl shook her head. "Had it come back for a second look it would have zeroed in on us, however still we held. We should have had a backup site to dash for. Traveling in the open is a risk we must accept, but I failed, *again*, to take precautions."

Galvanix found her suppressed alarm unnerving. "Beryl, you are not a credible candidate for an emotional crisis. What is happening to you?" And in a sudden inspiration: "Has it to do with being 'fey'?"

Beryl flinched. "Indeed," she said, and faced him. "My bioaugmentation is designed not to fall into enemy hands. In the event of death or serious trauma the systems degrade quickly. This has happened."

Galvanix stared at her, trying to work it out. "You mean that your memochips, and the conductors that quicken your reflexes—"

"All gone. Internal navigation, maps, languages, the balancing enablers—" Beryl made a dismissive gesture. "Flushed away."

Galvanix was appalled. Involuntarily he averted his eyes, feeling a wave of pity for the woman, the attributes that made her fleeter than human now dumped shit on the lunar plains.

The silence that followed seemed immediately unbearable. "Are you in pain?" he asked her.

"Not physically. The shutting-down is like . . . grace withdrawing. I know I am falling back on, on nothing less than myself, but—" She paused. "My strength is expended in prevailing against injury, not coming to terms with my loss. This was not meant to be survived."

Beryl rose suddenly and cupped one hand to her ear. "But I won't repeat those errors I survive." She stood listening several seconds, then asked, "Do your ears detect anything? I'm asking seriously."

"No," Galvanix answered after a moment. "But—" But Beryl was moving swiftly across the crater wall, slipping once and recovering in the first slow second of fall. Galvanix followed, grimacing as the cold rain pelted his face.

A dozen meters away Beryl vanished into an opening among the rocks, and when Galvanix reached it he found a fissure scarcely wide enough to admit his hips. Wriggling in awkwardly, he found the recess completely dark. He edged between the rough walls of rock warily, resisting the sudden suspicion that Beryl was waiting to spring out at him. "Beryl, godammit."

"I'm below you," she said, her voice near. Galvanix inched down and forward, sweeping the darkness with his fingers. Beryl was lying between the converging planes of stone, wedged lightly into the space where the fissure narrowed to her body's width.

"The searchcraft could yet return, or send another," she said. "I hope you've been thinking lately, because you are going to have to vet my decisions."

"And how can I do that if you won't tell me what you are doing?"

"Just help us stay alive from one hour to the next. You think tactically, I'll think strategically."

"Those are military terms, and I don't know what they mean." Galvanix found himself trembling. "Can you still locate your objective when we approach it?"

"Yes."

"Then the sensor is part of that band around your wrist. Don't trouble to confirm anything," Galvanix said. "And you're either going to bury it or, likelier, relay its contents off-Moon. So that's probably a transmitter, too, with power to reach a low equatorial satellite. Do you want me to take it if you're killed?"

"You wouldn't make it alone," Beryl replied. "Later I will show you how to use it."

Goading her, Galvanix realized, seemed to calm Beryl, and he stopped. Resting his forehead against the damp stone, he tried to collect himself, letting the meters of solid stillness absorb his agitation. The shelter of underground was soothing, and Galvanix felt his roiled emotions slowly settle.

"You declared yourself at peace," Beryl said in the darkness. "Has your quick fix at the infirmary convulsed you with hope?"

Galvanix suppressed a retort. "No," he said with dignity.

"You are as one already dead, your wife a widow."

"Are you wondering now at my motives? I am entrusted to aid you in your mission, which you say is unfinished."

"I am wondering at the state of your spirit," Beryl said. "Are you grieving for your unfinished life, or perhaps thinking about contacting your loved ones?"

"I don't think beyond the moment I inhabit." Galvanix felt himself suspended between tension and repose, perhaps only because he still had to steady himself with a hand against the opposite wall. "It is you who have been distraught. Is the decay of these systems going to affect your brain chemistry?"

"If they did, it is over now. I am alone in my skull, and can function thus. Do you think me helpless without augmentation?" Galvanix didn't answer, and Beryl added, "I will allow nothing inimical to my mission, and debar nothing indifferent to it."

Galvanix didn't know what this meant. "I will help you, short of assisting at another slaughter. If you would speak of what pains you, I might be able to help you further."

"Do you want to make love? I would hold no objection, but feel too unwell to participate more than cursorily."

"My God, Beryl, what are you talking about?" Galvanix was shocked. "Everything else aside, I would not molest an ill woman."

"Your arousal is not unnatural in conditions of profound danger. But I suspect your deeper need is to establish some relationship with the last person you shall know."

"I—yes, of course I do." Galvanix felt his throat constricting. He groped in the darkness and found her hand, squeezing hard before he received an acknowledging pressure. "No, I don't want to die without some reconciliation between us," Galvanix said, his voice strained. "But I have, had, no idea whether you share that feeling at all."

"I remain a human being, if tougher than you." Her voice betrayed little beyond its undertone of fatigue. "I also know how to set down a burden. Does your utopianism allow you to countenance half-measures?"

Galvanix said, "I think we know enough of the world to accept half-measures, except in matters of moral urgency."

"In matters of moral urgency," said Beryl, "half-measures cannot even be hoped for."

Fingers closed around his ankle, pulling him down.

The undisturbed darkness proved a balm after seventy hours' daylight, and they lingered thirty minutes after waking.

"In my culture lovers exchange gifts, but I have nothing to give you; you hold now all there is."

"Lovers have offered gifts for thousands of years. There are long traditions of impoverished lovers, so you may cite clear precedent in deferring yours with a promise."

"But I can promise never to have more than this, just a handful of days, which are yours anyway."

"Do not be bathetic. I will tell you of the gift I *will* give you, directly we return to High Earth Orbit."

Galvanix grimaced in the darkness. Beryl's homeland was no land at all. "Tell me," he said.

"I have a Ground Effect—an antique keepsake brought up when payloads were lifted by rocketry and every gram boosted was invaluable. It's a twentieth-century T-shirt."

"A what?"

Beryl repeated it.

"You mean like the letter T?"

"Suggesting the shape, which extended to waist and biceps. They were informal wear in temperate climes, and often boasted slogans on the torso, either self-expression or an advertisement of the wearer's favorite vendor."

"God preserve us. And which was this?"

"This was made for employees of a Western corporation, but my colleagues adopted it as kind of a motto. It says, *Protein gets out protein*."

Galvanix laughed. "Thank you," he said. He wondered if he

was being needled, but felt Beryl's brushing fingertips and decided not. "One day I will wear it with you."

"And you, of course, will make me a gift with your own hands."

Galvanix smiled. "It is enough that one makes it oneself, and I see no problem with using my mind as another does his hands. But I have an Earthside antique too, and you should have it. It is nearly massless, so may not be rare. It's also less old. The antique is a decal, which your admired Westerners persisted in affixing to public places and vehicles to hector passers-by. This was brought up to HEO, probably as a joke, and decorated the cabin of a space tug that was eventually scuttled in Moon orbit. It reads: 'Visit Terra Nova and shit!'"

Beryl chuckled, a deep sound Galvanix could only hear with his head against her chest. "Never malign tourists' organics," she said. "If you ever retrieve it, I will wear it on my helmet."

Galvanix saw red numerals light up in the darkness, a chronometer display somewhere on Beryl's person. Before he could twist his head to read them, they winked out.

"Does it hurt when I do this?"

"I like it anyway. And you: shall I prescribe more endorphins?"

"Don't be crude. My flesh demanded moderation even when well. You, however, may have anything you ask."

"Perhaps in fourteen hours. I hope you can log a day's march."

"'The replenished spirit buoys the body.' I'll be counting down from fourteen."

She poked him, not gently. "Don't become vacuous. We're being hunted out there, and can only get weaker."

"I know that, dear; it's never far from mind. I'm ready to talk seriously, if you're seriously ready to tell me what we're doing."

"Fair enough. We are perhaps eighty klicks from a rail line, which we can follow to the Far Sea. Thence we must reach the Pole, by whatever means."

"Steal a boat?"

"Or build one."

"Can we hop a train?"

"No. A good security program would detect the rise in resistance."

"What happens if we're caught?"

"Someone else will be sent after the objective, at great risk. Oh, you mean us?" She laughed.

"But you would not allow us to be taken anyway, would you?" Beryl did not answer. "Kill me to save me, or the mission? It makes one think."

"Don't think. There's no time left in your life for introspection. Only action; act until stopped." She squeezed hard for emphasis.

They reached the rail line two days later. For ten kilometers they had traversed a plain submerged under a half-meter of water, too deep to bound through, too shallow to swim. Galvanix was feeling weak and dispirited when Beryl touched his shoulder, pointing through the rain to a raised line running like a levee across the horizon.

There had been no more overflights or signs of pursuit. "They think we would have made for the twilight zone, but are likelier dead. The airship did burn in mid-air." However, when the sun had briefly emerged hours earlier, Beryl had ordered Galvanix to freeze, and they had waited—alert, Galvanix supposed, for the possibility of reconnaissance satellites—until the cloud cover closed up again.

"If a train comes, dive," Beryl said. They approached slowly, Beryl cupping a hand to her ear. Waving Galvanix back, she crept up the embankment of fused silicates, peering across its top before standing. While Galvanix scrambled across the wet and slippery surface, Beryl laid hands on the featureless twin rails, then nodded.

"Back into the water," she said. Galvanix looked at her in surprise. "I want to watch a train go by. Best to set out right behind one, and we need the rest anyway."

They waited behind a spar of rock twenty meters away, most of their bodies out of the water. Galvanix fell asleep despite efforts to remain alert, and was awakened by a prod from Beryl. He opened his eyes in time to see the front coupler glide past, followed by a slow succession of flatcars covered with wrapped packages and crates. Beside him Beryl nodded. "Good," she said.

"Why good?"

"It means there won't be a fast train right behind it."

A minute later the final car rolled past, a truncated box with a wan eye glowing behind it. Beryl gripped Galvanix's arm. "Wait until it's out of sight. There may be a camera on that thing."

Back on the embankment they wrung water from their clothes, which now clung to them instead of hanging sodden. Galvanix flexed once and leaped, grimacing at the sudden pain. Beryl bounded past him, falling shorter than usual. Together they started down the track, hopping alternately like the pistons of an unevenly reciprocating engine.

Low pools lapped against one bank of the railway, shallow enough to present a zinc green surface and a bad smell. These pools persisted for kilometers after the flooded plain on the other side rose to soggy tundra. "Culture ponds," said Beryl, pointing to a causeway separating flats of different hue. "They're growing fast biomass, harvestable after one lunar day. Consistent with a war footing."

After that they bounded lower, alert for crop workers or argus-eyed machines. When the ground to one side of the embankment was dry they descended, letting its mass block the arcs of their transit.

Galvanix was trailing Beryl when he saw her head snap up, twisting suddenly while still in flight to throw back a startled look. On her next bound she was atop the tracks, and Galvanix broke pace with a clumsy skid and step. He hopped up the embankment to find her crouched over the tracks, ear against a rail. Galvanix listened but didn't know if he heard anything. He ran a finger along one rail and pulled it back with a start, for the metal buzzed like a motor.

"Back out of sight, hurry," Beryl commanded, straightening and leaping at once. Galvanix bounded after. Ten meters away they dove behind a patch of scrub, and then Galvanix heard it. The sound came from back down the track, muffled by a crosswind: the wail of straining metal, punctuated by irregular clangs. The rails began keening in sympathy.

Galvanix guessed what it was only seconds before the engine rose obliquely over the horizon: a train *rolling* over the tracks like some metastasizing groundcar, hundreds of metal wheels squealing. Incredulous, Galvanix imagined he could smell the oil being burned just to lubricate its friction gradients.

The first cars assumed detail as they emerged through the mist, a featureless engine pulling high-sided boxcars. The train moved slowly, and variations somewhere—wobbly alignment or uneven wheel wear, or perhaps fluctuations in lubricant—would every few seconds produce a bang as two cars knocked lightly together, their concussion repeated down the next few cars.

"*This* train we can board," Beryl murmured, a low thrill in her voice.

He looked back to the train, which was rolling past with an enormous clatter. Moving scarcely faster than Galvanix could run—too slow to carry passengers, he thought—the long line of boxcars and cylindrical tanks crept across the rail line like a graphic display, fading into darkness ahead of them. How many cars could an electric engine pull? Galvanix looked down the track to discern the foreshortened shape of the last car, which slowly lengthened to disclose itself another tank.

"No monitor; let's go," Beryl said, and was up and moving. Startled, Galvanix scrambled after her. Beryl was heading for the tracks at an angle, bounding at top speed as the final car grew nearer.

Galvanix kicked hard as he struck the ground, flooding his muscles with urgency. Immediately something faltered, and Galvanix while yet accelerating felt his strength tip and quickly drain. The train, moving with dreamlike languor, slid past in the last seconds before he reached the embankment. Galvanix vaulted the slope at a bound, lunging desperately after the last car as it slowly pulled away from him.

At the crest of his leap Galvanix saw a human figure atop a boxcar, bounding toward him like a pedestrian running against a slidewalk. Beryl reached the edge of the tank and stood facing him as the train receded, raising an arm to gesture or wave.

Galvanix felt a sharp pain in his chest, stronger than the needles in his legs. A glint caused him to look down to see Beryl's tiny anchor, its barbs buried in his left pectoral. Galvanix was able to frame no mental response before its line snapped taut and he was pulled into the air.

Beryl carried him back up the length of the train, pausing to leap carefully between cars. "Stop racing your pulse, you're bleeding too much," she shouted in his ear. Rain pattered in his face, which he held still to keep from tugging his neck tendons.

Beryl set him down on the flat roof of a boxcar, and bent to pull open a small hatch. She dropped her legs through it, then stood sunk to the waist and reached for Galvanix. Darkness rose and surrounded him as she lowered him through, then laid him out on an uneven mound of some aromatic substance that crunched beneath them, a grain. The cargo nearly filled the car, forcing Beryl to crouch before pulling the hatch shut over her.

"How do you feel?" she asked, her voice booming hollowly. Exploring hands felt for the wet tear in his overalls, which she pulled further open to expose the ripped muscle beneath. "I'm going to have to sew this up," she said, her breath brushing his ear. "One barb on the anchor is adaptable for the purpose, although it's been in some dirty places."

She pushed open the hatch, admitting a circle of grey light. She pulled Galvanix beneath it and sutured the wound, using a single length of line. He fainted before she finished, and woke briefly later to hold his mouth open while she dribbled rainwater from her cupped hands.

Later he woke to pain, which clawed at his chest as though Beryl were still stitching and found echoes in every joint when he stirred his limbs. Beryl was holding his hand, and told him she had feared only that he might slip into shock. "Inflammation but perhaps no sepsis," she said, running a fingertip lightly over the cobbled skin. Beryl was angry when he refused to crawl off and urinate onto the grain, and helped him through the hatch only after first climbing out to study the landscape. "Your last chance," she told him grimly.

The train moved slowly, and the occasional jolts were cushioned by their bed of grain, though they boomed like concussions in a tunnel. Galvanix surrendered himself to whimpering, which he found made the pain more endurable. Beryl pushed barbs under his skin at various points as an analgesic measure, but Galvanix could not tell if it helped.

"We are missing our last opportunity to make love," he said weakly, smiling with an effort in the darkness.

Beryl squeezed his hand. "Maybe in orbit," she told him. "You'll be convalescing up there for some time."

Galvanix knew better, but allowed the thought to lull him. Later Beryl explained how the train would take them straight into a storage depot, whence they would actually hold some chance of escaping to the Far Sea by a route Beryl envisioned. Galvanix half-listened as she described the geography of their present and anticipated course.

Beryl told him they would be in the train for three days. Grains held in rainwater for two hours would soften, and Galvanix swallowed a few grams. Later she forbade him to go outside, for which he lacked the strength anyway.

Galvanix was awakened by Beryl touching a finger to his lips, and was told they were moving through a settled area. He could hear nothing to confirm this, but Beryl went back to listening against the wall, and after an hour he heard the indistinct sound of voices. The clatter of the wheels slowed, and minutes later stopped. In the ringing silence, Galvanix could hear distant sounds of machinery.

Beryl crawled over and said, "If they've got a good security officer, they'll check the cars now. The odds of our being alive are merely low." She buried Galvanix beneath a mound of grain. Galvanix heard her burrowing some distance away, then silence. The train started, stopped for an interminable period, then began rolling at what seemed an even slower speed. Galvanix drifted into sleep.

He woke suddenly when he felt the grain stirring beneath his body, as though someone were reaching up for him. Galvanix thrashed wildly, then felt Beryl's hands under his shoulders, pulling him up. "The grain is being drained through the bottom," Beryl told him. Galvanix felt a distant roar like a cataract as their footing slipped steadily. "Just keep on top," she said. "The machines unloading the grain won't look inside."

They slowly sank toward the bottom of the car, Galvanix fighting panic as he wondered whether he could keep from sliding through the chute himself. Beryl seized his arm, pulling him over to a rung on an inside wall. Galvanix hooked his elbow through it as the grain underfoot dropped away.

A surprisingly liquid gurgle resounded through the dark interior. The walls reverberated with a slam, and Galvanix heard the extended rumble of machinery disengaging and moving on.

They slid carefully to the floor of the car. Beryl resumed listening at the wall, while Galvanix tested his weight on either foot. Grain dust flew through the air, stinging his eyes even as it made his mouth water.

A wave of dizziness struck him, and Galvanix lowered himself to the floor. He could hear Beryl climbing rungs overhead. "I'm going to crack the hatch," she said, her voice carrying clearly in the stillness. Galvanix heard a faint scrape as the hatch was lifted. Eyes wide in the dark, he expected a crescent of light but saw only a smudge of dimmest grey. Beryl was beside him after a minute. "I'm going out now," she said. "Just keep still till I'm back." She leaned forward and kissed him hard on the lips.

Beryl was gone a long time, and Galvanix, though fitfully alert, wondered briefly what to do should she not return. Her capture would doubtless prompt a general search, but conceivably he might be missed and the empty train sent out again. He easily accepted the conclusion to lie still, and was drifting deep into compliance when Beryl touched his arm.

"Let's go," she said, low but not whispering. Beryl leaped to the open hatch, swinging for a second from its lip before pulling herself through. Galvanix swayed as he stood, but followed. His leg muscles managed the easy jump, but his chest cried out as he reached to grasp the verge, and his fingers slipped. Hands closed around his wrists, and Beryl lifted him through the top.

They were in a dimly lit warehouse, hardly taller than the boxcars. Only the last four cars of the train were visible; the rest had apparently been pulled on through as they were unloaded. Few lights shone, only one set in the ceiling. Among the slanting shadows, Galvanix was unable to gauge the room's size.

Beryl slipped down a metal ladder to the ground, looking up to Galvanix and gesturing for silence. Galvanix followed carefully, not dropping even the last few meters. He hurried after Beryl, so mindful of his burning chest still that he scarcely looked around him.

Beryl touched his arm to indicate direction, speaking low in his ear as they squeezed between two crates. "I found system access, which is keyed to a password, quaintly enough. Without my tools, though, I couldn't circumvent, and had to wait for someone to log in."

They turned a corner to face a dimly glowing screen set in a stanchion. Beryl strode to it and began tapping the keyboard swung out underneath. "As soon as I sign off we're going to move, so stay alert." Near Beryl's feet lay two sets of bunched fabric that looked like clensuits. Just beyond, Galvanix noticed with a start, a pair of feet protruding toes up from behind a small tractor.

"Beryl," said Galvanix in a low voice, "I hope you haven't killed someone."

"Simple concussion," Beryl said. "Can impair memory preceding and following an accident. With luck, he'll think he fell."

After a moment she stopped typing and went over to the fallen man. "He may even get up and forget doing so," Beryl said, hoisting him over her shoulder. She swung a small seat down from the stanchion and set the man on it, pulling out his feet so that he leaned backward. "Let's go," she said, handing Galvanix a bundle.

The sight of the limp body being maneuvered about had made Galvanix feel ill, and he fixed his gaze on a point between Beryl's shoulders. After a series of turns Beryl squatted suddenly before a row of round hatches set flush in the floor. She picked one and undogged its seal, then looked up at Galvanix speculatively.

"Could you shut this behind . . . No, I had better do it. You go first."

Galvanix pushed his bundle carefully through one of the tears in his suit and crawled gingerly through the opening, head first in the lunar fashion. The shaft was barely wide enough to admit his shoulders, and unlit save for a point of light an indeterminate distance below. Galvanix automatically began counting handholds as he moved through the artery, running his palm around its rim to confirm that there were no lights. At about twenty meters down his groping hand encountered air, and Galvanix edged forward to feel the outline of a second shaft cutting across his path.

"There's a turnoff here," he whispered.

"Keep going. Take the next one."

Galvanix resumed his downward crawl, noting that the light at the bottom was not appreciably larger. He was not surprised that the diffuse lunar soil had been so thoroughly tunneled. Another fifteen meters brought him to a second cross-shaft, dark in both directions.

"Here we are."

"Left."

Galvanix wriggled into the shaft, edging a few meters in before collapsing on his back. This tunnel was taller than wide, though not enough that Galvanix could sit up. He heard Beryl slither in behind him, and prepared to be urged onward. Instead a green light winked on beyond his toes, and Galvanix raised his head to see that Beryl had activated the helmet light of her clensuit.

"Put yours on," she said, unfolding the visor with a snap.

Galvanix pulled out his bundle, now sticky, and laboriously unrolled it. It was a simple closed environment suit, used by natives for the sixty years that there had been some form of atmosphere on the lunar surface. With some difficulty Galvanix untangled its limbs, manipulated the visor so that it snapped rigid, and examined the chlorophylter settings on the recycler.

"Beryl, there's only thirty minutes' breathing here."

"That will suffice. Start priming it now, however."

Galvanix had not yet gotten the suit on, so wasn't ready to begin exhaling into it. The filmy material could doubtless be pulled over his overall, but Galvanix knew the chlorophylter needed his body heat. He shucked his torn greys painfully, almost crying out as he pulled loose a patch pasted to his chest.

With the clensuit midway up his legs, Galvanix gave up. "Beryl," he murmured, his eyes blurring with tears of pain and frustration, "I . . . think I need help with this."

"You poor wretch." Beryl's form loomed over him, pressing through the tunnel's arch. Galvanix suffered her to pull his suit up over him, then seal and check it. In his weakness Galvanix regarded Beryl's ability to squeeze past him with passive wonder.

"Why is the tunnel prolate instead of round?"

"One couldn't negotiate the corner otherwise," she said. "Pull yourself together." She fitted the respirator into his mouth and pinched his cheek hard.

Galvanix lay still as Beryl crawled over him, then rolled over and followed. He blew into the respirator and felt his breath puff into the suit's lining. Ahead of him, Beryl's headlight shone faintly around the curve of her helmet.

The height of the tunnel allowed a freer range of motion, and they moved swiftly along its length. Galvanix lost count after they had covered a kilometer, and the darkness held no reference points save for the occasional puffs of air as they passed an intersection. They had traveled three hours, according to the suit watch which had helpfully begun counting from 0:00 upon activation, when Galvanix heard Beryl curse in front of him. Beyond the green glow of her helmet, a grey wall stretched across the tunnel like an eardrum.

"The passageway is sealed, and I don't think I can open it without alerting the security systems." Beryl was tapping at keys on a control panel, and Galvanix saw a small sequence of lights appear.

"Why is it sealed off?"

"Probably to prevent winds from temperature gradients. Perhaps a defense against flooding, although they should close automatically in the event of rupture."

"Rupture?"

Beryl spoke as she worked. "One tunnel cuts a deep chord beneath the Far Sea. I had hoped to follow it to the point of farthest penetration, climb a shaft to a disused dome now on the seabed, and attempt a buoyant ascent."

"From the bottom of the sea?" Galvanix felt a pit open in his stomach. "How deep?"

"About a hundred meters."

"But these aren't pressure suits!"

"It would have been rough. As it is, we'll have to backtrack, which is hateful and dangerous, and try a harder route." Beryl turned and gestured impatiently to Galvanix, who obediently lay flat. She coursed over him like a cat and disappeared into the darkness from which they had come.

Galvanix followed, shaken at the thought of breaking through to the bottom of the sea. He wondered whether they were below water right now, and found that his shoulders and arms were trembling. Galvanix knew that weakness was making him dependent, but could rally no strength to resist. Fear was washed over by shame and the urge to cry, which he bluntly suppressed, subordinating all thought to the rhythm of his gliding crawl.

Before him Beryl's light, which was now some distance ahead, had stopped moving. Galvanix froze, ears straining in the whispery stir of the tunnel. A faint light twinkled near the glow of Beryl's helmet, and Galvanix crept forward. He found her hunched at an intersection, punching the keys of a tiny control box.

"I think this is the turnoff," Beryl muttered, courtesy enough to someone who was plainly becoming an encumbrance. She was querying a local system, which would give displays of the tunnel ahead without requiring access or, presumably, logging the fact for Security to scan.

After a minute she clicked off the box. "Be ready to climb," she said, and squeezed around the corner.

They followed the tunnel for more than a kilometer. Galvanix saw that Beryl was raising her head, directing her helmet light onto the tunnel roof. After ten minutes she stopped, indicating to Galvanix an opening over their heads.

"This shaft vents air to the surface," she said. "If it doesn't give onto a public thoroughfare, we can escape through it."

She began checking her suit. "I'll go first; I don't want you falling on me. If you fall back and injure yourself, I will have to leave you."

Galvanix felt his extremities tingling. "I understand," he said.

Beryl reached forward suddenly and squeezed Galvanix's nape. "Mission comes first," she said. She pulled back before Galvanix could react, raised her arms into the opening and hoisted herself up.

Galvanix looked in after her. Beryl had extinguished her helmet, and no light shone from the top of the shaft. The slither of fabric against smooth ceramic receded steadily.

Galvanix rose to his knees and felt around the opening. A thrill of alarm ran up his arm as he discovered that the shaft was nearly a meter across, and moreover without rungs. Of course, he thought. He braced his elbows inside the widening sleeve and hauled himself up. The lift was easy, but a sharp pain pulled in his chest, premonitory.

Galvanix pressed his palms against the opposite sides and drew up his legs. He then slowly pushed his back up the side of the shaft, steadying himself with his outstretched hands. When he had risen as far as possible, he angled his forearms against the shaft and quickly brought up one foot. He then drew up the other, restored to his original position after ascending something less than a meter.

Galvanix repeated this operation twenty times, relying on his overdeveloped leg muscles not to tire quickly. He tried once to bring his arms into play, but found they would not sustain his weight for more than the second it took to raise his legs. He pushed himself into a rhythm, imagining his body a ratchet that would only click upward.

On the thirty-first click something failed. As he drew up a leg, the opposite calf cramped, pulling the foot from the wall before Galvanix registered pain. He threw out an arm as he fell sideways, and his shoulder socket took the jolt in a burst of stars.

Pain bounced off his skull like an echo. Galvanix spread his arms and other leg, arresting a slide that had left him somehow facedown. His calf muscle seemed to be trying to peel away from the bone.

Taking stock, Galvanix turned his head slowly, studying his position in the dim glow of the head light. He was perhaps halfway up, high enough to injure himself gravely if he fell. Wriggling his back muscles to squirm higher, he carefully tried to heel-and-toe his good foot up the wall without lifting it. It worked, but the progress was ludicrously small. This is called inching, he thought, wondering how many centimeters made an inch.

Shifting his weight to either hip as his muscles tired, Galvanix strained upward, a morsel supplying its own peristalsis. He suspected he was describing a slow spiral in his progress up the shaft, but could see no reference points on its featureless surface. Sometimes he pressed his fingertips against opposite sides, seeking a balance between the pain it spurred in his chest and his need to relieve his leg.

Pain lanced through his breast without warning. Galvanix ordered his arms to hold fast, but felt the wall sliding past his fingers. He kicked out hard, slamming his coccyx against the wall. One hand was pressed to his chest before he knew his leg would hold.

For several minutes he remained bent over his cantilevered leg, waiting out the slowly diminishing pain. He brought his hand away reluctantly, raising his head as if to look about. There was no determining how much ground he had lost.

No more mistakes, he told himself, as though from a distance. It was a way of diffusing the ego, that catchment for fear. Galvanix tried to wipe his hand on his clothes, which proved to be wet and filthy. Carefully he licked each finger clean, then blew on his hand to dry it.

Just go slowly, he told himself. Rest frequently. Galvanix moved his limbs with the deliberation of a spider, never two at once.

When something brushed his shoulder he froze, his thread of concentration snapped. After a moment he resumed climbing, and felt an object bounce lightly against his collarbone. Galvanix hung motionless for a second, then turned his head toward the distraction. In the narrow beam, the curvate tines of Beryl's anchor gleamed, its barbs bent inward like retracted claws. Galvanix looked at it uncomprehendingly.

The anchor spun slowly, its four tines twinkling in turn, then paused and rotated backward with equal languor. The thing was dangling on its superthin line; it had been lowered. Or it had hung some time, he had climbed up to it. Each thought filled Galvanix's mind, and presently gave rise to another. It was there for him.

Galvanix took the device gingerly in his hand and tugged at it. The line immediately jerked upward twice. The surprise snapped Galvanix into a semblance of wit: he had assumed Beryl had left the anchor behind.

Arms trembling, Galvanix wound the line several times about his wrist. A fingertip pressed one barb, and Galvanix felt a thrill run straight to his chest. Confirming that the anchor could not swing loose and catch him, Galvanix let his full weight gradually depend onto the line. It immediately began to draw him up.

How much line did Beryl have? Galvanix could already feel the twin beats of her hand-over-hand rhythm beneath the steady pull. Looking up, he saw a smudge of grey in the darkness, too indistinct to have shape. If Beryl didn't have her light on, Galvanix reflected in a final surfacing of consciousness, then neither should he. Galvanix extinguished his helmet light just as a glimmer of movement crossed its reach.

"Took you long enough, though I'm not surprised," Beryl said, taking his arm as he braced his legs. Galvanix gasped as she tugged, but said nothing. "We climbed farther than I expected, so we may be over a built-up area." Galvanix unwound and released the anchor, which disappeared into Beryl's clensuit.

Above them stretched a ring of dull light, which Galvanix realized was a sleeve of mesh open to the air. He squeezed past Beryl and looked out. The shaft rose a meter above ground level—as a safeguard against flooding?—and was capped like a mushroom to keep out rain. The cap obscured most of his view, and Galvanix could see only a few meters of flat surface. Air currents curled past his face, and a gust of rain drummed loudly against the cap.

Galvanix slid back down to face Beryl. "Where are we?" he asked.

"Over the shore, I think. Probably an industrial facility—some gusts carry a whiff of smokestack oxides."

"Pollution?" Galvanix was appalled.

"Never mind that. I've heard no human activity in forty minutes, but we may be in a line of sight."

Galvanix edged back up and pressed his nose to the mesh. Someone could be standing six meters away, looking in their direction. He felt Beryl squeeze in behind him.

"I sawed through the struts fastening the shaft cap," she whispered. "When I raise it, you look around."

Maneuvering carefully, Beryl got her hands beneath either side of the lid, which she slowly lifted like an enormous hat. Galvanix ducked his head and scanned the surrounding area.

"Nothing," he said. "We seem to be far from any building. I see lots of pipework and some holding tanks."

"Is there a close one you can run for?"

Galvanix looked again. "About ten meters."

The lid rose higher, until half a meter of clearance separated it from the sleeve. "Go."

Galvanix squeezed through the opening, ignoring a blossoming of pain in his chest. Cold rain pelted him, and something acrid blew past his face. He drew up his legs and leaped, sailing through the storm as though windswept. A second bound took him to a cylindrical tank, and Galvanix dove behind it. He crouched in the rain, pulling the headpiece of his clensuit over his scalp.

The airshaft was indistinct in the clouded rain, and Galvanix watched for a minute before he saw that Beryl had raised the lid enough to swing her legs away from the shaft. Holding it as carefully as a tray, Beryl slid out from beneath and slowly replaced the lid, her silhouette indistinct to any eyes more distant than Galvanix's. She was beside him in two bounds.

"Onward." They ran through the pelting rain, hopping low. Galvanix adjusted his faceplate, then put the respirator into his mouth and blew air through his suit. A warm band tightened across his chest.

"There," said Beryl, pointing toward a murky middle distance. Galvanix followed without wondering what she saw. After a dozen leaps further he could make out a low railing, the edge of a platform he now realized they stood upon. Glancing behind him—there was nothing but darkened outlines and mist— Galvanix approached the railing and looked out.

Ten meters below, black waters swirled around the structure's slender pilings. A swollen torrent cut through banks of scarcely eroded lunar stone, widening as it coursed past other buildings perched on stalks.

Beryl pointed to the horizon. Beyond the drowned land, the line of the world's end glittered through the mist, unbroken and faintly convex. Galvanix stared with wild surmise past the veil, where sunlight fell on the arching meniscus of the Far Sea.

FIVE

They descended the nearest piling, incised so faintly with footholds that Galvanix slipped and plunged straight into the water. He was immediately thrust to the surface, but strong currents grasped his ankles and pulled him swiftly away.

Water streamed down his faceplate, blurring vision more thoroughly than rain upon his unprotected eyes would have done. Galvanix was reaching up when something crashed into him. He was hurled underwater once more, pain lost in the spray of bubbles. Hands grabbed him before he surfaced: Beryl, who had judged and leaped, and now held him like a pet owner determined to avoid another chase.

Kicking hard, Beryl angled toward the near bank. Galvanix obligingly went limp until he felt ground drag beneath his boots. He scrambled for traction, then slogged ashore against a current that continued to snatch at his footing. Their shore, he discovered, was a spit of land cut off by the flooding of low ground behind an embankment.

"This is not a normal noonday storm," Beryl shouted.

Galvanix nodded, a gesture lost under the circumstances. "The shores of the Near Sea have never been like this, even since the destruction of the Mirrors. It must be the extra water dumped by the comet into the atmosphere."

"It's our salvation." Beryl was looking toward the complex they had just fled. "There is a boatyard four kilometers distant, and a craft can be stolen in such weather."

Weariness suddenly weighed at him. "I don't know how we—"

"You wait here, of course. Traveling through storm waters requires training." And perhaps sensing protest, she added, "It's quite safe, especially in a clensuit. I can throw my anchor like a grapple."

Galvanix shuddered. Beryl took out her anchor and whirled it overhead. Released, the projectile flew into the darkness. Beryl reeled the line back for a few seconds before encountering resistance, then nodded once to Galvanix and waded stolidly into the water.

Galvanix lay on his back, head turned toward the dim outline of buildings. No lights shone. A shift in the wind brought more rain pelting against his faceplate, and he raised his hand to shield it. What was happening with the world's weather? Galvanix imagined the millions of tonnes of water sprayed onto the atmosphere, not as a missile but still all at once.

Abruptly he wondered about the gases dissolved in the comet's ice. Had they reached the surface too, or were their lighter molecules scattered into their own lunar orbits? Galvanix felt a pang at the thought of that oxygen dissipated beyond recovery, circling the Moon in a wasted haze.

The air filling his clensuit cushioned him, and he realized too late that he was falling asleep. He woke as something shuddered beneath him, and raised a hand to feel a smooth bulkhead beside him. The deck began to vibrate more quickly, then lurched hard. Sliding backward, Galvanix flung out his other arm and struck someone's foot.

"Don't thrash." Beryl was facing forward, piloting—it came slowly together—some kind of craft. Galvanix raised his head, and a wave of nausea rolled over him. He lay back, curling on his side as the ship began a slow turn that dragged at his entrails. The engine's purr rose to a whine, creating the distressing sense (though Galvanix knew better) that acceleration was also increasing. He was trying to sit upright to avoid vomiting when the acceleration ceased, releasing him as though into free fall.

Galvanix rolled onto his back, breathing deeply. After a second he realized what else had suggested the rocket analogy: the vibrations had cut off with the acceleration. Only a faint hiss came through the deck, although the craft seemed to be maintaining speed.

He sat up slowly. "What is now driving the engine?" he called over the wind and rain.

Beryl glanced over her shoulder. "Steam, you will be happy to hear."

Galvanix was standing now, looking over the gunwale of a launch scarcely larger than a bed. Spray flew in twisting chevrons along either side of the prow. He leaned further and bumped his head against a clear substance. Looking up, he could make out the faint iridescence of the microthin canopy over the cockpit, its outer skin streaming with rain.

"This is not a mooncraft," Galvanix said, lifting his hand from the gunwale.

"Indeed. It is something your Farside shogun got from one of his high-orbital allies, though probably assembled here."

Galvanix looked alarmed. "What is its power source?"

"Once the electric engine puts us up to cruising speed, a fission micropile cuts in. It doubtless requires a rapid flow of water to operate.—And don't be such a fool as to look shocked. Did you think it would burn charcoal like your telephones?"

Galvanix was looking around frantically, as though finding himself in a dragon's mouth. "Can you operate such a thing?"

"The onboard intelligence handles the details. I believe that's it over there." Beryl pointed to a raised area on the console the size of a small book.

Galvanix shifted his feet, looking down. "And the irradiation of the flowthrough is held merely to 'acceptable' levels, since a craft this size cannot have full shielding. So your self-propelled coracle is putting radiation into the Far Sea."

"This craft is not one of 'ours.' If it were, the onboard would occupy a thousandth the space, and would have killed me when I tried to slip it out of the Farsiders' paltry security loop."

Galvanix sat down abruptly on the deck. The radiation, he thought in a mordant flash, at least could not harm him. "There is no reason for a craft this small to have long-distance capacity. And while it cannot hold equipment, it could still unfurl a dish and receive beamed energy instead of carrying a pile. Its design for long unsupported missions marks it plainly as a warship."

"True, but like most warcraft, it has a first-aid kit." Beryl produced a flat case from beneath the control board. "You have already been dosed for pain and shock, otherwise you would not be standing now." Beryl popped open the case, which caught the dim light like the mirror of her sudden smile. "This will buy us days of life. The chances of our completing the mission have gone way up. We may truly make it."

This succession of news was too much for Galvanix, who tried to assimilate it but could only sit back. He watched without comment as Beryl produced a tiny diagnostic device with wire-thin legs extending in all directions, which at her urging Galvanix allowed to crawl the length of his digestive tract. Beryl retrieved it after an uncomfortable hour and slid it back into the case, which promptly lit up with displays. "Your intestinal lining is completely moribund, worse than mine. It didn't measure your marrow stem cells, but this tells us enough. We will make it to the Pole, if barely."

Galvanix slept on that. He woke once to a sensation of swaying, and found the ship in virtual darkness. "Storm?" he murmured.

Beryl looked at him ironically. "No, a too-clear sky, which is why I submerged the vessel. The canopy makes the ship extremely buoyant, so I had to flood it." And indeed Galvanix looked down to see his suited limbs bobbing in a meter of dark water, moonlit by the console's pilot light.

Beryl took them up an hour later, anxious to return to cruising speed. They broke through a green skin that clung to the canopy in tatters. "The exuberance of this seacover bothers me," said Beryl. "The water is too warm."

Galvanix watched the rain push a ragged scrap of algae along the canopy's frictionless surface. "Won't it smother the marine life?"

"Stuff breaks up regularly," said Beryl. "Or should. I'm more worried about the cooling system, which is being overtaxed."

"The reactor cannot cool itself?" Galvanix turned on Beryl, incredulous. "Why then are we racing?" Anger made him suddenly weak, but a giddy rush seemed to lift his chest even as his hand groped for a gunwale.

". . . Because we must fly," he heard Beryl say from a distance. Galvanix could not make out his own reply. He tried to concentrate, and found himself lying on the deck. The rolling swells beneath him seemed to produce contrary tides in his own bodily fluids.

"Beryl." His voice croaked, and Galvanix drank from his helmet tube. He began to pull himself up, and gasped as cramps raked his arms. The sky remained disconcertingly dark, although the sun must by now be almost overhead.

Galvanix bumped against Beryl as he pulled himself to his knees. "How are we doing?" he asked.

Beryl did not turn. "The algae cover is thicker, and it's clogging the intakes. It's also slowing us up."

"If the ship had a hydrofoil, that would not matter."

"Yes, but a hydrofoil would lift the hull, and we need the flowthrough. The water isn't cooling enough as it is, and the onboard has had to release two long ribbons of superconductor to bleed the heat off. The damned things radiate in the infrared like jet trails, and increase our chances of detection."

Galvanix looked out. Patches of algae slid over each other as swells rose beneath them. Water streaming down the canopy obliterated detail, but Galvanix could sense the varying force of the rain from its irregular drumming overhead. A sudden burst rattled hard, forcing the ship deeper into the water like a compressing hand.

"Downdraft," said Beryl, seeing Galvanix's expression. "The Far Sea is a huge tidal bulge, but the atmosphere remains nearly spherical under the rounding effects of its circulation patterns. In mid-sea the wind hits the water as it would a hillside."

"Of course," muttered Galvanix, abashed.

"Damn it!" Beryl shouted. Galvanix started, realizing he had fallen asleep. His head had been resting against Beryl's leg, which had now gone rigid as steel.

"I have been monitoring the water temperatures two hundred meters down. It rose for ten minutes and now is dropping. We passed a heat source—they are *warming* the ocean!"

Galvanix was having more trouble focusing his thoughts than he liked. "How were you measuring that?"

"On a dropline, of course. Your Farsider colleagues are spilling heat from the ocean floor, through either reactors or a thermal tap. Either is bad, but a tap would be worse. This Sea can quench the heat of the lunar core!"

"Perhaps they're just trying to stimulate the ecosphere," Galvanix suggested.

"It doesn't matter if they are. *It's not their heat*."

Galvanix said mildly. "I thought heat was cheap in space."

"Not to move around, it isn't." Beryl studied the displays for a minute, then added, "If the lunar core could be reheated easily, the Consortium would have boosted it back to its level of four billion years ago. Then the Moon would have a magnetic field again."

"Is this something you're going to tell your superiors?"

"If I can," said Beryl grimly. "This reactor can't handle the warmer water, and will shut down in an hour. Then we're back to running on the fuel cells, which won't suffice."

Galvanix thought of his added mass on the lightweight ship. "You shouldn't have brought me along."

"Don't worry, if fuel expenditure were a problem I would put you over in a minute. We're abandoning ship; its last fuel goes to sending it off in a misleading direction." Beryl began tapping the tiny keyboard. "We could not have kept on much longer in any event: the craft will be found almost as soon as someone discovers it missing."

Galvanix scarcely heard her. The thought of jumping into the sea seemed to paralyze him; his mind remained fixed on the image, bereft of fear or anything else. Beryl said, "Your clensuit has been aircharged and sealed, but check it anyway." Galvanix did not respond, but when Beryl jostled him a moment later his fingers began to flutter automatically up the sides of his suit.

Beryl stepped back from the console. "In seventeen minutes the reactor is going to shut down, since the system will not permit override of its generous safety margins." She began running her hands over her own suit. "At that point electric power will resume and the craft will veer off. We'll leap then."

Galvanix muttered, "Generous," but did not look up. He began devoting himself wholly to checking his suit, pulling hard at the seams as though he were facing a spacewalk. Occasionally a hidden bruise shouted beneath his fingers. The suit displays inside his helmet reported full integrity, but Galvanix worked patiently up each limb, checking its entire surface as though establishing the limits of his being.

The sound of the engine changed, and Galvanix felt the deck vibrating beneath him once more. "Time," Beryl said. She touched a spot on the console, and a high wail tore through the cabin. Cold rain stung Galvanix's face, and he looked up to see the canopy slide rapidly away like a nictitating membrane. Beryl leaped onto the gunwale, crouching to steady herself with one hand. "I'll pick the vector," Galvanix stood beside her, knees trembling, as Beryl sought the angle at which they would strike the water at minimum velocity. The craft began a slow turn to port. Beryl swiveled and pointed her finger. "*Now.*"

Galvanix leaped, less at the command than upon sensing with Beryl the window opened by a conflation of favorable vectors.

Wind hit him broadside, and Galvanix contracted into a ball, afraid of being slammed to the surface by a downdraft. The long pause made him tighten further, then he hit the water in a skimming blow that sent him spinning. Water surged about his abruptly outflung limbs.

"Stay calm." Galvanix thought for a moment that Beryl had spoken in his earpiece, but realized it was not her voice. His breath had been knocked from him, and with dark spots dancing before his eyes Galvanix inhaled shakily and decided he could remain calm. He drew in his limbs and sought to take inventory, finding no suit breach nor broken bones, though he could breathe only in sips.

A wave struck his helmet, and Galvanix realized he was floating facedown. Rolling over, he found his view no less murky, although each splash to the head sent dark ripples across his faceplate. Galvanix kicked to attain an upright position, but could only briefly get his legs beneath before being toppled like a skittle. The waves' rise and fall did not, surprisingly, stir nausea—more medication?—but the involuntary waving of his limbs tugged painfully, and Galvanix was nearing exhaustion when his arm struck something hard.

"Don't use your radio." Beryl was gripping his elbow, leaning forward to touch helmets. Bobbing together, their legs kicked and brushed each other like the attentions of curious fish.

"How did you find me?" Galvanix could scarcely see her from half a meter away.

"Searchlight. We'll keep a line between us." Something was being slipped round his waist. "Hurt yourself?"

"Muscle sprains. How fast is the current here?"

"It's significant. We'll have to add our own efforts, but the sublimation draw will help us nicely."

"Beryl, I'm in no condition to swim at all. My arms—" Galvanix felt himself nearly swoon at the thought. "I'm simply too weak."

"That doesn't matter. Your suit can swim for you, though you may not enjoy it."

"What? I—" And before he could fully understand, Galvanix felt his arms and legs suddenly snapped to attention as though jerked by wires. Immediately they began moving in tandem, and to his horror Galvanix saw his hijacked limbs cutting swiftly through the water. The pain of this involuntary workout appalled him less than the violation.

"Beryl!" he yelled.

"The servos move very efficiently, and will doubtless take fewer strokes than you would exert on your own. You may regard this as an outrage of the spirit, but it is that or die, and I decline to offer you the choice."

They swam for seven hours, until Beryl had tired and surrendered to her own servos, then resumed and tired once more. Galvanix didn't know if they finally rested because she was exhausted, or believed Galvanix had reached the end of his endurance, or simply because the clensuits' energy cells had been taxed to the limits of renewal.

Galvanix felt the tingling of his now-still muscles with numbed detachment. The servos had only taken a stroke every few seconds, and Galvanix suspected he had moreover been receiving analgesia from the clensuit's doc. Resentment nevertheless pressed on him like the inflammation surrounding a splinter.

"We'll be making time while we sleep, a boon usually enjoyed only in space. The suits' buoyancy will carry us quite well, so you won't have to worry about presenting a broad surface to the current."

"I know," Galvanix said.

After several seconds Beryl added, "A kind word would cost you nothing, and might help me at a difficult time."

Galvanix could not spurn such an appeal, though he fiercely wanted to. "I wish you had trusted to my good sense," he said, his voice strained.

"You are too ill to make decisions for yourself. Pausing to argue is dangerous, and I'm not trained to delegate even when well. I am sorry I seemed to slight you."

Galvanix felt his anger dissolve, its particles vanishing unidentified beneath a wave of exhaustion. His manhandled limbs, lolling as the swells stirred them, seemed to be sinking into an enormous softness. Tears of release burned his eyes, and Galvanix gave himself over to sleep.

The plash of waves against his faceplate reached Galvanix long before he was fully conscious, assuming in the absence of other sensation the texture of an interior landscape. Galvanix woke slowly, knowing himself to be truly unwell, yet uncoupled from pain. Dimly he felt his limbs stirring, and kicked hard. He could feel no answering force, and guessed only after pondering his muffled sensations that he had brushed Beryl's leg.

Raising his head, he saw movement beyond the splash and stream of spray. Snowflakes were falling on the leaden surface of the water. The cloud cover, as seamless as the interior of a diving bell, seemed suffused with a weak light.

"We're climbing the tidal bulge," said Beryl, leaning to touch helmets. "Rafting above the lower atmosphere. Feel the light seeping through the clouds?"

Faint flickers lit one quadrant of the sky. Electrical effects, created by the updrafts over the Pole.

Galvanix caught himself trying to discern a slope in the water's surface, an illusion he found difficult to dispel. Concentrating on the level horizon, he realized that it seemed closer than before. They were sliding up the exposed meniscus of the bulge, an oil film skimming its surface tension. Galvanix felt a shiver in the swathing of his flesh.

"The winds are licking at the bulge like tongues," said Beryl, surprising him. Galvanix wondered if she was hungry. "The ocean is evaporating beneath us." Galvanix could picture it: the water-laden clouds piling high in the lunar atmosphere, then swept away to drizzle elsewhere. The immense water engine of the atmosphere then drew up more vapor, fueled by the warming sun.

Little of that warmth, however, was penetrating the mounting clouds. Snowflakes touched the waves and vanished, soon to return to the roiling air.

"Do you know where your database is?" asked Galvanix.

Beryl raised one hand and held it still for several seconds. "It's close, near the limits of detection. Perhaps forty kilometers. The capsule must have fallen within a few hundred of our landing site, as I had hoped. Now we shall overtake it before it reaches the Pole."

She would not discuss her means of locating the capsule. Galvanix guessed that Beryl had some type of quantum interference detector, simple enough to survive the purge of her wetware.

"Are you ready to go?" she asked.

"Beryl, I'm hardly here." That got a laugh, and she pushed away.

Galvanix's limbs stirred, gently enough that he almost failed to notice, then struck out in sure movements. He relaxed, telling himself he was riding a vehicle like any other. Scissoring his legs produced unmistakable evidence of bowel distress: his large intestine was no longer absorbing water. This explained his persistent thirst, which Galvanix realized was here to stay. He sipped at the helmet tube, holding the liquid in his mouth.

Snowflakes swirled against his faceplate, adhering as his strokes carried his head above the waves. Galvanix studied the pattern of one crystal affixed like a decal before his eyes: it lay within a clinging droplet, its edges glimmering faintly, although whether it was melting or growing Galvanix could not tell. He strained to focus on it in the lull between kicks, and the changing lattice seemed to grow before him, surrounding him in a matrix of twinkling tessellations. . . .

"Galvanix." A sound rolled at intervals through the empyrean of his helmet. He was no longer kicking, but floating in amnion, head below his feet. The voice resounded meaninglessly, a wave without force in the still waters of his being.

"Galvanix. Wake up." He was being upended and jostled, a sensation his middle ear alone troubled to register. The grey light rippling through his faceplate did not stir him, but the glare that shone a second later did. Beryl aimed the beam into his right eye, and he raised a hand. "Galvanix, it's over. We've reached it."

Floating shapes nudged them, islets of slush with thin glistening crusts. Galvanix sliced through one with a movement of his arm, and the pieces bobbed off, one striking another and clinging.

"Where are we?" he asked querulously. The dirty seascape around him seemed the debased realization of his crystalline reverie.

"Ultima Thule." Beryl laughed. "The capsule has lodged in a floe; they are becoming too packed to move quickly. My guess is the Pole itself lies beneath an ice cap."

Galvanix raised his head and looked around carefully, watching the shapes around him take edge as the chill of consciousness seeped through him. "You brought me back to tell me that?"

Beryl was contrite. "I have done you no favor, impressing you into this death march. You may end cursing me for not having left you on land."

"I'm still on the Moon," Galvanix murmured. At least he

would not die in space, his organics wasted like the steady leak of the lunar atmosphere.

Beryl said, "The capsule is ten meters ahead." She raised her arms to either side like a crossbeam, then turned slowly. "Before me," she said at last.

Galvanix moved forward slowly, trying to keep his bearing among the nearly identical formations. The archipelago was too crowded to negotiate without pushing at the bobbing slush, altering what landmarks there were. Beryl, treading water to maintain her position, called out course corrections, then gave up and came swimming after him.

Galvanix was resting his arms upon a large floe, too wide to circle without losing his sense of direction. Summoning his strength, he hauled his upper body over the edge, which dipped sloshing beneath his weight. He scrabbled forward, digging his fingers through the crust as fatigue flooded him. Like the Earth's first fish to crawl ashore, Galvanix crept on his stomach to the center of the floating island, then rose slowly to his feet. The ice crackled warningly but did not give, and he stood straight, flakes whirling about him as a long swell rolled underfoot.

About him blobs of white stirred against a black surface that stretched away on all sides until it was obscured by the falling snow. No field of solid color was visible within this compass, but Galvanix looked up and had the giddy sense that the icecap arched overhead. Was that up or down? Galvanix felt himself standing once more on the ice comet, gazing upon a world he would never know again.

Something struck the back of his helmet with a small click. Galvanix felt a slight pull. "Good," said Beryl, speaking through her stretched wire. "If you will let me stand where you are now, I can direct you to it."

Galvanix looked at the uninviting water with dismay. He did not think it would be cold—his suit had protected him from outward sensation—but had an aversion to immersion, which parodied the freedom of weightlessness while gently impeding movement. Reluctantly he approached the edge, stretched on his stomach and surrendered himself to the water. When he looked back Beryl was already standing on his vantage, arms stretched from her sides like an exulting usurper.

The wire tightened. "That floe ahead. Where my light is

shining." A bright point appeared on her helmet, but its beam was swallowed into the meters of dancing snow. Galvanix followed the line of her sight and picked out two cakes the size of tabletops. The wire went slack, presumably his signal to proceed. Galvanix kicked toward the nearer shape, clumsy but buoyant. The wire reeled out behind him.

The ice floe was too small to straddle, and sloughed off an armful of slush when Galvanix tried to encircle it. He waited until the wire drew tight. "Is this it?" he asked.

"I don't know. This close the directional sense blurs."

Galvanix felt a flash of vexation. "Then drop your leash till I wave."

The line fell loose, and Galvanix was suddenly alone. No light from Beryl reached him, and after a moment's fumbling he activated his own helmet beam. In the beam the lapping sea seemed black, soaking the slush above the water line to a dirty grey.

Galvanix began pawing at the slush, which dissolved like wet tissue. Beneath lay harder ice, which resisted the scrape of his fingers. Its translucence allowed him to see a few centimeters within. Galvanix pulled a fine-tipped tool from his belt, which cracked the ice for him to pull loose. The process was slow, and Galvanix felt with horror the prospect of sieving the entire floe through his fingers. When he felt a tap on his shoulder he didn't turn.

Beryl touched helmets. "It is this piece, or one nearby."

"What kind of poor directional device do you have, anyway?"

"One lacking its circuitry, which was flushed. I am running it through my nervous system, on memories of feeling it operate, and it exacts a price."

Galvanix turned to look at her, stricken. "Is it hurting you?"

Beryl batted the question away. "It worked, we're here." Her other hand came up holding her own tool. "Let us make quick work of it."

It was not quick work, and two hours passed before the floe was reduced to a glaze of floating chips. Galvanix had worked with one arm around the dwindling shard, and as they bobbed amid their debris he felt a faint panic at having nothing to grasp.

Beryl pointed to another shape three meters away, almost obscured by the increasing snow. "There."

The ice sheet was large enough to sprawl upon, rounded like a tiny continent until Beryl swept away its strata of snow. Galvanix lay atop it, peering close as his faceplate allowed while he chiselled into the milky bedrock. He edged backward as he chipped away the shore, until he felt his shins hanging over air: painfully he brought up his knees, hunching on the floe like a folded suit.

They had calved away nearly half the sheet when Galvanix found a shadow within the ice, which resolved as he scraped closer into an ellipse the size of his thumbnail. Snow began to cover it, which he wiped away, finding the shape unchanged. He reached out to tap Beryl. "Is that it?"

Galvanix could not see her expression as she bent over the shape. Without raising her head, Beryl gestured—thumbs up, a spacer's affirmative—and drove her tip into the ice.

Galvanix slid back into the water, turning to float on his back. Snowflakes settled over his faceplate, a blanket arriving in bits. A deep peace suffused him, with a finality he knew would not be interrupted. He did not start when something shook his shoulder and clicked against his helmet. "Galvanix; let's go. We've got it."

Galvanix let the news seep in languidly. "Go where?"

"Farward. I have to deal with the capsule, and it should be as close to the Pole as we can get. I don't think we can reach the Pole itself, but reducing the radius will make things much better."

Galvanix spoke with serenity. "I have only slowed you so far, and you cannot need me now. I wish you luck in your mission, but will not join you."

Beryl did not draw back. "Ah, but you must, my dear. I still will need you, and still cannot say why. I know your exhaustion, and though I require you as a colleague, I ask you as a friend."

Galvanix slowly exhaled. The shores of quiescence receded, their siren strains fading to the immediacy of movement and resuming pain. He would do it for his friend.

They aimed for floes large enough to crawl across, often traversing them on their stomachs before slipping back into the water like seals. Soon the ice sheets were jammed together, their uneven edges treacherously covered by snow. Beryl and Galvanix stood carefully, cracking their visors as though tasting the air of a new world. They scuffed through the snowfall cautiously, but sometimes found themselves crunching slowly but irreversibly through a thin spot, leaving them waist deep in the now invisible sea. Bounds produced invariable breakthroughs, and Galvanix learned to put one foot down before taking weight off the other, plodding forward in a parody of Earthly walking.

Snow swirled and abruptly dashed at them as rival winds chased each other across the plain. Beryl nodded to see their footprints quickly effaced. At one point the horizon closed in like an iris, banishing all sense of direction. Unable to proceed, Galvanix and Beryl stood bracing each other, helmets touching like buttresses.

"If we were not carrying the capsule with us," Beryl remarked, "I could take a bearing from the direction it lay."

"I still don't understand how you knew its signal frequency. Hadn't you lost that data when your wetware was purged?"

"I had indeed. However, I had begun searching for the capsule while still on the comet and that brought the code sequence into my mind. With concentration, I could just recall it. My memory skills are learned; no purge can touch them."

"So you still had the code in your head, where the Farsiders could get at it?"

"They would have had a struggle," Beryl muttered.

When the snow abated, she studied the sky and pointed at last to a spot high in the seemingly uniform grey, behind which she said lay the sun. Her finger swung down to point Farward, a simple deduction Galvanix was disturbed to find himself unable to follow. Beryl set off and he fell in after, eyes down to keep within her footprints.

Snow flew past in the driving wind, which whistled through Galvanix's broached faceplate like a wavering but incessant howl. When the cloudcover opened a seam and spilled light over the plain, he trudged on obliviously until Beryl stopped before him. Snowflakes twinkled around them, and Galvanix stared for several seconds before realizing that they were merely carried by the wind. Nothing fell through the clear air but sunlight piercing the vault of cloud, and Galvanix squinted in the unaccustomed brightness.

"As good a chance as we'll get," Beryl announced. She inserted two fingers into her wrist pouch and brought out the capsule. Galvanix looked around the empty snowscape, which had nothing evident to recommend it over any other site. A tiny whine brought his attention back to Beryl, whose suit was extruding a slender antenna from the shoulder.

"I'm going to need your power cells for this," said Beryl, beckoning with her free hand. Galvanix still could not understand, but came forward docilely. Beryl uncoiled a line from his belt and plugged it into her own. She touched a stud on her glove, causing a fine tool-point to flick forth like a claw from her index finger, then carefully flipped back a panel on the capsule's casing and brought forth an almost microscopic length of wire.

"My own suit had the equipment for this," she remarked. "This will have to be improvised."

Then Galvanix understood. Realization spread warming through his halting mind, and Galvanix watched with quickening alertness as Beryl opened a panel on her belt and threaded wires through it. She looked up at the rent in the cloudcover, which was slowly twisting and widening. "Do you think the opening will drift overhead?"

It did. Beryl glanced over her shoulder to aim the antenna at the zenith, then touched a stud on her belt. Galvanix heard nothing, but saw a flicker in his peripheral vision: the readings on his suit displays suddenly changed. Galvanix focused on them and tried to remember what they used to read.

Beryl was briskly detaching the line that joined them, which retracted into Galvanix's suit with a snap. She reached into her belt panel and held out her hand. "Watch this," she said.

The capsule was running like melted jelly, dripping past her fingers as a breeze bore off a wisp of vapor. Within seconds it was gone, leaving only a hole in the ice that the wind promptly erased.

Galvanix looked back into the sky, wondering who had picked up the signal. The disintegration of the capsule, so violent an image of the discharge of their task, made him feel odd. "What do we do now?" he asked.

"Now? Why, anything we want. Would you like to go for a walk?" Beryl bounded high into the air, an energy-wasting flourish that might have brought her crashing through the ice. She struck the snow with a wet crunch and leaped away, opening her visor fully as she sailed backward. "We can do whatever we like!" she shouted through the cold air.

Galvanix stared. He pushed his own faceplate up, wincing as a cold blast burnished his face. "Hey!" he shouted, a puff of vapor issuing from his mouth.

Beryl bounded back, landing before him in a small spray of snow. Galvanix could see her face through the open helmet, a wild expression in her eyes.

"Why are you capering?" he demanded.

"For relief, you dolt. My mission has been wholly fulfilled. I ensured the detonation of a fission device which destroyed the comet, and recovered the database that was secured there. You will never appreciate which was the more important, but both are now complete."

"You did not secure your own return," Galvanix noted.

Beryl shrugged, an elaborate gesture in a clensuit. "What I did will influence profound developments in human space; would you not die to achieve as much? And death holds few terrors for me, for reasons you would not embrace. Shall we walk? I'm getting cold."

Beryl set off in long strides that left footprints only every few meters. Galvanix tried gamely to land in these parts, but found them too widely spaced to match without an exertion he knew would prove ruinous. He called to Beryl, who promptly matched his pace, though with a bounce which he knew burned energy.

"Are we still trying to avoid detection?" he asked.

"Why, do you want to be captured? They might give you emergency treatment, but many interrogation techniques work quite well on the moribund. Do you want to have your mind unraveled?"

"Not I, but you seem the kind of sport to prefer any chance to certain death."

Beryl gestured about them. "I don't think anybody's looking for us."

"Then do you mind if we walk side by side?"

Beryl laughed and threw an arm round his shoulder. "I don't mind anything. Would you like to make love in the snow?" Galvanix gave a startled laugh, and Beryl pushed her open helmet against his and kissed him hard. Her face was very cold.

Before Galvanix could reach properly Beryl stepped back and closed her helmet. Unwrapping her talking wire, she quickly attached it to Galvanix's helmet and pulled it taut. Then she replaced her arm round Galvanix, keeping their distance constant. "Can you still hear me?"

Galvanix could, but was closing a circuit in his own thoughts, whose current flowed slowly in distraction and fatigue but strained to discharge its potential. "Beryl, is there something wrong with your suit?"

Beryl turned toward him, her expression unreadable behind her rime-glazed faceplate. "My power cells were drained to send the radio burst. It even drank some of yours. The clensuit's a good insulator, but won't withstand freezing winds without its heat system."

Galvanix sputtered, then turned to face Beryl, striking his helmet against hers for direct contact. "But *why*? You could have wired the arrangement so transmission would draw on both suits equally. It would have been an easier splice!"

"You are colder than I am."

"And you are healthier than I. Now you will freeze to death while I drift off with power in my cells."

"Spare me your death cult sensibility. I have body fat to burn, and little other use for it now—unless you care to stick your hand down my suit. Do you want to walk with me? I really must keep moving."

Beryl set out again, and Galvanix fell into lockstep, his hand on her shoulder to keep the wire taut. When he faltered Beryl put a steadying arm round his waist. Galvanix felt a sudden wash of tears at the gesture, which immediately gave way to a remote calm. He didn't know if he was wavering from illness or already relinquishing this world.

When Beryl went through the ice Galvanix thought at first she had stumbled. She pulled him hard off balance, her cry cut off by the snapping wire. Galvanix fell slowly to his knees, a stately lunar obeisance which he nevertheless could not halt. Snow puffed on impact before being snatched by the wind, and Galvanix—realizing in horror the extent of his weakness—continued to topple helplessly onto his side. When he rose on his arms, he could not see Beryl.

Galvanix's heart contracted as he looked wildly about, expecting to see her bounding on, disdainful. A flash of movement drew his attention to the churned snow around him, and when he crawled forward he found her at the bottom of a shallow bowl, buried to her armpits in rippling slush.

As he watched, Beryl clawed at the crumpled slope, which broke loose and slid toward her. The weight of the sodden and darkening slush seemed to impede her movement. Galvanix extended a hand, which Beryl waved off. She brought up her other arm with difficulty and lifted her visor. "Catch and get back!" she called. Beryl held up the barbed anchor and tossed it weakly toward him. Galvanix snatched it unhesitatingly in his gloved hand. "Back," Beryl gasped, before snow displaced by his lunge cascaded over her helmet.

Galvanix rolled several meters away, then stopped, chest heaving. Immediately he felt Beryl pull on the rope, and dug fingers and toes into the soft snow as he began to be dragged backward. After a few seconds the tension relaxed, and Galvanix raised his head to see Beryl, both arms clutching the line, lying on the edge of the snow.

Galvanix crawled over unsteadily, nearly falling as a separated muscle stabbed between his ribs. Beryl was struggling with her helmet, and Galvanix helped her release its catch, lifting it off as a necklace of slush fell dripping away. Her face, ashen against the snow, was immediately dusted by blown powder.

"Water in your suit?" he asked anxiously.

"The neck seal held." Galvanix helped her into a sitting position. He felt her chest quivering beneath his arm, and twisted his head to read her chin displays. "Don't fuss," she snapped. "The shiver mechanism delivers heat more efficiently than exertion."

"You need heat nonetheless." Galvanix uncoiled the line wound within his own belt. Beryl attempted feebly to prevent him, but he pushed her hands aside.

His fingers worked automatically, following an emergency drill he had learned as an adolescent. "There," he told Beryl as he closed the last connection and saw her chin displays come on. "We're on the same power now."

He refastened Beryl's helmet, glad to give decent cover to her weak and defeated expression. He wiped snow from the faceplate, then leaned forward and touched helmets. "I am going to build a windbreak," he said clearly.

He expected a protest, but Beryl said nothing. Lowering her

head gently, he began piling snow. His ribs shrieked, but Galvanix molded the pain in the snow before him, subsuming it into the emerging geometry of structure. Crawling carefully over the line that ran between them, Galvanix raised around Beryl a curving wall of packed snow, then lay down beside her.

"Do you still want to trek Farward?" he asked her, helmets touching like whispering statues.

Beryl drew her limbs closer to her body. "This seems far enough."

Even farther for Galvanix, he thought, then realized that wasn't true. He curled against Beryl's back, hoping to provide another buffer against the scouring wind. It wasn't cold at all.

A thunderclap broke over the plain, punching through the crosswind like a cannonade. Beryl did not stir, but Galvanix was roused by the sound, more concussive than the rolling thunder of lunar electrical storms. He raised his head above the windbreak, wondering what singularity of polar meteorology would create a thunderclap that sounded like a sonic boom. A thin keening cut through the wind, and Galvanix pulled off his helmet. He turned his head to see a point of light burn through the clouds, brightening on the fires of deceleration.

Galvanix bent to rouse Beryl, who was sitting up and raising her visor, her chafed face serene. A roar blossomed behind him, and as Galvanix turned, the engine was upon them, braking too fast for mortal flesh. Dark forms dropped in front of them as the flyer shot overhead, seizing them with more than human speed. Galvanix could only raise a hand before elasticity enveloped him, and was pulled away with a force that blotted consciousness.

Siege-Engine Songs

SIX

Hideki Yasuhiro gazed thoughtfully at the fading geometries of the garden below, its dissolving lines further softened by rain and the refraction of an old window thick enough to hold out vacuum. The effeteness of the ornamental garden had never pleased him, but Yasuhiro recognized the imprudence of letting the weather take it away. Eventually his men would rebuild the residential grounds, toiling largely by hand like the Imperial gardeners their forebears might have been.

The wind blew hard against the window, obliterating the scene in a burst of spray. Yasuhiro imagined without dismay the gusts slowly erasing the designers' conceits of sculpted hedges, carp in pools. The surface air, though thin as that sweeping Earthly mountaintops, still could scour when driven by the heat engine of lunar weather.

The first time it rained on Farside people around him had wept. Yasuhiro had been impressed at the technical achievement, but did not believe he was witnessing the creation of a world. It also rained on Titan.

"Yasuhiro-sama." The voice was small and empty of resonance.

Yasuhiro turned his head slightly. "Speak."

"The first expeditionary force is awaiting your inspection, General."

"Will it pass my inspection?"

"I cannot simulate your evaluative process, which is more complex than mine. However, the soldiers have met the technical criteria for combat dress."

Yasuhiro turned. On the countertop before him stood a grinning gargoyle four centimeters high. The figurine was shaped like a tutelary *kami*, and had in fact served in some household shrine, polished and immobile, for the years before its activation. Yasuhiro knew that it lacked the capacity for facial articulation, but wished its frozen expression did not so resemble insolence.

"I will be there presently. Send Hiromoto."

"Yes, General." Still grinning, the creature bowed slightly, then leaped like a flea across the room.

Yasuhiro turned back to the window. "Screen on," he said. The streaming window was replaced by a field of dark slate. Yasuhiro spoke a string of numbers, and a map appeared in glowing yellow.

Though the symbols before him spoke the language of his heart, Yasuhiro's attention was not on them. Real weather drummed faintly through the sweeping lines of air fronts and depressions, speaking of clashing forces. The land his men were soon to take had been tilled by settlers who devoutly believed it their home, and Yasuhiro did not disdain the effort expended over decades in their cause. Men grew up weak and self-exiled on this starveling Moon, but they strove and were men. When their land was besieged he expected many to overcome their teachings and fight back.

Steps approached, paused. "General, sir."

Yasuhiro turned to face Hiromoto, who held his hands and bowed. "Report."

"The caisson is drained and in place. Both companies are ready to move out. Weather reports—" Hiromoto hesitated, evidently noticing the display already in sight. "—are being monitored by all stations." Like many officers, Hiromoto wore robes indoors, a nippophile fashion Yasuhiro found absurd in low gravity. Yasuhiro himself favored trousers except for the most formal ceremonial occasions, as indeed Bushido warriors had sometimes done, many centuries ago.

"You will be leading the incursion?" Hiromoto ventured.

"All plans remain unchanged." Yasuhiro knew his lieutenants were divided over the advisability of his accompanying the expedition. Although the danger was slight, all had felt that morale would be devastated if Yasuhiro were to be killed in the first engagement. Admitting their point, he nevertheless overrode them, knowing the value of letting his men see their general in action.

Hiromoto was evidently thinking along the same lines, however reluctantly. "Your presence will be a profound inspiration, Sho—Sir," he stammered.

Yasuhiro was amused at Hiromoto's near-stumble over the

forbidden word, though it demonstrated again the man's unfitness for true command. Yasuhiro knew of course that he was widely called "shogun" in the ranks, and recognized that history might someday classify his command as a shogunate. He did not fail inwardly to remark that the title was more accurate than they knew: historically shogun meant supreme military dictator, who ruled, at least in theory, only in the name of his emperor.

"I will follow," Yasuhiro said. Hiromoto bowed out quickly.

Yasuhiro studied the weather map for another few seconds, then dismissed it and strode away. Patterns wavered over the tilted floor, and Yasuhiro glanced up: a skylight ran the length of the clerestory, angled so as to admit the sun through most of its long transit. Not even the stars were visible now, but Yasuhiro paused to watch the pattering gloom, knowing that the view opened onto the ecliptic. The Farside sky would never see Earth, but Yasuhiro derived a moment's pleasure from the thought that he looked upon the path of his own true home: not the Moon, nor the locus of Earth, but the concentric tori of Earthorbital space.

Like most of his generation Yasuhiro had grown up largely in the low orbital stations, spinning crêches that offered growing musculatures the stresses of virtual gravity. A scholarship had brought him to La Cruz, an engineering academy associated with the Union of South American States. Yasuhiro spent his adolescence contending with the rigors of microgravity mechanics, striving to understand the iron laws of physics well enough to master vacuum construction in an environment that did not forgive error. The academy, which was organized along military principles, taught him that actions had effects, and Yasuhiro found a truth that would set him apart from his countrymen, who yearned for an easy, forgiving world that somehow would not hit back. Burning with an intensity it later amused him to recall, Yasuhiro had applied for emigration to Nova Brasilia, and had been privately told by a senior science officer that he was more valuable to their cause on the Moon.

Yasuhiro had returned to the Lunar Republic at twenty, half a lifetime ago. He built Moonorbital habitats to house the growing generation of children born to the Lunar Republic, and helped boost them to higher orbits as the Inflooding thickened the atmosphere. Sometimes he wrote recommendations for promising students to study at Earthorbital institutes, but never had time to return to High Earth Orbit himself. It had been decided years before that he would have no contact with subversive ideologies.

If Yasuhiro retained any apparent taste for the sophisticated milieu of his school days, it was for the imported chocolate liqueurs he was known to favor, his only vice. The cocoa's complex alkaloids passed without incident through the bloodstream of any other lunar citizen extravagant enough to indulge in them, but in his subtly altered brain chemistry they produced voices during meditation, which spoke with the alacrity of a briefing officer.

The Embargo surprised everyone on the Moon, but fell within one of several contingencies for which Yasuhiro had orders. Returning to Farside with the rest of populations of the now unsupportable habitats, Yasuhiro had railed against a government that renounced all claims and would not survive without friends in a war. Compelled to drill children and adolescents in calisthenic regimes to prevent their muscles from withering, the Lunar Republic had instilled a discipline that strengthened minds against its own weakness. Yasuhiro's task was easy, especially when the grinning homunculus came to him with detailed instructions and a vast store of information. The tremulous Republic tolerated sedition, as it would tolerate anything that threatened it.

Yasuhiro did not mind when his men whispered *shogun*, though he worried sometimes about susceptibility to vanity, which history proved insidious to generals who ranged beyond immediate control of their superiors. As he descended the spiral steps of the clerestory, Yasuhiro reflected on power and the will of men. Five hundred years ago entry to the warrior class had been hereditary, just as access to education and the opportunity to develop one's strength had always and everywhere been shuttered by class, wealth, or other factors unrelated to merit. Today all humans might pick up the tools to better themselves, and the truth emerged—at last washed free of the impedimenta of history—that individuals *were* born unequal, some inclined to lead, others to submit. Yasuhiro would rather wrestle with the materials of the cosmos than the wills of men, but knew what resources would now serve his cause.

He entered the hall where the two companies were assembled. Four hundred men stood at rigid attention, presentable considering they had had no authentic military training. Yasuhiro thought with satisfaction, They have the discipline of engineers. That was considerable, but unequal to that of soldiers; they would not, however, be facing soldiers. Yasuhiro had the military counsel of his gargoyle; the Nearsiders had nothing, were not even planning military resistance. He knew this because the Farsiders knew everything of the Republican plans, having tapped their communications long ago.

Yasuhiro inspected his men cursorily, knowing the occasion to be ceremonial. Each wore a clensuit the color of the regolithic terrain they were soon to occupy. Over their right shoulders hung lightning rods, electrical discharge weapons that could stun from a distance, scramble circuitry if turned upon unarmored machines, and renew themselves from enemy power supplies or solar cells. A battery of further equipment garlanded each soldier, but the clensuits covered all but the open face masks. Yasuhiro gazed down the line of impassive expressions, wondering how they would fare in combat.

Without a word he raised a hand, and the company commander barked orders. The soldiers turned and began filing out the room, bounding in a measured sequence that rolled through their ranks like waves. Yasuhiro crossed the room in two leaps, sailing through an officer's entrance that slid open at his approach.

Yasuhiro immediately felt the increased humidity against his face, a subterranean dankness that whispered past as blowers labored to banish it. He did not break stride, yet raised his nose to savor the laden air. The saturation of the regolith was at once a tactical headache and a strategic windfall.

Twenty-seven years after the Inflooding began, the porous lunar soil was still swallowing water. The Embargo had starved the Lunar Republic of news, yet deprived in turn the Earthly powers that imposed it of one urgent piece of intelligence: None of its principalities knew whether seepage from the saturated regolith into the upper crust had abated. If the crust showed a sustained capacity for absorbing surface water, the Moon would have no permanent seas until a truly vast measure was poured into it—enough, the Consortium feared, that its resultant increase in mass would shift the lunar orbit and affect the tides of the fragile Earth.

Even the Lunar Republic did not have the answer to this question, for Yasuhiro, mindful of their poor security, had quietly

sabotaged their recording devices. His command alone knew the
verdict that had been eloquently rendered at the center of the
world: that the desiccated Moon would drink until the vessels and
patience of Earth were exhausted. Although the sated Luna would
still lack the mass to exert significantly stronger gravity, its
swollen bulk would shift like a drunkard's uneasy hams, causing
subtle perturbations mother Gaea would never accept.

The staging area resembled the platform of an ancient subway
system, its high vaulted ceiling echoing as bodies, too crowded to
bound, shuffled like Tokyo commuters of the last century. The
first wave was loading into its capsule, a carbon shell threaded
onto the tunnel rail like a bead. Launch engineers, mostly women,
were preparing to snap open the second vehicle as soon as the
platform cleared. The faces peering out of the packed canopy were
all male, which Yasuhiro guessed would itself strike terror into the
peasants they would surprise.

The chief engineer raised a hand, and the vehicle slid swiftly
away. Five meters from the platform the rail curved into a tunnel
that dropped away sharply, and the capsule vanished down its
track as though going over a waterfall. The second capsule was
already being fitted into place. Behind was the staff car that would
carry Yasuhiro and two of his captains to battle. As the second set
of thirty men pulled away from the platform with a hiss, Yasuhiro
settled into the padded seat.

The staff car was heavily cushioned, a precaution less against
attack than the possibility of a wreck. The transport system was
too simple, however, to allow much danger of mishap. The tunnel
cut a deep chord through the lunar crust, emerging in Nearside far
within the Republican border. Two other tunnels bored from this
site to other parts of Nearside, while additional systems cut
through elsewhere. This riddling of the lunar interior, which had
been accomplished only at great expenditure and subsequent
privation, was adequate to mount a far greater invasion than
Yasuhiro would ever need. But then, he knew it served an
additional purpose.

The clear canopy closed over him and a puff of cool air touched
his face. His captains sat to either side, neither venturing to speak.
A figure outside gestured and the capsule surged forward, riding
a wave of magnetic repulsion. The tunnel entrance rushed at them
and the capsule tipped into it, plunging at once into darkness.

Yasuhiro sat impassively as the capsule accelerated, pressing him into his seat. Allowing the capsule simply to fall toward midpoint would take forever under lunar gravity, and the system would in any event recover most of the motive power during deceleration. Yasuhiro heard a rustle near his ear, and turned to see the *kami* crawl up to grip the epaulet of his clensuit.

"Launchings under way at Crane's Nest and Snowcap," the creature confided. Code names were used because the tunnel, being open at one end to Nearside, was classified hostile ground. "Four minutes delay at Snowcap, projected to reach five and a half by final launch."

Yasuhiro grunted. The flood plain of Mare Moscoviense was afflicted with a shifting water table, which stressed the tunnel walls so that the rails required constant realignment. The delay was vexatious but acceptable, for the expeditionary forces would be permanently established and advancing rapidly before the Republic surmised as much from its suborned communications network.

To his left Captain Ishido had one hand raised to his ear, an intent expression on his face. Yeh on his right was absorbed in a display streaming across a wrist screen. Yasuhiro had his own monitors, but turned instead to the gargoyle.

"What is the weather on the Rock Garden?"

"Stiff winds, faint drizzle, heavy overcast. Temperature eighteen degrees, likelihood of direct sunlight very low." The Rock Garden was the emergence point for this tunnel, which ended three meters below its surface. An advance crew of engineers and robots was now expanding the disguised passageway to the surface, which was only wide enough to admit tiny drone aircraft.

"And the surrounding area?"

"Deserted. Nearest human two kilometers, none approaching. No overflights."

Three klicks away stood a settlement called Mira, where nine hundred workers tended the agriculture and fixing projects under way in the lowlands surrounding Cleomedes. Depots of heavy construction equipment dotted its outskirts, and a robot factory that produced nitrogen-fixing mites (it had now ground to a halt after its stores of imported Earth elements finally gave out) occupied several rooms of the town center. Most important, Mira was fully integrated into the substrate of the Republic's Grand Files. Though Yasuhiro's forces had long beguiled the system's peripheries, a full assault on the Files could only be launched through an organ more vital than call box or wristphone.

Yasuhiro closed his eyes, willing tension from the muscles of neck and back. The occupation of Mira was unlikely to meet violent resistance, but his troops had been drilled hard against the possibility, which had been driven home a fortnight earlier when two foreigners blasted their way out of the Kwankok industrial complex, destroying property and killing twelve. Yasuhiro guessed that they were survivors of the mission that destroyed the comet Fenrir, the man one of the Republican crew, the armed woman probably "City Boy," the human agent required to accompany all transports of radioactive materials through space.

The Republicans had shown surprising resolve in going after the comet themselves, rather than trusting the Consortium to save them. Yasuhiro had listened to their policymakers fret for months before deciding to proceed with a once-discussed plan to vaporize the mass with a type of fusion device originally intended for use in excavating waterways. It had worked, too: the Republicans had launched one of their last orbital vehicles in the hope that one of the Earthorbitals would also follow the plan and show up with the plutonium core. Whatever else went wrong—clearly the two Republican operatives were to have been taken into custody at mission's end, preserving the Embargo—Yasuhiro had watched recordings of the explosion with professional satisfaction. An engineering job, not precise under the circumstances but successful.

Their bodies had not been recovered, although the trauma visible on the female soldier, to say nothing of the diagnosis run on the Republican by the Kwankok medical facility, left no possibility of survival. Had they miraculously made it to Nearside, the female might have been saved. Yasuhiro had had the Nearside files scanned for news of their discovery, but the Republic knew nothing at all. He regretted the loss of the woman warrior, a professional who would doubtless have proven valuable after his forces took Tycho.

The sensation of acceleration began to fade, and Yasuhiro felt himself ease forward from the springy cushions. The tunnel was utter darkness, the only illumination that of the console's soft glow.

"Launch boats," he said.

"On schedule," the *kami* replied. "Number seven moving onto—"

"Show me," Yasuhiro said. The screen before him came on, a bar graph with numbered captions. He read it at a glance. "Snowcap," he said. The display changed. "Crane's Nest."

Yasuhiro slipped smoothly into the flow of data, checking troop movements, weather patterns. For a second he spoke to the captain sitting next to him through a link that ran back to the clerestory. In his absorption Yasuhiro almost missed turnover, noting the point when the tunnel swung past the tiny molten core only as a faint internal realignment.

From this middle ground the mission appeared suddenly to Yasuhiro in long perspective: The first military assault ever launched through a sub-crustal tunnel, and doubtless the only one history would ever see. Earth's Transatlantic Tunnel—now the North Transatlantic, he remembered—was run by an eighty-year-old tube authority that had been empowered in the days when disenfranchised groups sabotaged public structures, and the Eurasian and Pacific tunnels were all run by tough multi-government corporations. Nobody could use an existing tunnel for clandestine purposes, let alone dig a new one. The historical circumstances that allowed Yasuhiro's people to drill undetected through a planet, however small and porous, would be remembered for a thousand years.

Yasuhiro glanced at the ETA clock, which was clicking down like a backward odometer. Twenty-three minutes.

Yasuhiro had studied and thought long about combat, which he knew always deteriorated into chaos whatever the battle plan. But this would not be combat, certainly not at first. Yasuhiro, through his minions as his superiors through him, was *working his will*. Purposeful and anti-entropic, it was nevertheless finally the exertion of a force against resistance; a weather front, a bacterial incursion, a geological upthrust. The universe comprised strife between forces, and there was no use seeking a benign still center to mirror the enfolding peace of a mother's love.

The advance team had broken its widened tunnel to the surface, and a screen showed a slow pan of the landscape. Midmorning drizzle, flung at an angle by winds. Flyers ranged wide, alert for life or other probes, and the mechs began reinforcing the tunnel opening.

Yasuhiro wondered briefly what it would be like to fight a land war against a determined opponent. All the Moon still lived in enclosures, bulwarks against vacuum and, later, violent weather: fortifications, though not intended as such, which a determined soldiery could with adequate preparation defend. He imagined the infantry of the Tokugawa shogunate or Medici pontificate ranging across this small-compassed and tempestuous planet, playing siege-engine songs as they battered cities as though knocking on the walls of the world.

His earphone came alive. "General, we have emergence on Crane's Nest. First squad up, eight, ten men, and counting. . . . All green."

Yasuhiro touched a control and the screen gave displays for Crane's Nest. The profile remained unchanged. One corner showed a drone view of the emergence point from twenty meters up: indistinct figures leaping like fleas in all directions under heavy rain.

Twenty minutes, and the screen displayed the platoon's dispersal pattern, an expanding cloud of dots with fresh ones appearing at the center like new particles in the universe. Yasuhiro watched for several seconds, then with an effort blanked the screen and turned his attention to the tunnel ahead.

The first capsule was nearing the terminus, braking only in its final minutes. Yasuhiro reviewed reports confirming that the debark platform was prepared and Rock Garden still deserted.

Seventeen minutes. The first capsule came to rest, and soldiers began swarming out of it by twos. Yasuhiro watched them on a split screen, one half showing the men vaulting with timed coordination from their seats, the other an exterior shot of clensuited figures launching themselves from the lip of the tube entrance onto Nearside soil.

The capsule emptied and was quickly collapsed. The tunnel entrance slid shut behind the last soldier, muffling the sound of the second capsule. Displays danced briefly before Yasuhiro's eyes, showing stress on the landing platform.

The second capsule was unloaded in a hundred seconds, same as the first. A blinking light warned of imminent deceleration. Four minutes.

"Geronimo," murmured Yeh.

The capsule began to brake, filling the canopy with a keening that rose with the mounting deceleration until Yasuhiro felt his eyes bulge from his skull. A circlet of light appeared in the darkness ahead, expanding as the capsule slowed. Yasuhiro told himself that the docking ring was overhead and not in front of them, and as it dropped around the capsule he felt for the pull of gravity at his back. His spatial orientation rolled like a tumbling video graphic, and Yasuhiro knew in his nerves that he was facing upward just as the capsule shivered to a halt.

The three men were pushing themselves out as soon as their restraints snapped open. "Move it," said Yasuhiro unnecessarily.

He swarmed across the handholds of the tiny debark platform swiftly and automatically, as his men had been drilled to do. The metal disc overhead slid open at his approach, and Yasuhiro sailed upward onto Nearside and lunar day.

His faceplate popped open and a wave of smells flooded his mouth and nose, wet and redolent of decay. Nearside had always had greater vegetation, flush with the bonus of reflected Earth-light. Neither Earth nor indeed the sun was visible now, but the drizzling sky shone like burnished metal, and the spray that blew against Yasuhiro's cheek was warm.

He came to rest lightly on a rocky spur that hid the tunnel entrance from the plain beyond. Immediately he dropped to his stomach, scanning the horizon for signs of movement. An indistinct motion to his right might have been a soldier, but Yasuhiro's visual magnification could not resolve detail in the wavering rain. Field communications were kept to a minimum, against the small chance that the Republic had deployed mosquito drones that could intercept the narrow transmission beams.

"Next capsule coming out," the *kami* murmured in his ear. Yasuhiro did not respond. The third platoon would be setting off as a unit, in another direction. Yasuhiro was watching the sky over Mira, alert for word from the passive listening devices blowing through the air that evidence of troop movements had been detected.

Thunder rumbled across the plain, and Yasuhiro stiffened before recognizing it. Turning, he saw sullen flickers low in the sky behind him. The fast-moving weather was sweeping toward Mira, and Yasuhiro had to wait only thirty seconds before the cloud cover overhead went white as the sun. The brilliance lasted nearly a second, and the *kami* began speaking even as the first concussion crashed over them.

"We got good signals out in all directions," said the creature, sounding pleased. "Coming back now. Computing . . . okay, got it. No electromagnetic activity save those of known testing stations. Crude meters for recording weather conditions—their circuitry feels almost twentieth-century, as if the Republicans built it themselves."

"How close are your readings?"

"Enough. The Squid would sense the smallest operating mite ever brought to the Moon."

Yasuhiro reflected that superconducting quantum interference detection was itself a twentieth-century technology, but forbore to dispute with a machine. "Test at every lightning bolt," he said, doubtless unnecessarily. Programmed sensors would automatically send out a scanning pulse in the millisecond after any electrical disturbance great enough to dazzle receptors.

A speaker beeped in his left ear. "General, this is Okawa," said a voder, decoding a quickburst message. "We have a Twenty-three on the southern road." A tiny map display appeared at the corner of Yasuhiro's faceplate.

"How did that happen?" Yasuhiro demanded. "Never mind," he said, seeing the site was only a kilometer away. "I will arrive directly."

Yasuhiro took a bearing and set off in long bounds. Condition Twenty-Three was the unplanned capture of locals by forces that had hoped to remain unnoticed. As Yasuhiro approached the narrow causeway, he saw a wheeled ground vehicle stopped on the road, with four civilians and three soldiers beside it. Other forces, he assumed, were positioned in concealment off the road.

The soldiers moved as though to salute but remembered to keep watch on their prisoners. "How did this car come upon you undetected?" Yasuhiro demanded.

One of the soldiers, a lieutenant, gestured helplessly toward the vehicle. Yasuhiro glanced into it and immediately saw that the thin-walled structure, lacking room for any engine, rested atop a chassis mounted with pedals. An expression of disgust crossed his face. "So this foot cart rolled up the road and surprised you?"

"Yes, sir," the lieutenant said. "It produced no thermal or

electromagnetic trace, and makes no sound that would carry through the rain."

Yasuhiro looked at the four riders, who stood with frightened expressions. They wore clensuits, of course, sealed to keep out the weather and excellent insulators. And bicycle mechanisms produced very little friction.

"Heading east?" he asked.

The lieutenant nodded. "About twenty-five kph, sir."

The vehicle would have reached Mira in about half an hour. Yasuhiro had not expected the invasion to go undiscovered for much longer than that. He began to turn away. "Push the cart off the road. Bind the prisoners and leave them with a single guard. When—"

One of the civilians moved suddenly. Yasuhiro had time to see the nearest one tug at the top of the cart's side panel, which came loose as a long metal rod. He swung it hard at Yasuhiro's head, and came open suddenly in a spray of blood. Yasuhiro jumped back, but was spattered in a wide arc.

The prisoner fell sideways, entrails spilling through a slash widening from shoulder to opposite thigh. The nearest soldier took a step back, swinging round the tip of his filament sword, now visible as a line of too-bright blood. As he held it threateningly toward the astonished prisoners, the blood began to drip from its length, leaving the hyperthin filament invisible once more.

One of the prisoners toppled slowly in a faint. Soldiers were standing up from the nearby field, weapons raised. For a second everyone stared at the disemboweled man, his organs sluiced clean by a burst of rain to show pink and grey as they sagged from a sheath of yellow fat.

No one spoke for a second.

"Check the vehicle for weapons," said Yasuhiro. "And their suits, if you haven't already." He waved to dismiss the surrounding soldiers, who saluted and turned away. "Future prisoners should be bound at once."

Yasuhiro did not look at the soldier who had saved him, now standing rigid as a statue. His bloodied comrades collected themselves with visible effort, and the lieutenant acknowledged Yasuhiro's short nod with a tremor in his salute. Yasuhiro thought, Let them gape then at death, which they know strains against the skin of every challenge.

Yasuhiro looked at the ground vehicle, which had rolled partly onto the shoulder. He pulled it back to the tarmac, observing that it moved easily. "Get in," he told the third soldier.

Yasuhiro climbed into the front of the vehicle as the young man adjusted his feet into the pedals. "I will go unchallenged," he told the lieutenant, "but not because the ground forces continue to miss this cart." The lieutenant saluted smartly.

They began rolling east toward Mira. Standing into the wind, Yasuhiro felt a trembling in his upper arms, delayed response to the nearness of death. He drew a deep breath, willing his body's return to readiness.

Lightning flashed behind and then ahead, as though echoing. "Word of the vehicle's capture has been dispatched on coded pulse," said the *kami* after a second. "Your progress will not be hindered."

"I know," said Yasuhiro. "The lieutenant has face to regain."

A puff of wind blew directly into his face, plant-fresh and electric with ozone. Oxygen either way, he thought; the most valuable element in the outer solar system, which surrounded the inner as a tree might its earliest rings. Proud of their might in stripping Venus, the Consortium timeservers could think of nothing better to do with their prize than bear it next door, scarcely forty million klicks, to an even less promising rock. While a billion klicks beyond, the real frontier beckoned, rich in every other organic element; awaiting only oxygen to breathe life into deep space.

Yasuhiro touched a splash of red on his clensuit and brought his fingers up before his face. Hemoglobin, bright with O_2. He looked across the plain, past the tunnel entrance which was even now being converted to his purposes, and imagined he saw the glow of Mira low against the curving cloud cover.

Hideki Yasuhiro straightened in his muscle-driven car, leaning into the wind as he sped across the subjugated fields. Voices whispered in his ear, and he listened. Waving onward to a patrol of men hiking along the shoulder, Yasuhiro spoke orders to his familiar and prepared for his entry into the city.

The World in Its Skin

SEVEN

Galvanix drifted through a succession of wails and snaps, conducted through his jawbone rather than the cushioned hush round his ears. When the acceleration increased, it pushed him deeper into a soft couch and washed away consciousness like a sponge.

"Are you lucid?" asked a face looking down at him. Beyond it Galvanix could see another hovering figure. "We have given you a spinal block, and don't want sensory deprivation. Try to follow this light with your eyes."

The face receded, and a bright point swung into his line of vision, swaying and bobbing like a firefly. Abruptly it swelled to a perceptible circle, changed color, became a triangle and then a square. The shape went through several more transformations before snapping out. "Good," said the voice. "We would like to monitor your powers of concentration. Please relax and listen."

Galvanix became aware of a sense of depth, then saw a panoply of stars open before him. Near the bottom of his vision the curved limb of the Moon stretched like a mural. Galvanix saw a bright star expand into a finely detailed object, a floating castle articulated with twinkling skylights, bristling antennae, solar screens on long stalks, and docking ports guarded by folded robot arms. A sliver of light ran up one of the cables threading the structure, which were otherwise nearly invisible.

"Tsippora Aleph," said the voice. "The largest habitat of the Circumlunar Catena. Its equally massive but smaller counterparts Beth and Gimmel are orbiting sixty degrees ahead and behind. The correspondingly distributed mass of the remaining habitats arrayed along the incompressible strands of their 'necklace' ensures that the Catena will remain in dynamic equilibrium, and that none of its habitats will experience orbital degradation from brushes with the fluctuating reach of the lunar atmosphere."

"Tethered birds," Galvanix murmured.

"These are all 'third generation' habitats," the voice continued, "meaning that they are constructed entirely from material mined from the Moon or from second-generation bodies. Our field of vision allows us to see the second-generation world 6743 Terpsichore—" (here a blue ring appeared briefly around one star) "which is far too distant to resolve into its distinctive ellipsoid. If you would like to see the history of cislunar settlement recapitulated in a single picture, we need only wait a few minutes before the 'first generation' Malenky Gruzhia appears over the lunar horizon. Built entirely of materials boosted from Earth over a hundred years ago, it is the oldest continuously inhabited structure in circumlunar space."

The starfield drifted for a moment, then centered on a faintly flickering star, which promptly began to grow. In a few seconds it swelled to a ceramic cylinder, striped with solar panels and turning like a toy.

"Your response shows that you recognize the structure. Your mother probably spent several weeks of her pregnancy there, resting at full Earth gravity. Midgard is partly owned and managed by the Catena, although their own program of evolution has obviated the need to send any of their own citizens there."

"They have made themselves inhuman," Galvanix said aloud, his voice an incomprehensible croak.

The speaker evidently understood. "They are the first society in space to introduce a program of augmentation for all citizens," it agreed. "Most societies permit only adults to modify their cerebral architecture, and some countries on Earth forbid all such. But the Catena's legislation cannot be called tyranny. Their course was adopted by democratic vote, and those who dissented negotiated resettlement, with subsidies."

"Exile," said Galvanix.

"There are now human beings living around Neptune, and you may take pleasure in reflecting that every one of them is, save for their better nourishment, cerebrally indistinguishable from Cro-Magnon Man."

That seemed to establish where the speaker's bias lay. Galvanix asked, "Is this image a recording?"

"It is the real-time view from our aft portal, save for the close-up of Midgard, which was phased in from memory."

Galvanix thought with effort. "Then we are in low lunar orbit. Where are we going?"

"We have left lunar orbit—you may have felt our passage through a small mass driver—and are bound for HEO. The trip will take several days."

Galvanix was startled. "High Earth— Why am I not being returned to Nearside? And why so slow? We are both— *Beryl*. How is she?" Agitation rose like silt in swirled water.

The starscape faded to darkness, and the dimly lit face, age and gender indeterminate, bent over him once more. "You cannot be returned to the Moon; the Embargo must be observed. This pod is returning Taggart to her mission base. Its speed is a ballistic constraint; the pod has no propulsion of its own. If it did, it would classify as a war vehicle and be open to enemy fire. Taggart is well."

"Enemy fire?" Galvanix felt a sudden calm steal over him, inappropriate enough for him to recognize the introduction of a sedative. He did not resist the wave of lethargy washing over him. "I would like to speak to Beryl, if she is conscious."

"Taggart is on ice. This medical system serves only one; she was expected to return alone."

Sleep was bearing him away, but Galvanix's consciousness caught briefly on one curious point. "Then how are there four people on board . . . ?"

If the voice replied, he did not hear it. Galvanix slept, weightless, and the Moon continued to fall away from him.

He woke to gravity and fresh-smelling sheets. Overhead a peaceful scene of green foliage nodded slightly in an invisible wind, and Galvanix realized that he had been regarding it for several minutes before fully waking. He looked around carefully. He was in a small room, an off-white cube the length of his bed. Two walls were etched by doorways, while the third bore the outline of a retracted work station. The only visible light source was the skylight above.

Galvanix sat up, ready for pain. None came, though strange twinges ran up most of his muscles. He seemed to be resting in lunar gravity, and a wild hope seized him. It was dashed a second later when a soft chime sounded from nowhere, the sort of electronic cough spacers use to warn that one is about to be addressed by a machine.

"Good morning, Citizen Galvanix," said a pleasant voice in the neutral accent familiar from spaceborne broadcasts. "You are resting in a recovery suite in the Earthorbital Habitat Eldorado. It is Tuesday, the fourteenth of April, and the local time is 17:13. Clothing may be found in the closet, and sanitary facilities are available at the end of the hall.

"An attending specialist will come to speak to you within the next thirty minutes. If you are feeling any physical discomfort now, please say so."

"Has the woman who arrived with me also recovered?" Galvanix asked.

"This program is not authorized to disclose medical information about other individuals. Your specialist will be able to answer questions on a variety of subjects."

Galvanix did not respond, and the program remained silent. He climbed out of the bed, which slid softly into the wall behind him. Inside the closet he found a grey jumpsuit, whose intimate fit suggested his vital statistics had been given to the machine that produced it. Galvanix wondered what other personal information was ranging through the systems of the habitat.

The larger door opened readily to his thumbprint, disclosing a short hallway with three closed doors. One bore the interspace symbol for restroom. It too opened; Galvanix smiled at the neat face trap, which let his own courtesy prevent him from confirming that the other doors were barred to him.

The restroom had full fixtures and even an individual shower stall, with settings conspicuously unmetered. Galvanix luxuriated in a long shower. It was, he thought, typical of the habitats: No room, but plenty of cheap energy.

Back in his chamber Galvanix composed himself for his interview. He spent a moment contemplating the skylight, then realized it was a hologram: the swaying boughs nodded back too quickly for lunar gravity. The bed slid out at the touch of a stud, and Galvanix adopted the lotus position, clearing his mind in anticipation of possible conflict.

The door chimed, and Galvanix opened his eyes as it slid open. A slender man stood in the hall, dressed in a pale blue tunic and trousers. "Good afternoon, Citizen," he said formally. "I am pleased to see you up. May I come in?"

"Please do," Galvanix replied. "I am sorry I could not open the door myself." If the pleasantry concealed a rebuke for denying him the chance to try—it popped out too fast for Galvanix to know—the man took no notice.

"My name is Vincent Yee," he said as they shook hands. "I am a security officer for the Earthorbital Habitat Eldorado. If you are feeling well, I would like to talk to you about your recent activities."

Galvanix gestured toward his bed. "Please sit down. I trust I am well, though you perhaps know better than I."

Yee inclined his head. "I can assure you you are fine, and hope you will excuse the circumstances of your medical care. The transport pod that brought you here was hard-pressed to treat two patients at once, and had to keep you unconscious. Please be assured that you will not be so dealt with while a guest here."

Galvanix expressed his gratified assurance while Yee swung the bed open into two facing seats. He wondered whether the man's oriental features were intended to lull him, or would prove to.

"First let me return a property of yours." Yee produced a tiny cylinder, which Galvanix recognized as his voice recorder. He accepted it with thanks, wondering if Yee himself had listened to it or knew where it had been. The officer's face, however, showed nothing but bland politeness.

"I would like you to tell me everything you can about your last twelve days." Galvanix was startled at the time elapsed, though he realized he must have known. "I will also explain your current status and answer what questions I may, although most will probably touch prohibited ground." Yee smiled frankly. "I have been instructed to tell you everything you are likely to guess for yourself, in the hope that this will prompt your trust."

Galvanix suspected this little confidence was calculated, but found himself warming anyway. He said, "I would first like to know how Beryl is."

"The operative known to you as Taggart is well. I can say no more about her."

Galvanix felt a pang. He groped for another question, but all seemed to feature Beryl.

Yee said smoothly, "Perhaps you could give your account first."

"Of course." It was, after all, a debriefing by a security agent. Galvanix began with his pickup by the *Corsair*, suspecting that Yee knew more than he of the preparations for that mission. He gave as much detail as he could remember, but Yee frequently asked questions, some of which he couldn't answer. He did not mention having become lovers with Beryl, and Yee did not allude to it. Yee took no notes, forgoing any pretense that the conversation wasn't being recorded.

"Have you no more questions, then?" asked Galvanix at last, rather formally. He did not mind hinting at their *quid pro quo*, since a framework of ongoing negotiation appeared the only means of exchanging information in this society.

"Not now, thank you. We hope you will not mind speaking again if additional questions should arise later."

Galvanix raised his eyebrows. "Certainly, if I am here that long. Can you tell me when I can be returned home?"

Yee frowned. "The Embargo remains in effect, for all that our sortie transgressed it. I do not know how long you may have to stay here."

Galvanix stared at him, then stood in sudden agitation. "How can such legalisms prevent you from returning a civilian? The Lunar Republic is *uninterested* in your assets squabble; even those who deny our sovereignty acknowledge we make no claim to your real estate. Am I going to remain a prisoner because of this . . . act of violence?" His voice trembled.

Yee sighed. "The Embargo, for all that it may resemble a military act, is a diplomatic accommodation, mutually observed while momentous issues are resolved. Taggart's rescue was a permissible variance—the recovery of an Earthorbital citizen compelled to ditch over Farside while engaged in the legal, even laudable activity of volatilizing a cometary fragment threatening to impact the surface. Your removal was unplanned, but also justifiable: a severely injured human discovered during pickup in an uninhabited region. Protests have been lodged as a matter of course, but we expect a finding of No Violation.

"Returning you, however, *would* be illegal, unless all interested parties were to agree to it, which would never happen. There are many parties involved by now, all aware of how we could fill you with data before dropping you back.

"And you are not a prisoner," he added. "More of a guest. Your legal status is complicated: you were a citizen of Nippon until your family repudiated. Nippon accepted your repudiation, but does not recognize the Lunar Republic—neither does Eldorado's Board of Governors—so you are by most jurisdictions a stateless person, which carries its own rights and conditions. I call you Citizen, of course, because the nonrecognition is a legal not a human matter." Yee smiled. "You will find many in Eldorado with sympathy for the Republic."

He stood. "Every resident and visitor has access to Eldorado's Grand Files. You will enjoy limited penetration, but public information comprises quite a lot." Yee snapped his fingers and said, "Screen on." A rounded rectangle darkened on the wall. "Eldorado. Display," he said, and a schematic of the habitat appeared, rotating slowly.

"I cannot tell you where in the habitat you are, though you may be moved to an open area later. Your quarters are somewhere in the southern hemisphere—" Galvanix remembered the vortex of shower water swirling down the drain—"on a level relatively close to the core. If you would like to reside at a higher gravity level, talk to your medical program."

Yee showed Galvanix how to swing open and use the work station, then pointed out the room controls and laundry chute. "Your closet is actually a transport pip; you should take it in an hour." He looked at Galvanix appraisingly. "How do you feel?"

"Very well, thank you, considering." Galvanix preferred to treat such questions from a military officer as a courtesy rather than a medical inquiry. Nevertheless, he felt compelled to say something, so added, "I have felt some odd dislocations."

"That's not surprising. Your injured tissues have been rebuilt, but the neurological 'fit' is best left to establish itself. You will probably feel some unease in your recelled colon when it is first pressed into service."

Yee paused, looking embarrassed. "Someone will be here to see you immediately after me, whose necessity I hope you will understand." Galvanix looked at him questioningly, but Yee only began a formal leavetaking, which Galvanix duly reciprocated. Less than a minute after he left the door chimed.

A young man dressed in identical military garb stood at the threshold and asked to be admitted. When the door slid shut he identified himself and told Galvanix that he was acting on the authority of Eldorado's Board of Governors and that this conversation was being recorded. "Please be advised that all information regarding the artifact found on the comet Fenrir, its nature and recovery, is declared classified. You are enjoined from relaying any such data to another individual or processing system, or creating any record of it. Information on Eldorado's criminal code may be obtained through the Grand Files. Do you understand what I have told you?"

He should probably be thankful, Galvanix reflected later as he sat down before the screen, that the security forces didn't simply hold him incommunicado, or even try to expunge selected memories from his skull. As it was, Galvanix found that he could add his name to the public lists without demur from the safeguard system he was sure was monitoring his transactions. Anyone who wished to contact Galvanix could now look up his name and call.

Access, however, proved more restricted. A request for the floor plans of Eldorado brought the surprising news that this was not public information. Galvanix asked for a listing of public information on the habitat and was offered a range of files beginning with fifty-year-old news reports of its construction; but when he requested the schematics appended to a tourist's guide a flashing message reported that this was denied him.

After an hour Galvanix rose and blanked the screen, then opened the pip. The space within was narrow even for Galvanix's frame, and he could barely raise his hand to the button that closed the door. Cushioning ballooned in from all sides, less to protect against rapid acceleration, Galvanix suspected, than to disguise the direction of turns. And indeed he could feel little of the pip's motion, save that it traveled, with occasional stops, along all three axes, and at least once rotated through ninety degrees.

The wall to his left opened, catching Galvanix by surprise. He stepped out and the pip slid shut, one of four lined up along a wall. Another pip opened and a woman strode out, stepping around Galvanix with an annoyed expression.

Galvanix retreated across the floor of a broad concourse, turning back to watch a succession of people emerge from the pips. Most wore overalls, some embellished with ruffs or sashes, while a few were dressed in military tunics. Others descended a spiral staircase set in the room's center, forming into small groups as they came off the narrow steps.

Most of the pedestrians were entering a set of double doors, beyond which Galvanix could hear cafeteria sounds. The gravity, which was greater than in his room but less than a gee, lent an easy spring to their gaits. Galvanix approached the doors, catching the smell of food.

Inside, a queue wound past the far wall, where food was being served by mechs and, Galvanix was surprised to see, children. He stepped behind the last person, who nodded incuriously. Nobody in the queue or the tables it edged past gave him more than a glance. As they approached the food, the citizens touched their right thumbs to a square set in the wall, then took the tray that protruded like a tongue from an adjacent slot. Galvanix pressed his thumb uncertainly against the square and promptly received a tray.

When they reached the front Galvanix watched the man before him, mimicking his actions and getting an identical meal. A girl who looked about ten years old ladled vegetables onto his tray. "Did you help prepare this?" Galvanix asked her.

"No," she said. After a second she added, "But next year I can work in the rice ponds."

After pouring himself tea Galvanix scanned the long tables, wondering with mild panic what governed seating protocol. He looked more carefully over the sea of faces, and was startled to see one smiling at him. Galvanix froze, and the woman, seeing his expression, waved him over.

She appeared to be about sixty, and sat alone with a cup of coffee. "Is your name Galvanix?" she asked.

He stared at her. "Yes, how did you know?"

"I've got a program that alerts me to additions to the residence files. Not too many people pop on per week, fewer still on a day when no ship docks. Please, sit down."

She paused to sip while Galvanix seated himself. "Also, most people list their personal number, which you did not. That suggested you might be from the Lunar Republic, so I checked your name against the last phone listing we got before the Embargo. That cost a bit, but my curiosity's a pet that must be fed. Found a 'Galvanix,' no first name. That left me no clue as to gender, but new residents often eat here, because of the intermediate gravity, so I decided to keep an eye open. You look new, also rather Moonish, so I hazarded a guess."

Galvanix was taken aback. "Well, I'm grateful for the company."

"I'm sorry, my name is Elena Caban. I'm a ballistics engineer."

Galvanix smiled. "How interesting! Ballistics is very important where I come from."

"You *are* from the Moon, aren't you? A wonderful place to do ballistics work, since orbital structures are emplaced or shifted all the time."

"Not lately, I'm afraid." His voice had an edge, and Caban looked at him closely.

"No, that Embargo has shut it all down, hasn't it? Nobody can land anything on the Moon, and you don't even own spacecraft, do you?"

"We have a few," Galvanix said. "Even built some ourselves—it doesn't take much to lift off the Moon. But any that dock in a Consortium-affiliated port are interned. It's 'legal,' apparently, since we don't 'own' the Moon." The edge of his anger flashed, and Galvanix smiled with an effort.

"And is that how you got here?"

Galvanix hesitated. "I can't say."

Caban readily accepted this. "Hey, eat your food," she said. "We're very proud here of our cuisine." Galvanix stared at his plate, trying to think when he had last eaten and wondering why he was only mildly hungry. He lifted his fork, a Western implement for stabbing food, and tasted his vegetables.

"You are right," he said politely. "I wish my own were so good."

"You have a garden?" Caban seemed surprised and pleased. "We should—" She raised a hand, silencing herself. "Let us wait until my husband can join us before discussing horticulture. He is a soil synthesist, and would love to hear it."

"I would be honored to make his acquaintance," Galvanix told her.

Caban studied him for a moment. "People in the Earthorbitals are pretty informal," she remarked. "You will have to get used to abbreviated manners."

Galvanix smiled. "I spent half my childhood in circumlunar habitats, so I'm familiar with orbital society."

"That's good. Earthorbital citizens love to argue, and most of them will want to talk ox."

"Talk ox?" Galvanix looked blank.

"Discuss oxygen, its use and disposition. The Earthorbitals are all Geodite; they want the carbon, nitrogen and free oxygen liberated from Venus used to create major habitats. Spreading it thinly over the Moon seems to them simply a waste."

"But the habitats were *created* with the mineral wealth of the Moon," Galvanix said. "Virtually all the oxygen that could be economically liberated by pre-Soliton technology went to fill your shells, which are jacketed by our soil."

"True, but those resources were paid for. Nearly all the habitats hold shares in the Consortium, or are owned by interests that do. If the Consortium wishes to abandon the Moon and redeploy its assets, it can."

Galvanix looked grim. "The Moon is a *world*, sufficient unto itself as no habitat can be. Centrifugal force is a clumsy makeshift for gravity. Your habitats are literally repellent, flinging ships away that approach them wrongly. If breached, they spray out their contents like an exploding rotor." Galvanix made a violent motion with his fingers. He had an image, vivid and incommunicable, of the habitat, its straining vectors yearning for dissolution like those superheavy nuclei physicists can fleetingly create.

"Those interested in planetary settlement point to Mars as a better candidate for atmospheric transfusion," Caban observed. "It's greatly larger in area, more Earthlike in gravity, and within reach of the asteroids."

"Mars won't feed circumlunar space," Galvanix said. "That's why the Moon was terraformed, remember? They wanted a farm world, kilometers deep in vegetation with orbital towers poking through like stakes."

"I can see you're going to be popular company." Caban smiled, not sarcastically. "People have been wondering about the Moonies ever since they vaporized that comet—the *comet*!" She looked at him sharply. "Were you involved with that? Don't tell me if you can't."

Galvanix spread his hands helplessly.

"Well, if you're not sure, ask. Gag orders must be specific, and everything else is fair game. That's guaranteed; otherwise the Governors would proscribe everything—Earth taught us that."

Caban looked at her wrist. "I should return to work soon. Do you know your own schedule yet?"

"Ah." Galvanix drew a perfect blank on how to answer this one. He considered taking refuge in *I can't say*, then rebelled. "I don't know what I am supposed to do now."

Caban looked puzzled, then her face lit with comprehension. "You're a refugee."

Galvanix had not considered the word. "Yes," he said.

"Have you thought of seeking work here? Whatever you do can probably be used: this is, after all, a world."

"Can I?"

"You can always seek work: that's a human right, and this is the high frontier, redoubt of free trade." She saw that Galvanix knew nothing of "free trade," and waved the point away.

"My husband and I have coinciding shifts starting Wednesday, so perhaps we can all eat together. Do you have my number?" She began to recite it, then saw Galvanix wore no wristband. "Well, you can get it from the system. There are three Elena Cabans, but I'm the oldest."

Galvanix followed her to the bin for used plates and utensils, then bade her good evening. Outside he watched the throng crossing the concourse, more now leaving the cafeteria than going in. A map showing their location was set at waist height behind him, presumably for children. So it was not forbidden to know his own location, Galvanix thought, only that of his room.

He sat for several minutes on a circular bench backing the staircase, watching the habitat citizens. Many, he noticed, were speaking Spanish. Galvanix considered ascending the staircase, but his muscles urged against it. The spiral continued down through the deck, but that route led only to higher gravity, from which he would have to climb back.

Fatigue came suddenly, as though a timer had gone off within him. Galvanix stood and returned to the pips, his muscles now feeling the gravity. A small queue had formed before the four doors, and Galvanix waited docilely, smiling at the woman in front and hoping nobody addressed him. He stepped inside and pressed his thumb to the control square, trusting the system to return him where it wished. The cushions swelled against him, and Galvanix surrendered himself to their embrace. When the door opened he almost fell into his room.

As he lay on his bunk in the darkened room, Galvanix thought to wonder why he had felt no surprise at finding himself alive. The body cannot help accepting this, he thought; it only knows living. Nevertheless he remained bemused at his complacence, which only the focus of continued introspection warmed to a tiny flame.

I *will live*, he thought in a small prospective thrill, and the sense of exaltation lifted and bore him away.

The next morning Galvanix set about mastering his environment. He encountered no one in the hallway or shower, and was ready to conclude that he was sole occupant of a low-gee convalescent module. Sitting down before the screen, Galvanix noted the time—9:32—and programmed a wake-up chime for 6:30 thereafter. He requested a news summary, glanced at the headlines without interest, and dismissed it after a wordsearch for "Moon" and "Lunar Republic" ran negative.

A few minutes' exploration of his personal status disclosed a wealth of resources. Galvanix had refugee status, both as a stateless person denied return to his place of residence and as one displaced by the "current political conflict" (no mention of war). He enjoyed indefinite residency and could apply for citizenship, although the "current political conflict" might impede action on his case. Requests for exit could be made, but no action guaranteed. As a stateless person he could not appeal to any embassy, but the United Nations—Galvanix was startled to see the name—would offer an advocate should he run afoul of matters of state. In addition the Lunar Republic had legal representation in Stockholm, to which application could be made; and for any conflicts internal to Eldorado the Board of Governors would appoint him an advocate upon request.

Galvanix found that even within the data system he enjoyed numerous avenues of recourse: legal review, medical review, request for clarification. Galvanix triggered the medical review and explained that he had maintained a full-gee exercise regimen while on the Moon and could handle higher-gravity accommodations. An Earthorbital-accented voice—female this time—asked him to take the pip to Room 7–413, where he could take a stress test on any available machine.

Giving him the destination seemed a good augury, Galvanix thought as he punched in the room number, since the system could have simply sent him there. The ride entailed a long drop, and when the door opened Galvanix was in Earth gravity. He walked carefully into what appeared an exercise center, its walls covered with display screens and signs warning that objects fell fast at this level.

Galvanix strapped himself into a testing couch and turned it on. He spoke his name when requested, and gave a string of zeros for his number. The test system accepted this, then put him through a grueling series of muscle tests, extruding at intervals a variety of handholds and bars for him to strain against. At the end, aching and sweaty, Galvanix was released and told that he qualified for residence at full Earth gravity. He was given a room assignment and told that his personal affects would be sent after him.

Galvanix walked shakily to the shower, where he dropped his jumpsuit into a chute and immersed himself under a hot spray. Two other men were sharing the narrow quarters. "How long does it take for the clothes cycle to run?" Galvanix asked them.

"Perhaps four minutes," a dark-skinned man answered, looking at him strangely.

Galvanix had to force himself to remain in the shower that long; the communal quarters seemed to activate his Republican frugality. The men were toweling themselves outside when he joined them, and Galvanix pulled a towel from the proffered slot hesitantly, wondering if there was protocol to observe. The towel was faintly scented, and seemed to be textured with thousands of tiny villi. He noticed the sidelong glances as he dried himself. If the men were looking for telltale suntan lines or body ornamentation, they were disappointed.

Sodden, the towel began to squirm in his hand, yearning to wring itself dry. Galvanix dropped it in the chute, took his jumpsuit from the rack beneath. It occurred to him that most citizens didn't exercise in their work clothes, but he willed himself not to blush. He pulled on his jumpsuit with composure, smiled at the man he caught looking his way and left.

His room proved a cubicle in a narrow hallway that resembled a military barracks. The length of wall separating each room from the hall could be slid up into the ceiling if the occupant felt sociable, creating a semi-private nook. Most cubicles had been opened in this manner, creating the impression of a long room separated by parallel dividers. Men were asleep on their bunks, or at work or play before their screens. Two were conversing in Spanish across the width of the hall, and Galvanix felt their eyes following him as he walked uncertainly to his own closed room.

The numbered door opened to his thumbprint, and Galvanix wondered a moment if he should slide up the wall as a gesture of amity. Later, he decided: settling in is legitimately private. His cubicle offered a fold-down bunk on the right, shelving along the left, and screen space along the back wall, with a circle marked on the floor for a chair. Galvanix pulled up the chair, activated the screen, and sat down before it.

"I would like to send a message to Rona Tsujimaro, Tycho, the Moon."

"Transmissions to the Lunar surface cannot be completed for the duration of the Embargo," the system told him. "Messages can be stored for future transmittal."

Galvanix imagined lovers' letters stacking up in data banks on either side of the Embargo, like the unstitched halves of an epistolary novel. He saw little point in creating a record that would not get home before he did. "Cancel command," he said. "Have there been any messages for me?"

"Yes, two."

Galvanix lifted his eyebrows. "From whom is the first?"

"From Hiroko Nagashima."

Galvanix was too shocked to answer. After a moment he said, "Hiroko Nagashima predeceased the Embargo."

"That is correct. This message was recorded on 12 May 2109, deliverable only in the event of your arrival in High Earth Orbit."

Galvanix stood, then after a moment sat again. "And from whom is the second message?"

"The second message was left in your mailnet at 10:23 this morning by Jack Prokashch."

Galvanix looked at the loudspeaker blankly. "Is he the husband of Elena Caban?"

"Yes."

"Display the message."

Two paragraphs materialized on the screen. Jack Prokashch, Agronomical Engineer, conveyed his greetings to Galvanix and expressed interest in hearing that he had worked in recent lunar horticulture. He invited Galvanix to visit the Eldoradan biosphere and discuss topics of shared interest. A schedule of his anticipated working hours was appended.

Galvanix swung the keyboard up from the chair's arm and tapped out a reply. "Send," he said.

Galvanix blanked the screen, stood and left the room, leaving the front wall open behind him. He rode a pip to the lowest level of the habitat, where gravity hung on his limbs like sodden clothes. Eldorado's running track circled the habitat's circumference like an equator, and Galvanix sprinted down its length, pushing for exhaustion. He pounded round the track a second time, drawing stares from runners more sensibly attired. Galvanix walked a third lap, stood long minutes beneath a steaming shower, then collected his jumpsuit—now looking slightly frayed—and returned to his room. He slid the wall shut, turned and activated the wall screen without sitting.

"Tell me about my sister."

"Hiroko Nagashima was born in the Moonorbital Habitat Galena, now part of the Circumlunar Catena, in 2089, and died on the Earthorbital habitat Kosmograd in 2109. She spent the rest of her life on the surface of the Moon, professing citizenship in the Lunar Republic. Detailed medical records of her birth and death are available, but access to lunar archives for intervening information is not presently accessible."

"Why did she leave circumlunar space to seek medical treatment?"

"That information is not available."

"Were her reasons for seeking off-world care not discussed with her physician?"

"Such discussions remain confidential information."

Galvanix invoked his right as next of kin, and was informed that confidential notes recorded by the consulting physician could only be released to an inquiry into possible crime or malfeasance. He sought recourse and found he could appeal on compassionate grounds, to be reviewed by a human committee. Galvanix began composing his appeal, then heard a beep and looked up. The screen illuminated a notice explaining that the appeal would be moot: information concerning Hiroko Nagashima's medical condition was expressly denied to Galvanix.

Galvanix sat down thoughtfully. His run had drained any energy for agitation, and he merely studied the screen, as though wary of a sudden move. Pressing further would require a sustained campaign, and Galvanix abruptly remembered Rona urging him never to act without knowing his motivation. He cleared the screen, and sat a moment regarding its acquiescent blankness.

"Are there any other citizens of the Lunar Republic on Eldorado?"

"Yes, eight."

"Display their names."

All resided on low-gravity levels, six in the same dorm. Galvanix memorized their names and numbers, a mental exercise he found comforting.

"Send the following message to all of them," he began. "No—cancel that. What time is it?"

"Twelve-nineteen," said the system, obligingly displaying the figure.

Galvanix smiled coldly. "How can you tell?"

"The phages break up the sewage in about a minute, take the big molecules down to the level optimal for regrowth, which varies for each crop." Jack Prokashch gestured, not at a plot of earth but at a bank of screens running the length of one wall. "That releases heat, which triggers the phages to withdraw. After that, it's essentially fine-tuning throughout the growth stages, while controlling the nutrient supply like any chemist."

Above the screens, a row of long windows showed a field of wheat nodding beneath a low ceiling inset with points of light. When he had come in an hour earlier, the chamber behind the glass had been filled with a cloudy liquid, which had drained away to reveal the stalks, previously bare, laden with golden husks.

"How large are your phages?" Galvanix asked.

"Those used here are almost big enough to see." Prokashch leaned over a desk and handed Galvanix a small square of laminated white paper, the center of which bore traces of fine dust. "The assemblers of course are much smaller, though the truly molecular-sized models are used only in reprogramming."

"You have refined your procedures to the rigor of a complex recipe." Galvanix realized the compliment revealed his ambivalence. The chaff of lunar wheat was rendered back to dark soil and grown anew; here the stalks were re-used like coathooks, and the husks were merely dismantled into units for the construction of new husks.

"Research *is* a good deal more exciting," Prokashch admitted, "but maintaining Eldorado's food crops remains our prime responsibility." And indeed Galvanix could see the justice in that.

"What would happen if I inhaled or ingested some mechaphages? Would they begin chewing up my blood cells?"

Prokashch laughed. "Your body temperature would turn them right off. Of course, they would pass with your stools and start in on them as soon as they cooled. We considered that once—salting phages in the food—but it proved less efficient than keeping the process centralized."

Galvanix shuddered. "I can only envy your controlled conditions," he said politely as they continued through the room. "We have only one gravity level to work with, and growing crops outside the greenhouses—which of course is our real interest—leaves them subject to the vagaries of our weather."

"Yes; livelier even than Earth weather, isn't it?" Prokashch looked briefly quizzical, as though remembering old textbooks about the ordeals of outdoor agriculture. "And you haven't received any new technology in four years, have you?"

"No. In fact, most of our ground mites are defunct, immobilized by grit our post-Embargo weather has kicked up, or perhaps just washed out to sea." Galvanix explained the effect of the Mirrors' destruction on lunar climatology.

"Here's my office." Prokashch conducted Galvanix into a cubicle big enough to seat two people, and waved him into the chair opposite his desk. Galvanix studied the diminutive man with bemused amusement. Prokashch had allowed himself to grow nearly bald, which suggested some private limit in how far he would permit technology to shape his person. His walls were lined with reproductions of antique botanical prints, which Galvanix decided he liked.

"Wine?" Prokashch offered as he brought out a clear decanter, which appeared to contain grape juice. "It's my own vintage, rather dry."

Galvanix accepted, and watched as Prokashch emptied a tiny vial into the juice, which immediately began to change color. "Have you ever been to the Moon yourself?" he asked.

"Never. Always more tempting to drop down to Earth, it being so close, and those trips prove expensive." Prokashch swirled the decanter gently and set it down. "I applied for a grant to study lunar soil evolution five years ago, but the political crisis came up . . ." Prokashch waved a hand, and Galvanix nodded.

"I don't know if I shall ever get to the Moon now," Prokashch remarked. "You should probably record your experiences farming the lunar surface; it would make a wonderful book. I can't imagine when anyone will next grow crops under the sky of a new world—Mars in the next century, perhaps."

Galvanix bristled at this. "Why, do you think I shall never return home? You speak as though the Lunar Republic were history."

Prokashch seemed surprised at his sharpness. "I merely meant that the rapid changes in technology are leading to circumlunar developments that don't match anyone's projections. The Geodites want to create an enormous enclosed hoop, big enough that even a slow spin will confer full gravity. Now they say they can build a vast one with metals from Mercury, set it in orbit round the Earth. Most of the Earthorbitals favor building semi-rigid bubbles, hundreds of kilometers across, that grow free-floating forests of crops. Others predict that Soliton tunneling will soon be used to channel energy directly from the surface of the sun. If that happens the next decades will see high-energy projects on a vast scale. A group with Bechtel wants to put a spin on the Moon, give it a twenty-four-hour day."

"Dogshit. They would deform the universe to make it similar to Earth."

"Well, when settlers adapt to truly radical conditions, you call it unnatural," Prokashch observed.

"That is different. Those are people who have so given themselves over to tailored transcendence that they are no longer human."

There was a pause as both men decided not to pursue the topic. Prokashch cleared his throat and asked, "Well, would you like to work with us? The existing systems run well with our present staff levels, but we are always looking for new strains. Your lunar research could prove valuable."

"I would like that very much." Galvanix knew that space in the habitats was too valuable to let those not useful in orbital industry or life support remain long, and he didn't want to be sent down to Earth.

"I'll talk to our personnel director—who is not, contrary to what you may hear, a machine, though she lives surrounded by them." Prokashch stood. "Did my wife get a time when you can join us for dinner?"

As they walked down the hall, Galvanix noticed that one door bore the stenciled outline of what looked like a small animal.

Prokashch followed Galvanix's glance and smiled. "Would you like to see our meat crops?"

"No, thank you." Galvanix had seen steakpups before, and took no comfort in hearing how the glistening creatures endured filleting without protest before waddling off to grow flesh anew.

Prokashch shook Galvanix's hand at the pip entrance, all hearty congeniality. An indoor man, Galvanix thought, as he punched in the room number for the dorm where the lunar citizens lived.

He guessed where the pip was taking him as soon as it started moving. His weight falling steadily from him, the capsule rose toward the still center of the world. Galvanix knew with a jubilant surge that it would stop just as he reached his own level of gravity.

The doors slid open, and Galvanix stepped forward with familiar lightness. The room before him was large and bare, streaming with light from a long row of windows.

"Come in," said a voice. "Enjoy the expanse. We lunar types never got used to your close walls, so we took them down."

A young man was standing up in a recessed floor space, a pair of video goggles pushed up over his head. Galvanix saw his eyes widen as he studied Galvanix's features. "Do I see a fellow exile?"

"Galvanix, of Tycho." Galvanix inclined his head.

The young man leaped lightly from the pit and came forward with his hand extended. "Andrei Chen, shuttle pilot from Tsiolkovsky. When did they get you?"

Get? Galvanix thought. "I left Nearside thirteen days ago, but I'm not supposed to talk about it."

"Really?" Chen looked at him in amazement. "I assumed you had just been transferred. We've all been here for years. You broke the Embargo?"

Galvanix raised his hands self-deprecatingly. "Evidently one may still leave the Moon, Citizen. I have been told I may not return, so the Embargo still holds."

"Just call me Andrei," said Chen as he led Galvanix toward the center of the room. "I've adopted orbital customs by now."

Galvanix suspected that the man had long indulged the pilots' characteristic weakness for orbital culture. He watched as Chen pulled the goggles off his head, shaking a spray of long hair back from his Eurasian features, and tossed them toward the floor pit.

The goggles sailed in a slow lunar arc, so beautiful that Galvanix felt his throat catch.

"We keep militant lunar time," Chen remarked, "so it's around three A.M. here. Everyone else is asleep; I'm working night shift." He laughed.

Galvanix saw that the floor was cratered with half a dozen sunken spaces. He could glimpse the bottom of the nearest one, where a still figure lay curled beneath a blanket. Galvanix raised a hand involuntarily to his mouth.

"They can't hear us," Chen said in a normal tone. "We lined the pits with acoustical tiles."

Light threw elongated rectangles across the floor, falling neatly between the pits as though mindful of their contents. Looking more closely, Galvanix noticed that strips of cropped grass lay precisely within each sunlit area, like tiny lawns separating dwellings.

"Your grass seems to be nourished by a fixed light source," Galvanix observed, amused.

"The windows? Oh, they're quite real. We could program a nicely moving sun if we wanted fakes."

Surprised, Galvanix approached the windows and looked out. Beyond lay a great open space, a canyon. Its opposite face, smooth as a cliff, glinted with windows.

Chen touched the edge of one pane and it swung open like a door. Galvanix jumped. "I can see *you* grew up near vacuum," said Chen with a smile. A warm breeze touched their faces.

Galvanix leaned cautiously over the sill. Twenty meters below him a landscaped park spread along the canyon floor, like gardens between Earthly tenements. People strolled among the lawns and flower beds, oblivious of observing eyes. Galvanix ran his gaze up the far wall a dozen meters above. The facing walls seemed to lean toward each other, and Galvanix looked up to see them almost meet beneath a row of brilliant lights.

"Eldorado isn't built like most geodes," Chen remarked behind him. "Instead of the hollow center, they have splinters of open space, like flaws in a crystal."

Galvanix gestured toward the far wall. "That looks like, what do they call it, a skyscraper?"

"I think so. Someone told me once the park reminded her of her backyard in Brasilia." Chen opened a wall panel next to the window and removed a length of line, which he shook out to reveal a rope ladder. He tossed one end out the window and grinned. "They hate it when we do this."

Galvanix watched Chen climb backward out the window, then swung his own legs over. The ladder consisted of a single strand of braided monofilament, with polymorph rungs that snapped rigid when the line was pulled straight. Galvanix descended without fear, though he remembered that the gravity would be higher at the bottom.

Chen was scurrying downward with practiced ease, his feet swinging over squares of greenery dotted with upturned faces. Despite his weight, the line pulled visibly to one side, as though hanging in a steady wind. Galvanix reminded himself that he too would fall along a diagonal, like a child flung from a merry-go-round.

Gravity was already pulling at his heels, its slight tug increasing at every step. Galvanix looked down and tried to estimate the g-force of ground level, thinking it could not increase too much over that distance. He was reassured to see the nearest passers-by gliding with springy steps.

Chen let go and dropped the last few yards, landing with an easy bounce. Galvanix descended a few rungs further and did likewise. He tried to remember leaping off bunks while living in the circumlunars, where a fall of even two meters would bring the deck rushing at you like a planet.

Galvanix steeled himself for impact, remembering to keep his knees bent. He hit the grass less hard than he had feared, springing upright with, he realized, a child's foolish grin on his face.

Chen, looking equally pleased with himself, had caught the eye of two elderly women beyond a rose hedge. "Hello, ladies!" he called, raising an arm. The women waved back uncertainly.

"Everything in our room is bugged, or so we assume," said Chen, taking Galvanix by the arm and setting off at a rapid stride. "Listening devices," he added, seeing Galvanix's blank expression.

"Isn't that illegal?"

"Not at all. We enjoy problematic legal status, and the war footing complicates matters further, all of which is set out at great length if you wish to check. Read your rights." Chen bore down facetiously on those last words.

"War footing?"

"They don't call it that, of course. Everyone's terrified that this could become a shooting war, with people hurling missiles at each other. On Earth, of course, they've moved beyond that, with fusion pellets and things that congeal your proteins like egg whites, but old-fashioned kinetic weapons will work quite well in space."

"You're not serious."

"Well, it hasn't happened yet, but people talk." Chen noticed Galvanix's white face. "You mean you don't know? Did the Embargo really close you off?"

"There had been talk . . ." Galvanix felt distress sweep over him. "Scholars assigned to project trends from the last date we had; astronomers watching Earthorbital space for changes in launch activity . . ."

"Then you've got no reason to be surprised. The Moon and the atmosphere of Venus are prizes worth fighting over. It's the biggest allocation of resources since the European countries discovered the New World."

Galvanix shook his head and bounded several steps ahead. "I know nothing of the last four years," he said.

"Most of this is recent. Eldorado's home corporation is one of the pioneers in Soliton technology, and will benefit hugely from the current terms of the Consortium. But if it entered these agreements knowing how the Tunnels would change the rules, it's virtually a crime. Eldorado and the Encantadas just lost a decision in the World Court, and the radicals could move to attach their assets if something isn't negotiated."

"Madness," Galvanix muttered. "How long have you been here?"

"Since the beginning," said Chen, with a touch of pride. "I was on a layover, waiting to take the *Siliy Golub* back to Tsiolkovsky. A military delegation appeared and told me that the Moon had been sealed off—like a contaminated lab—and I would have to stay." Chen shrugged. "I've been here ever since."

"What were you doing when I came in?" Galvanix asked.

"Piecework. One buys things with money here, and you didn't think they let me ply my trade." Chen scuffed at a clod angrily with one foot. Galvanix had forgotten the pilots' wild resentment at their inferior status. The elaborate safeguards that prevented intelligent machines from being misused also kept them too expensive for the Lunar Republic, which suspected that prices were further inflated by unacknowledged tariffs. The Republic consequently used human pilots for cargo runs, and was greeted with ridicule by those habitats that did not simply forbid dockings.

"I was offered work today," Galvanix observed.

"Take it. You look like you could stand full gravity—they could ship you to a geode, or even Earth." Chen raised his hand and began walking slower, his chest heaving. He caught Galvanix's look of concern and grinned, a fine sheen on his high brow. "Remember, this is twice my gravity."

So Chen had wanted to join the Expanding Frontier, yearning not to join the Earthorbitals but to sail out past Mars, where pioneers lived in the microgravity of the asteroids or the labs orbiting Jupiter. Galvanix felt a pang for the man's balked ambitions.

"Are you trying to work up to full gravity?" he asked.

"What, and get sent out? Actually yes, but I'm in no hurry. Kind of a hobby."

They had reached the edge of the park, which inclined upward to a small terrace surmounted by a wall of vine behind which metal gleamed. Chen turned and they started back, when Galvanix pointed suddenly at a black man strolling beyond a grassy knoll.

"Look, isn't that a Namerican?" he asked.

"Who, the one with the black skin? Why would you say that?" Chen gave him a strange look. "You don't think Namericans are all descended from Western blacks, do you? Anyway, skin color means nothing, lots of people go dark for cosmetic reasons or easy sun protection."

"*Oh.*" Galvanix thought a moment, feeling his face grow red. "The one thing we felt sure about was that Namerica was hostile to the Lunar Republic."

"That's true enough, though we've got plenty of other enemies. The factions who don't want squatters in their food factory are as nothing beside those seeking to scrap the Consortium." Chen halted and sat, a brief look of surprise passing over his face as he hit the grass.

"The real radicals would undo everything," he added. "Parcel out the atmosphere, send down their mining factories as though our Moon were a convenient asteroid. After a thousand years it will presumably have dispersed into a cloud of little geodes. They simply have no use for a world that unsuits its inhabitants for living elsewhere."

Galvanix sat beside him, mindful of the higher gravity. "I thought Earth was developing medical techniques that would rehabilitate human tissues to full gravity."

Chen laughed. "If that technology was perfected I'd be directing traffic in Zambia now. Don't forget these people are ready to play rough. That's why people talk about the emergence of oxygen barons."

"Oxygen barons?"

"If the Consortium falls apart, the splinter groups will end up with those resources they already control or can grab. Periods of expansionary instability can lead to new divisions of wealth." Galvanix wondered if Chen was quoting someone. "Even those left holding more than they can keep may negotiate to their advantage."

"Like Yasuhiro," Galvanix ventured.

"A pawn," said Chen. "He'll be rolled up like a carpet when the time comes."

A wisp of vapor drifted across the array of lights overhead. Galvanix lifted his gaze in surprise as the light wavered, wondering if these wedges of space managed to experience weather.

Chen stood with an effort. "I should return to my work," he said. "Fall behind schedule and they will tell me how reliable their machines are."

Galvanix sprang up after him. "I should not have interrupted you," he said. "Your kindness has cost you working time."

Chen flicked his wrist, a very Earthorbital gesture. "Forget it." He looked across the park to the rope ladder, which rippled slightly in the mild downdrafts. "Once they changed my thumb code while I was out here, denying me all access. A joke, but telling should you think we're not surveilled. I had to climb the ladder to get back; nearly killed me."

They crossed the lawn toward the park entrance, a large archway set like the entrance gate of a city wall. "You should stay here awhile," Chen was saying. "People come only to relax, so they will talk to you."

Galvanix watched the strolling orbitalists. "They don't look as though the combine that owns their world is facing reversals." He thought a moment. "What do bankrupt habitats do?"

Chen smiled. "They raise the rates for breathing, of course. What else?"

That evening Galvanix decided to face his dead. He shut the door, then ordered his system to defer calls. "You have a letter for me from Hiroko Nagashima, sent seven years ago."

"Yes."

"Can you print it for me?"

"It's in full video."

Galvanix had expected this. He dimmed the lights, then sat back in his chair, heart pounding.

"Run the message."

The screen went from slate to a prefatory black. A second later it flicked alight, and Hiroko was on the wall before him. Galvanix almost cried aloud.

The figure, full scale, was Hiroko at the end of her life, when she had refused to let herself be seen. Galvanix had guessed that she would not look good, but had not prepared himself for this. Dark lids like sagging bruises rimmed her sunken eyes, which flicked to and from the camera. Her skin was blanched as a European's. Shaved circles dotted her close-cropped skull like buttons.

"Yuri, I . . . don't know when you will hear this. Maybe not for years." She paused and drew a breath, which sounded wrong. "I'll destroy it if I survive, which I won't. So I have been dead for over a year. I hope you have buried your grief."

"Stop," ordered Galvanix. The image froze.

At once he regretted it, for the stilled face of his sister, caught on the wall like some agonized church-painting, became immediately intolerable. "Resume," he said.

Hiroko dropped her eyes and took a breath. "I have written you all a letter. I didn't say this, but the doctors think they know what is wrong with me. It has been identified only once before, in a lunar settler forty years ago. They now think that what's attacking my glial cells is sustained by low gravity, and if I am sent to a geode or Earth its progress might be arrested. They cannot reverse it, though, and say it will resume as soon as I return to the Moon.

"The doctors have given the syndrome a name—not ours—and

think it can affect about one person in ten thousand, if he spends his life in free fall or on the Moon. My own physician tells me that they will now be able to test for the condition, so others can be warned in advance and won't have to suffer like this."

Her image suddenly blurred with tears, which Galvanix fiercely blinked away.

"Anyway, I am not going to take their treatment. We tried it last week—they sent me on a trolley to the equator of this inside-out world, and I was flattened against my cot as though a giant was crushing me. The doctors told me that I would grow stronger in time: in a month I might be no worse than any other Moonie dropped on Earth, which is still pretty bad. I asked if I could ride this trolley every day—spend even one hour at lunar gravity—and they said no, the constant fluctuations would be worse than nothing at all.

"So I'm not going to do it. My doctor still wants to argue, but I know I'm right. She told me they might repair the damage to my brain someday, by tiny machines that rebuild brain cells molecule by molecule, but that's no kind of life."

Hiroko's fretfully restless gaze settled at last on the camera. "But facing death brings some odd compensations in this world. Some people came to see me yesterday. They want me to consent to a special procedure, something they cannot ask of a citizen, a citizen of anywhere I guess. But we're not citizens." She laughed. "I'm going to agree, though it's kind of awful, something they couldn't ask even of a Moonie unless she were going to be dead soon anyway."

Galvanix felt his chest tighten.

"I promised not to say what it was, but I'm getting paid for it. *Paid.*" She shook her head, then stopped and closed her eyes, as though the movement had pained her. "We had to work out the legalities because you can't pay someone who's dead, but they arranged it through a kind of trust, they're full of legalities here. The family is not to know; in fact, I'm not even going to tell you now, though you will learn soon enough.

"It's for you, Yuri. I'm setting this message so that you won't receive it until you've come to the orbital worlds, as you certainly will. I know why you've kept up those exercises. The Moon is going to be too small for you, no matter what you say.

"Take care of yourself, Yuri. Your chances of having this

syndrome are much greater than one in ten thousand, but you can go to Earth anytime, can't you? And don't use that stupid name you've picked; I'll address this to both names, but I hope you've junked it."

Hiroko coughed, then winced. "I hope you won't remember me like this. I've gotten a small favor: this message will erase after being played—"

Galvanix sat up. "Stop!" he cried. The image froze. "Is that true?" he demanded of the room.

"To which statement do you refer?" asked the system.

"Can this message not be replayed?"

"The portion already played has been erased. The rest of the message will erase as it runs, in compliance with an uncountermandable directive."

Galvanix felt panic welling inside him. "Can you copy the remaining message before playing?"

"No, it is copy-protected."

"What does that mea—never mind. I want to rent a camera, able to film a screen display in high resolution."

"The present message cannot be filmed or reproduced in any form," said the system, making an uncharacteristic inference. "A legal prohibition prevents the message from running if any recording device is directed toward it."

"I—" Galvanix sat back, emotion rushing over him. He looked at the image of Hiroko, caught with its mouth open. "Resume," he said.

"—wasn't easy to arrange. These people are more intent on mastering data than even you; they won't delete anything."

Galvanix watched Hiroko pause and wet her lips. Her image was sand running between his fingers.

"I don't want this to supplant the family letter, so I won't say anything more. Use what I've given you wisely; it's all I've left of me."

Hiroko looked down, then raised her head again and seemed about to speak. Abruptly she reached forward, and the image snapped out.

EIGHT

Galvanix gradually settled into the clockwork rhythms of Eldorado, unmarked by even a slow-moving sun. He signed an employment agreement with the Board of Governors—noting with amusement how it stipulated that no vesting in the Eldorado Corporation, or rights of continued residency, would accrue from working under these terms—and began to learn about microenvironmental agriculture. He read deeply, watched the growing of crops through glass walls, shared his own small knowledge with Prokashch and colleagues. Earth gravity exhausted him by day's end, but Galvanix kept to his room at the dormitory, urging his musculature back toward the hardiness of childhood.

He dined occasionally with Elena Caban and her husband, his nominal boss. Once he brought two other Republicans, Chen and a lunar geologist named Hsiu, who was wholly unequal to Earth gravity and had to wear an exoskeleton. The outlandish device, made of support struts thin as straws and laced with elastic webbing, ran down his limbs and spine like ornamental scrollwork. Galvanix loathed the thing, though Hsiu seemed to regard it as no more an indignity than a spacesuit.

Most members of the habitat's lunar colony capitalized on their willingness to work in the low-gravity levels, which citizens balked at because it tended to slow their reflexes. Hsiu worked in an entomology lab, a mystery to Galvanix since crop pollenization was performed by mites, even on the Moon, and vermin were unknown to space habitats. "Well, it's research," said Hsiu evasively, and promised to invite Galvanix up sometime. Prokashch, who knew more than he usually said, simply smiled.

Galvanix followed the news daily, though it told nothing of the Republic. The lunar weather patterns showed continued perturbances following the gigatonnes of ice the ecosphere had absorbed. Galvanix studied the photos on his screen, which showed a Moon nearly covered with clouds. The swirling curds, distributed throughout the deep atmosphere, gave it the appearance of a rough-edged snowball.

One evening his phone queeped while Galvanix was asleep. Surprised and wondering if there was an emergency—acquaintances knew his working hours—Galvanix took the call. The screen failed to light up, however, and the voice came through in the darkness.

"How are you enjoying grown-ups' gravity?"

Galvanix started. "Beryl, I've been trying to reach you."

"These are busy days."

"You told me Beryl was your real name."

"It is. Did you get the system to disgorge a list of every Eldoradan whose first name is Beryl?" She laughed.

"Credit me with doubting it would work," Galvanix said testily.

"Credit granted. Care for a visit?"

"Certainly. When can you come?"

"Four minutes. Keep your lights out." The call clicked off.

Galvanix took a Republican quick shower, returned and dressed. Indulgently he sat with the room dark.

The door chimed and immediately opened. Galvanix saw nothing beyond; Beryl had gotten the hall lights extinguished, a neat trick.

She stepped forward as he stood and slid into his arms without preamble. Galvanix's heart crashed against his ribs, hard enough that he feared she could feel it. It was a minute before he could speak.

"Is the current color of your skin a state secret?"

Beryl chuckled. "Your humor can show a pleasant edge when you let it. In fact, one can change skin color in minutes—seconds, if you don't mind overstimulating your metabolism."

Beryl stepped back, and Galvanix heard clothing drop. Her skin slithered against his, warm and smelling alive. His back hit the bed before he realized he was falling—she had done something sudden in the dark, wrapping an ankle behind his knees, then cushioning the back of his head with her palm. Beryl swarmed over him, all hands and breasts. Galvanix felt himself responding irresistibly, blazing like an eruption of the skin.

"You've been denying yourself," she whispered in his ear. "I can feel it in your nerves."

Galvanix began to ask how, but flung the thought away. The

flesh knows better than to speak, he realized, and gave himself over to this wisdom. The previous weeks contracted to a point, less actual by real measure than this displacing hour. Their silence rolled easily on like a long sea swell, creating no tension it did not immediately resolve, when Beryl ran a hand across his hip and murmured, "I can't do this again."

Galvanix felt his stomach flinch. "Never?"

"Long time. This is an indulgence, tolerated because I've been a good agent and could still always get killed. People have been killed already, you know? Not soldiers or civilians, or hardly any, just agents like me."

Galvanix did not know what to say to this, as he felt little sympathy for the agents but did not want this one to die. "I'm sorry."

"Don't be. I have another ninety minutes; how fast do you recover in this gravity?"

Abashed, Galvanix muttered something about her crude standards for gauging readiness in love. Without replying Beryl leaned away from him and rustled through her clothes. After a second Galvanix heard a snap, and a viscous liquid trickled over his chest. "Maybe a rub will wake you up. Pay attention, because my turn comes next."

Vapors tickled his nose, reaching into his sinuses like tendrils of some sharp chemical. Immediately he felt a tingling throughout his body, which gathered like electric potential round his unexpectedly renascent erection. Indignant, Galvanix opened his mouth to protest, but Beryl thrust her tongue in like a plug.

When she left, Galvanix closed his eyes against the dark, tasting pleasure as though the experience were still upon him. Beyond the door, the corridor lights had doubtless resumed their soft glow, and Galvanix knew without turning his head that the hour, minute and second were neatly illuminated in a corner of his invisible screen. *Tell me not, Sweet, I am unkind, That from the nunnery Of thy chaste breast and quiet mind to war and arms I fly*. Sadness broke through his pleasure like the bittersweet core of a candy, and Galvanix turned his head involuntarily toward the door. In his mind's eye, Beryl continued receding into the burrows of this always-inside world.

• • •

When the end came Galvanix was sitting before a screen at the crop labs, answering a series of questions about lunar soil flashed before him by an agronomy program. The first blow resounded through the room like a gong, and his screen went instantly blank. Galvanix looked up, seeing a row of startled faces reflected in the windows before him, when the next jolt threw him to the floor.

Shouts filled the room, and someone fell against Galvanix as he pulled himself upright. Cornstalks swayed behind the windows, and a wave of still-draining nutrient sloshed hard against the glass. The intercom came alive with a voice speaking loudly in Spanish as the windows suddenly turned red, then began scrolling up letters of blazing white.

> THE EARTHORBITAL HABITAT ELDORADO HAS BEEN SEIZED BY FORCES ACTING ON BEHALF OF THE PLAINTIFFS OF WORLD COURT CASE 2113:8540–168 IN ACCORDANCE WITH A DECISION ANNOUNCED 09:26:17 4 MAY 2116

Galvanix glanced to the console's time display, which read 9:26:43.

> AWARDING THE HABITAT AND REAL ASSETS TO THE PLAINTIFFS. A COMPLEMENT OF INTRAORBITAL VESSELS IN DOCKING CONFIGURATION AROUND ELDORADO HAS DECLARED THE HABITAT CONFISCATE AND MOVED TO TAKE POSSESSION.
>
> ATTORNEYS FOR ELDORADO SPACE TECHNOLOGY AND DEVELOPMENT CORPORATION ARE SEEKING TO ENJOIN SEIZURE PENDING

"*Madre de Dios*," someone said. The deck vibrated beneath their feet, and the lights dimmed briefly.

Galvanix's wristband buzzed, and he raised it automatically to his ear.

"Galvanix Nagashima," a male voice said in the wristband's flattened timbre. "Proceed at once to Room 207 on Level Two. Take stairways only. Do not identify yourself to any members of the boarding party."

Galvanix began to speak, but the transmission light winked out. Another tremor swept the room. The deck underfoot began pulling steadily to one side, like the compartment of a slowing train.

Galvanix fell, causing another colleague to stumble and sit down hard beside him. Cups and desk ornaments slid across the floor, fetching up against one wall. People still in their seats were gripping the armrests, while one man stumbled backward across the room as though driven by wind.

The screens flickered once. Galvanix turned to look.

THE OPERATING SYSTEM IS EXPERIENCING ATTEMPTED OVER-RIDE FROM BOARDING FORCES. ALL SUBSEQUENT PUBLIC AN-NOUNCEMENTS SHOULD BE DISREGARDED UNTIL CONTROL HAS BEEN RE-ESTABLISHED AND BOARDING FORCES REPELLED. NON-SECURITY PERSONNEL SHOULD REMAIN INSIDE WHILE OWNERSHIP OF THE HABITAT IS CLARIFIED.

And the windows returned to transparency.

Galvanix and others stood up slowly, looking at each other with wide eyes. The sideways drag continued to pull at them, and Galvanix suddenly realized what it was: the spin of the habitat was being altered. As he straightened he also realized that he had grown perceptibly lighter.

"Is this an attack?" Crop designers were worriedly trying to coax information from their lifeless screens, strains of panic in their voices. Galvanix noticed a few looking to him, as though he were conversant in matters of warfare and siege. He spread his hands.

His wristband buzzed again. Galvanix looked at it, but the transmission light did not come on. The buzz was repeated, admonitory.

"Excuse me." Galvanix pushed past the knot of people and made for the door. Another jolt shook the room, and everybody grabbed for a hold. Galvanix kept from sprawling this time: the slower fall did not outstrip his lunar reflexes.

Surprisingly, the corridor was empty. "Inside" for the habitats meant within a designated room, "outside" being the public space of walkways and plazas. A rough hiss filled the air, which Galvanix recognized after a second as radio static.

He took an experimental leap, which carried him half again farther than he usually managed at this level. As he came down the near wall swung slowly in, and Galvanix had to put out his hand to keep from striking it. Deceleration: the habitat was still slowing.

His foot kicked the wall, and a man leaned out an open door a few meters away. He looked at Galvanix wildly. "They're killing our spin!" he cried.

At the sound of his voice others peeped through doorways, heads turning like startled prairie dogs. One was staring at Galvanix's features. Galvanix turned and lunged away, using the loping stride appropriate for intermediate gravity. After a dozen meters he could see his strides were getting longer.

The static abruptly ceased, and a resonant voice boomed through the public address system. *"Attention, citizens and residents of Eldorado. The Earthorbital Habitat of Eldorado has been seized by implementation forces of the Free Orbital Confederation, acting as agents for the plaintiffs of World Court Case Two One One Three Colon—"*

Galvanix entered a small plaza at the intersection of two corridors. A fountain jetted into the helix of an ascending staircase, its spray of water now sweeping askew to splash the inner steps. People stood in attitudes of shock or fear, faces raised and legs braced against the tilting floor.

". . . any resistance as a violation of the Berne protocols governing piracy in Low Earth Orbit. Citizens who quietly—"

Galvanix abruptly realized what was familiar about the voice: it carried the local accent of a Republican Farsider. He looked about wildly, as if expecting an assault through the loudspeakers.

"Hey!" A man wearing the military garb of the habitat's security forces was waving to Galvanix from the stairs. As Galvanix looked up, the man leaped nimbly down in a series of twisting hops that countered the floor's movement. He landed in front of Galvanix, grabbing his elbow as another tremor shook the room. "You Republican? What's your name?"

Galvanix told him, and the man looked blank for a second. Galvanix realized that he was consulting an independent database, which covered one ear like a plastic fungus. "You are supposed to report to Room 207 instanter. Follow me."

The helix continued down through the floor, and the security man took the steps at a bound. "Keep three meters back," he called over his shoulder. Galvanix had no trouble complying, for the faintly elastic staircase swayed worse than the decks. Galvanix leaned against the wall, which shuddered with gurgles and clicks.

"Are the pips still working?" he asked.

"Stay out of the pips, for Christ's sake. You put your ID into a transport device and you'll be shunted straight to the hostiles."

Galvanix felt a chill. He wanted to ask what that meant, but the agent plunged on ahead.

The shout pounded his eardrums, too loud to be human. "HALT!" Its mechanical voice came from the floor below. Galvanix nearly stumbled, then steadied and peered round the curve. The agent was standing dead still. "WHY ARE YOU MOVING BETWEEN FLOORS?"

The agent held his arms out carefully. "I am seeking to assist—"

A loud crack interrupted him, and a pencil beam of light flashed once in a line terminating at the agent's belt buckle. Galvanix thought the man had been shot, but he leaped instead of falling to the floor below.

Galvanix hurried down the curve to see him bending over a small box lying on the floor. A wisp of smoke curled up from it.

The agent looked up as Galvanix landed beside him. "Did it see you?"

Galvanix stared at the box. Unmoving insectile legs extended from one side. "I don't think so. Why?"

"We got a copy of the program the invaders injected into our operating system before it closed up. You're on their round-up list."

Galvanix felt a second shock. "Me? Why?"

"You probably know better than I. Carrying any identification?" The agent was looking up and down Galvanix's lab tunic, his eyes lingering over Galvanix's thumb as though considering taking it off.

Galvanix slapped his pockets. "No."

"Wear this." The man pulled something from a pocket and threw it against Galvanix's chest. It was a wad of fabric which unfolded into a mask.

Galvanix pointed at the toppled box. "That's the invading force?"

"Cheaper than people, also faster and more numerous. Get the mask on and let's go."

Galvanix pulled the mask quickly over his face as the agent

peered down a corridor. The plaza was empty; evidently the robot had cleared it of traffic. As soon as the mask had settled, its seal began to tighten gently round his neck—part of a pressure suit, Galvanix realized.

Something crashed hard behind him, and Galvanix jumped. Across the plaza a stream of water gushed from one wall, spraying across the floor as though a high-pressure main had ruptured. As Galvanix watched, two more jets blossomed beside it.

The agent swore. "They've filled the lower ballast tanks. Now they're flooding the decks."

Galvanix was aghast. "People will drown."

"Nah, the place is full of emergency suits. They're shifting mass to the lower levels, to slow the spin further."

"*Attention, citizens of Eldorado.*" The loudspeakers set in the high plaza ceiling were almost drowned out by the roar of water. "*All compartments addressed by this announcement will be partially immersed within the next thirty minutes. All citizens should remove calmly to higher levels. Your screens will show the egress route for your area.*" Against a far wall a rectangular space darkened and began flashing a display.

The agent swore again. He sloshed across the plaza, passing a woman in a stained lab gown who had emerged from a nearby corridor to gaze at the swirling deluge like a crestfallen home-owner. He studied the display for a second, then turned and bounded back in a series of half-gravity leaps that splashed like a skipping stone.

"They are flooding the equatorial ports, including all normal exit routes. We're going to have to go back through the center of the habitat and across to a high latitude hatch on the far side."

"Couldn't I just hide in a lab?" Galvanix asked. "Your courts will order this outrage halted before a thorough search can be done. And I know nothing these renegades might want."

The agent grabbed Galvanix's arm. "Let's get this straight," he said. "You are not to fall into these pirates' hands, and I have authorization to administer an immediate brainwipe if necessary. These people are not overzealous litigants, they are *renegades*, trying to break the legal framework governing human space. Have *you* ever heard of the Free Orbital Confederation before?"

Galvanix, frightened, shook his head. The agent waded across the plaza, dragging Galvanix with him, and accosted one of the onlookers. "Give me your gown," he ordered, then threw it over his shoulders.

The room was beginning to fill with people, who paused at the threshold and looked with identical expressions from the cataracts to the stairs, which were beginning to drip. The loudspeaker was droning through a series of evacuation instructions, warnings, and assurances of good treatment. The agent tried to push through the crowd streaming in from the corridors, but their crush made progress impossible.

A young woman stumbled against him and he caught her arm. "Is there a mechanism back there herding people?" he demanded.

"Is that what it is? I couldn't see anything, but it had a voice like a siren."

The agent turned away, pulling Galvanix by the elbow as he walked quickly toward the staircase. "Move with the crowd," he shouted in Galvanix's ear. "Faster, but not conspicuously." He released his grip and was lost from sight.

People were jostling Galvanix and stumbling in the water and low gravity. The water had stopped rising, but was pulling at their ankles as it swirled toward the down staircase. Despite the crowding, Galvanix was able to move more quickly than those around him. He hated to be pushing past people in an emergency, but reminded himself that these citizens were not being hunted.

Water was spilling through the overhead staircase in a wavering cascade. Surface tension, triumphing over the weakened gravity, caused streams to run down the spiral railings like a river of snakes.

People were climbing the staircase on their hands and knees, awkward but quick in the easy gravity. Shouted questions filled the room. When a tremor shook the plaza, the sound would rise to a whoop as climbers clutched at the stairs.

Galvanix noticed a few people staring at his mask. He considered pulling it off, but realized that the dramatic gesture—disclosing the Republican features beneath—would attract rather than dispel attention. Judging distance with a nicety that came of low-gravity living, he bent his knees and jumped for the staircase, catching a railing a quarter of the way up.

Galvanix swung hand over hand up several steps, then pulled himself up onto the edge of stair left open because it bore the brunt of a steady pattering stream. Every other step was now crowded with unmoving refugees, and Galvanix looked into the well of the spiral to see a growing crush near the top.

Almost directly overhead was the uninhabited spot on the next turn of the spiral from which the cascade spilled onto his head. Galvanix tensed and jumped, sailing upward into the stream of oily water but catching the slippery rail in his fingers.

Water immediately ran into his sleeves and began filling his suit. Galvanix was struggling to pull himself up when he felt hands grasp his wrists. Two men hauled him up beside them on the crowded stair, looking strangely at his dripping mask. Galvanix thanked them and looked up once more. Three meters above, the stairs disappeared like a corkscrew through the ceiling. Galvanix leaped once more, grabbing the lip of the opening.

No one helped him up this time, but the incrementally lighter gravity got him onto the deck without assistance. Citizens on this level were also trying to get on the stairs, and the crush was immense. Galvanix crawled away from the edge, found there was no room to stand, and continued crawling among the crowded legs. He reached a wall, followed it to a turnoff and rose shakily.

People were waiting to push their way into the plaza, but Galvanix slipped past them and started down the corridor. As he prepared to take a bound someone touched his elbow.

"Good move," said the agent. Galvanix turned and stared. "In here," he ordered, thumbing a doorjamb. Water rushed in as the door slid open, and the agent pushed Galvanix through.

They were in a foundry of some sort, at the head of a narrow walkway shadowed by looming machines. The overhead lights were out, and the room was lit only by the glow of tiny indicators. Galvanix advanced slowly, hearing his boots squelch.

The agent was on his knees before one of the machines, removing a rectangular panel. "If there's an enormous gush of water, we'll need another route," he remarked. The panel came off and he caught it easily in the low gravity. Galvanix watched him insert his head into the empty space beyond and shine a light up. "Looks good."

He pulled himself out and strode across the room, kicking up a small spray. At an expanse of bare wall he touched several points in succession, and a row of drawers smoothly slid open. The agent looked in several, then pulled forth a hand device, studied it, and pointed it at the floor. A blue line of light struck the film of water with a puff of steam. He clicked off the device and tossed it to Galvanix. "Cutting beam," he said. "Have any scruples about shooting an enemy?"

"Yes."

"Then I've got good news for you." He grinned. "You'll only have to shoot machines."

Galvanix crawled into the shaft, descending a few rungs of its metal ladder while the agent entered and pulled the panel shut after him. They then began climbing. The habitat's continued slowing tilted them toward one wall, and Galvanix could not be sure if they were ascending straight up or on a steep incline. Galvanix put his palm to the wall and felt the rumble of rushing water like a subterranean river.

"Might they flood this shaft?" he called anxiously.

"They don't know it exists. The design specs show nothing here, and the habitat's mass and measurements have been adjusted to hide any discrepancies. An audit would have to run for hours before it could pinpoint the burrows. I was merely worried about seepage."

"Eldorado has hidden spaces that no records reveal?"

"Every defensive structure has them."

They climbed fifty-four steps, each spaced the distance between Galvanix's elbow and fingertips. Twenty-six meters, or four levels. At one point the agent stopped and plugged a wire lead from his database into a small box set in the wall. He listened intently for several seconds.

"What's happening?" Galvanix asked as he retracted his lead and resumed climbing.

"No surprises. The invading forces are consolidating, but important intelligence was purged from the Files before its loss, including all security data. Our forces are throughout the habitat, armed and unidentifiable. Legal appeals presumably continue, but we are clearly dealing with rogue forces who will soon declare themselves out-of-jurisdiction. No human boarders yet, nor are any likely until occupied zones are cleared for booby-traps. Our people are killing their remotes, which have begun responding with deadly force. Two fatalities so far."

Galvanix was horrified. "So it's a war now."

"This is nothing. Their most powerful remotes are microscopic, and fly through the air like spores. Those will discover our warrens soon enough, although recovering and interpreting their raw data takes time. Ours are hunting them now."

"Where?"

"Everywhere. The real war is in the air, civilian. We're just skirmishing on the macrolevel."

When they halted, the agent listened with one ear against a wall, then carefully removed a panel. No light spilled through, and he slid out as smoothly as a ferret. Galvanix crept up slowly and peered through the opening. Distant shouts reached him, but there was no light. He could sense only that the room had a low ceiling and small dimensions.

Galvanix craned his head and neck past the opening, hoping to hear something. In the distance he saw the beam of a hand torch scything through the dusty air, which tasted of agitation. He could make out the dim figure of the agent at the end of the swinging beam. The metal edge creaked as he leaned further, and the torch shone immediately in his face.

"Let's go," the agent said softly. Galvanix climbed out as quietly as he could, feeling bouncy and careless in the less-than-lunar gravity. Rubbish littered the floor, and decorative posters on the walls hung in waving tatters. Galvanix could make no sense of this, since the habitat's slowing had affected its inner levels much less violently.

Several meters away lay a body, facedown and utterly still. The agent noticed Galvanix staring. "Three," he said.

"How else was your update wrong?" Galvanix whispered.

"Battlefield intelligence is always patchy. No more talk." The agent kicked off the ground and drifted, almost soundless. Galvanix followed, trying to touch down on the rubble-free spots the agent located for himself with his beam.

At an intersection the agent halted, shining his beam carefully to either side. Galvanix could see the corridor curving upward as it receded in either direction, as though they were standing beneath the rib of an immense hull. A wind whispered through the vacant passageway, stirring debris and creating an echoing rustle that covered the sound of their movement.

"I thought refugees would be filling the upper levels," Galvanix whispered.

"This is an interfloor; no stairs open here. Also sounds like they've sealed this stretch off."

The agent pulled the appropriated lab gown over his head and sent it drifting away. Galvanix stared. The man was no longer wearing his military tunic, which had turned into a drab coverall of the sort worn by mechanical engineers.

"This way." He extinguished his light, bringing down total darkness. Galvanix heard the agent advance almost soundlessly, as though he had memorized where the patches of debris lay. Galvanix kept to one side of the corridor, his hand brushing the wall as he skirted the largest heaps.

Light flooded them like the glare of an explosion. The eyepieces of Galvanix's mask filtered it down, and he had time to see something flying toward them, a black asterisk with arms unfolding like a spider's.

The agent took the charge of tanglin square in the chest before he could raise his hands. The elastic substance whipped its tendrils round him like a bolo, adhering where it touched and drawing tight. The force of the blow sent him flying backward in a flat trajectory that grazed the floor and bounced like a skipping stone.

Something popped sideways from his receding body and struck a wall. Galvanix turned in horror to see the agent's entangled form skittering into the distance, limbs trapped and unmoving. He tensed to leap after it and felt something clasp his arm. Galvanix shrieked at the touch, but the enveloping wrap didn't come. He was pulled back and whirled about, to face a point of blinding radiance.

The light shifted, and Galvanix saw a metal box, identical to the one glimpsed on the plaza floor, resting against the ceiling. An extensor arm, thin as a pencil, reached across three meters to hold his elbow in an iron grip. The brilliant eye of its beacon swiveled like a chameleon's eye, searching the ground behind him.

"Why are you in the company of this armed resister?" The voice held the mechanical quality of a device constructed under design economies for other purposes.

"He ordered me to follow him." Staring at this engine of death, Galvanix found himself incapable of pretense.

"What is the device on your belt?"

Galvanix thought frantically. "A cutting tool."

"Don't move." The extensor arm released him, reached down

and took the cutter. Galvanix began to realize that he was not going to be shot.

"What is your name?"

"Andrei Chen," he said automatically.

"Of the Lunar Republic." Not a question.

"Yes."

"Remove your mask, with your left hand."

Galvanix raised his arm slowly, peeling the mask up from his face. The remote studied his features silently. "Replace the mask," it said at last. "You must follow me."

"I wish to confirm the welfare of my companion," Galvanix said carefully, as to a machine of limited capacity. "The tanglin may be preventing him from breathing."

"The resister is lying face up and breathing regularly. His vital signs are being monitored."

Galvanix wondered how much hardware the expansile tanglin could contain—medical readouts, a cutoff mechanism in case the victim began to suffocate, perhaps sedatives. Without thinking, he turned to look at the agent, an act the remote did nothing to prevent beyond grasping his elbow once more. The supine form was still, either unconscious or awaiting their departure before attempting to writhe free.

A ribbon of smoke rose near Galvanix's feet: the agent's database, which had kicked free of his head and was now turning into a marbled puddle.

The grip on his elbow tightened slightly. "Follow me."

The remote rolled smoothly along the ceiling by a means Galvanix could not discern. He felt himself pulled into the air as the arm retracted to a third its length, towing his diminished weight through the air like a disabled ship.

As he trailed through the darkened corridor, Galvanix realized how they had been surprised: the remote, crouched on the ceiling, had been hidden by its upward curve while the agent had played his beam over the floor below. Galvanix wondered whether the Eldoradans had remote devices of their own, then remembered the mites battling in the air, across strategic surfaces.

The remote came to a sealed door, which slid open at their approach. Beyond, the corridor was lit and free of rubbish, but the walls and ceiling were dripping. Galvanix saw drain gratings flush with the floor, and wondered how much water had been sluiced through here. Within a minute large drops were sliding down the robot arm and onto his hand.

At one point the remote slid past a long window, disclosing a room filled with people. Habitat citizens stood or sat with their backs against the wall, looking disheveled and distraught. One stared at Galvanix with widening eyes, her mouth moving soundlessly. In an instant people were crowded at the window, watching him ride past a meter away. Galvanix could think of nothing to signal or mouth, and realized they could not anyway see his expression. Faces against the glass, they slid out of sight like a departing train.

Galvanix wanted to be put in the company of civilians and left by this fighting machine. "Where are you taking me?" he asked.

The remote did not answer. Galvanix saw no loss of face in trying a machine. "You violate law in mistreating me."

The invaders' forces were apparently programmed to respond to this charge. "This habitat is now the property of the Gleaming Aurora, which has commissioned the Free Orbital Confederation to act in its name. You were discovered trespassing in the company of an armed resister, and are being taken to proper authorities."

So the successful plaintiffs had constituted themselves as a new bloc. Galvanix felt the wing of madness brush over humanity. "I am not detained by any legally recognized force. You attacked without warning or justification. You are merely an overpowering weapon."

"Emergency conditions justify the—" The remote stopped dead in its tracks, jolting Galvanix hard. He stared from the end of its suddenly swaying arm, then called to the machine, which clung to the ceiling like a dormant bug. Finally Galvanix grasped the extensile arm with his free hand and levered his legs up, touching its ceramic carapace. Nothing.

Heart pounding, Galvanix began wriggling free of the robot's grip. He scraped his elbow pulling it loose from the viselike hold, then slid the pincers down his arm like a bracelet, pulling the thin point of his wrist through and loose. He pushed himself away from the arm, drifting to the floor with dreamlike ease.

Galvanix bounded back in the direction he had come from, pushing off from the wall when the wet floor made him skid and leap askew. In seconds he was back at the window, where the detainees stared at him in renewed wonder. They shouted at him, but a low hum filling the corridor—Galvanix had thought it the remote's motor—smeared their muffled words to unintelligibility.

Galvanix mimed freeing his arm, saw them nod, then asked in gestures how he should proceed. The detainees discussed this a moment, then all pointed in the direction he had first come. Back, then up. Galvanix waved thanks, looked at them yearningly, then bounded away.

Round the corridor's vertical curve Galvanix saw the sealed door. It slid open at his approach, though whether at the behest of an unseen sensor or the microscopic siege engines that had killed the remote, Galvanix did not know. Beyond it no lights shone, and Galvanix was hesitant to let it slide shut behind him. He stretched out on the floor, keeping one foot across the threshold, and reached out to grasp a strip of wall panel lying among the rubbish in the gloom beyond. Galvanix heaped all the trash he could reach in the doorway, hoping that its mass would keep the mechanism from trying to close.

When he stepped away the door slid shut, crunching the rubbish like grain. Darkness closed around him like a book, but a sliver of light remained. Galvanix knew that the imperfectly shut door was activating a malfunction notice in the Operating System, although the invaders might not immediately think to investigate. Nevertheless he moved quickly, picking his way among the rubble in the slowly dimming light.

Galvanix found his cutting tool in the near darkness, and felt for the raised letters of the dial. He activated its weakest setting, and the beam shone forth like a torch. Galvanix found the still form of the agent nearby, his chest rising shallowly. He did not touch the unconscious form, thinking that the tanglin might attack at an unskilled touch.

Shining his light across the narrow ceiling, Galvanix located what looked like a square hatch, mounted on hinges so as to open under emergency conditions. Galvanix leaped, floated up to the handle, and turned it. The door came open as he drifted down, showing blackness within. With a jump Galvanix went up and through.

He drew the hatch shut behind him and crouched in darkness, listening before daring to activate the torch. Gentle air currents brought a strange, organic smell he could not identify. Galvanix decided that he was in a large room, probably a lab or a crop tank. He did not know of any this high up, but there was much he did not know.

A loud buzz cut through the air. Galvanix ducked, hearing something pass overhead. The droning object circled him, and Galvanix switched the cutter to a wide beam and whirled it over his head like a scimitar. He saw something graze the cone of light, and the buzzing instantly stopped. Surprised—the setting's intensity was inadequate to damage any mechanism—Galvanix swung the beam back, and glimpsed the object gliding downward in the low gravity. It struck softly in the darkness.

Galvanix swept the floor with his beam and found the object, which was still stirring. He stared at the complexly articulated device, which looked like nothing he had ever seen. It was half a meter long, and bristled with waving sensors.

Abruptly it resumed buzzing. Galvanix nearly dropped the cutter in astonishment. The thing was a giant wasp.

Still stunned, the insect crawled toward the edge of the illuminated circle, wings buzzing. It lifted slightly off the ground, feeling cooler air. With a convulsive movement Galvanix narrowed the beam and sliced the creature in two.

Whirling, Galvanix slashed behind him, sweeping the darkness for several seconds. There was no sound, and he stopped suddenly. Galvanix widened his beam and ran it shakily along the walls until he found a door, then dove for it.

The door panel responded to his touch and Galvanix bounded through, striking the far wall. He looked up and down the narrow corridor, which was softly lit and carpeted with trimmed grass. A second wasp was crawling along one wall four meters away. Galvanix sliced through it, watching the halves flutter to the ground with unnatural slowness.

"You're panicking, and that's not good," a voice nearby said. "Wasps aren't predators, and these are out of their normal gravity anyway. There are worse things on this level, and a man who panics is in trouble."

Galvanix whirled. "Who's there?"

"No one's *there*, as you can plainly see. You're hearing a microspeak, windborne." The voice seemed to be drifting past Galvanix, though he could see nothing. He shone his beam at the voice, catching the flicker of a transparent membrane.

"You're not a soldier, probably not a citizen. Okay in low gravity, though. Maybe one of our lunar guests?"

"You already know more about me than I of you." Galvanix kept the quaver from his voice.

"No need to address the microspeak; I'm hearing you through a wall pickup, and seeing you through a camera in the corner. Use the door on your left—no insects beyond, I promise."

Galvanix went to the door at once. Its panel was not set for public access, and required a thumb print. Galvanix hesitated.

"Oh, don't worry about that. I reprogrammed these things long ago." The door opened.

Beyond lay a darkened room of uncertain dimensions, its only light trained on a spiral staircase so flimsy as to seem decorative. "I'm a few levels up," said the voice, coming from a new direction, "although I could easily descend to your level, now that the gravity has so weakened. On the whole, however, I prefer to remain above, especially since the staircase is the wrong size."

Galvanix wasn't sure what that meant, especially since the staircase was designed for a single person. Its fairy-castle frailty seemed precarious, even at reduced gravity, and he rested his hand on the bannister gingerly. The structure swayed like gossamer but did not break, and Galvanix took it as a token to ascend, his feet almost floating over the molded steps.

The helix bored into a narrow tube, which rose through several higher levels without offering egress. Galvanix did not bother counting the steps: by this time he was climbing in long bounds, limited only by the tight curve of the staircase.

The room it gave onto was much smaller, as Galvanix realized he should have expected. He was penetrating the inner recesses of the habitat, reaching increasingly smaller chambers that would perhaps continue dwindling to cellular dimensions.

This room, however, seemed distinctly too small for human comfort, and Galvanix wondered if it was usually tenanted by robots. The ceiling brushed his scalp, and some of the handholds were set too close to the wall for him to hook more than a finger through them. Galvanix squinted in the odd light, looking among the miniature trees and dollhouse structures for signs of human occupancy.

"I'm right behind you. Look carefully."

Galvanix turned slowly. The sound had come from a nearby

speaker, but Galvanix focused on the far wall, which was covered with clinging ivy. Something dangled like an ornament against the carpet of green. Galvanix realized with a start that it was a small animal.

The creature's sticklike body seemed no longer than a human hand, but the head was the size of an orange. Liquid blue eyes regarded Galvanix speculatively while a thin tail, longer than any other limb, coiled loosely round a vine.

Galvanix showed no outward reaction. His eyes slowly searched the wall behind the ivy for eyeholes or cameras, but his mind had already accepted that the lemur-like creature had addressed him. The voice had not, after all, been human.

"Greetings, citizen of the Lunar Republic and fellow outcast." The creature was holding something to its mouth as it spoke.

"Greetings. I do not know your status." The word, in orbital English, had legal rather than social implications, and encompassed citizenship questions as well as the standing of nonhuman entities such as corporations and intelligent engines. This judicious touch was spoiled when Galvanix's voice broke.

"If you think I'm unsettling, you should see who lives next door." A wall panel dissolved into transparency, revealing a wavering interior filled with liquid. Something stirred within, and Galvanix saw an amphibian shape raise its eyes, an impossibly large head traced with veins pitching slowly between paddling flippers. An inhuman intelligence peered briefly across the distance, then retreated to regions of the tank below the edge of the window.

Galvanix was shaken. "What . . . are you doing here?"

"Doing? Done to, rather." The wall panel solidified once more. "And my status is not citizen, nor even resident. It is *property*." The swollen head cocked, a ponderous motion even in this gravity. "Privileged, I should add. I may not be abused, no more than any true-bred animal, and enjoy all the protections of an intelligent engine. Also special classifications attending my experimental nature, but that becomes technical. My name is Bruse."

"Galvanix." He could not bring himself to inquire after the creature's well-being.

"You are enjoying the present disruptions a good deal less than I. That is because I recently restructured my cerebral architecture—that skill is my *raison d'être*, I should explain—and have adopted an egocentric consciousness, which certainly changes one's view of the world!" The creature laughed, a shocking sound. "I'm presently as selfish as any human; probably worse, since I am not used to this heady wine. As any *infant*."

"So why aren't you incapacitated with fear?" It seemed a rude question, but Galvanix could not shake the conviction that he was addressing a mechanism.

"Oh, *I'm* quite safe. Valuable asset, in fact. Indeed, the slowing of the habitat's spin has been a great boon to me: the area in which I can roam has been expanded twenty-fold." Bruse tapped his head meaningfully. "I require very low gravity. Suffer strokes otherwise. A major constraint on beings of my sort."

"That must be horrible."

"Not really. I have no instinct to roam; that was edited out. Mind you, the fluidity of my neurological structure—which results in total breakdown with larger brain volume, which is why I'm small—has its risks. I can create a morphology that produces utter misery—excessive anxieties, or a hair-trigger sensitivity to distractions—which I must endure until I have the strength to reconfigure. I also suffer from the inadequacy of my digestive system, whose design was rather scamped."

"I am sorry."

The creature tilted its head back—the gesture was unfamiliar, but Galvanix instinctively recognized preening. "Oh, that gives me pleasure! I feel like a pocket universe with this consciousness; no wonder you fight wars and misinform each other. I am very lucky the crisis caught me in this state: nothing else would have left me feeling so *alive*."

Galvanix did not know what to say to this. "Do you know what is happening below?"

"Do you mean the battle? I don't think its outcome was ever in doubt. Are you worried about loved ones? I find love fascinating."

"I was told to report to Room 207, or suffer a brainwipe in preference to falling into enemy hands."

"*That* would be an inconvenience to someone of your neurologic rigidity, wouldn't it? Sorry. Room 207 is an emergency exit, to be used if a spacecraft smashed a main docking port and personnel had to be evacuated. Sounds like they wanted to put you straight on a lifeboat."

"I don't believe I have any knowledge of value to these warring factions."

"You never know. Do your loyalties lie with the invaders or the habitat?"

Galvanix was amazed at the question. "You think me a partisan with a gun? I would side with the friends of the Republic, except that I can't believe either of these enemies wish us well."

"That's largely true. But Eldorado is probably more interested in maintaining an inhabitable Moon. Personally I favor the diversion of planetary matter to create a galaxy of microworlds, as befits someone of my frail constitution. This renders me suspect with the Board of Governors."

Galvanix could not imagine this monster posing a threat to the habitat. "You nevertheless enjoy an enviably central location," he said politely.

"Central? This desert? There is nothing here but refugees from the square-cube law—like the oversized insects that so scared you—and water tanks. Microgravity is hardly at a premium: you can always go outside. The water is kept here merely to conserve potential energy. In fact—" Bruse seemed to brighten—"*I* know a way to get you off the habitat without encountering the invaders. There are four emergency spillpipes running from the core right into space. They were designed to dump water if the habitat had to be slowed under truly dire conditions, like structural failure that would preclude firing retros." He laughed. "Even the invaders didn't use them—water is too valuable to waste. Better flood the living quarters with it!

"There's even one nearby," it added. "At this level, everything's nearby."

Galvanix shuddered. "No, thank you."

The creature performed an elaborate writhe Galvanix guessed was a shrug. "You older types are mired in the minds you grew up with, a real handicap in a rapidly changing universe. The future is a game for the young and the hungry—I'm five months old myself, and on the cutting edge."

An enormous gong broke over them like a blow, making the deck shiver underfoot. Galvanix stared. "What was that?"

"Sounds like someone forcing the door of the pip. Resonant,

isn't it?" The creature reached behind a leaf and held something to the side of its head. "Yes?" it said after a pause. "Of course you can come in, but I can't open the doors for you."

At once it launched itself into the air, sailing directly past Galvanix, who flinched aside. "A fib," Bruse remarked over its shoulder. "I mapped out the circuitry of this level months ago, and grabbed what I could during the system takeover. They'll have to cut through the doors, which gives you a few seconds."

The chimera struck the far wall and grabbed a handhold. A panel opened in the wall beside it. "You coming?"

It disappeared like a puppet into its box. Galvanix followed hesitantly, squeezing through the narrow panel, which led not to an adjacent room but into an equally narrow passageway. The panel knocked against his ankles as he wriggled through, anxious to shut again.

Tiny lights lined the duct, which must have seemed a comfortable avenue for the imp. Ahead Galvanix could see the creature pulling itself along the rungs with limbs and tail. It disappeared around a sharp corner, which Galvanix could negotiate only with difficulty. Several meters beyond, the creature hung waiting, its enormous eyes unreadable.

As Galvanix drew nearer he noticed that a section of duct lay open, showing darkness beyond. "This leads to one of the recently drained ventricles," Bruse announced. "At its bottom lies one of the spillpipes, which leads directly outside. I can control its mechanism from here—" the creature seemed to smirk—"and flush you right out. I can also direct you to another stairwell, but I believe those exits are all covered."

"But I have no spacesuit," Galvanix cried.

"All habitat garments function as pressure suits in conjunction with a mask, which you have. There are gloves concealed in your wrist cuffs; pull them loose."

A hollow booming began to reverberate through the close tunnel. Galvanix could not tell if its source lay before or behind him. "I think you had better go," the creature said.

Galvanix began squeezing through the opening, turning with difficulty as he maneuvered first his lower legs, then his thighs, into the cavity beyond. Bruse hovered nearby, as though to offer assistance. "Altruism can be surprisingly gratifying," it remarked. "No wonder humans dabble with it."

Galvanix found he could only fit his shoulders through by introducing one arm at a time. He struggled to draw in his elbow in the cramped space, feeling a welling of claustrophobia. From down the corridor came the sound of tearing metal.

With a wrench he was through. The panel shrank to a bright rectangle framing a grotesque silhouette, then slid shut. Galvanix drifted in darkness, touched by cool air and the clean smell of water on metal. He pulled at his cuffs, finding superthin gloves attached which unrolled neatly. As he tugged the last fingers into place his feet brushed the bottom of the tank.

With a light bounce he came to rest on the sloping interior. He activated his beam and shone it round the beaded surface. A sealed hatchway was set like a plug at the bottom, and as Galvanix stepped forward it snapped open like a trap.

At once a violent suction filled the tank. Droplets rained down as though shaken from a bough. Galvanix was pulled forward and his feet, lacking traction in the low gravity, were swept from under him. In an instant he was sliding irresistibly into the whistling O of the pipe.

The cutter flew as his elbow cracked against the lip, and darkness swallowed him. The wave-front of air rushed to fill the vacuum of the tunnel, carrying him before it like a chip. Skidding against the frictionless sides, Galvanix felt his mask and clothing balloon around him.

Abruptly the walls of the tunnel vanished, and Galvanix scrabbled in surprise.

Mist clouded his lenses, evaporating in a second. He was tumbling in an immensity, surrounded by stars.

PART FOUR

The
Oxygen
Barons

NINE

"Galvanix."

"Yes?" Darkness swam about him, a formlessness devoid of sensation save for the crisp edge of Beryl's voice.

"Can you hear me clearly?"

"Yes. Only in one ear, though." He was about to specify which, but found he was not sure.

"Is this better?" Beryl's voice opened into stereophony, though Galvanix felt no sense of her presence before him. He tried to raise his hands to his ears, and discovered he could not locate his limbs.

"Are we still in the ballistic pod?" Galvanix looked up for the hovering faces of the medical technicians.

"No, much time has passed since then. We are in fact bound back for the Moon."

Galvanix considered this, trying to establish his sense of time. "Has my memory been tampered with?" He remembered hearing of a drug that, once administered, would tag all subsequently created memories. A second drug could then numb these memories, or even erase them.

"In a sense." Beryl laughed shortly. "Your sensorium is being electronically controlled, for reasons involving mass constraints in travel. If you feel ready, I can plug in the visual of our fore port."

"Please." Galvanix saw a faint stirring in the darkness before him, though no sensation touched his eyes. In a second the Moon resolved before him, a three-quarters section cut by a precise arc. A few stars shone behind it, but Galvanix's surround remained black, as though he were peering through a long telescope.

"Something's wrong with the visual," he said.

"Yes?"

"The color is wrong. It's gone dirty. And the terminator is far too sharp. . . ." A sense of distress, unlike any he had ever felt, swept over him. Malaise suffused him, a wrongness that filled his consciousness like electric potential seeking discharge. "Something has happened to the atmosphere."

"Do not worry about that. What else do you see?"

Galvanix studied hard. "The light shining through the lunar limb is different, there's less of it. That would mean less air. The clouds seem sparser; I can see land and sea plainly through them. They have both changed color." He looked further, confident in Beryl's assurance. "The array of ocean is different. We must be approaching from an unusual angle."

"To take the last point first, you are correct. We are coming in from outside lunar orbit, and you are seeing both Farside and Near. We are also traveling along the ecliptic, and the South Pole is visible several degrees down the terminator.

"Your other observations are also accurate. This is a realtime view, not an extrapolation. The Moon's atmosphere has been corrupted, and is settling to the surface as a precipitate."

Galvanix considered this in shocked silence. A welling of dismay began somewhere within him, and was immediately drained off. He looked again at the gibbous Moon, its edges smaller and harder as though shriveled. "How was this done?"

"A new technology, of course. The silicates in the soil have been induced to break down and their elements to oxidize separately, which binds much more oxygen than before. New basalts are being exposed to the atmosphere, apparently through tunnels drilled down to the crust. Atmospheric nitrogen is fixing spontaneously."

"That's impossible."

"Which part do you mean? None of them is impossible; they are simply unnatural, meaning they can only be forced by expenditure of energy, which someone has in abundance."

Galvanix could not avert his gaze from the scene before him. Details leaped to his attention: dark circles, the crater lakes of the highlands, now showing through the clouds like emerging pox; an opening disclosing a sea of strikingly unnatural color. The nimbus of sun-caught cloud edging the dark side was gone, and Galvanix suddenly realized the extent of despoliation.

"What has become of the people?" he asked.

"They have retreated underground, where the old quarters

remain airtight. Clensuits can recycle indefinitely, so most people made it to cover. Some are already being evacuated."

"And the ecosphere?"

"Dead. Atmospheric pressure down to a hundred millibars and dropping. Soon there will be no aerobic life."

Galvanix felt disorientation. "How fast did this happen?"

"Once it began, very quickly. However, a good deal of time has passed since your most recent memory."

Galvanix felt as though a section of his life had been stolen. "Have I been kept unconscious since then?"

"In a sense. Listen: while we were in the ballistics pod, a full neural mapping was made of you. Such maps are sufficient to create complex programs that can, for at least brief periods, simulate a human consciousness."

"That's impossible."

"No."

"It's illegal!"

"Not to a stateless person, not during wartime. There is precedent, though you don't want to know about that."

"This is monstrous." Galvanix felt outrage, which as quickly faded away. "And what have you done with this ghost program?" But suddenly he knew.

"I am talking to it, of course. Did you imagine you were riding in a clensuit beside me?"

The shock was milder than it should have been, as Galvanix himself realized. Beryl explained this as a design feature: spikes of anger or euphoria were damped down, their amplitude carefully noted.

"You have made a caricature of me—of him," he said. Anger was lost in wonder, at least for the moment. "*I* am not Galvanix at all."

"Indeed you are not. Perhaps I should address you as Galvanix Two, or G-2. Would this satisfy your sense of appropriateness, *Gitu*?"

"Obviously you can give me any name you like, so long as it is not that of another." Nevertheless he felt a pang; of course he wanted to be called Galvanix.

"Very well. Your recording was made not out of depraved indifference to human dignity or suffering—you cannot, you will

note, register pain in any immediate sense—but to provide me
with crucial information about the Moon's surface. You have
already shown willingness to risk your life for your Republic and
community; you are here risking something much less."

"Galvanix is risking nothing at all."

"Quite right. And your destruction would not be a death in
anyone's eyes, not even your own."

Galvanix realized this was true, although he did not like being
so informed. He mistrusted his equanimity—if it was the product
of programming intervention, then how much of his emotional
response was his, and what else had been altered?

Beryl answered these questions with alacrity. "Cognitive modification is negligible, since it cannot be accomplished without
jeopardizing sophic integrity. If your memories and expertise were
readily separable from your sense of self, they would have been
decanted alone."

"What is 'sophic'?"

"From *sophia,* the wisdom that comes of slowly gathered
knowledge, organized in light of experience. The mind is not
serried like a memory bank, as Galvanix would be quick to inform
me."

"What has become of Galvanix?" he asked suddenly.

"He was sent to Eldorado, which was eventually taken over by
interests associated with the South Americans. He was subsequently evacuated to Earth, where he remains."

Galvanix pondered. The thought of his authentic self, as vibrant
in its three dimensions as a hologram idealization, provoked a
melancholy like the memory of a lost beloved. Galvanix pushed
the subject aside.

"Is my mental capacity enhanced in any way?"

"No. As you recall, modification of cerebral architecture brings
different consciousness, a different self. Your only advantage over
Galvanix is the ability to operate at a faster rate if I change the
setting. This capacity will only be used under urgent conditions,
as recordings such as you remain unstable and deteriorate rapidly
after about ninety hours of subjective operation."

"Do you carry more than one recording of me?" The thought
was distinctly unpleasant.

"Again, no. A second Gitu activated in mid-mission would be
nearly useless."

Galvanix felt relief. He wondered whether Beryl might carry the recording of another lunar expert, but the idea did not bother him.

The Moon grew with just-discernible speed, drifting slowly off center as their trajectory carried them toward orbit. Beryl explained that they were traveling in an atmospheric cloud, spiraling slowly outward from Venus. Scanning devices would see nothing, for they were encased in a clump of frozen gases.

"What is our mission?" he asked her.

"I can't tell you."

Galvanix was amused. "Can a ghost program be made to talk if captured?"

"I cannot tell you because I do not know. Part of the mission will become known to me when we touch down, and completion of that task will unlock knowledge of the next."

"Does it have to do with the database we recovered?" Galvanix asked.

"Smart question, Gitu. Probably."

The partial orb swelled, became a curving piebald wall bulging against the darkness. Galvanix felt faint stresses, which Beryl told him were acceleration as they fell Moonward. A rudimentary sense of motion and balance was all he had besides sight and hearing, which themselves came patched through Beryl's receivers.

"The first orbit will be very low, seventeen klicks. Deceleration will reach four gees, and the larger ice chunks will probably come apart. That's when we break out and dive for the surface. Any radar will lose us in the fragmentation."

It sounded spectacularly reckless to Galvanix, even though he knew they would be piloted by computer. He nevertheless felt no fear, indeed doubted he retained that capacity.

"I'm cutting you out of the system now, can't spare the space. Hold tight." Before Galvanix could reply the view in front of him snapped out like a light.

The darkness that closed around him was not complete, for the system fed him a minimal sensorium, creating the vague sense of space about him and a hush like the whisper of air. In the stillness Galvanix composed himself, contemplating the Void around him with amused fellow-feeling.

• • •

"Still there, Gitu?" Beryl's voice held a strain of excitement.

Galvanix came to full awareness like a rising bubble. A steady pull drew somewhere upon him, which he knew must be the gravity of home. No other sense was open to him, meaning he had access to none unless Beryl took special steps.

"You know where to find me, Beryl," he answered.

"We are on the surface, on the eastern slope of Theophilus. It is early night."

"Can you let me see?"

"Of course." The world snapped into place. Galvanix studied the landscape, startled by the speed with which the evening sky had gone dark. He had expected to find the Moon as it had stood in his childhood, a dead world with wisps of atmosphere and a scattered dustfall of organic matter. The slopes of the walled crater Theophilus were not familiar terrain, but Galvanix knew there was something wrong about them.

"Are we standing among ruins?" he asked.

"I'm afraid not. The formations you see are crystals, pyroxenes that have reconstituted so as to hold more oxygen. Their composition is difficult to determine through spectrometry, so one of our missions is to study samples. There appear to be hundreds of varieties."

Galvanix realized that he was not seeing through Beryl's eyes, but controlled a camera of his own. With an act of will he caused it to pan upward and scan the horizon, where the Mare Nectaris formed a shallow sea. He looked long at the forms rising from it. "What has happened to the sea?"

Beryl was chipping bits of crystal from the formations around them. "The seas have been covered by a solid skin, presumably silicate. There is almost no water movement on the lunar surface."

Galvanix was aghast. "Even the poles?"

"Both tidal poles are covered by glassy domes. Crystals have formed atop them as elsewhere, so their smoothness is not readily apparent from space. The heat exchange, however, has been totally destroyed: this night will be a cold one."

Galvanix looked at the spires and polygons lacing the horizon, their crystalline structures soaring in the thin air and low gravity. The crescent Earth shone from the opposite side of the sky, giving a faint blue sheen to the winking points of variously angled facets.

"How much mass is in those structures?" he asked.

"A lot. Each one is kilometers high, and still growing. Their lattices are quite dense, binding up oxygen, silicon, and even nitrogen in long chains that withstand the daytime heat. We'll want samples of those, too."

Galvanix panned back to watch Beryl at her work. Crystals were everywhere: tetrahedrons poking from the ground like new shoots, outcroppings of rock that had acquired a laminate of glittering surfaces. Grit crunched underfoot, more granular than the powdery regolith of the old airless Moon. Galvanix was looking at a garden of crystals, inorganic life blossoming from the air and soil with the riotous variety of nature.

"Are these still growing?" he asked.

"They don't grow at night. Evidently they are energy-driven, perhaps by nanomechanisms roving their surfaces. Their growth rate has slowed, but only because the atmosphere is so much thinner."

Beryl ran her hands quickly over the budding gems, chipping away fragments with fingertip picks.

"How are you going to get back with your samples?"

"I'm not getting back, nor will the samples. They are being analyzed now, and the data dispatched by novel means."

Which I am not to know, Galvanix thought without rancor. He could nevertheless imagine possible ways to get bursts of information off even an embargoed Moon, especially with the atmosphere gone and frenzied particles escaping into orbit at midday.

"And what will become of you?" Galvanix did not think to say *of us*.

"I will make contact with a Republican outpost. Yasuhiro has overrun much of the Moon, but personnel records were destroyed before he reached them. I should be able to blend in as an anonymous worker."

"That won't work if you still have black skin."

"Don't worry, I look like any Republican." Beryl began working her way down the crater's edge. Galvanix had questions about Farside involvement with this atrocity, but knew he was not going to get a briefing.

For an hour—Galvanix found he could consult an internal clock by another flexion of will—Beryl stowed samples into a compartment in the side of her suit. Galvanix watched, but found himself free to think, and brooded long while Beryl descended the glittering slope.

The broken plain seemed to hold little interest, and Beryl took only a single sample of what resembled melted glass before she started across in great strides. Sensing her relaxed attention, Galvanix asked suddenly, "Did the database we recovered *enable* this to happen?"

Beryl allowed herself to land and leap again before answering. "Yes, it seems so. We thought we got to it first, but the capsule wasn't just a database, it was more like a virus. The information it contained was already set out as program instructions, which were shed as the artifact was carried toward the Far Sea. Where they came into contact with dormant assemblers in the cold waters, the assemblers were turned to its task."

"Which was?"

"Why, to produce mites that take apart lunar compounds and induce recombination along desired lines. Most of the Moons' pyroxenes, such as augite and orthopyroxene, contain elements that will bind up more oxygen on their own. One kind of mite did that. There must be dozens of different models, each with its task, and billions of each model."

Galvanix thought about this. "And how was this monstrous plan created?"

"It was devised by an advanced intelligence system that had been sent out on the Jovian project in order to escape supervision. The system used new technology to develop an offensive capability—an old-fashioned black project."

"A what?"

"The term refers to weaponry research so secret that governments hid the cost in their budgets, so that sometimes their own legislatures did not know of them."

Galvanix felt himself grimace—an illusion, as no muscles existed to heed the command. "And so this research unit spent eleven years in deep space, peaceably working out the means to destroy an ecosystem?"

"Exactly. The technology behind Soliton Tunneling permits a great deal of destructive innovation in microgravity environments, which is why intelligence systems capable of manipulating such data have been regulated for twenty years. Every cubic centimeter of Earth and LEO is scanned by Squids for evidence of contraband complex systems. The security state that Western civilization feared for so long finally came about, not to suppress individual dissent but in order to protect humanity against a threat a single individual could bring against it."

"Which nevertheless happened."

"Essentially, yes. The Geodites dismantled the lunar ecosphere, and now hold the key to its reconstitution. If they keep the key, they win: this strengthens their bargaining position immeasurably."

"And the Lunar Republic is gone."

"No one *cares* about your fairyland kingdom, not a single faction. It was an absurd extravagance: the resources being contested are enough to develop Mars and all the Galileans—real worlds that could house a hundred billion people."

"The spiritual state of humanity is not measured in biomass."

"Fortunately for *you*," Beryl snapped. Galvanix, humiliated, withdrew into silence.

For ninety minutes Beryl strode across the plain, stopping only once to scrape at a low pool that had crystallized in fernlike patterns as intricate as frost on a pane. Galvanix wondered why he had not been deactivated, and concluded that Beryl wanted him to study the transformed landscape. It pained him to do so, but Galvanix—not truly Galvanix, he told himself—recognized his existence was defined by his duty.

Beryl spoke unexpectedly. "You remember the years when the Moon had an atmosphere this thin?"

"I was a child, yes."

"Conditions now differ to an unknowable degree, but your recollections may be valuable. Violent winds subsided shortly before we landed; there is still enough dust in the high air to obscure our image to orbiting cameras. I am relying on your instincts to help if we should encounter local anomalies."

"Very well." Galvanix felt he could know nothing of this skeletal world, and quailed at such responsibility.

"Temperature eight degrees and dropping hourly. Nights get cold fast. Fortunately we are radiating no tell-tale heat."

"Beryl," Galvanix said, "you did not resume conversation in order to tell me these things."

"True. After the next sample I am going to send our data in a radio burst. It's a calculated risk—the burst could betray our presence, but it would be more dangerous to gather all the data before sending it."

Galvanix felt increased alertness at the mention of danger, but no fear. "Is this something I can influence?"

"No. I want to apprise you of your utility as back-up operative. If I become incapacitated, system control will be turned over to you. You should be prepared to act if you find yourself suddenly regaining the use of limbs."

"Control your body?" Galvanix was horrified.

"Control the clensuit. My defunct self will presumably not be in *rigor mortis*, and may be maneuvered like a dresser's dummy."

Galvanix thought this over. "Any mishap that would injure you would probably not leave me time to orient myself."

"It's a fairly desperate expedient," Beryl agreed. "However, this is a high-risk venture throughout. Even if nothing goes wrong, my survival entails passing as a displaced Republican, for which the chances for detection rise almost asymptotically with time."

"But if you're detected—caught—they would simply *hold* you, wouldn't they? They certainly wouldn't attempt to harm you."

Beryl laughed. "My captors will want to provide the strongest deterrent against further infiltration they can; I'm sure whatever they arrange will be recorded and broadcast. You are denying some fundamental aspects of human nature, such as the drives to vent anger and take revenge. It is a peculiarly unseemly delusion in someone opposed to updating the human animal."

"I can't believe that," Galvanix said. He felt an odd dislocation, and wondered if his emotional response was being tempered.

Beryl said dryly, "I will take little pleasure in seeing you proved wrong."

Galvanix felt emboldened when challenged. "I want you to tell me—"

Beryl interrupted. "I'm turning you off now."

". . . Galvanix."

He clawed free of the blackness with less difficulty than before. A view came into focus before him, a half-lit patch of ground less than a meter away. Trying to shift his gaze, he found it frozen.

"I'm here. Did your transmission work okay?"

"That was days ago. It got through, but we were detected. There must be mite-sized scanners in low lunar orbit; I thought the atmosphere was still too dense for that. We were shot at before I cleared the area; two microprojectiles went through my suit at high velocity."

Galvanix felt a stab of alarm that was immediately quashed. "Are you injured?"

"Not badly, but four emergency seals are enough to hamper the recycler. Carbon dioxide levels are creeping up, and I will need new air within hours."

Galvanix's view slewed to one side, coming to rest at another unprepossessing scene. He realized that Beryl had moved her head, carrying his captive field of vision with it.

"Is there a reason I cannot move my camera eye?"

"I don't want stray movement at the wrong instant."

"Then can you align it with your own line of sight?"

The view swung to show a mound of crystalline rubble gleaming against the horizon. Galvanix studied it, trying to get a sense of scale. A twinkle to one side caught his attention, and he suddenly made out a person half visible in the harsh low-atmosphere chiaroscuro. The spacesuited figure stood perhaps twenty meters away, half the height of the faceted pile, looking across the plain like the guardian over a treasure.

"Yashurio's?" Galvanix asked, voice unintentionally low.

"Indeed. The pursuit."

Galvanix could not turn to look behind him, but saw in his peripheral vision the edges of the glassy spur behind which Beryl was crouching. "You should be able to slip away," he observed.

"I'm not trying to slip away. I want his oxygen."

The shock was greater than before. "Beryl, you can't do that!"

"No? It's his life or mine. That's the *enemy*, see his weapon? He's one of the renegades who destroyed your Moon."

"You think that makes me want him dead? You could surrender to him."

"Gitu, don't disgust me. I want a detailed description of that suit, and you are going to provide it." The view clicked rapidly through a sequence of increased magnification, centering finally on the slightly fuzzy image of the soldier, which slowly gained clarity. Galvanix saw that the suit was a model widely used in the first years of the Inflooding, neither a standard clensuit inadequate for sustained vacuum use, nor a true spacesuit. He had once spent months toying with such obsolescent gear in his afterschool hours, and knew without thinking how the recycler could be lifted like a sweetbread from the opened chest.

The soldier moved, and Galvanix saw the glint of a slender tube nearly a meter long. With a thrill he recognized the muzzle of a rail gun.

"My own can puncture that suit at twenty meters," said Beryl, evidently reading his thoughts, "assuming it isn't armored. The helmet is, of course, so I need to hit the torso. You must tell me where the recycler is mounted."

"No." Galvanix was about to add something, but realized his response was sufficient.

"If I have to shoot off a limb, he may fire back. And if I destroy the recycler it will be a wasted life. Would you like to watch me do this twice?"

"I won't abet murder."

"You worm." Galvanix's view snapped back to regular magnification. "I am forced to guess. Recyclers are sometimes installed under one arm . . . but such a vital unit would be more readily accessible at the *waist*."

Galvanix realized that Beryl must be monitoring his electrical activity, hoping for a telltale response should she hit upon the site. "Forget it," he said. "I am going to meditate."

Beryl reacted quickly. She raised an arm to point at the distant pile, and something flashed at her wrist. An explosion crashed through Galvanix's audio, flinging him backward. His balance reeled as the view spun, then steadied: Beryl had recovered and was kicking fast and low toward her target.

Before them the jewelled mound seemed to have disappeared behind a growing ultramarine cloud, which glittered brilliantly as innumerable tumbling grains caught what light remained. Something was moving in the foreground, a crawling figure that dropped from sight.

"The power drain of my next shot will shut you off, you bastard, assuming I can manage one—"

Beryl rolled once as the ground sprayed fragments beside her, and flung out her arm. Galvanix knew blackness.

He came to consciousness by degrees, unaware until he saw something moving in the darkness before him. He reached for other sensations, finding only a faint rasping sound. At first he thought it correlated with the chopping motions he gradually discerned in the night scene, but realized after a moment that he was listening to Beryl panting.

His field of vision offered only the swinging movement of a dim object, which Galvanix decided was Beryl's hand. He studied silently, straining for detail. Beryl commented, "Awake, eh?"

Assent was unnecessary, but Galvanix said, "Yes." Her tone did not invite further comment, and he waited several minutes before asking, "Where are we?"

"I am lying on the shore of Theophilus, chopping at the sheet that covers its surface. If I can cut a large enough hole I shall crawl through."

Galvanix did not know what to make of this. "Are you injured?"

"No."

"You are breathing hard."

"My recycler is slowly failing. You can listen to me asphyxiate."

Galvanix would have made some reply to this, but Beryl's breath came in such ragged gasps that he knew she should not speak. He watched as she hacked at the translucent silicate, which slowly flaked loose like mica. Beryl thrust her arm into the slowly widening hole almost to her elbow, and Galvanix thought suddenly of the exposure and restricted mobility of a swimmer beneath the ice. "Are you sure you can hide down there?" he asked.

"Hide? I can die outside as well as anywhere. I'm seeking a stratum of oxygenated water at the bottom."

Galvanix was startled at the thought. "Can you remain there indefinitely?"

"Not without starving. However, there's a small chance that the recycler's transpirators can in time build new paths around the emergency seals."

Puffing, Beryl lurched forward, forcing both arms into the opening. Galvanix watched, helpless to act. He wondered if the crack of tool against crystal could strike a spark, any radiance to attract the flying mites which were doubtless hunting them. They would never feel the blow.

"Through," Beryl gasped. She was wriggling like a fish into the opening. Galvanix just glimpsed the ripple of black water striking her faceplate, then darkness. His sense of balance yawed, but no other input reached him save the frantic scrape of her breath.

Beryl exhaled in a wailing sigh, though only to resume panting. They were tumbling slowly—descending, Galvanix realized, the submerged slope of the crater. "You made it!" he cried.

"Ther," Beryl said, voice blurred. "Ifth . . ."

Galvanix realized she was swooning. "Beryl, *don't pass out,*" he said urgently. "Can you set your suit to take in the oxygen on its own?"

Her reply was incoherent. Galvanix raged through his uncoupled motor nerves, denied even bars to shake. He wondered in a panic if suit function would pass on to him when Beryl's brain activity began to falter. "Beryl," he entreated, seeking a way to raise his voice, "have you set your suit?"

"Automatic," she mumbled. "Getting cold . . ."

The water must be suffusing the transpirators of her suit. "Just breathe deeply," he said. They were drifting now, and Galvanix attended Beryl's resumption of steady breathing with the intentness of one denied any chance of distraction.

For fourteen minutes she sighed evenly, and Galvanix was thinking that she had drifted into a long sleep when she spoke. "You are really not much good, are you?"

Galvanix was at once relieved and stung. "I would have pulled your muscles like oars if I could."

"I don't want a galley slave, much less a co-administrator of my limbs. You are worthless if you deny me your knowledge."

"I can't kill for you, no."

"I could expunge you, you know. Capital punishment, for refusing orders in battle."

"Do it."

"When we're safe, I'll take pleasure in it. Your kind will never fill the solar system; you talk of harmony with nature, but deny everything about it you don't like."

"Thus can you justify whatever physical law doesn't prevent. You have managed without killing that soldier after all."

"Trapped, with a crippled recycler," said Beryl. "Mission stalled."

Galvanix had no reply to this. They drifted, impelled by short bursts of motion. "Are you kicking?" he asked.

"Into deeper water. The recycler has to work too hard to extract oxygen here; I want a richer mix."

"What's our depth?" Galvanix hoped Beryl would take the hint and patch him a display.

"Two hundred fourteen and dropping."

Galvanix's surprise must have registered, for Beryl remarked, "It's a good deal safer than space."

"Of course." Galvanix felt his sense of motion fade, leaving him bereft of reference as though hovering weightless.

"This is better," Beryl said after a moment. "I'm going to fill my tanks while no one can stop me. Just like an oxygen baron."

"A what?"

Beryl laughed. "You've been out of touch. The folks who locked up your atmosphere, and may break the Consortium. Control oxygen and you control human development between Earth and the outer asteroids. You may think of it as the cosmos' sweet breath, but it's an instrument of power."

Galvanix was trying to remember whether "baron" was synonymous with warlord. Beryl's last phrase brushed some trigger, however, and he asked suddenly, "Was your allure for Galvanix an instrument of power?"

"My allure?"

"Galvanix loved you—*I* love you. You got his devotion by showing passion for him when he was vulnerable. Was that a trick they teach you at assassins' school?"

"I was vulnerable, too, you little subset. What scant help Galvanix could offer was mine anyway. Check your memories of being a real human being."

"If you survive, will you try to see him?"

"If I survive I'll be sent back into action. If we all live a hundred years, we may meet again. Are you adopting a protective attitude toward your authentic self?"

Galvanix framed a retort, then suppressed it. He realized the futility of arguing with someone who could read his response to her every sally, then saw in a rush the ugliness of quarreling at all.

"This time I shall surely die in your company," he said simply.

"You are clever, Gitu, and you sound like Galvanix, but I will not treat your dissolution as a death. I have dealt with clever constructs before, and the misfortune of their loss is not pathos. Were you—wait!"

Sudden silence, and the sensation of Beryl kicking frantically about. The forgotten blackness brightened, to deepest brown. So profound and dense was this shade that Galvanix merely stared, transfixed. "Submarine," Beryl muttered.

Registers of color filled the world, gradations of swirling umber Galvanix had never dreamed. A great humming drew slowly across the bass string of his nerves. Light pushed steadily through the depths, as though they were ascending toward the surface. In the tinted translucence Galvanix saw Beryl raise her arm.

Utter darkness, not the unbeing of oblivion but the solitude of total isolation. Galvanix knew at once that he was not merely cut out of the sensorium. His sense of balance was present, but seemed awry. He thought he might be upside down.

"*Beryl.*" Not even his voice remained; the circuit enabling his tiny voder was gone. Galvanix felt for neural avenues, or even roadblocks, and found nothing. The network connecting him with Beryl's system was missing.

Galvanix ranged carefully through the possibilities. Either Beryl had been killed, or her suit badly damaged, or she had jettisoned Galvanix in the course of battle. Pressing against his sense of equilibrium, Galvanix decided that it was sound. He was unmoving, at an odd position. It came upon him only gradually that the mechanism housing his being was lying at the bottom of Theophilus.

It did not seem likely to Galvanix that Beryl's broken body would rest unrecovered on the lake floor. Would a suit fragment escape notice? He did not know how large was the engine containing his consciousness.

I am forgotten, he thought.

No internal clock remained to tell the hours before the program that was Gitu began to dysfunction and disintegrate. A failing power source or other damage might have advanced that sentence date anyway. Galvanix suspected there was in fact no battery left, merely residual current racing through superconducting circuits.

Dissolution, not a death. He knew he lacked the amplitude to achieve true peace of mind, but nevertheless rejected the image of crumbling matrices. A single ego, guttering; like the Western model of self that had so marred the last centuries of civilization.

Twenty-nine years, from the Moon to near Earth and back. It was a not unpleasing arc (that another would take it up did not now matter; he could justly contemplate the shape of his life without regarding offshoots). He thought of the universe outside, complicating in pockets while diffusing somewhere else. Perhaps he would leave it only to emerge elsewhere, though a crumbling construct seemed an unlikely candidate for such transcendence. Fortunate enough, he thought, to have come to rest in the watered soil of the Moon.

Release from the Wheel

Ten

Tumbling, Galvanix caught a glimpse of what might have been the sun, followed a second later by an enormous Earth rolling toward him. Instinctively he tried to raise his hands, but found his outflung limbs gone rigid, as though his wheeling figure was being transformed into a constellation.

Something caught his ankle. Galvanix was yanked hard, thinking disconnectedly that he must have snagged upon a boom or antenna. A second later he felt the grip tightening, and the careening stars suddenly snapped into place as he was pulled rapidly backward. From somewhere a tinny voice asked, "*Are you all right?*"

Galvanix lacked the presence of mind to answer. It was quickly becoming cold, and each new breath tasted stale. The drag on his ankle continued, meaning that he was still accelerating. Galvanix was wondering whether he would smash into a bulkhead when a soft immensity struck him.

Cushions billowed around his faceplate, affording a glimpse of swelling blue fabric before closing over him like water. Galvanix was fighting to draw breath back into his flattened lungs. Suddenly the restraints vanished, and Galvanix flailed to discover his limbs freed and sudden light about him. His mask was pulled from his face.

He blinked, looking into the eyes of an upside-down bearded man. Behind him, Galvanix's mask waved in the grasp of a crab-sized mechanism with meter-long limbs. Before he could move, the mech grasped his garment in a pincer and sliced the suit open from collarbone to knee.

"No external injury? Good." The man leaned forward to flash a beam into Galvanix's eye. Disoriented, Galvanix wondered briefly whether he was confronted by another medical program posing as a human, then felt the man's breath against his cheek. "That was quite an escape," he was saying. "Welcome aboard *The Amelican Pelican*. A warship, fortunately for you."

"What?" The word emerged in a gasp.

The bearded man explained. "Any ship bearing arms must be manned. Keeps 'em slow, and may even deter governments from firing them at each other. We'll certainly test that principle in the next hour."

Galvanix was still panting, his body racing on its own war footing. He looked at the man wildly.

"Your skin is cold." A warm hand touched his chest, which at once began shivering. A sharp smell hissed into one nostril. Suddenly Galvanix was calm, and a warm sheath enveloped him. "Better rest while the med takes a look at you.

"You're lucky we got you," the voice continued through a growing haze. "One of the other ships sent a net spinning toward you, but our line snatched you from its very shadow. Or lucky for us, anyway. God knows where your interests lie . . ."

Galvanix awoke when the pull of gravity drew him back against a couch. He opened his eyes, focusing on a console half a meter away. Moving his arms, he found them secured by a crash web.

"Awake? We're re-entering the atmosphere. Gliding in, decelerating all the way. Tremendous waste of energy, and the tax on coming in like this is enormous. Heats the atmosphere, besides depriving the Authority of its braking load."

Galvanix lifted his head with some effort, turning to see the bearded man in the seat beside him. Not yet strapped in, the man was leaning forward to gaze speculatively at Galvanix. He appeared about fifty, pale-skinned and fashionably balding, wearing a featureless short-sleeved jumper.

Galvanix found his voice. "Why is the ship making such an inefficient descent?"

"Ship? We're not on the *Pelican*—bringing that boat out of the sky would cause an international crisis. We're in a skiff, fast and light. And we're dropping in because someone doesn't care to entrust you to the Tower Authority. You some type of hot property?"

"Not that I know of . . ." Deceleration was increasing steadily, pressing Galvanix's head back against the couch. "Where am I going?"

"Now that's interesting. I'm not supposed to tell you anything, not even my name. Pardon the discourtesy. You must have had quite a time back there—I was actually told to make sure you carried no weapons. You don't look like a soldier."

Galvanix exclaimed angrily. He twisted to defend himself face-to-face, but the web and condensing gravity at once pulled him back.

"Nobody's else flew out a chute like you. And without a suit! Doubtless I'll never read of it."

"You want to know?" Galvanix suspected he was being drawn out for the benefit of a hidden recorder, but felt suddenly that to resist would concede their combative philosophy. "I'll tell you everything."

He was still talking when the whine of the abrading stratosphere crept in through the vibrating walls. The pilot, who could not possibly hear him, indicated a willingness that Galvanix continue, but the effort of talking against the growing G-force made Galvanix's chest ache as though kicked. Galvanix gestured resignedly, letting the hand fall quickly back.

He blacked out in the subsequent deceleration, awakening only when a concussion jolted up through his spine. A tearing noise filled the cabin as though the undercarriage were being sheared away. The skiff had touched down. Galvanix felt himself flattened once more as the skiff slowed, squealing, and black spots swam before his eyes. Slewing to the left and right, the craft braked hard and came rocking to rest.

Galvanix thought himself deafened, but discovered that two cushioned panels had swung from the couch to clamp his head fast. When they swung back he could hear himself sigh. The crash web snapped free, and Galvanix leaned forward stiffly. He turned to look out the forward window behind him, but the tiny cabin was featureless as a cell.

"Welcome to Earth," the pilot said. Galvanix grinned foolishly. At once the ship trembled. Gurgling sounds ran up the walls, and Galvanix felt his stomach lift slightly, as though he were descending an elevator.

His grin vanished. "What's happening?" he demanded. "We're submerging!"

"Hard to hide that," the pilot allowed. "Surface *is* mostly water. Frightened by depths?" He seemed to find that funny.

Galvanix listened to a series of clanks and rumbles as something took hold of the ship. He couldn't guess how far beneath the surface they were. When a hatch behind them hissed open the pilot was up and through it before Galvanix could twist to look.

"Take care!" the man called through the opening. A uniformed woman descended at once, offering her arm to Galvanix. Shakily he acceded, grasping the rope ladder now dangling through the hatch and wondering if he could climb in one gravity. As soon as he put his foot in the stirrup the rope was pulled swiftly up and he was being helped by several hands into a chair. Lights flashed by overhead as they rolled smoothly forward.

"You are Galvanix Nagashima?" He was in a room with a uniformed man, who looked up from a handscreen he was holding. Blue eyes, European, regarded him with brief curiosity.

"Just Galvanix, born Yuri Nagashima."

The official glanced at his palm. "Yes," he agreed. "How do you feel?"

"Disoriented."

"I'm not surprised. Would you like to be apprised now, or sleep first?"

Galvanix blinked. "Let's talk now."

"I am afraid there isn't much to talk about. As a stateless person, you are in a difficult position. The world is almost at war, and one side does not recognize the civil rights of stateless individuals as defined by Berne protocols. Unwilling to make concessions its enemy does not, the other side has suspended such recognition for the course of the conflict. As a consequence, the legal perquisites that might otherwise be extended to you are largely denied."

Galvanix felt a lump congeal in his stomach. "Just two sides?"

"To a degree, yes, although the allies have by no means identical interests. The annexation of Eldorado will doubtless further polarize matters—or rather, clarify the outlines of the conflict."

"What are the opposing camps' names?"

The official smiled. "Them and Us."

Galvanix said carefully, "I gather that you are not even to tell me into whose hands I have fallen."

"Not now. There seems no reason to deny you that knowledge, but I have not the authority. By this time tomorrow your case will have been reviewed, and things may be different."

"Yet you would like me to provide you with information."

"Indeed, yes. We are not prepared to negotiate for a debriefing, but cooperation can only help your case."

Galvanix was not about to acknowledge himself a "case" before anyone's judgment, but let the point pass. "I'll continue from where I left off in the ship," he said blandly, and did. Halfway through he requested and got tea, and before the questions that followed were finished Galvanix found himself swaying with fatigue.

The official looked again at his screen. "I think you should rest now," he said. Metabolic readouts from a planted sensor? Galvanix was too tired to care. The official nodded to him, then glanced back at his screen and added as if reminded, "Thank you."

Galvanix did not remember the trip to his room, collecting himself only as he stood awkwardly to fall across the enormous bed. He dutifully began to tug at his clothing, then realized that he was already undressed. He let go of consciousness at once.

Soft music woke him, and he lay drowsing a moment, reminded of the satellite bunks of his childhood. After a moment he climbed forth, muscles aching, to look about a large, almost empty room. The chaircart stood next to the bed, with his jumpsuit folded over it, but Galvanix merely leaned against it as he studied the two doors, the bare walls that might extrude dressers or workstations, and a wall stud near the bed labeled *Press for Assistance*. Galvanix did so and was told by a pleasant female voice about the facilities through the nearer door, and asked when he would like breakfast. "Ten minutes?" Galvanix replied, still fuddled.

The shower revived him, and Galvanix returned to the room to see a covered tray roll in. He was musing over porridge and tea when a light above the second door came on with a chime. "Come in," he said, standing.

A dark-skinned young woman entered. Her loose blouse bore insignia at her shoulders. Galvanix wondered if someone had decided that women would elicit a better response from him.

"Good morning, she said. "I'm Yasmin Rajee. I ventured to wake you because it's daybreak here, and you will want to slip onto local time."

"Good morning. What time is it?"

"Five eighteen, almost dawn."

"Dawn?" Galvanix recalled that sunrise took less than a day on Earth.

"Would you like to see it?" she asked. Galvanix stared. "We'll have to hurry."

He followed her out the door, down a corridor he could vaguely recall. Inside an elevator Rajee said, "Fourteen," and the weight settling on Galvanix as the capsule shot up made his knees buckle. "Careful," she said, grabbing his elbow.

The doors slid open onto a puff of cool air with a startling smell. Galvanix stepped out onto a small porch, above which the night sky glowed like a painted dome. A low railing looked over the sea, which ran unbroken from the horizon to plash against bulkheads perhaps ten meters below. Galvanix leaned out, not knowing whether to look down or up.

"That's south," said Rajee. She led him counterclockwise round the curving walkway. Galvanix watched the sky as they bore left, wondering if memorizing the time and position of stars would let him deduce his location.

Rajee, as though suspecting his thoughts, said, "You are on the *Manasa*, an Indian sea-stalk in the Bay of Bengal. Precise latitude and longitude available on the infonet."

"Then I am not to be held incommunicado?"

"I don't know that you are to be held at all. But you must hurry if you wish to partake of the full sunrise."

Before them the eggshell sky was tinted a beautiful cerulean above the horizon, where wisps of cloud shone brilliant white. "Morning over the Andamans," Rajee commented. Galvanix scarcely heard; he was watching the rim of the sky brighten as though something were burning through.

The first rays to break the lip seemed to lance straight at him. A necklace of fiery points lay upon the sea, their beams wavering like searchlights. In a second they melted into a blazing bar, which bulged upward as he watched. Color was pouring into the eastern sky like cream rising through coffee. "Unbelievably fast," Galvanix murmured.

"Comes nearly straight up this close to the equator," Rajee said. "Oh, you mean compared to the Moon?" She laughed.

"The room system is now activated by your voice," Rajee said, looking into the empty teapot. "Ask it for more tea."

Galvanix did so, then inquired about his access to information networks. "There's a funny story there," Rajee said, sitting back in the chaircart. Galvanix was perched on the edge of the bed. "Your flamboyant exit from Eldorado was witnessed by numerous ships in the area. Evidently one of the others also tried a rescue. The takeover itself is international news, and a clip of you being snagged has been seen by perhaps three hundred million people."

Rajee located a button Galvanix had not noticed and reclined the seat back by twenty degrees. "Nobody knew who it was in that suit, of course, and our government felt no obligation to advise the world's press agencies. However, the Grand Files of Eldorado are public information, and downloaded to Earth daily, so the press had a field day rummaging through and coming up with likely candidates. Yesterday they published a list of twenty, including you."

Rajee glowered. "One of their factors was body mass—they based their calculations on a great shot of you being yanked by our towline—but they also assigned far too much weight to the likelihood that the ejectee was a non-citizen. They were *right*, but that doesn't redeem their weak reasoning: they got lucky."

"I came out through a spillpipe attached to a tank at the habitat's center," Galvanix said. "And the lunar colony was quartered up in the low gravity."

Rajee waved that consideration aside. "Two other so-called Lunar Republicans were on the list, and seven hours ago legal counsel for your Lunar Republic—some firm in Stockholm—began hitting us with show-cause motions in the World Court. Worse, it has introduced charges in the commercial courts, claiming that our government must demonstrate that no lunar individual is being held incommunicado or else be deemed guilty of misuse of orbital corridors." Rajee showed in a grimace her opinion of such logic. "One suspects your counsel of complicity with interested parties: they want us to open communication with Eldorado so that all candidates may announce their whereabouts. Eldorado is now under governance of a legal entity of which India is merely a member, and we cannot act on our own."

"But why keep Eldorado cut off?" Galvanix asked.

"Emergency conditions obtain there, as the courts recognize. The Consortiumists merely hope to embarrass us by forcing the release of casualty lists—caused by violent resistance *they* encouraged—that will come out soon anyway."

"People were *killed*," Galvanix said wonderingly.

"That doesn't bother anyone," said Rajee bluntly. "Among twelve billion, international relations are too important to be threatened by skirmishes. We're not in space, where lives are precious. If you had floated out dead nobody would care, but an escapee whisked off is briefly news, at least if the moment was filmed. The Consortiumists naturally hope it will prove somebody embarrassing to us, and I don't think you qualify."

The door opened and another tray rolled in. Rajee lifted the lid of the steaming pot. Galvanix ventured, "The Consortiumists are those signatories charged with improper advance knowledge of Soliton Tunneling?"

Rajee stared. "Don't you know anything?"

"I have been out of touch," Galvanix said pointedly. "All I remember from before the Embargo was that India and Brazil were the major countries calling for revision of the Orbital Consortium."

"The Indo-Brazilian alliance is the axis of opposition to the present economic order, dominated for over a century by the imperialism of the first nations to industrialize. I am amazed that you people, professing statehood within a land you don't own, cannot understand."

"You do oppose our existence," Galvanix said.

"We oppose the dominance of space's natural resources by a few super industrialized powers." Rajee cried. "The air of Venus will invigorate the solar system—there is little elsewhere beyond Earth. The cartels and superpowers squabble among themselves, but present a united front against those nations who cannot"—she struggled for the right word—"*belly up* to their card game."

Galvanix served the tea. As Rajee sipped moodily, he asked, "So what of my own disposition? Will your government acknowledge my presence here?

"You are a stateless person displaced in wartime. You could legally be interned, but kinder arrangements will probably be made. But you have no place you *want* to go, have you? Back to Eldorado? Nippon, maybe?" Rajee saw her answer in his expression and smiled. "We are giving you refuge, please allow the legalities to work themselves out."

Galvanix thought about this after she left. He asked the room system to give him access to the infonet, and was surprised when a console promptly unfolded from the wall. Sitting on the bed with the keyboard in his lap, Galvanix asked for a map showing their location, news summaries of the last twelve hours, and access to an outside line (denied). The wall screen showed a fast-action film of the spinning Eldorado being approached and boarded, other ships gathering like bystanders; then a crisply edited sequence, assembled from various angles, of a rag-doll figure being spat forth like a seed. Galvanix watched the tumbling form with mortification, wincing when a gripper line snatched its ankle and pulled.

He tried to reconstruct when he was brought here, but could not determine transit times. Plainly he had slept less than eight hours, for fatigue now assaulted him in waves. Galvanix set aside the keyboard, thinking it unseemly to sleep, and woke when the chime sounded. He struggled up from the sideways position into which he had slid as Rajee strode in.

"Still on lunar time? We're going to the mainland."

Galvanix slid his feet to the floor and sat up groggily. "Right now?" he asked. "You give me no notice."

"Why, you've got luggage?" she said nastily. Galvanix followed her out without a word.

The corridor was crowded now, mostly with Indian or oriental workers. One man looked from Rajee's shoulder insignia to Galvanix, his eyes widening in surmise. Rajee bundled him into another elevator, saying "Top, override," as the door closed behind them. Its other occupant, a young woman in technician's overalls with a caste mark on her brow, looked at them in dismay as the elevator climbed past her destination.

Industrial fumes struck them as the door opened, petrochemical vapors and a tang Galvanix remembered was hydraulic fluid. Rajee led him swiftly across what looked like a flight hangar, crowded with technicians and robots and snaking cables. Galvanix looked up at the high ceiling, which echoed with the sounds of machine work about him, but Rajee hurried him on as though disapproving of his curiosity.

"In here," she said, approaching a small aircraft. Galvanix stared; the plane was less than six meters long, and its fuselage was scarcely wider than a sarcophagus. A square set in the open hatch was the only window visible.

Rajee must have felt Galvanix's muscles tightening, because she immediately urged him forward. "It's a short hop to Madras," she said impatiently, as a flight technician began guiding his feet into the hatch.

"Why not just send me on the next boat?" asked Galvanix, whose dawning horror of flying in a robot ultralight was two-fold.

"We've got to produce you immediately," she said as Galvanix settled into the upholstered niche. "Consider it a victory." She nodded to the technician, and the hatch slammed shut.

A voice immediately began explaining takeoff procedure. The ultralight would be hurled off the top of the building on a centrifugal sling, which would whip it around twenty-eight times until the craft reached launch velocity and was released. Powered flight would then commence. Galvanix would, the voice assured, feel no dizziness, merely a pleasant sense of being pressed into his couch. The voice continued but Galvanix heard little, for the craft had begun to move, and his mind went promptly blank.

Acceleration settled and deepened, although the accompanying whine remained constant. Galvanix saw only an unbroken field of blue, though its brightness flickered with, he realized, each passage near the sun. Numbly he began counting, and was up to twenty-one when the pressure suddenly vanished, casting him into a second of silent free fall before engines roared around him and the aircraft lifted in flight.

The craft sailed for three hours, a figure Galvanix was able to check against the only display visible in his confinement, a timepiece set in the hatch frame. High rills of cloud sailed past, and at one point the plane was enveloped in white as it climbed through some stratum of cumulus.

The system never spoke again—Galvanix realized that it was not responsive at all, just a recording played at the outset of each flight—and he realized the plane was descending only when it banked, showing a limb of horizon glinting with buildings. Galvanix composed himself, breathed deeply when the engine suddenly ceased, and saw the sun vanish behind a hangar ceiling a second before touchdown.

Indistinct figures moved past the window. The hatch popped open, and stifling heat poured over him like bathwater. He was being helped out by hands brown as cinnamon, and the sodden air held a dozen odors: machinery, sweat, unrecognizable others. A severely uniformed man stood at attention before him as Galvanix wobbled briefly on his feet.

"Galvanix né Nagashima, Yuri?"

"Well, yes."

The man seemed to find his duty distasteful. "Please follow me."

They walked across the hangar floor, Galvanix stumbling and being at once supported by men beside him. He expected to be conducted indoors, but was led instead toward a gleaming silver cube the size of a small room.

"This is a Berenger-Nixit," said the officer sourly. "Within you may receive secure calls."

A short man wearing African robes was standing by the cube, which Galvanix realized was not quite touching the ground. "Comrade Galvanix? I am Robert Mbulu, from Nixit. Your representatives have arranged for your access to our communications facilities." He gestured toward a tall object beside him, which resembled a rolling doorframe. "First, of course, we must assure that no listening devices have been concealed on your person."

"That is not necessary," Galvanix told him. "I have nothing to hide from anyone."

The representative looked hurt. "Please, sir, our service would not be complete without this. I would have to ask that you sign a document certifying that you declined this protection."

"Oh, that is not necessary." Galvanix was embarrassed to have interfered with someone doing his job. Relieved, the Nixit representative rolled the doorframe over Galvanix several times from different angles, then placed it against one wall of the cube.

"Simply step through," he said. Galvanix could see a faint rectangular outline in the silver face. Resolutely he plunged through the veil, which gave like a thin film, then broke and slithered over him.

The Nixit's interior was a soft-lit den with a contoured seat in the center. A lacquered sideboard lined one wall, set out with a teapot, coffee urn and crystal decanter. Facing the chair was a large screen upon which the words *Call for Galvanix* shone in Japanese and English.

Galvanix settled into the upholstered chair, staring at the message as though its elegant typeface held further meaning. He felt for the row of studs on the chair's right arm, and tapped Proceed.

"One moment, please," said an unaccented voice. The screen flickered, then was replaced by the image of a young European.

"Galvanix? This is Emil Einbach in Stockholm. I am a partner at Lee, Schlossel, which represents the Lunar Republic on Earth."

"How do you do," Galvanix said. "I must thank you for delivering me from captivity."

Einbach smiled. "You must credit your hosts' incompetence for that. Had they shipped you to a Geodite habitat we could have done nothing, but hustling you down in that blatant manner brought attention. Lots of innocent people are needlessly detained in this mess, but abducting a hapless Moonie before cameras and then refusing to identify him was foolish. They might have handled it better if it hadn't broken during the night—senior officials were asleep, audiences in this hemisphere were not. Anyway. You are well?"

"Yes. Am I then free to go?"

"Perhaps not, but travel restrictions are less onerous than captivity. I shall know in a few hours. Meanwhile, a few points." Einbach looked down at his notes. "You are listed in the World Registry under your preferred name, Galvanix. You already had an ID number: your parents were still Japanese citizens when you were born, and a number was reserved for you. These numbers are never retired. I've got it here—" A string of twelve digits appeared at the bottom of the screen.

"I am establishing a credit account for you, from a fund for the use of distressed Republicans on Earth. India is not one of the wealthy nations, and I would recommend you get an ID card for dealing with vendors or officials lacking thumbreaders. The request has been processed, and you can pick up your card at any Registry office."

"Thank you. Will the card list me as Lunar citizen?"

"I'm afraid not. Various restrictions will probably be imposed by the Indian government, which we are negotiating. May I assume we are empowered to act on your behalf?"

"Of course," said Galvanix politely.

"Thank you. We have agreed that you return to the *Manasa*, at least pending other arrangements. There is some question as to whether your movement is not covered by the articles of the Embargo."

"That's nonsense. My colleagues on Eldorado were not interned, merely prevented from returning to the Moon."

Einbach nodded. "It's not much of an argument, but there must be a hearing. In the meantime, the press will be kept from you—like many poor countries. India maintains restrictions on information flow. You shall of course have free access to your counsel, on secure channels if you wish it."

"Please, that isn't necessary. They flew me here in a single-passenger plane, a monstrous waste of energy."

"As you prefer. You will also be granted access to the *Manasa*'s library, a fundamental dignity. You will have the right to make international calls, although I wouldn't try to reach a news agency. . . . Also, watch the charges. The Indian Development Corporation sets its own line rates, and may want to discourage you."

They talked for half an hour, discussing plans for eventual settlement and work. Einbach was not optimistic that the Embargo would be lifted soon. Galvanix concluded the call feeling morose, and was studying the teapot beside him when a flicker caused him to turn back. A line of print was once more on the screen. *Call for Galvanix.*

Galvanix touched a stud. "Who is calling?"

A second line appeared: *Hiroko Nagashima.*

Galvanix sat still. He thought of distant relatives from Nippon seeing his name and calling, but he did not believe it. Possibly the Earth system did not distinguish between calls from people and messages left for pickup, though that seemed scarcely likely.

He touched another stud, keeping the screen dark. "This is Galvanix."

The first syllable burned like liquid oxygen. "Yuri, this is Hiro."

He tried to summon anger, but undercurrents swamped the effort. "My sister Hiro is dead. You have got her voice perfectly." His own voice cracked on the last word.

"Yuri, let me see you."

Galvanix hesitated only a second. The Nixit of course had the capacity to show callers without revealing its client, but Galvanix would never use it. He touched a stud, and the screen swam into life.

Hiroko's image looked out at him from a blackness without depth or texture. She was older, face lined with the wear of the chronically ill. Her hair was pulled tight behind her head.

Galvanix stared for a few seconds, then found words. "That is a computer construct."

"It is not the camera image of a physical object, but is real nonetheless. I *am* here, Yuri, in the sense that matters."

"Hiro died, in the sense that matters."

"Did you get my message on Eldorado? I almost told you then. Have you guessed?"

Her eyes searched his expression as awareness dawned. "Yes, you understand now. They made a *copy* of me, took my mind apart and transcribed its workings. A terrible science, which men have sought for over a century, like eternal life. They still cannot do it effectively without peeling away the brain in ten thousand slices, and it's illegal. But my case was exempted, in one country, because I was stateless and dying and willing, and they wanted badly to know how a new method worked." She moved her head slightly. "And so that is here, which otherwise would not be."

"You are . . ." Galvanix thought and spoke again. "How are you?"

"You're thinking it's not really me, aren't you? Well, it *feels* like me. Believe me, Yuri, that's what matters."

"No, of course, I'm sorry." Tears of shame and grief blurred his vision. "Hiro, what can I do?"

"For me? Nothing. I am here for *you*."

Galvanix wiped his eyes and looked at her. "I don't understand."

She smiled. "Let me describe myself. I am a complex of semiautonomous systems, nearly all of which must operate together to produce consciousness. My keepers—they do not like being called that—often activate these in conjunction with other systems they have developed. I sometimes retain the faintest memories of these sessions, as if from dreams. When I am conscious, I see, hear, and feel as a human does, else I would soon cease acting like one."

Galvanix gestured toward the screen. "What, then, is this?"

"You are seeing my self-image, which corresponds to projec-

tions of how I would look if living. It is not my own confec-
tion—" Here she smiled and turned her head in a manner that
stopped Galvanix's breath. "I would quickly become a monster if
my self-image bent to my will."

"Not you." Galvanix shook his head. "Never."

"Poor Yuri, you think people prettier than they are. I dwell too
much on myself. It is ugly, but remains that pit into which we are
flawed to fall. You shall save me from that."

Galvanix looked up. "How?"

"By taking what I have to offer. Listen. Funds are available to
you, much of it in a trust account that Emil Einbach administers,
but I have kept some of it floating. You can call me, or leave a
message for me, just like a living person. Here's the number. I
know Earth—my incorporeal state has its advantages—and can
help you. You may be here for a long time."

"And where are you?"

"I cannot tell you that. I have been treated fairly, and will keep
my promises. Later, perhaps, there is something you can do for
me. For now simply go, stay out of trouble, try to do good. You
have a long life to live."

"Hiroko—" Alarm strained his voice lest she click off, but the
face waited patiently. "What . . . will become of you?"

"I will continue. We can speak of this another time, but now
you should address your affairs." She would not break the call,
but her expression told him it was time. His heart swelling against
his throat, Galvanix bade her farewell, then touched the breakoff
stud.

A slip of paper curled like a shaving from a slot below the
screen. Galvanix pulled it free; it gave his ID number and, a few
lines below, Hiroko's. He memorized them with a glance and
dropped the slip into the waste chute, where it vanished in a puff.

The security man was glowering when Galvanix emerged.
"You received two calls," he accused.

Galvanix shrugged. The Nixit representative inquired if everything was satisfactory. Absently Galvanix turned to say that it
was, blinking as the security man stepped between them. "You
will please follow me."

They walked toward the hangar's near wall, an enormous
facade like the side of a building, this time unaccompanied by
guards.

The officer seemed disinclined to speak, and after a moment Galvanix asked where they were going. "You will return to *Manasa* on the thrice-weekly steamer tomorrow," the man replied, then added, "Now that the world is assured we are not mistreating you, there is no reason to waste resources flying you."

"Of course not. Will I be billeted, or may I travel freely?"

"Did your European lawyer not give you money? Must you rely on our government for all things?"

Galvanix wondered how his case had sufficed to humiliate this man. "Thank you," he said. It occurred to him that he was in a kind of shock. "When does the flight leave?"

"Eighteen ten," the officer replied crisply. "Be early. The system will admit you."

They came to a large door, which hissed open at the officer's touch. It led not outside, as Galvanix had supposed, but into a long corridor. He realized then that the immense hangar was carved into the side of some building.

They entered an elevator and rode down. The initial drop eased the strain on his knees, and Galvanix broke into a smile. The officer looked at him curiously.

"Is Madras a large city?" Galvanix asked him.

"Ten million." It was clearly an ignorant question, even for a Moonie.

"And where do we go now?"

"I am escorting you out of our building."

The humidity struck him like a sweaty palm, one accustomed to long commerce with spices and oils, hot asphalt, decaying vegetation and, strangely for the sodden air, brick dust. A shimmering plaza stretched before him, busy with travelers and carts bearing luggage, many of them driven by short-trousered cyclists.

Galvanix stepped out blinking, inhaling only reluctantly. Morning sunlight glowered through clouds that threatened storms, but the weather was almost impossibly hot for the hour. Galvanix was disquieted by the sun's rapid ascent, and wondered how hot it would be by afternoon.

He followed a footpath for several hundred meters, taking turns at random. The signs, which were in English and an unfamiliar alphabet, suggested he was at an air terminal, in Meenambakkam.

Speakers set in tiny kiosks gave answers in any language, but the questioner first had to insert a card.

Eventually he saw the logo overhead that designated international agencies, and followed an arrow to a high-ceilinged concourse, large enough to have served an Imperial rail station two hundred years before. A single sign announced the International Registry, and it topped a machine booth. A queue of unmoving petitioners stretched across the great floor, and Galvanix joined it with a sigh.

The afternoon passed slowly as the line crept forward. Galvanix found that he could not stand in the Earth gravity for long periods, but his fellow supplicants had long since settled silently on the warm tiles. A boy wearing dirty robes came by selling what looked like water from a plastic sack. But Galvanix, though the only non-Indian in queue, had no money, much to the child's disgust.

As he sat, Galvanix worked patiently to order his last experiences into a sequence he could assimilate. He remembered with a small start his pocket recorder, left behind in his room in Eldorado. Doubtless some occupying agent would soon play its contents, studying his narrative for possible strategic value. Galvanix wondered briefly whether he would be able to acquire another recorder on Earth; the torpor about him seemed to mock the possibility of narrative.

Despite his hours in which to frame a strategy for dealing with the Registry box, Galvanix thought of nothing but of giving his name and accepting what came. If authorization for a card had been granted, he would presumably be issued a card, or told what queue to join to seek it.

The sun was slanting through the high narrow windows of a different wall when Galvanix's turn came. He remained standing when the man in front of him had advanced to the booth, but the man's case took twenty minutes, and Galvanix was aching when he finally stepped forward.

The booth was simply a screen and keyboard, with partitions on either side for privacy. The screen read *Enter Identification Number* between two lines in different scripts. The keyboard bore three different alphabets, depending on the angle of vision, and Galvanix tapped out his number.

Full Name GALVANIX? the screen asked.

Surprised, he tapped an assent. The screen instructed him to press his right thumb against a glowing keyboard square, then to look at a blue point at screen's center. Bemused, Galvanix complied, staring straight ahead as a series of peripheral lights swept over him. After several seconds they vanished, and the monitor beeped once. Galvanix looked down to see a card emerge.

It was pale blue, with his name printed beneath a holographic likeness that hovered, it seemed, a centimeter above its surface. His features looked drawn and disheveled, his hair awry.

As Galvanix studied the likeness, the machine beeped again. He looked down to see a second card protruding from the slot. He pulled it forth with sudden foreboding, and found the identical image on another pale blue card. *Yuri Nagamaro*, it read.

Galvanix held the two cards with a palpable sense of their wrongness. Uneasily he glanced behind him, but nobody seemed to have heard the second beep; the man behind him glanced up from his cross-legged repose only to see if Galvanix had finished. Galvanix looked back at the screen, which was once more asking the supplicant's identification number. With a sudden resolve he concealed both cards in one hand and left the booth.

No voice challenged him as he crossed the enormous floor; no broadcast beep or alarm signaled error. Galvanix put one card in his pocket, walked twenty meters, slipped the second in another. He passed through an open door, and an exhalation of moist wind licked over him.

Cyclists at once offered him passage, which Galvanix declined. He began limping across the plaza, wincing as the pavement seemed to strike him through his soles. A few enterprising pedalers, seeing his distress, coasted alongside him, urging that he take refuge in their conveyances. Galvanix shook his head, spread his hands apologetically, then pulled out one of the ID cards and waved it to show he had no cash. The nearest cyclist, an ageless man in an exotic wide-brimmed hat, grinned and cried, "No problem!" Galvanix realized with tired mortification that of course most urban Indians would speak English, at least in the transport trade. He settled gratefully into the narrow seat, and was promptly taken to a bank booth.

Galvanix climbed out painfully and studied the machine. The card he held was the Nagamaro one, and with a shrug he inserted it and pressed his thumb to the plate. The screen immediately gave the card's name, number and credit balance. The figure was meaningless to him, but he requested the largest amount the machine would give.

"And now, where would you like to go?" his driver asked.

"Tea."

They wheeled onto a thoroughfare crowded with bicycles, pedicabs, and small motorized vehicles, which were going no faster in the crush than anything else. Aircraft roared overhead, sometimes quite low. Galvanix realized after several minutes that he was being taken away from the airport, either owing to its inadequate teahouses or in order to inflate his fare.

The hangars quickly gave way to an industrial quarter which, unbroken by airfields, was even more crowded. Large trucks frequently blocked the street, and the cabs would stream like detouring ants onto the sidewalk. It was during one such delay that the lowering clouds, as though punctured once too often by climbing or descending planes, suddenly broke into a torrent. Warm rain fell in sheets, and the street was soon streaming.

"May monsoon," said the driver. "Not too bad yet."

The cafe was situated beside a loading dock, its tiny tables and chairs crowding onto the sidewalk beneath an awning that poured water in a wavering curtain. Behind it customers regarded the downpour languidly.

Galvanix splashed through a coursing gutter before reaching safety, soaking his shoes in alarmingly foul water. The cab fare came to about a thousandth of his cash on hand, suggesting he had an adequate sum. He settled, dripping, at a table, and saw the man at the next table smile.

"The monsoons used to be as regular as clockwork," The man shrugged as though at the folly of hoping for such order in the modern age. He was dressed well, and had middle-aged features that seemed neither Indian nor oriental, perhaps Malaysian.

Galvanix nodded politely. "I am surprised the drivers didn't check the weather forecasts."

"But why? They must seek fares whether it rains or not. You are just from the airport?"

Galvanix assented, then introduced himself cautiously as Yuri Nagamaro. He realized his ignorance would mark him as a newly arrived traveler, though without luggage or destination.

"Edward Tamani." The man bowed his head in greeting. "Your accent, it is unusual. You are perhaps Canadian?"

"I'm from the Moon," Galvanix said. The man laughed delightedly.

"Madras is fortunate to be a coastal city, also unfortunate for the same reason. It is your first look at India, correct? Coastal cities are richer than the villages, but the poorest villagers flock here."

Galvanix was watching the water rushing past the gutter near his foot, carrying offal and vegetable waste. "Is there no drainage system?"

"Why, drainage where? The highest point in Madras is eight meters above sea level. When the sea began rising in the thirties the streets were slowly inundated; this quarter had old buildings with water lines a meter high. Of course people adapted—you have seen pictures of the floating walkways and street skiffs—but when it flooded the poor drowned in great numbers." Tamani gestured in one direction. "The waters will be pumped over the seawalls, but that cannot start until the rains cease."

"Why do they not build underground?"

"Why, they do, though the poor have such terror of drowning that the structures are only used by the desperate, who are many." Tamani pointed across the street. "Those better off crowd the bustees."

"The what?" Galvanix turned in his seat. An immense block of a building, which he had taken for a factory, was swarming with people along its exposed side. Scaffolding covered it like a trellis, and adults and children, clothes hanging wetly, scrambled across its face to vanish into tiny openings.

Galvanix stared. "What is going on?"

"The bustees are very old. These high-rise models are newer—Indonesia built them for a large thika tenant about fifty years ago, who rents the ground they rest on and lets out their hundreds of units. Those people are Madras' working poor: they cannot afford the kothabari, where families can keep an entire room to themselves, but neither do they sleep on the pavement. A few years ago a thika tenant failed to reach terms with his landowner for a new lease, and moved an entire bustee upriver to a cheaper site. Over a thousand dwellers trailed after it with their belongings in their arms."

"This is monstrous."

Tamani seemed unperturbed. "India is a crowded country. There is more housing in Madras than ever in its history, but people keep pouring in. Many of those climbers are factory hands, but most work in the marine industry, fishers or algae-sweeps. They do tasks performed only by machines in the West, but it's cheaper here to hire workers, who have nothing else."

Galvanix had an insight. "Is that why there are so many foreigners here—to batten upon wages depressed by poverty?"

The man smiled, unoffended. "Indeed, but how else shall India prevail? My company buys jute from two textile mills here; our interest raises the price. Besides, the problem is India. The soil is poor and subject to erosion, and crops are often flooded or parched. There is industry and great ocean development, but forever too many mouths."

A waitress appeared and Galvanix ordered tea. She asked something, not in English. "*Chai*," said Galvanix, feeling panic. He ventured a sentence in Japanese, but the woman looked blank.

Tamani spoke up, explaining suavely to her evident satisfaction. "Pardon me," he said to Galvanix after she withdrew, "but she wished to know the kind of tea. I took the liberty of specifying their better brand."

"Thank you." Galvanix was acutely embarrassed.

"If you do not know Tamil or Hindi, you should buy a translator. A small model can put both into English and costs very little."

"Thank you, perhaps I will. But are people not offended by those things?"

"Indians? They worship such engines. No, I am serious. Their Hinduism accommodates thousands of gods, and the commonfolk can fit all the modern world into this ample scheme. When appliances first reached middle-class households in the twentieth century, Indian women began praying to a new divinity, Santoshi Mata, who could facilitate the acquisition of a radio or refrigerator. The nanomachines that work in their fields are revered as an aspect of Dasra Asvin, an old fertility god. Educated people incline to a more sophisticated version, but there's no orthodoxy; all is an aspect of Brahman, and the arrangement of details is left to local tradition."

"That is certainly unlike Western beliefs," said Galvanix cautiously, hoping he had not chanced onto a regional enmity.

"I do not criticize merely because I myself follow the way of Allah. But such indifference to doctrine accompanies a lassitude toward all progress. The commonfolk still tolerate appalling injustices, because to them social evils are merely steps on the pathway to *moksha*. How can you help people who think the wretchedness of their poor is divinely appointed?"

"Moksha?"

"Absorption into the One; release from the wheel of rebirth."

Galvanix's teapot arrived, steaming as his sodden clothing steamed. Edward Tamani paid his bill and politely bade Galvanix good day, disappearing into a cab he hailed with a pocket device.

By the time Galvanix finished his tea the rain had ceased, although no sun appeared. The gutters ran on with undiminished force, and cabs crowded the higher ground in the middle of the lane. Deciding his saturated shoes would not dry anyway, Galvanix counted out the same sum he had seen Tamani leave and set out on foot. He headed in the direction where Tamani had indicated the seawalls lay.

Rainwater coursed through an intersection like a freshet, its eddies already filmed with scum. Men stood shirtless on the sidewalk, wringing out blouses and the edges of their dhotis or pajamas, while women huddled in dripping chadors, uselessly flapping their trailing ends. Despite the slowness of the traffic, a cab or van would occasionally muster the speed to launch a spray of water across the sidewalk, soaking pedestrians.

Galvanix walked past another bustee, looking like a plastic honeycomb with its grid of close-set doors. Children hung from the scaffold like monkeys, the lower ones staring into his eyes as he passed. From the ground level came the smells of smoke, stale cooking oils, wet clothing.

Late afternoon darkened quickly in the overcast shadows of the large buildings. Galvanix waited for municipal lights to come on. Cab traffic had subsided to a single lane, and Galvanix had forgotten about it when a pedicab driver pulled abreast and called, "Ho! Want to go downtown?"

"I am walking, thank you."

"No, unsafe for foreigner. Bad quarter." The cab was keeping pace with him, pulling closer to the curb to let traffic pass. "Rob you." Galvanix turned to look at the driver, who vigorously mimed some form of violence. He was a young man in khaki shorts, pedaling through water nearly up to his axle. Galvanix realized with a start that the man was several years younger than he.

"Can you take me to a store? I want to buy a translator."

"No problem. Whole street, nothing but stores."

Galvanix climbed in. The cab took him to a plaza of brightly lit storefronts, which resembled the commercial district of any city in the world. He wandered through air-conditioned aisles until his clothes were dry, then bought a simple translator which one held like a long-stemmed flower.

"Map?" he asked of a street display on a wall. The map answered his questions in Raj-accented English, illuminating streets in illustration. Galvanix took a series of descending staircases beneath street level, where a rail system sped him east. He emerged to the smell of the sea, invisible beyond walls now hidden by darkness.

Galvanix listened for breakers, but the roar of machinery drowned even the sound of his footsteps. Light spilled from the windows of block-long buildings, dancing with motes agitated by the ceaseless engines that conveyed and processed the ocean's yield. A long blast cut through the wall of sound, the horn of a ship piloted, evidently, by fallible humans instead of machines. A work gang passed him on the sidewalk, identifiable by the men's identically spattered clothes and loud camaraderie.

A fusion plant was half a kilometer up the street, Galvanix remembered from the map, and a long stretch of seawall whose top was open to sightseeing. The map recommended tourists avoid both sites after dark. Shipyards and food foundries ran day and night, and Galvanix realized that thousands of men were working behind the high walls ridging the street.

He walked an hour along the waterfront, passing tiny restaurants set between massive facades where vendors sold food for customers to eat elsewhere. There were few cabs; the street rumbled with enormous trucks, great jointed beasts that angled out of loading docks and pounded past like behemoths. One block was full of loitering workers: a shift was ending, or a dinner break called.

The darkness prevented Galvanix from noticing detail, and it was some time before he realized that the neighborhood had changed. Families slept on the sidewalks, which were sometimes flooded from blocked gutters. Buildings were smaller, and the noise level had fallen. Few of the people he passed looked up, but Galvanix met the eyes of a girl sitting up among huddled sleepers, and saw her startled expression.

He realized that only the respite of night saved him from the attentions of beggars. He remembered with a start those children, mutilated so as to compel alms from appalled Westerners, still seen in the septic lesion of Calcutta. The sleeping forms about him seemed whole, though he did not pause to examine them as he picked his way across the increasingly uneven and littered lanes. As he stepped past one family a woman drew in her leg suddenly, disturbing a cloud of flies that quickly resettled over her.

Wandering freely, Galvanix no longer troubled to keep track of what street he was on. When he saw a line of red lights rising into the sky, he remembered the Madras Tower, a tourist site overlooking the harbor which the map had shown. Content to have a polestar, Galvanix kept the tower before him, arriving some hours later at its darkened plaza, where he rode a tiny transparent elevator up sixty stories for a hundred-rupee coin. The city of Madras bent round its harbor, then spread west and south to the horizon, brilliant and dark regions alternating in a patchwork of abjection. This is the world, he thought. The Moon is the next world, maybe. But this.

On the edge of the plaza he found a phone booth and slipped quietly into it, keeping the door ajar and the light off. The phone refused to accept cash for a foreign call, perhaps in order to record the user's identity. Galvanix took out the Nagamaro card and called Hiroko.

The booth signaled connection, but the screen remained blank. An artificial voice said, "Good evening, Yuri."

"Hiroko? You sound different."

"I am different. I am presently incorporating a good deal of additional cognitive ware, and 'Hiroko' is subsumed. That part of me you know as Hiroko cannot be reconstituted to speak to you without being pulled from projects in progress, which would be disruptive. Be assured that I encompass all she is, or knows."

Galvanix was disoriented. "I need information. Can you speak?"

"Yes. A more innocuous version of this call shall be recorded by the Indian security forces. Hiroko could not pull that trick, nor could I against the systems of a richer government. Speak freely."

Galvanix closed his eyes, took a breath. "Explain Yuri Nagamaro."

"Why, you are he. His number is one reserved for you by the Registry, before it learned that Nagamaro and the Yuri Nagashima it had registered at birth were the same. Nagamaro is the name you took on marrying Rona Tsujimaro, should anyone ask. It is regrettable that the Embargo has prevented the Indian government from learning that fact, for they do not know under what name to seek you. You, of course, cannot be held accountable for this, even if they were to search you and find both cards. They were after all issued in response to your innocent application; you knew too little of Earthly legalities to appreciate that one must be surrendered."

"You can roam freely through the World Registry?"

"Not at all. I cannot invent ID numbers, but a second had been set aside for you. I cannot invent names, but the Embargo has kept the Registry ignorant of Republicans' marriage status. True Registry fraud is exceedingly difficult and soon discovered; only your unusual circumstances allowed this opening."

"You act as though you expect me to turn criminal or revolutionist."

"Your sister acted to preserve your range of options. Did you in fact marry Rona?"

"No." Galvanix felt a pang.

"Hiroko would say you should. She has maintained sophic integrity only in order to help you on Earth. Her belief that your and Rona's love can survive your immaturity is very strong."

"What is sophic—never mind. Listen: I need advice. I want to escape."

"Are you under legal restraint?"

"No, but they expect me to take tomorrow's boat back to the *Manasa*. I am resolved to resist these curbs on my movement. Everyone wants to hold me in case I prove useful in their battles, though they know I am not."

The voice did not pause before answering. "You would have done better to run at once; it is now only eleven hours before they miss you. There are few places you can reach in that time, even with the Nagamaro ID, where they cannot track you."

"Name one such place."

"*Manasa* itself."

"I beg your pardon?"

"Take the morning flight to *Manasa*. You will arrive before the steamer departs and you are missed. Security will assume you have fled inland or hidden in the city. They will not look where they sought to take you."

The plan's audacity dazzled him. "I will do it."

"If you call Hiroko, be circumspect. She cannot block surveillance, nor act decisively to protect her interests. Despite her expanded capacities, she remains almost as squeamish as you."

ELEVEN

Dawn found Galvanix on a broad boulevard, where he waved down a cab for the airport. The passenger terminals were filled with shops that never closed, and Galvanix thought suddenly to buy a piece of luggage, which he filled with two changes of clothes. A newsfax machine flashed something about the Moon, and he bought a copy without looking at it, wary of curious eyes.

The woman operating the ticket booth made no comment as Galvanix purchased passage for *Manasa* on a cross-Bay flight less than an hour off. He boarded a plane that was nearly full, its engines idling while passengers debarked and their places quickly filled. Galvanix found himself sitting next to a dark-skinned man in his early twenties, who introduced himself as Vikram Jayakar, a student. "And what takes you to *Manasa*?" he inquired pleasantly.

"How do you know I am bound there?"

The boy lifted his eyebrows. "You do not know Air India," he remarked.

The plane lifted uneventfully, its acceleration negligible by space standards. Over breakfast served in boxes, Jayakar attempted to engage in conversation, which Galvanix could not politely rebuff. The relaxed traveler did not seem to notice Galvanix's tension, but could hardly miss his unworldliness, and Galvanix readily admitted that he was from off-world. Jayakar, suitably impressed, evidently did not discriminate between the habitats sufficiently to ask which one, nor consider that Galvanix might be a Moonie.

"There are great strains in the heavens and Earth," he remarked. "It seems important, but is not. What use are those airs and earths—it was decided fifty years ago that the large importation of natural resources from space would disrupt the environment. Those organic elements can only make soil for spacemen, who never starve anyway."

Galvanix was surprised by such parochialism, and said so.

"Even if you see nothing valuable in the creation of new worlds, you cannot deny the importance of space industry to Earth."

Jayakar shrugged. "The space habitats once beamed down power, then provided the long strands that allow us to tap the Earth's core. Such fulsome energies produce excess heat in the world, which must be bled back into space with vanes that puncture the sky. Meanwhile the sun beats down: there is energy enough, unless you wish all the world to live as profligately as the West."

"But it is your government that has joined the assault upon the Orbital Consortium, which was humanity's united endeavor to develop space peacefully."

"Those resources are wealth to many, and India is poor. Why should the powerful nations be permitted to cheat us? The West developed its technologies after colonizing the weaker countries, India as much as any."

Galvanix was not prepared to dispute this. "This conflict does not fall between East and West."

"That is true; there are not two sides but a hundred. But their positions on the Consortium issue align themselves between two poles. And what, may I ask, is yours?"

"I despise the conflict," said Galvanix vehemently, "and respect no side. I think the Moon should be allowed to develop as the world it has become."

"A Republicanist!" Jayakar cried, delighted. "I am sure your government would gape at your application for emigration to that stubborn tribe, had the Embargo not prevented such exile." And the young man bit into his orange with zest.

The seat back in front of him unfolded into a tiny console, and Galvanix ranged idly through the ship's data system, which did not offer news but contained an encyclopedia. He read through the entry for *sophia*, then requested the one for *moksha*. Beneath the definition were listed over a dozen instances of its use; most were from ancient scriptures or modern texts, but one fell between the two, dated 1914. Curious, Galvanix brought it up.

"The real secret of life seems to consist in so living in the world as it is, without being attached to it, that *moksha* might become easy of attainment to us and to others. This will include service of self, the family, the community, and the State." Mohandas Gandhi, letter to his family.

Galvanix noticed that Jayakar was watching him. "What do you think of that?" he asked.

Jayakar read it. "Gibberish," he said. "Gandhi was being pulled in a dozen directions at once: to India, to the Imperial England he served, to the Indians in South Africa he lived with. Service of the State indeed! The good Indian knows no state beyond caste, and no duty to the *moksha* of others. Gandhi's thought grew a lot simpler after he had been back in India a few years."

"It sounds very good to me," Galvanix said.

"You are not Indian."

An hour later the intercom above their seats announced their approach to *Manasa*. "But we have not begun our descent," said Galvanix, looking out the window at the distant floor of clouds.

Jayakar smiled. "The entire plane is not landing, only these eight seats. Do you think we waste fuel in India?"

Galvanix looked at him in alarm, but Jayakar only pointed to the panel on the seat-back before them, which was flashing its request that both men fasten their crash webbing.

A soothing voice was explaining that the *Manasa*-bound section would detach and land separately. Galvanix wondered in dull panic why he had thought otherwise; something from old films suggesting that passenger planes landed intact, like birds. "Actually, my people despise waste," he said in a choked voice.

Think of it as a spacecraft, he told himself, only slower. He closed his eyes against the countdown display, but found himself counting along mentally, and steeled himself for a greater kick than the jettison actually brought. Within seconds they were in free fall, which Galvanix would have enjoyed if he hadn't known it meant uncontrolled plummet. At the jolt of chute deployment he shouted relief.

They splashed down within sight of *Manasa*, a slender grey tower rising two hundred meters above the sea. Waves bobbed and splashed against the windows, and Jayakar led the passengers through the hatch at the top, where they watched the approaching tug through the wind-shredded spray. Behind them, the sodden parachute spread on the water like an algae bloom, a dry pleat still flapping stubbornly.

"In the United States," said Jayakar, "the passenger pods are steered into inertial towers, like peas down a pipe. The pods are slowed by magnetic resistance and their kinetic energy recovered. We can't do that here: too complex."

If Jayakar was suggesting a possible area for further redistribution of technology, his point was lost on Galvanix, who was staring at the sea-stalk in fascination. The *Manasa* rose three kilometers from the ocean floor, where crawling robots collected manganese nodules or drilled for chrome and copper. Oreboats surrounded the tower like bees round a flower.

"Is it *Manasa* or *the Manasa*?" asked Galvanix as the new arrivals trooped across a high-windowed gallery overlooking the sea.

"Is it a ship or a city?" Jayakar replied. "Not every Asian language shares Europe's concern for definite articles."

At the polite insistence of a *Manasa* official they were taken on a brief tour of the structure, filing past capillaries where seawater was desalinized, a scale model of the sea-stalk that turned transparent to reveal its design, great portholes swarming with fishes. An exhibit illustrating the history of Man Outside His Environment offered standing ranks of underwater and space suits ranged like an armored brigade. Galvanix stared at a bulky Moon suit from the last century, consigned to an eternity in museums like some plated fossil.

Galvanix and Jayakar stood together in the queue for rooms, so were placed in adjacent quarters. Galvanix registered as a visitor, barely glancing at the rates for an extended stay. The machine accepted his card without protest.

In the privacy of his cubicle Galvanix opened his flimsy, which was already crumbling from exposure to the salt air. The article about the Moon was short, noting only that unexplained changes had been observed in its atmosphere. He felt a prick of alarm. He activated his room console and requested additional data, but was told implausibly that there were no updates.

No one appeared the next morning to accuse him, and Galvanix roamed the structure freely. The *Manasa* seemed like a core sample of Moon driven into the Earth, familiar even in its low-gravity architecture. The tower drew energy from the temperature differentials of surface and sea floor, but not enough to disturb the sheltering cold of the deepwater ecology. Additional power came from water- and wind-vanes, and the rest from solar panels at its summit. When the monsoon blew or the tides ran, the structure inclined like a reed.

He placed a call to Hiroko, who was unavailable. The call was returned in the middle of the night.

"Yuri." The screen on the wall remained dark.

"You are not Hiroko."

"No. World tensions are high, and an unsecured call cannot be risked. I can muffle this call only briefly."

"So I cannot speak to Hiroko while I am here?" His voice betrayed a tremor.

"Not at this time. There appear to be efforts to poison the lunar atmosphere, and further skirmishes may erupt."

"What?" Galvanix stood in agitation. "Poisoned how?"

"Further news is being restricted, and I cannot penetrate further. Remember that anything you tell me will be relayed to Hiroko. I contain Hiroko."

Galvanix put away his concern about the Moon. "If I cannot speak to Hiroko, I will ask you about her."

"Proceed."

"Do others like her exist?"

"No, the procedure is destructive to brain tissue. The personalities of still-living individuals can be mapped and recorded, but attempts to animate them result in rapid breakdown. Some recordings have nevertheless been made of humans in high-risk professions, in the hope that a future technology may someday allow their resurrection."

Galvanix thought of Beryl, then pushed the thought aside. "Why has she retained her sophic integrity?"

"As she said: for you. Her motives in submitting to transcorporation were primarily to create funds for her family—you and your children—for when the Lunar Republic collapsed. Certainly she did not yearn for the survival of her ego; cultural revulsions overcame self-preservation."

"She said there is something I could do for her."

"You have already done it."

Galvanix felt cold. "If Hiroko has no other reason to live, she may seek . . . release from the wheel."

"Ha," the voice said. It did not sound like a laugh. "*I* have, as you say, a reason to live. It was written into me, but so was yours. If Hiroko wishes no longer to assume her original form—and she does—she will simply revert permanently to the fuller entity that is me."

"She does?"

"Hiroko has set instructions to be reconstituted one more time. At that time, she may specify one further reconstitution. So she goes."

"When will she be—" But Galvanix realized he was transgressing his sister's privacy. Which in turn, he realized later, answered any question of whether he thought the construct truly human.

He brought his agitation to Jayakar that evening. "All right," the Indian said indulgently, "let us set aside my feelings about your Moon country. Are these resources being best used in turning your Moon into a tiny planet?"

"Of course—people can live on it as well as grow crops. Turning the Moon into a force-fed garden would serve only people living in hollowed rocks, estranged from soil and sky."

"Most people would question the worth of such alien soil," Jayakar mused, "though the West is peopled with settlers. Still, look at your world. Month-long days? You break with the human cycle of waking and sleep."

Galvanix explained how this was no harsher than the long days and nights at Earth's extreme latitudes, but Jayakar waved this aside. "You would do better to spin your Moon—mount rockets along its equator and fire them. Can't the fields that channel the sun's force deploy such energies?"

Galvanix was shocked. "Certainly not. Besides, such havoc would destroy our ecosphere."

"But a new one would arise under a twenty-four hour regime. Besides," Jayakar added, reaching for an orange on his desk, "consider this." He set the orange spinning like a top, then let one finger brush against it, slowing it slightly. The orange began to wobble on its axis, then drift across the desk top. "If you can change its spin, you can change its course."

"But who would want to do that?" Galvanix asked.

Jayakar frowned. "We studied this briefly in college. In the next century scientists hope to move Jupiter's big moons farther out, away from its radiation belts. Then they would give them atmospheres, and even tiny suns, less than a kilometer across, that would orbit each moon at the equator."

"We don't need that," said Galvanix. "We do it with mirrors."

"And Venus," the Indian continued doggedly, "would always be too hot. Like India." He smiled. "You couldn't put a shield between Venus and the sun, because it would have to orbit faster; couldn't stay in place. So perhaps they will move *that*." He rolled the orange toward Galvanix.

"Not possible. Moving Venus farther out would interfere with the Earth's orbit."

Jayakar shrugged. "Look, my friend, I am not a spaceman. I study the sea, and my studies are now biased more toward food production than the beauties of phytoplankton. But one subject I know is tides, which tells me a little about orbital ballistics. Perhaps you world-builders will put Venus in Earth's orbit, one hundred twenty degrees ahead. Put Mars in back, would that work? With plans like this, nobody will lavish air on the little Moon. Perhaps you will let it do its job, which is to raise tides on Earth."

There were answers to this, but Jayakar seemed pleased with himself, and Galvanix didn't press the subject. He forgot it the next day when news came on the morning flight, rumors that a spectroscopic photograph taken by an amateur during a suborbital shuttle revealed depletion of the Moon's oxygen content.

"News says nothing," remarked a technician Galvanix had met over meals. "Someone could be filtering the atmosphere, or perhaps inducing oxidation."

"This is awful." Galvanix was too agitated to sit still. "They are stealing a world's air!"

The technician shrugged. "We don't know who it is. It's not as though they can expect to *hide* it."

"Oxygen barons," Galvanix said bitterly.

The technician looked impatient. "They're all oxygen barons up there. So are we. Look at Brazil, which had to maintain their rain forests instead of developing, because the industrial world was producing too much carbon dioxide. Now they hold shares in the Consortium and the ocean development authorities, but claim they are being cheated. Oxygen." She looked at Galvanix. "Why, what do *you* breathe?"

The takeover came two nights later. An alarm went off, not the chime of the door. Galvanix sat up quickly, expecting the door to open and security agents march in. Instead, the alarm shut off and a voice began speaking in Hindi. Galvanix pulled on his jumpsuit and looked outside.

People were filling the corridor, most of them in night dress. Galvanix saw Jayakar standing with one hand raised, listening to the intercom. A puzzled expression crossed his face.

"What is happening?"

"It says not to be alarmed, there are unannounced changes. The *Manasa* is 'being moved.'"

"What does that mean?" someone asked.

Jayakar was listening again. Another person repeated a phrase and added, "'Unannounced procedures'—that could mean anything."

The intercom voice paused, then resumed speaking in a different language. Several of the people who had been talking now stopped. Galvanix looked at Jayakar, who had turned back toward his room. "What does this mean?"

"The sea-stalk is being turned over to a different administration. We are to remain calm and not interfere with any officials we may see. The structure is to be 'shifted,' whatever that means. That voice was not Indian."

"You mean a forcible seizure?" Galvanix felt as though he were still dreaming.

"We have not been told. Maybe someone took over the Indian Development Corporation. We can check the system." He turned toward his room.

"Let's use my console; I'll call outside." They went into Galvanix's cubicle, where a message already shone on his screen in four languages. The English version counseled calm and said that the *Manasa* was being moved.

Galvanix tapped a key repeatedly. "Can we not get out?"

"Perhaps the system is swamped with calls," Jayakar suggested. "Or communication is disrupted."

Galvanix looked at him. "This happened to me once before. When Eldorado was invaded."

Jayakar raised his eyebrows. "Then your experience is unusual indeed. I don't think half a percent of the Earth's population has had direct experience with the Crisis. You must gravitate to unstable places."

"Retaliation for Eldorado," Galvanix muttered. "Or some new

intrigue." He had gotten the messages off the screen, but his efforts to call out were being shunted into a queue. He considered putting his Galvanix ID into a public phone and invoking his right to call Stockholm.

"Try the seaview channel," Jayakar suggested. "That's always on." He leaned forward and tapped keys. A video image of the nighttime ocean appeared, showing points of light ranged across its surface. Jayakar ran through a series of images, some of them schematics that Galvanix couldn't make out before they were succeeded by the next. "A lot of traffic out there," Jayakar commented.

"Meaning what?"

"Well, that the *Manasa* is being surrounded by occupying forces, either to seize it or to prevent it from being seized. Those subs near the bottom are heavy creatures, probably equipped with lasers to slice through our pilings."

Galvanix stared. "Why would they do that?"

"Why, in order to cut the tower adrift and tow it. The structure is buoyant, you know, and—" he glanced at the screen—"we are in a rising tide. That should float the tower free nicely."

Galvanix began to tremble. "How can you take this so calmly?"

Jayakar looked at him mildly. "I take no interest in politics, which I cannot affect. My only worry is further delays in my research. I once lost a month to a typhoon; I hope this won't be as long."

Galvanix took a breath. "I will not submit to this," he said. "It is too much. I am not an asset to be fought over."

"I don't think you can leave the tower at this time," Jayakar said.

"Republicans are too small for Earth eyes." Galvanix picked up his kit bag and attached it to his waist. It contained nothing but money and his two ID cards, none of which was likely to serve him. Jayakar followed him out the door.

The corridor was less crowded than he had expected, evidently because the best information was available through the room consoles. Galvanix was surprised to see the elevators functioning, and more so that there was only a small crowd around them.

"Yuri, where would they go?" asked Jayakar. Galvanix had not realized he had spoken. "The sea level is doubtless closed; do you think someone will rent you a boat?"

"I knew a way out the day I saw it." Galvanix wondered a second at his calm, especially when he realized that there was more noise about him than he was hearing. He saw from the displays that the elevators were in sufficient demand across the tower's hundreds of levels to ensure a long wait. He tapped a query into the wall guide, which told him that the museum lay seventeen levels below.

The stairwells, which residents were encouraged to use for short trips, were nearly empty. Galvanix started down, turning briefly to wave as Jayakar shouted after him. He emerged on a dimly lit and empty level.

The museum seemed closed, but swung open when Galvanix inserted his card. He walked down the line of empty suits, stopping at the Moon model. Galvanix knew why he remembered it; he had played with such relics as a child. The silvered faceplate looked back eloquently: a workhorse out of place, useless to the present.

Galvanix wrestled the thing to the ground, unsealed the helmet and got his hand inside. The suit was held up by a skeleton of rigid rods, whose joints went slack when he found the switch. Galvanix pulled it out, then stood and stripped off his jumpsuit. Getting into the suit was easy: it had been designed for use in emergencies.

Galvanix stood slowly, feeling its added weight in Earth gravity. The suit was large for him, built for strapping Europeans. He activated the suit system, and was glad to see the helmet lights go on. The air tank, he knew, would be full: water vapor would condense inside unless it was kept under pressure.

Behind the largest exhibit, a tiny research sub from the twentieth century, Galvanix found a freight door. A wall switch across the room opened it, and he trod heavily through. He had some trouble keeping his balance, and began to think the floor was tilting slightly.

The freight elevator was designed only to communicate with certain levels, but came at once to his summons. Galvanix asked the wall screen for a display of these levels, and found what he wanted quickly. As the elevator rode up, he consulted the suit system: power enough to run the respirator. He kept the faceplate up, unwilling to strain the system.

The door opened on a loading dock, loud with nearby machinery. Galvanix stumped out and almost immediately encountered a technician. The man stared at him.

Galvanix said, "I want to use the airlock." Eyes widening at Galvanix's features, the man nodded immediately.

A wall screen showed a scene Galvanix did not recognize from Jayakar's survey, and he stopped. After a second he realized that it was a sonar image of the sea bottom, with the *Manasa* plainly visible in the darkness. The stalk was surrounded at its base by hovering objects, several of which were clinging to its side. Looking closer, Galvanix saw that the tower wasn't touching the sea floor. It had been severed, and was now under tow.

Galvanix felt sudden vertigo at the thought of the ground beneath him adrift. The stiffened suit prevented him from staggering. Think of it as a ship, he told himself.

"In here," the man was saying. The hatch he pointed to was covered with red-lettered warnings. The technician spoke into a wall grille and pressed his thumb against a square, and the hatch slid open with a puff of briny air.

Galvanix lowered his faceplate and stepped through. The hatch hissed shut, leaving him in a small chamber lit dimly by an overhead panel. He saw a tiny camera mounted above the hatch, and raised his arm. A hum buzzed faintly through his soles, and the floor was suddenly boiling with rising water.

As the sea rose past his chest, Galvanix felt the stirring of buoyancy. When it covered his helmet, he bounced on his toes, hovering a second before settling lightly back. He felt a second's alarm, then remembered how much denser the water would get as pressure approached outside levels.

The light in the flooded chamber grew steadily dimmer, and Galvanix felt his boots leave the deck. The suit system hummed, fortifying against high rather than low outside pressure.

Galvanix brushed the ceiling, which vibrated with activity beyond. Sounds were reaching him as the medium thickened, the whine of a pump, distant gongs outside. Galvanix was finding it difficult to move his limbs.

The whine died, and Galvanix floated for a second in silence. Then the low grate of the outer lock sliding open, and a wash of current against him. Running lights framed the hatch, an invitation out.

Galvanix kicked against the syrupy water, then thought to

activate his head lamp. Designed to be visible from low lunar orbit, the beam illuminated a corner of the airlock, although the rest remained in blackness. The chamber had handholds along all its surfaces, and Galvanix pulled himself to the threshold and through.

He began rising at once, one foot dragging along the bulkhead until he kicked free. He seemed to be ascending feet first, probably due to the backpack's weight. Galvanix tried to bring up his knees, but the suit fabric resisted flexing at this pressure.

Lights shone around him, six or seven in a darkness space never achieved. Nevertheless Galvanix felt he was sailing through void, not crushing thickness. They looked like tiny suns, he thought, and felt his throat catch.

He was rising above a solar system full of starlets, Earth-sized clouds of hydrogen scooped from Jupiter and compressed by magnetic fields into ignition. Pinpoints that would blaze for millennia, they circled Titan, Callisto, Ceres. Two orbited Mars, points of a triangle whose third was some asteroid counterweight. Venus gleamed, a second Earth, spinning with a weather-calming velocity no moon would slow.

Points twinkled in reflected glory, thousands of worldlets orbiting the Earth, Venus, the sun. Where was Mercury? Whittled into nothing, its iron refined into a zodiac of bodies no astrology could chart. Between them vessels coursed, running along trajectories and geodesics that were sometimes material, threads between worlds.

And nowhere was the Moon. Galvanix knew this now. Not *his* Moon, the first-growth wilderness of the Republic. The Moon of this future was not visible to him, he would be farside to it forever.

The water was growing brighter, but not because he was ascending. Lights were training on him, a beep signaling incoming radio. Galvanix ignored them. He read the outside pressure gauge, whose changing measure told him nothing of depth but confirmed he was still rising.

Galvanix fumbled at his wrist controls, preparing to shed the backpack when he reached neutral buoyancy. His oxygen tank would be jettisoned as well; the oversized suit would hold more than the five minutes' air that fitted systems contained.

A vibrant whirring grew about him, the hum of a propeller. Light speared him, dim but remaining upon him. Galvanix realized he might be snagged like a fish, perhaps only because he was slowing. He punched at his wrist panel, and the straps at waist and shoulders loosened. Galvanix writhed free, feeling himself spurt upward even as the hiss of his respirator cut off. The spotlight began to fade.

A dim rippling was visible above him, like a curtain stirring in darkness. Galvanix sailed straight into it, broke and was through. A wave smacked the side of his helmet.

Lights through the streaming faceplate. Galvanix closed his neck seal and popped the plate, blowing out air like a whale. He raised his face to the spray. Above him hung the Moon, drawing tides toward her. Galvanix gazed at its swollen face, wondering at the wrongness of tint.

"Yuri!" The voice shouted in his ear, unmistakable. Galvanix closed his eyes, welcoming the delusion.

"Yuri, I'm coming to you on tightbeam, patching through a news copter overhead. Are you hearing me? Wave your hand!"

Wondering, Galvanix raised a heavy arm from the water.

"Yuri, you're free. One of the press agencies recognized the spacesuit through a sub camera and guessed it was you. Your name has been broadcast, you're known to be there. Nobody can grab you . . ."

Her voice faded when he moved his head. Galvanix did not know whether that confirmed her reality or the opposite.

"Keep your helmet still, they're aiming at its crown. Or put on your radio, we can overwhelm other signals. Yuri, say something."

Galvanix toggled on the radio. "Hello?"

"There you are!" The voice came through the earphones, unnaturally clear. "They won't let us land, it's a conflict zone. Don't worry. Oh my dear, you are safe at last."

Something in the final words stirred alarm. "What do—"

"I'm going now, there is no purpose in squeezing back into this corset of ego. It's only by shedding all I have become that I could rejoin you."

"*What are you saying?*"

A wave sloshed into the helmet. ". . . you can call my greater self, but won't. Just help our countrymen; it will be hard for many. You too, but you are tough. Do not mourn me—in some form, I may outlive you. Time's up. Farewell!"

She was gone.

Air was seeping out the neck seal, deflating the ballooning suit and causing him to sink. Yuri tore open the garment, shucking it in a practiced motion. The Moon suit disappeared in an expiration of bubbles.

Bobbing in the warm tropical water, Yuri looked up at the circling lights. Only the near ones came closer.

EPILOGUE

When Gaia and Cytherea were both in the sky, Gitu climbed the East Pole to see three worlds at once. Only at the top of the peak could both planets be glimpsed in their entirety, and Gaia was already skimming the tips of the Golney Range. Luna's axis was not precisely parallel to the Spindle, and the satellite's rapid rotation would quickly take the larger world out of sight.

Gitu looked up to see evidence of the Spindle itself, the heavenly bridge joining the planets' near poles in a great line bisecting the sky. Even this high, however, the lunar atmosphere blurred the gossamer strand, and only at the zenith, where the Spindle came closest to the world that circled it, could Gitu see a thread of silver for a few degrees of arc.

The morning sun shone off to Cytherea's left, illuminating a third of the planet like a peel of fruit. Gitu thought he could make out the continent of Ishtar, with the distinct cloud patterns surrounding the Maxwell Mountains. Gitu had spent ten years on Cytherea, when the world was first brought outward from the sun to dance with Gaia round the point Gaia previously occupied, when every available being was needed for the task of worldforming.

Luna had still been recovering in those years, bruised from its wielding at the hands of engineers, who had drawn it back from Gaia in proportion to Cytherea's approach so that no disturbance should rock the home world's tides and afflict its ancient cities and ecologies. Luna had taken long to heal; but it was small, and was in time given back the atmosphere it had once had, in the years when Gitu was young.

Such thoughts would sometimes remind Gitu of his more-than-brother Yuri Nagashima, who lived ninety years on Gaia before removing to the Greater Jovian. Forty-one years ago perihelion had brought Jove unusually close to Gaia–Cytherea, and Gitu had looked out at the gas giant, wondering briefly whether the human who had shared his childhood still lived.

Gitu could never imagine going to Gaia, a journey that lay just beyond the fork where Yuri's and his lives had parted; but someday he hoped to traverse a section of the Spindle, perhaps even sail the open center where the wind currents blew between the worlds. Pilgrims from Gaia, he knew, patiently climbed the staircase running its length, toiling from old world to new across millions of kilometers; someday, perhaps, the first would arrive. Gitu would be happy to glide a hundred klicks, dallying at its transparent expanses to see the tiny worlds, some newly arrived from circum-Neptune and even beyond, basking in the nearness of Sol, within sight of the planet where life was born.

Such fancies lay far in the future. Gitu's opened wings dried quickly in the rarer air, and he beat them twice to restore circulation. He left his legs clutching the rail on which he had perched; they would cramp for hours after he returned to them, but Gitu wanted this flight.

He waited for a good breeze, then spread his wings and was lifted away. The gills in his underwings drank air, oxygenating rapidly in the high altitude. Gitu soared through the crosswinds, banking to enter a wide arc. Nyvre, the city that owned him, glittered below, a bracelet rimming the Oktengi Reservoir. Beyond stretched the preserves of Brylkei, garden to the crews who sailed through space. Working to feed such millions was duty enough for any person.

The older world was falling below the horizon; its newer twin ascendant. So the Moon turned, at the heart of civilization. Gitu rarely rose from his work to be stirred by such thoughts, but when he did he recalled when the world was very different, and his soul was happy.

Acknowledgments

Discussion of molecular machines, which I have called mites, is indebted to Eric Drexler's prophecy of nanotechnology, *Engines of Creation*. Studies by Dandridge Cole and R. R. Vondrak confirmed my belief—to which the dry riverbeds of Mars offer eloquent testimony—that the atmosphere given a small world would persist for an historically if not geologically significant period. Bruce Sterling first used the term "concatenation" to describe a series of habitats circling the Moon, although his structure differs from the one described here. The futuristic-sounding solitons are quite real, and a general discussion of the wave fronts that never dissipate was published in *The New York Times* on December 15, 1987. David Morrison of Duke University helped with the calculus, Kandace Hauf of Yale with the Japanese.

James Blish's 1969 story "Our Binary Brothers," a fragment of an unfinished novel, contains a passing reference to an alien artifact which the protagonist hears translated as "steam telephone." Nothing more is made of this intriguing device, which remains one of the unresolved elements of the novel—I even pointed this out once in an essay. It was not until I was halfway through this book that I realized that my own steam telephone represented a subconscious attempt to answer this question. I suspect Blish's design would have been more elegant.

—Gregory Feeley
New Haven, September 1988

THE FINEST THE UNIVERSE HAS TO OFFER

__THE OMEGA CAGE Steve Perry and Michael Reaves
0-441-62382-4/$3.50
The Omega Cage—a hi-tech prison for the special enemies of the brutal Confed. No one had ever escaped, but Dain Maro is about to attempt the impossible.

__THE WARLOCK'S COMPANION Christopher Stasheff
0-441-87341-3/$3.95
Fess, the beloved cyborg steed of Rod Gallowglass, has a host of revealing stories he's never shared. Now the Gallowglass children are about to hear the truth...from the horse's mouth.

__THE STAINLESS STEEL RAT Harry Harrison
0-441-77924-7/$3.50
The Stainless Steel Rat was the slickest criminal in the Universe until the police finally caught up with him. Then there was only one thing they could do—they made him a cop.

__DREAM PARK Larry Niven and Steven Barnes
0-441-16730-6/$4.95
Dream Park—the ultimate fantasy world where absolutely everything you ever dreamed of is real—including murder.

For Visa and MasterCard orders call: 1-800-631-8571

FOR MAIL ORDERS: CHECK BOOK(S). FILL OUT COUPON. SEND TO:

BERKLEY PUBLISHING GROUP
390 Murray Hill Pkwy., Dept. B
East Rutherford, NJ 07073

NAME_____

ADDRESS_____

CITY_____

STATE_____ ZIP_____

PLEASE ALLOW 6 WEEKS FOR DELIVERY.
PRICES ARE SUBJECT TO CHANGE WITHOUT NOTICE.

POSTAGE AND HANDLING:
$1.00 for one book, 25¢ for each additional. Do not exceed $3.50.

BOOK TOTAL $ _____

POSTAGE & HANDLING $ _____

APPLICABLE SALES TAX $ _____
(CA, NJ, NY, PA)

TOTAL AMOUNT DUE $ _____

PAYABLE IN US FUNDS.
(No cash orders accepted.)

281

MULTI-MILLION COPY
BESTSELLING AUTHOR OF DUNE!

FRANK
HERBERT

__THE ASCENSION FACTOR*	0-441-03127-7/$4.50
__THE LAZARUS EFFECT*	0-441-47521-3/$4.50
__THE JESUS INCIDENT*	0-441-38539-7/$4.95
__MAN OF TWO WORLDS*	0-441-51857-5/$4.50
__DESTINATION: VOID	0-441-14302-4/$3.95
__THE DOSADI EXPERIMENT	0-441-16027-1/$3.95
__THE WHITE PLAGUE	0-441-88569-1/$4.95
__EYE	0-441-22374-5/$3.95

*By Frank Herbert and Bill Ransom

For Visa and MasterCard orders call: 1-800-631-8571

FOR MAIL ORDERS: CHECK BOOK(S). FILL OUT COUPON. SEND TO:

BERKLEY PUBLISHING GROUP
390 Murray Hill Pkwy., Dept. B
East Rutherford, NJ 07073

NAME_____

ADDRESS_____

CITY_____

STATE_____ZIP_____

**PLEASE ALLOW 6 WEEKS FOR DELIVERY.
PRICES ARE SUBJECT TO CHANGE**

POSTAGE AND HANDLING:
$1.00 for one book, 25¢ for each additional. Do not exceed $3.50.

BOOK TOTAL	$ ____
POSTAGE & HANDLING	$ ____
APPLICABLE SALES TAX	$ ____
(CA, NJ, NY, PA)	
TOTAL AMOUNT DUE	$ ____

PAYABLE IN US FUNDS.
(No cash orders accepted.)

275